CURSE
OF THE
SPECTER
QUEEN

JENNY ELDER MOKE

CURSE OF THE SPECTER QUEEN

A SAMANTHA KNOX NOVEL

HYPERION

LOS ANGELES   NEW YORK

First Hardcover Edition, June 2021
First Paperback Edition, May 2022
10 9 8 7 6 5 4 3 2 1
FAC-025438-22077
Printed in the United States of America

This book is set in Fairfield LT Std/Adobe
Designed by Phil Buchanan

Library of Congress Cataloging-in-Publication Number
for Hardcover Edition: 2020030926
ISBN 978-1-368-06699-0

Visit www.hyperionteens.com

SUSTAINABLE
FORESTRY
INITIATIVE

Certified Sourcing

www.sfiprogram.org
SFI-01054

The SFI label applies to the text stock

To Max,
MY FAVORITE COFFEE SHOP WRITING BUDDY

CHAPTER ONE

Sam let the first door chime go unanswered, occupied as she was with the stack of delicate books cradled in her arms. The second chime earned a grunt of displeasure from her as she scanned the shelves for the first edition of John Locke's *An Essay Concerning Human Understanding* she had repaired last week. She spotted it, tucked safely between Kant and Machiavelli. The third chime rang so insistently that she tipped the book forward too hard and it dropped to the floor with an ominous *crack*.

"Oh dear," she said, crouching down to retrieve the book. "Mr. Locke, I apologize. And I swear to you if it's the butcher's boys again, I will take the broad side of his cleaver to their rear ends myself."

The spine appeared unmarred, which was more than Sam could say for her disposition as she stacked the book on top of the others and jostled to a standing position. She tottered to the front of the shop and set them down on the desk. In the window stood the rounded figure of Clement's postman, his face pressed to the glass and obscuring the gold lettering across the door. She checked off each book on her inventory list, letting him freeze in the early January snows of rural Illinois, before crossing to the door and unlocking it. A blast of cold drove it open like an unwanted guest.

"Yes, Georgie, what is it you need?" she asked, shivering back from the chill.

"Got your mail," Georgie huffed, bustling past her to drop his sack on the desk. He trod in drifts of snow across her pristine carpet, and she swept the more offensive piles back out the door as she swung it shut.

"That's why I had the package drop put in, Georgie," Sam said. "So you can leave them in a protected box without them getting soaked by the melting snow you're tracking in."

"It's colder than a brass toilet seat in the Arctic out there," Georgie replied, leaning against his mailbag like he planned to stay. He peered into the stacks behind Sam. "It's toasty in here, though. Must be nice for you, being tucked up in this place all day."

"We keep the temperature stable for the books," Sam said, her patient tone fraying at the edges. She had plenty to do before her long walk home in that same snow, and she couldn't do it as long as Georgie was here chewing the cud. "Extreme heat and cold damage the leather. You said you had my mail?"

"Oh sure." Georgie ducked his head into the thick canvas sack. "Couple of these are too big, wouldn't fit through the slot."

Sam was sure his bell ringing had far more to do with the warm interior of the shop than with any oversize packages, but it was too late for that. Here he was already, invading her space and upending the careful equilibrium she maintained. He didn't care that there was the rest of the inventory list to get to, plus the packages to prepare and send to Mr. Peltingham in London and Mr. Burnham in Oslo, never mind the repairs to the copy of *Medieval Remedies for Cistercian Monks* they had received at the shop last week. She didn't have time for Georgie Heath and the trail of muddy snow he dragged everywhere.

He pulled a small collection of boxes from his sack—none of them, as Sam suspected, too large for the mail slot—with an exotic array of stamps across the front. Sam's heart rate picked up when she spotted Mr. Studen's scrawled handwriting. He always had the best finds in Paris. She grabbed her letter opener and sliced through the thick paper.

"Books," Georgie said, in the same tone his father used when talking about the neighbor's marauding hogs. "Always books, isn't it?"

"Yes," Sam said with a happy little sigh, extracting Mr. Studen's letter along with his latest find. "We *are* a bookshop, Georgie."

Oh, clever Mr. Studen. She smiled at the first few lines of introduction, a jumble of letters and pictographic marks. He'd sent her another cryptogram, with a small note dashed off at the top that read *I'm sure to stump you this time.*

He wasn't, but she appreciated the challenge.

Georgie gave a snort. "I don't know what we need with a bookshop here in Clement, anyhow. We've already got a library."

"A collection of old family Bibles does not count as a library," Sam said, reaching for a pencil and paper. It looked to be a straightforward monoalphabetic cipher despite the distraction of the pictographic marks, but she didn't want to underestimate Mr. Studen so quickly.

Georgie shrugged. "I was happy enough to give that stuff up the second I walked out of Mrs. Iris's schoolroom for good."

"*Madame* Iris," Sam corrected.

"*Madame*," Georgie said in a gross mockery of the French madame's accent. "Pa says a book is only good for propping open a door or knocking a fella out."

"Well, I would expect no less from the man who led a town-wide protest when Mr. Steeling hired a Frenchwoman to teach at the schoolhouse," Sam murmured, making a list of the most frequent letter appearances and the most common letter groupings in the cipher. Georgie craned his neck around, squinting at Mr. Studen's neat handwriting.

"What is that?" he asked. "Some kind of gibberish?"

"It's a cipher," Sam said. "A code. It's meant to keep a message hidden."

The last word she said pointedly, looking up at the intrusion of his person on her space. If Georgie noticed her intention—which Sam was positive he did not—he didn't do anything to address it. Instead he scooted in closer, wrinkling up his nose like his father's prize hog.

"Well, how do you know what it says?" Georgie asked.

"You need a key," Sam murmured, writing out a few attempts at the letters she thought she might have deduced.

"Do you have the key?"

"No."

"Well then, how do you know what it says?"

Sam let out a sigh. "I don't, Georgie. Not yet. I have to decrypt it, which would be much easier to do without so much distracting chatter."

Georgie rocked back. "I get it, this is like those things you and Jo and Bennett used to do, out at the Manor, right? Those treasure hunts you'd make up."

"We didn't make them up, Mr. Steeling did," Sam said, setting down her pencil and folding the letter closed along with her deciphering attempts, away from Georgie's prying eyes. "And I haven't done those in years, not since we were children."

Georgie shrugged. "Maybe you and Joana can put one up now that she's in Clement again."

Sam drew back. "Jo's in town?"

"Yeah, didn't you know it? I figured she would have come to see you straightaway. You were the only one she ever bothered with. Maybe she's too good for you now, too, after being at that fancy academy in Chicago."

Joana Steeling was back in Clement and she hadn't come to see Sam. So, she was still mad about the fight. Sam had tried so many times to explain why she couldn't go to the academy with Joana—first in person, and after Joana left, through half-finished letters—but Joana couldn't understand. It was so easy for her, the heiress of the Steeling fortune, to spend late nights in shady speakeasies flirting with the boys, getting into and out of trouble. But Sam could never live like that. Most likely Joana had found her people at Marquart Academy. It didn't surprise her that Joana had moved on, but it did surprise her how much it hurt hearing about it from Georgie Heath.

"If you see Jo, tell her we're out at the old barn most nights, me and Pete and the gang," Georgie said, oblivious to Sam's discomfort. "They might have those swanky speakeasies up in Chicago, but nobody's calling the G-men on us. We do what we want, all night if we want it."

"Sounds a dream," Sam said tiredly. "But I've got work to do, if there's nothing else."

"Oh, right, got your newspaper here," he said, ducking back into the bag and pulling out a copy of the *Chicago Daily News*. Sam's attention snagged on a small headline tucked into the right corner of the front page: *TUT OPERATIONS RESUMED*.

"The curse of the mummy has been lifted," she murmured, leaning closer to read the rest of the article.

"Are they still writing about that thing?" Georgie asked, glancing at the paper. "The grave or whatever?"

"Yes, they're still writing about the tomb of Tutankhamen," Sam said dryly. "It's the greatest archaeological discovery of our time."

Georgie waved her off. "I don't see any point in all that old stuff. Who cares? They're all dead anyway."

Sam had no intention of explaining the historical significance of Howard Carter's recent discovery of Tutankhamen's tomb. No one in Clement would understand, except her boss, Mr. Steeling. He shared Sam's fascination with all things ancient and lost. He spent much of his time traveling overseas to exotic places like Greece to join archaeological excavations. Places she would only ever read about in the *Daily News*. She snapped the paper closed and placed it on the desk, looking at Georgie expectantly.

"Well, I suppose that's all," Georgie said, gazing forlornly out at the brutal white of the main street of Clement.

"Yes, well, enjoy your evening in the barn with the other boys," Sam said, picking up his sack and putting it on his shoulder, using the movement to push the rest of him toward the front door. They both squinted against the cold wind that burst through when she opened the door.

"All right, all right, I'm off," Georgie said, the winter wind turning him chapped and irritable again. "You tell Jo—"

"Will do, thank you, Georgie," Sam said, swinging the door shut and throwing the dead bolt.

She took a deep, cleansing breath of the temperature-controlled interior of the store, the soft scent of the oiled leather covers restoring her sense of self, before turning her attention to the stack of recent arrivals. Her eagerness to discover new friends outweighed her obligation to the packaging list or the pang in her gut about Joana returning home and not coming to see her.

She had just begun to sort the packages when a smaller one slipped out from the press of the others, the paper soiled and the corner torn away. It looked as if it had been through a monsoon, the writing so faded it was a wonder Georgie had known where to deliver it at all. And judging by the various interpretations of the address scribbled across the front, she wasn't sure the bookshop had been the package's first delivery attempt. How long had it been in the system, knocked from one place to the other, before it got to her? There was no return address. She held it up, a small puff of dry earth sifting onto the desk.

"What a terrible journey you've been through," she tutted. "Let's get you fixed up."

She carried the package to the repair room in the back. The work lamp there glowed a bluish white. A humidifier hummed beside it, giving the occasional ping in the relative silence. She sat at the worktable and opened the package. A little avalanche of dust and desiccated plant parts came sliding out along with the enclosed item.

The book was small, barely larger than her hand, the cover in such disrepair that Sam feared it would disintegrate if she so much as gave it a stern look. She had seen plenty of books in a variety of conditions since she started working at Steeling's Rare Antiquities, but this had to be the worst state of deterioration she'd ever witnessed. It looked as if the book had been buried in someone's back field and dug up by a stray goat.

"Who would do such a thing to you?" she wondered, her chest aching at the violence the book had encountered on its journey. "Well, whatever ills have befallen you, you're safe here now."

There was nothing in the package to indicate where it had come from, no letter of provenance or introduction from a buyer explaining what the book was or why they had sent it. The mystery of it had her pulling out her tools, for the moment abandoning the other new arrivals. She took her brush and went to work, tilting it up to sweep softly along the outside edges, collecting a tidy pile of earth and sediment.

Already she knew it would need a rest in the humidifier to loosen up the pages and hopefully restore the faded writing within. Once she had sufficiently cleaned the outside, she began her preliminary inspection of the interior. The pages were so waterlogged she could hardly pry them apart, but with the aid of a scalpel and a level of patience bordering on stubbornness, she managed to loosen one enough to pull it open.

The writing was, as she suspected, faded and illegible in many places, but that wasn't what drew her attention to the book. It was the hasty sketch of a cat on the open page, the graphite strokes thick and dark and tearing through the paper in some places. She could even see smudges where the lead must have broken. Whoever drew this cat must have had very strong feelings about it.

Except that the longer she stared at the image, the less it actually looked like a cat. At least, not like any ordinary house cat. The proportions were all wrong—the ears too sharp and pointed, almost like horns; the jaw too long and narrow, more fitted to a dog. And then there were the eyes. They were nothing more than blank page, but the longer she stared, the more they seemed to burn, two desolate holes radiating a promise of danger. Awareness prickled down her legs and across her arms, as if a wayward slip of icy January wind had found its way into the shop. But it wasn't the wind. It was the way the cat kept staring, even when she slid the book aside. Those sightless eyes were on her, always on her, and in a fit of fear she slammed the cover shut.

"Don't be such a fool," Sam muttered, though she made no attempt to open it again. "It's only an old book. What's the harm?"

Georgie was putting her on. He must be. This was exactly the kind of prank he and Pete and the other boys would pull back in Madame Iris's schoolroom. Leaving notes with rude poems, knowing she would mistake them for clues to a new treasure hunt at

Steeling Manor, the hunts Mr. Steeling created for his children and Sam. They must be bored to tears after the last snowstorm, getting pickled out there in his father's barn every night. They were probably watching through the front window, waiting to see her come tearing out of there screaming.

But there was nothing at the door save the whistle of the winter wind and the last rays of a dying sun. The darkness looming outside made the malevolence emanating from the book so much worse, and Sam was acutely aware of how alone she was just then. She hovered in the doorway of the workroom, not wanting to come any closer to the odd little book.

"What are you?" she whispered.

But whatever secrets the book had, it held them as tightly as the dust wedged into its pages. Sam chewed at one corner of her lip, weighing her options. She could try to chase down Georgie, force the book back on him, and make him deliver it to Steeling Manor. But the shop was the last stop on his route; he was probably halfway back to the barn by now, and halfway into a flask of his awful bathtub gin. The boy could be surprisingly agile when getting away from work. She could leave it until the next time Mr. Steeling came by to check on the new arrivals, but that could be weeks from now and Sam didn't want it hanging around.

No, there was nothing for it. She would have to deliver it to Steeling Manor herself. Which meant facing her fears, and potentially her former best friend.

"Oh, Sammy girl, what have you gotten yourself into?" she sighed, tucking the book into her satchel and pulling the strap across her chest like a battle shield.

CHAPTER TWO

Sam knew she had made a terrible mistake when the third car nearly ran her off the lane leading up to Steeling Manor. One car in Clement was an anomaly; two cars a statistical improbability. Three cars could only mean one thing.

A party.

Sam's fears were soon confirmed as she reached the large circular drive in front of the Manor and spotted the fleet of fine cars parked around the massive water fountain. Within it three women stood back-to-back, their bare arms raised to the sky, glittering daggers of ice dripping from the buckets in their hands. The facade of the manor house was no less impressive, painted in a brilliant white with a wraparound front porch held up by sweeping columns in the Greek Revival style. Freshly fallen snow lined the edges of the lawn, making it look like a Christmas-village set piece. The sight of the wide windows framed by robin's-egg-blue shutters made Sam's head ache, and even though she knew it was not the season for them she could have sworn she smelled Mrs. Steeling's English roses.

But she wouldn't think about those flowers, or the treasure

destined to be buried forever beneath them, or that last fateful hunt left unfinished. She had a job to do.

Now that she was closer to the house, she could hear what the crunch of snow under her shoes had hidden before—the tinkle of champagne glasses, the rumble of idle conversation punctuated by an occasional laugh. The faint strains of a horn.

Definitely a party.

Sam sighed, already regretting so many things, and waited for the recent party arrivals to disappear through the front door before braving the porch. She pounded a fist against the massive glass-and-steel double doors, entirely too loud and fast, and stood back to wait in a jittery silence. The butler drew the door open, his professional decorum covering up the half-second glint of surprise in his gaze.

"Ms. Knox," he said in his smooth English accent that always sounded slightly disapproving. Or maybe that was only ever directed at her and Joana. After all, he was always the one catching them using Cook's good ladle as a digging trowel.

"Hi, James," Sam said on a sigh.

"Are you here for the soiree?" James asked, his gaze sliding over the raggedy edges of her father's old winter coat and the loose pair of work trousers she'd put on under her skirt so the snow wouldn't pile up in her socks.

Sam shook her head, burrowing deeper into her coat. "Absolutely not. I received a strange book at the shop that I need Mr. Steeling to see."

A faint crease appeared along James's otherwise-smooth forehead. "I am afraid Mr. Steeling is indisposed."

Sam moved from one foot to the other, the resolute energy that had carried her there quickly dissipating under the butler's steady gaze. "Well, of course I can see that now that I'm here, only I didn't know it when I left the shop. Maybe I could just leave the book in the library? I'll be quick, I promise. I don't want anyone here catching sight of me either."

The crease in his forehead deepened. "I see. I will show you to the library."

"That's all right, James," Sam said, already moving past him into the foyer. "It's only been a few years—I still remember the way."

But Sam hesitated in the marble entryway, the cacophony of voices echoing against the hard floor like a physical impediment. Just beyond the foyer, the party guests moved, sparkling and sleek in their floor-length dresses and tailcoats. Deep within the house, a band played something new and heavy on the brass, the dancers whirling in and out of view as they moved their feet in double time to keep up with the tempo. Mr. Steeling had expanded his collection of rare goods since the last time Sam had been there; the walls were lined with numerous restorations of precious Greek pottery. And it seemed Mrs. Steeling had finally convinced him to swap out the massive stone lions that used to guard the staircase with tall porcelain vases. But underneath all those decorative changes, it was still the same manor house. Her second home for so much of her childhood, until she couldn't stand the sight of it anymore.

No, no, that wouldn't do. No need to retread those memories, not tonight. Sam took a deep breath, keeping her eyes wide open, and dodged through more arriving guests toward the staircase leading to the second floor. Several people looked at her askance, taking in her well-worn clothing and the drifts of snow still piled over the toes of her shoes. She increased her speed, practically running up the steps. She found the library straightaway, just past a full suit of English armor from the thirteenth century. Sam ran her fingers over the word BIBLIOTHECA in thick brass letters above the door handle before pushing it open, slipping in and pressing it shut. Only after she had inhaled the leathery scent of so much knowledge could she release the knot of tension twisting her gut.

At least until someone said her name.

"Sam?" The voice was warm and deep, like a swirling pot of chocolate, and terribly familiar. Sam stiffened and whirled about, her satchel banging against her hip under her coat.

"Bennett?" she said, the name slipping out halfway between a plea and a sigh.

Bennett Steeling rose from behind his father's desk situated in the center of the library, the shelves of books reaching another twenty feet overhead. He wore a black tailcoat, the shirt white and crisp and the jacket tailored to fit his broad shoulders and narrow hips. His hair was styled back in soft waves, nearly black like Mrs. Steeling's, his eyes the color of champagne by candlelight, a beautifully light brown with sparkling patches of gold. Sam cataloged all these details, comparing them with the precious collection of memories she had hoarded for the two years he had been gone to college in Chicago.

"I didn't know you were coming tonight," he said. He waved to the door, seeming to encompass the whole house beyond it. "I thought these kinds of things didn't interest you anymore. Jo said you hadn't even been to the Christmas party in the last two years. Between the two of us, I think my mother is starting to take it personally that no one but the mill workers show up for her parties nowadays."

He said it lightly, as a joke, but it prodded something deep and tender within her, a wound she preferred to leave alone. It had always been so hard to come back here ever since the telegram from the War Office seven long years ago. Her mother had walked the mile and a half from their house after receiving it, her hands still red and her dress still damp from the hot laundry. And there Sam had been, playing at being a code-breaking explorer, not knowing the war had taken her father and changed her life irrevocably. For those last fateful minutes, she was still just a girl seeking an adventure.

Sometimes she thought about getting a spade and digging up that last treasure, just to be done with it. It hung like a loose thread in the tapestry of her consciousness, always snagging her when she brushed past the memory. The urge was nearly overwhelming, even now, after so many years away. She hated the idea of anything left undone, especially the hardest of all their treasure hunts. But she never could do it. Maybe she didn't want to find out she had been wrong all along, and the statue was never really buried there. Or maybe she didn't want to dig it up after all these years and find out nothing really changed.

"Sam, everything all right?" Bennett asked, because of course it had been too many moments since he had said anything and she had stood there mired in a memory.

She was suddenly and painfully aware of the plainness of her appearance—her threadbare white shirt that had been through the wringer so many times the tint of her skin showed at the elbows; her thick khaki skirt that was too tight in the waist and came too far above her knee, but had no more fabric to let out; the hasty bun she had fastened that morning, trying to tame the kink of her auburn hair into some kind of recognizable shape. Bennett looked like a Greek god made flesh, a marble statue come to life, and she probably looked as if she'd spent the last hour tilling the back fields and cleaning out the feeding trough.

Oh, the work trousers. She should have slipped them off the second James sniffed at them. Maybe she could slip them off now without Bennett noticing. Except she and Bennett were the only ones in the library, as far as she could tell, and he was looking right at her. It wouldn't do to start shucking items of clothing now.

"Oh, yes, sure, everything's fine," Sam said.

He circled the desk and came to stand before her, his eyes sweeping down to her feet and back up to her face. One corner of his mouth crooked up. "You've gotten taller."

She could melt into the warm edges of the way he said that, swim around in the chocolate timbre of his voice. It had gotten deeper since he'd left, she was sure of it. It had expanded and aged like the fine French wines Mr. Steeling was always rumored to be smuggling into his parties. She could listen to Bennett talk for the rest of the night, but if she didn't say something soon, he would think she had been brained by their old mule in his absence.

"I . . . You're back? From Chicago? I didn't know."

Bennett tucked his hands into his pockets, that small smile still turning up one corner of his mouth and threatening to take Sam's knees out from under her. "Only for the evening. I skipped out on the Christmas party this year as well, and Mother gave me hell for it. Said that I came home so little these days she was starting to forget she even had a son. Which is ridiculous, of course, because she comes up to Chicago at least once a semester to do all her shopping, but you know my mother. She might have left the stage, but it never left her. Anyway, since I'll be gone for the semester, I figured I'd better come home and make the appropriate rounds."

"Gone?" Sam said, her voice pitching up in dismay. "Where will you be gone? I mean, why will you be gone? Where are you going?"

"To help one of my professors—Professor Wallstone—with a survey in Ireland."

Sam's eyebrows went up. "Professor Barnaby Wallstone?"

"You know of him?"

"Of course. I read his article in last year's *Archaeological Digest* about Linear B and the possibility that it could be a form of ancient Greek."

Bennett winced. "That article didn't win him any friends in Sir Arthur Evans's camp, especially the part where he criticized Sir Evans for keeping his cache of tablets under lock and key and thwarting the efforts of any would-be decipherers. He received a shocking amount of hate mail and nearly had his tenure revoked."

"Oh, but I think he might be right," Sam said. "He made some compelling arguments around the syllabary and its parallels to Mycenean Greek of the later time period. I know Sir Evans has first right of translation as the discoverer of the tablets, but he's been promising the next volume of Scripta Minoa for ages. It really has impeded progress, to Professor Wallstone's point. But I thought Wallstone's expertise was in Greek and the classics. What is he doing in Ireland?"

Bennett gave a small sigh. "Professor Wallstone has a bit of a reputation at the university for his . . . side projects. He spent a semester researching the standing stones in Ireland and Wales on a lark. The administration wasn't pleased about him abandoning his classes to graduate students, apparently. Now he's got it in his head that he wants to excavate a potential Neolithic passage tomb in the mountains outside of Dublin. He's convinced it might have been a worship site for the Druids. Don't mention it to my mother, but really I came home to raid Father's collection on Celtic lore and symbology."

"Which ones did you pull?" Sam asked, the topic shifting her attention away from how the collar of his shirt made his jawline look so appealing. She skirted around Bennett to examine the stack on the desk, reaching for the topmost book and propping it up on either side to take the pressure off the spine. She tapped the pages. "Conway is a good one, though I find his writing style a bit blustery."

"He does tend to go on," Bennett conceded, joining her on the opposite side of the desk. "After a year and a half at the University of Chicago, though, I'm used to it. All the professors talk at you like they're lecturing, even in casual conversation."

"Oh, you're studying ogham, too," Sam said, pulling the book out from beneath Conway's formidable tome. She traced a finger over the branch-like formations of the ogham characters on the page.

Bennett tilted his head up in surprise. "You know about ogham?"

He pronounced it differently than her, the *gh* sounding more like a soft *w*. She turned warm with embarrassment; that's what came of learning so much of her vocabulary from books. The pronunciations were always spotty at best.

"I read Robert Stewart Macalister's theory that it originated in Italy, based on secret hand signals the Druids used to communicate," Sam said quickly, hoping to move past her mistake. "Isn't it also called the Celtic Tree Alphabet?"

"Yes, the ancient Celts used it to approximate the characters of their spoken language, since they had no written language," Bennett said. "They mostly used it to mark graves and property lines with people's names. And there are these stones, all over Ireland and Scotland and Wales, that have ogham characters inscribed on them."

"It's so incredible," Sam said, "that these stones have lasted for thousands of years, with secret messages hidden in plain sight. Imagine finding one for yourself and discovering its meaning for the first time in centuries. What a thrill that would be."

Bennett's gaze turned warm. "You never could resist a good mystery. I remember you would go for hours, days, hunting down one of Father's buried treasures. You'd forget to eat, to sleep. It used to drive Joana nutty. I'm surprised you haven't flown the coop by now to seek your own puzzles to solve in the greater world."

"Oh, I . . ." She shook her head, as if that might shake some of the stuffing out of it. "No. That's all . . . It was just childhood fancy, those treasure hunts. I'm not going anywhere. I could never . . . The shop needs me. Who would tend the books if I were gone? Georgie Heath? His father would have the pigs feasting on their delicate interiors by nightfall."

Bennett laughed, the sound of it creating a sensation that expanded in her chest like a new collection of stars. "Yes, but imagine his dismay when they began quoting Chaucer the next morning."

Sam smiled, the heat of it radiating out of her skin. "It would finally class up the barnyard."

"Well, it's a shame the shop needs you so much, because Professor Wallstone could have used a mind like yours at the Hellfire Club," Bennett said.

Sam lifted both brows, the hairs on the back of her neck rising. "What is the Hellfire Club?"

"Well, technically it's called Montpelier Hill, but the locals call it the Hellfire Club, after a group of nobles that used to meet there in the early 1700s." Bennett moved the book with the ogham figures, tapping on an entry in the book below it. "It was a hunting lodge built in 1725, and local legend has it the man who built it tore out the stones of a Neolithic passage tomb to make it. The place is supposedly so cursed that a storm blew the whole roof off right after it was built. So they just tore more rocks out of the passage grave and put a stone roof on it."

"Cursed," Sam echoed, suppressing a shiver. No self-respecting scholar would believe in curses, even if she did want to draw a little closer to the warmth of the massive fireplace.

"It's all a bunch of superstitious nonsense, of course," Bennett said, leaning against the edge of the desk. "The curse, I mean. The passage tomb is quite real, or so Professor Wallstone believes. Convincing the rest of the administration has been more difficult."

"Why is that?" Sam asked, studying the squat, grainy structure of the Hellfire Club lodge in Bennett's book. Even in tiny black-and-white form, a sinister air hung over it. But maybe that was just the clouds looming in the background.

"The university just opened the Oriental Institute a few years ago, and their focus is on the Near East, especially now with Howard Carter's discovery of Tutankhamen's tomb. But Professor Wallstone is . . . very determined." Bennett frowned as if this were an argument he'd had with himself several times over.

"You think he's wrong?" Sam asked softly.

Bennett shook himself. "No, no, of course not. He's brilliant, and the excavation of a Neolithic passage tomb would have great historical significance. But sometimes his side interests become obsessions. And this one has been particularly engrossing. Anyway, he's gone off to Dublin to do a survey of the site himself, without a license or the university's support, but he'll need assistance. So I've agreed to go along. Someone's got to watch out for him."

"Oh, well, that's . . . something." Sam didn't know what *something* she thought that was. She didn't want to think about the searing disappointment of losing Bennett so soon after he'd finally returned to Clement; and she had absolutely no intention of examining the frisson of interest running along her spine at the idea of digging out the remnants of an ancient passage tomb. That part of her life was long past.

Bennett shook his head, straightening up. "But you didn't come here to listen to me go on about my studies. What was it you needed?"

"Oh, you weren't going on at all, I find it fascinating," Sam said, before catching the enthusiasm in her tone. "What I mean is, I hope you have a good trip. I got a book at Rare Antiquities, a strange one. There was no return address on the package, no letter of provenance inside, nothing. It couldn't have come from any of our regular sellers, and the inside of the book . . . Well, I thought I should bring it to Mr. Stee—uh, your father—right away."

She pulled the package from her satchel and handed it to Bennett. He frowned at the faint trace of handwriting on the front.

"This came to the shop, you said?"

Sam nodded, taking a half step forward and craning her neck to look at the lettering. Did she miss something? "Yes, just this afternoon. Why?"

Bennett tapped a finger on the package. "Because I recognize this handwriting. This is from Professor Wallstone."

Sam drew back in surprise. "Your professor? I thought you said he was in Ireland?"

"He is," Bennett murmured, sliding the book out. He made to open it, but Sam grabbed his arm.

"Please don't," she said, cringing back from the barest sliver of page visible beneath his finger. She gave a little embarrassed laugh. "I mean, don't open it while I'm here."

"Why not?"

Why not indeed? Sam could hardly admit her fears when he had just dismissed the superstitions of the locals so disdainfully. And she probably *was* being ridiculous. Too much time alone in the stacks, devouring all those articles about the curse of the mummy in Egypt. Still, she had no desire to look at that cat—if it could really be called that—again.

"I don't—" she began, but she was saved from her attempt at an excuse by the creak of the library doors and a confident, brassy voice just outside.

"Bennett, you old bore, Daddy sent me to shake off the dust and round you up for handshakes and baby kissing," said Joana Steeling, sauntering into the library like she sauntered into every room. With more confidence than Sam could have ever mustered. Joana looked like she'd stepped right out of the pages of a Butterick catalog, all tall and long, elegant lines in a brilliant scarlet evening dress. She had cut her hair short, the pageboy style popular with Hollywood starlets, the golden finger curls framing her face.

"Oh. Sam." Her expression softened in surprise, an awkward silence stretching out between them as Sam tried and failed to come up with something to say to bridge the gap.

Sam chewed nervously at her lip, running her hands along her satchel strap. "Jo, hello. Georgie said you might be home. I . . . You didn't say."

Joana's expression shuttered as she swept past Sam to link her arm through Bennett's like she was a prison guard tasked with his transport. The hem of her gown brushed over the piles of melting snow Sam had tracked in. "Yes, well, I'm not a dusty old book, so I didn't think you'd care. Bennett, Daddy's waiting. You know he hates waiting."

Sam drew back sharply, stung by the casual barb. Joana had always been the best at them, they'd just never been aimed directly at Sam before. Bennett frowned, glancing back at the stack of books even as Joana dragged him toward the door.

"I've still got a lot to do before I leave," he said. "I really don't have time for Father's kissing up."

"Make time," Joana said grimly. "If I have to laugh at another joke about the length of hemlines these days from a rotund bald man with sour champagne breath, I'll burn the whole place down. Give them something else to talk about."

"I've just received an important package from my professor in Ireland," Bennett insisted. They stalled at the library doors, and Joana glared at Sam like this was somehow all her fault. Which, to be fair, it was. But it wasn't like Joana could know that. "Sam brought it from the shop."

Sam cringed. "I didn't know it was from your professor."

"It's important that I go through it, Jo," Bennett said.

Joana rolled her eyes. "More important than making sure Daddy pays your tuition next year?"

"I wouldn't expect you to understand," Bennett said dryly. "Since you got yourself expelled from the academy after a single semester."

"What?" Sam gasped. "Oh, Jo, what happened?"

"Don't you 'oh, Jo' me," Joana said, stabbing a finger in Sam's direction. "That school wasn't worth my time anyhow. Full of dew droppers and killjoys, stuffier than a leather couch. Maybe if you had come with me I would have stuck it out, but I'm better off without it."

Sam took a full step back, the implication of Joana's words sinking into her chest and tugging at her heart. "I should go," Sam said, her voice shaky. "I've got to get back to the shop."

"I bet you do," Joana muttered. She gave Bennett's arm a little pinch, dragging him through the library door. "Read your little books later, Bennett. You know the way out, don't you, Sam?"

Joana didn't wait for Sam's answer, and Sam only waited long enough to be sure Joana wouldn't see the shimmer in her eyes before hurrying out of the library. She shoved past James, his surprise showing in the faint creasing around his eyes, but she didn't stop to apologize for her rudeness. She'd made a fool of herself, but that could hardly be helped now. At least she still had the shop—she would always have the shop. The books didn't judge her.

Her steps slowed as she reached the main street. It was so dark with all the storefronts closed up for the evening, the deep stillness broken only by the crunch of her boots through the snow. A single crow cawed somewhere in the distance, startling her enough that she doubled her pace.

A little restoration work was just what she needed to settle her nerves. She reached the front door of the shop, fishing for her keys as she grabbed the handle. But it turned freely, the door opening with a soft click. She was sure she had locked it. Something tugged at the edges of her awareness, a prickle of warning as she stepped into the darkened shop. Her eyes needed time to adjust, but her feet knew the way into the stacks. She was just outside the workroom door when a rumble of deep voices spilled out, along with the stray beam of a lantern.

Someone was in the bookshop.

CHAPTER THREE

Sam froze, not daring to put down the foot she had just raised, as the voices took shape. There were two of them, one low and rough like someone had taken a razor blade to the edges of it, the other smooth and hypnotic. Who were these men? What were they doing invading her shop? She tentatively lowered her foot but it felt off-kilter, the ground too soft. She looked down, her eyes adjusted to the dark enough that she could make out what she had missed when she first entered the shop.

The books were destroyed. Pulled off the shelves, knocked to the floor, piled in mounds all over. These books she had so lovingly pieced back together after their punishing journeys through time were now strewn across the floor like common paperbacks, their spines broken, pages bent, sections hanging loose from the binding. She sucked in a painful breath, the noise like a gusty tornado in the relative quiet.

"Someone is here," said the razor-edged voice in a thick Irish accent.

Sam cringed, shrinking back from the light that swept out from under the workroom door, which gave an ominous creak. More light spilled around the edges, and frantically she skittered past the piles of books, doing her best not to step on them. She darted around the nearest shelf, ducking low as the two men emerged with a lantern held high.

In any other context she might have considered them some sort of vaudeville duo, for they were opposites in nearly every way. One man was built like a granite slab, his shoulders filling the doorway and his head ducking just to clear the room. The other was more compact, his limbs short and wiry. They both wore long robes, the kind a monk might wear, their looming presence threatening and out of place. Sam caught sight of a pin fixed to the front of their robes, the gleaming edge of what looked like a heart made of metal, as their gazes swept the mess of the bookshop.

"Go that way," said the big man as he pointed in Sam's direction.

Sam scooted back, looking around desperately for a less exposed corner. She wove her way through the stacks on hands and knees as the lantern light continued its inexorable sweep. If she let herself imagine that light snagging on her foot, the panic would reach its iron fingers up and drag her down into its heart-stopping depths. So she only concentrated on putting one hand in front of the other.

"We know ye're here," said the big man. "Come along. Don't make us find you."

Sam choked back a sob, scrunching closer to the nearest shelf for protection. She didn't consider her satchel, though. It swung into the shelf, sweeping a collection of books to the floor.

"There you are," said the smaller man, rounding the shelf and standing over her. He raised his voice. "Found her, Brother Padraig."

Sam's heart rose into her throat, stopping any chance of her crying out for help. Not that there was anyone left on Mill Street to hear it. The big man, Brother Padraig, came around the stacks from the other side, trapping her. He held the lantern high, the blinding light obscuring his face.

"We don't want to hurt you, lass," he said. "But we will if we have to. Where is it?"

"Where is what?" she whispered, her voice trembling so badly it crossed two complete octaves on its journey out of her mouth.

"The book. Where is it?"

"Book?" She looked around wildly at the books on the floor and spread throughout the shop. "Which . . . ? We have . . . Can you be more specific?"

Brother Padraig crouched down, resting his arms on his knees. This close she could see the pin on his robe clearly. A heart on fire, the flames reaching out of the top.

"Don't play the fool, lass," he said. "We don't have time to waste. Where is the diary?"

Diary? Sam shook her head frantically. "I don't . . . We don't carry personal books. Unless you mean Samuel Pepys's secret diary? We had a copy a few months ago, but it already sold—"

Brother Padraig grabbed her coat and dragged her close. "Stop putting us on, lass. We know the professor sent it here. That book rightfully belongs to us, and we'll have it by whatever means necessary. Now give me Father Jacob's diary, or I'll have to find a more direct way of persuading you."

"Father Jacob?" Sam could barely put the two words together, much less comprehend their meaning. "I don't know. . . ."

But she did know, didn't she? Her brain had been doing the work in the background, the gears turning and clicking into place. She didn't believe in coincidences any more than Bennett believed in local superstitions. It couldn't be a coincidence these men with thick Irish brogues appeared in her shop demanding a diary the same day she received a package from a professor in Ireland with an old diary.

The diary she had left with Bennett.

"I don't know any Father Jacob or his diary," Sam whispered.

Brother Padraig leaned in close, his eyes like black glass. "Wrong answer, lass."

His hand disappeared into his robe and the hard glint of a knife flashed in the lantern light. Sam screamed and kicked out on instinct, her foot connecting with his chest. He fell into the nearest shelf, the glass of his lantern shattering in a terrific explosion. Shards of it rained down on Sam's head as the lantern dropped onto the nearest pile of books. Sam and Mr. Steeling had worked to build the shop to minimize the intrusion of humidity and sunlight, the twin destroyers of rare books. They kept the bookshop as cool and dry as possible to maintain their pristine condition.

Which made them the ideal tinder for fire.

The pile lit up like fireworks, pouring smoke into the air. Brother Padraig threw up his arms in protection. Sam took the distraction as an opportunity and crawled away. It wasn't until she ran up against the back wall that she realized the fatal flaw in her escape route. She had crawled into a dead end, and now there was a growing line of fire between her and escape.

She got low, pulling her shirt up over her face to keep the smoke from infesting her lungs, but it stung her eyes as the heat in the bookshop grew stifling, prickling at her skin and making her head throb. Somewhere on the other side of the fire the men shouted to her, their voices rough and urgent, the smaller man spitting curses as he tried beating back the fire with his robes.

"We have to go," came his voice, his words harsh in the swirling smoke. He pulled Brother Padraig back. "This'll all be ashes. We've got to get out."

"The diary!" Brother Padraig shouted. "Lass, give us the book and we'll save you!"

"The fire is too high!" the smaller man yelled.

Sam curled into a ball, trying to find a patch of clean air, but the shop was thick with the dispersion of incinerated pages. She coughed, her eyes watering. "Please, help me."

"The book!" Brother Padraig barked.

"It's no good, Brother Padraig," the small man cried. "We couldn't reach her if we tried. God have mercy on your soul, lass."

"No, please!" Sam cried out, reaching forward as another pile of books caught fire in a blinding explosion.

By the time she could clear the spots from her eyes, the men were gone and the fire had consumed half the shop. Sam curled up between the last two shelves. Her head pounded, her skin hurt, and she felt like she might throw up. There was no escape. These books had been her life, and now they would be her death.

But those men had escaped. And if they were looking for the diary, it wouldn't be long until their search led them to Bennett. If they were willing to let the bookshop burn down, what would they do to him? She had to find a way out.

She gazed up at the empty set of shelves above, the top lost in a thick cloud of smoke. Full of books it probably weighed a few hundred pounds, but empty it was light and wobbly, and easily unbalanced. She rose to a crouch and set her shoulder against it, shoving as hard as she could. Smoke swirled in warning as the shelf came crashing down, the top catching the next shelf and knocking it over in a domino effect, all the way to the front door.

She kept her shirt over her mouth and scrambled across the empty bookcases, knocking her shins and knees against the shelves as she went. The shop was so hot she could barely keep her eyes open. It was her last and longest departure, crawling over fallen shelves on hands and knees, but she didn't stop until she reached the front desk. She paused for a half second, wanting to gather the last new arrivals in her arms and save them, but the ceiling gave an ominous creak overhead, a crash from the back of the shop warning of its imminent collapse.

Sam stumbled for the door and spilled out onto the sidewalk. The snow sizzled against the heat of her clothes as she crawled for the general store on the opposite side of the street, collapsing against the storefront. A resounding *crack* split the night when the ceiling of the shop came crashing down, the inferno consuming the last of the books.

CHAPTER FOUR

Sam was little more than a smudge of soot stains and desperation by the time she reached the police station on the far side of downtown Clement. She used the last of her strength to pull the door open and collapse across Chief Higgins's desk with a puff of ashes and heat. The chief, halfway into a blissful late-night doze, startled upright at the specter of this demon come to seek vengeance on the living world.

"S . . . Sam Knox?" Chief Higgins said, surreptitiously wiping a line of drool from one corner of his mouth. He cleared his throat gruffly, straightening out the rumpled edges of his deep-blue uniform. "What are you doing here this time of night?"

"Fire," Sam wheezed.

Chief Higgins raised his bushy eyebrows at Sam. "You need a light to get home?"

"No," Sam said, gritting her teeth in frustration. "There is a fire—"

"Chief, you better take a look at this," said one of the deputy boys, peeking out the door where Sam just entered. "Looks like there's some kind of smoke or something, coming from the end of Mill Street. Might be a fire."

"It *is* a fire," Sam said desperately. "I'm trying to tell you—"

"Hang on there, Samantha," said Chief Higgins, bustling out of his chair and circling the desk to meet the deputy at the door. "We've got a situation here."

Sam rolled her eyes. This was what came of appointing a corn farmer as chief of police. "If you would just listen—"

"Oh hell, it looks like there is a fire," Chief Higgins said, running right through Sam's insistence that there was, indeed, a fire. "Heaven help us all if it gets to Mr. Steeling's mill again."

Sam wanted nothing more than to collapse and take a nap, but there was still the matter of the intruders at the bookshop. "Chief Higgins," she yelled out, following him around the station as he bustled to the phone to call the volunteer fire brigade. "There's something else. There were men, in the shop. You need to find them."

"Just a minute, Sam, I've got to— Hello? Mr. Steeling? We've got a situation down here. . . . Why, yes, I heard you were having a party, was planning on stopping over myself after a . . . No, sir, I didn't mean –it's only that . . . All right, I can hold."

Sam tugged at his sleeve insistently. "Chief, I need you to listen to me. There were men in the shop. They broke in, and I think—"

"We'll take care of all that, soon as we get the fire sorted," Chief Higgins said. "I'll get one of the boys to drive you home soon as— Mr. Steeling? Yes sir . . . Well, yes, I know there's a fire, that's why I called you. Sam Knox is down here. She's saying it happened in your shop there. I was— Yes sir, of course, sir. We'll see you soon as you get here."

"Chief, please," Sam begged, a wave of tears gumming up the ash in her eyes. "I need your help."

"You'll be all right here for a spell, Sam, while the boys and I work to put this fire out," Chief Higgins said, taking her firmly by the shoulders and steering her to his desk. "In the meantime, why don't you have a seat and rest? We'll take care of everything."

"No, Chief!" Sam called after him, but the man was already out the door with his deputies in tow. Sam sighed, collapsing into his still-warm chair as the silence of the suddenly empty station buzzed like a hive of angry bees in her ears. If she'd had the energy, she might have screamed or torn at her hair like the funeral wailers in ancient Greece. But luckily for her follicles, she did not have the energy.

They were gone, all of them. The books she had so lovingly restored, cataloged, and shelved, all burned up. Her present was on fire, her future in ashes. What would she do now, without her books? If she let herself think about it too long, the urge to scream grew exponentially. She could do all of that later, though, when she knew Bennett was safe.

She needed to get to Steeling Manor, somehow, but there was no way she could walk all that distance back to the house. It was possible those awful men from the store were already on their way, or even there. Maybe they were holding the whole family hostage. Except Chief Higgins just spoke to Mr. Steeling on the phone and he didn't make any mention of intruders or hostage negotiations, so maybe they hadn't arrived yet. Which meant she still had time to get to Bennett and warn him.

But with the adrenaline wearing off she was left weak-kneed and light-headed, a fatigue dragging at her bones worse than any from a long day spent hauling laundry with her mother or lugging new inventory around the shop. She needed to close her eyes, just for a moment, just long enough to gather her thoughts and uncoil some of the tension still making her lungs ache—a tension that exploded when someone grabbed her arm.

She shot up with a strangled cry, gripping at the hand, visions of hearts burning and black cats with ears like horns tormenting her. But it was Joana's face that appeared before her, lined in worry and fatigue.

"Sam, you damn fool, I'm so glad you're all right," she said, seemingly unmindful of the terror coursing through Sam's veins. "You look a mess and you reek like the ash end of a cigarette, but at least you're all in one piece."

Before Sam could think of any appropriate response—and really, was there one?—Joana dragged her into a fierce hug. "How dare you make me worry like this when I was so determined to be cross with you. You know what worrying does to my complexion."

"Sam, my girl, we came as soon as Higgins put in the call," said Mr. Steeling, barreling through the door in full business mode. He still wore his evening clothes, the bow tie tilted a few degrees askew. What a story there must be circulating with the cocktail shrimp. "What in hell happened?"

Sam's eyes filled with tears. "Oh, Mr. Steeling. I'm so sorry. The books, the shop . . ."

"Never mind them," Mr. Steeling said, gently but firmly. "I can replace books. I can't replace you. I've got to check on the men. Will you girls be all right here?"

"Of course," Joana said, putting a protective arm around Sam.

"Oh, Mr. Steeling, about the shop," Sam started, but Mr. Steeling held up a hand.

"Plenty of time to take inventory of the damage later, Sam, I've got to make sure the fire doesn't reach the mill. We can't have another disaster like the one during the war or we'll all be in the begging line again." Mr. Steeling pointed a finger at Joana. "No antics, all right?"

"Oh, Daddy, just go," Joana said with a wave. She waited in that same position, Sam tucked confidently under her arm, until her father left the station. Then she turned on her heel and held

Sam out at arm's length, looking her over critically. "We'll have to get you back to the Manor and cleaned up, *after* you tell me what happened."

Sam shook her head. "There's no time for that. I need to find Bennett."

Joana drew back in surprise. "Whatever for?"

"I think he's in danger."

"Danger? From what?"

How to explain all that had happened that evening, everything that had changed? She hadn't yet had time to comprehend it herself, much less attempt to explain it to someone like Joana. She feared that she had half imagined those men with their thick accents and old-fashioned robes.

"It's about the package I brought earlier," Sam said. "It's an emergency."

"Does the shop burning have something to do with it?" Joana asked, her gaze narrowing suspiciously.

"Please, Jo," Sam begged. "I need to talk to him right away."

"Well, you'll have to send a telegram, then, since he's halfway back to Chicago by now."

"Bennett left?" Sam asked, her stomach twisting.

"Yes, nearly on your heels. He's got to catch a train from Chicago out to New York to board his steamer to Ireland. It doesn't leave until morning, but you know how he is. If you're not early, you're late. I almost considered stowing away in one of his trunks. As it is, Mama will hardly let me leave the Manor, much less venture all the way across the Atlantic."

Sam shook her head. "No, Joana, Bennett can't go to Ireland, not now. We need to catch him, before . . ."

Before what? She couldn't think about that either.

Joana stood beside the chief's desk with her hands on her hips, taking on a no-nonsense air of determination inherent in the Steeling line. "Sam, stop giving me the runaround and tell me what's going on."

"I can explain everything later," Sam said, chewing at one corner of her lip. "But right now we need a car."

Joana lifted both brows. "Samantha Margaret Knox, are you suggesting we steal an automobile?"

"I wouldn't suggest it if it weren't absolutely nec—"

"Oh stop, I love it," Joana said, a light sparking deep in her eyes. "I haven't stolen anything in ages. I was getting rusty. Daddy's brought the Phaeton, freshly gassed, and I've been itching to take her for a whirl. We'll be in Chicago before sunup."

"How do we get the keys?" Sam asked as she did her best to scrub the ashes of her books from her neck and face with the sleeve of her ruined shirt. She was in desperate need of a bath, but there was no time. She beat the worst of the ashes out of her winter coat before putting it back on, trying to draw any of her father's strength from its woolen interior.

"I'm offended you would ask," Joana said, fishing down the bodice of her dress to pull out a set of keys. "Of course I borrowed the spare set before we left the house. I wasn't going to stick around the police station all night. We'll swing by the Manor for a quick change and be off."

Sam considered the very serious consequences of her decision—Mr. Steeling would never trust her again, they might actually get arrested, and she had very little confidence in Joana's driving skills. But all of that paled in the face of the danger that awaited Bennett if she didn't get to the train station in time to warn him.

"Let's go," Sam said. "Before it's too late and I lose my nerve."

Joana grinned. "Just like old times, huh? I should have gotten myself kicked out of the academy ages ago."

CHAPTER FIVE

"So, these men set the shop on fire for what?" Joana asked, pitching her voice up over the roar of the engine. "A dirty old book?"

Sam shook her head, bracing her hands against the dash and watching the stalks of corn whip past on the edge of the Phaeton's headlights. Joana drove with the pedal to the floor, the whole car rattling and threatening to dump them out every time she hit a dip in the road.

"I know how it sounds," Sam said. "But you didn't see the diary, Jo. It was . . ."

How to explain the sick wave of dread that washed over her at that one brief glimpse inside the diary? Father Jacob's diary, they had called it. But who was Father Jacob? And what other terrible secrets did his diary contain?

"If they wanted the book so bad, why didn't they just pay for it like everybody else?" Joana asked, ever practical.

"It wasn't for sale," Sam said. "At least, not yet. I'd only just received it at the shop this evening. It looked like it had been misdelivered several times before it got to me, so it was probably sent several weeks ago."

"Who sent it?"

"Bennett said the writing on the package was from his professor, Barnaby Wallstone. The one he's meeting in Dublin. But the diary had extensive damage, it looked as if it had been buried for some time."

"Why send it to the shop?" Joana asked.

"I don't know. Maybe Bennett told him we do repairs there? The diary is in bad shape, the worst I've ever seen. I'm not even sure I could recover most of the interior. Or maybe he thought it wasn't safe with him in Ireland. Those men at the shop wanted the diary so badly they were willing to let the entire building burn down, with me inside. I don't know what they will do to Bennett if they find out he has it. Oh, Jo, what if we don't make it in time?"

"We'll make it," Joana said, tilting her head down and pressing her foot on the gas. The engine growled beneath Sam's feet, a promise in every rumble.

The cornstalks edging the road flattened into great plains, then rose from the earth, first in the form of squatting houses and then into the lumbering form of great neighborhoods, and finally into the skyscraping monoliths of downtown Chicago. The hollowness that whistled through Sam twisted into a maelstrom as the buildings loomed over her and pressed in close, as if any one of them might topple over and crush them. Cars crowded the lanes as people filled the sidewalks, the thin light of dawn tinting everything a faint pink. A railcar came barreling past them fast enough to rock the Phaeton, its bell clanging manically.

"Jo, do you know where you're going?" Sam asked, her voice the only anchor in the growing chaos around her. She gripped the dashboard as hard as her bones would let her.

"Mostly," Joana said, gunning it around another car and slamming the brakes as a collection of young men in navy uniforms trotted across the street. Joana blew a shrill whistle out the cracked window, which earned her a salute from two of them.

"Jo, maybe we should . . ." Sam swallowed down the acid burn of the bile rising in her throat, pressing her eyes closed. But that only made the violence of the stop and start worse, so she opened her eyes with a sickening certainty. "Could we maybe stop? Or walk? I need . . . I think I'm going to . . . Jo, please."

"You'll be all right," Joana said, taking a hard right down a side street and earning a few shouts from surrounding drivers. "You get used to it."

Sam couldn't imagine ever being used to this if she had the rest of her life to try, not that she wanted to. Everything was so big, and loud, and menacing. She didn't know how anyone here took a deep breath, much less found enough room to turn about or stretch their limbs. And the buildings were just . . . *so tall*. Taller than Farmer Mason's new barn, or the oak in the back field that Papa had refused to cut down because it was older and knew better than the rest of them. Tall as the buildings were, they'd all been crammed into short stretches of city blocks, like cattle jockeying for the same patch of shade on a hot day.

They were huge and imposing, but they were also beautiful. Unlike the practical, squat buildings of Clement, these buildings sported high arches and needle-like spires and thousands of windows that shone in the rising sun. The sheer scope of them captured Sam's breath. She had seen pictures, of course, in the newspaper, but grainy little photos were nothing like standing among the architectural giants. She pressed her face to the thick glass, craning her neck to try and catch a glimpse of the tops of the buildings far overhead.

"How do you even hear yourself think here?" Sam asked.

"You don't, that's the beauty of it," Joana said. "Everything else is so loud, you don't have to put up with your own thoughts rattling your head."

"I like my own thoughts."

"Not everybody does," Joana said flatly.

Sam hadn't asked Joana what happened—how she'd gotten herself expelled, or the more important *why*. There had been more pressing concerns, but now it occurred to Sam that a good friend would have asked somewhere in the last few hours since they left the police station in Clement. A good friend would have written in the past six months, though, and Sam hadn't managed that either. Their fight seemed so silly now, Sam not wanting to go with Joana to the academy on scholarship. Maybe Joana was right; if Sam had been there, she might have been able to keep her out of trouble. But then Sam would have had to leave the bookshop, and Clement. Joana just didn't understand.

"Jo, about what happened before you left—"

"Bennett said his train to New York was leaving out of Grand Central," Joana cut in. She didn't look at Sam. "We should be there in a few minutes, if these lollygaggers would get the lead out."

Sam sank back into quiet as Joana shouted a few choice words out the window at another rude driver. She'd never been very good at friendships, considering Joana was her only real friend in Clement. And even then, it had mostly been an effort on Joana's part to draw her out of the pages of a book and into real life. She lost two years to the darkness of grief after her papa died, and when Mr. Steeling opened the shop and coaxed her into helping him run it five years ago, the shop became her only source of joy. A focus that turned into an obsession. She had become so engrossed with her duties that it had been a relief to shed all her other obligations. But had she shed too much? Had she lost Joana?

The few minutes stretched into twenty, but eventually they

pulled up under a clock tower that loomed thirteen stories above, the topmost numbers lost in the low early-morning clouds. Joana didn't find a spot so much as she made one, angling the Phaeton into an empty stretch of street with signs Sam was sure said NO PARKING. But the clock tower chimed five, and there was no time for dithering over parking laws. They needed to find Bennett.

Grand Central Station of Chicago took up as much room as all of Mill Street in Clement, a sprawling complex built of deep-red bricks and filled with Gothic archways, gleaming stained-glass windows, and that imposing monolith of time rising up to connect the ground to the sky. A massive sign in red letters announced the station as a central hub for the Baltimore & Ohio Railroad. The wind here cut like a dagger of ice, and Sam was grateful for her coat despite the lingering scent of smoke within its folds.

She hesitated at the bottom of the stairs leading into the station, surveying the crush of passengers crowding the entry doors. "Jo, how are we going to find him in all these people?"

Joana frowned up at the station entrance. "It *is* bigger than I remembered." She clicked her tongue. "We'll just have to go inside and find his train. Come on, I once found an heirloom ring in the snow at two in the morning. This is nothing."

Sam hurried to keep pace as Joana took the stairs two at a time, her heel clicks lost amid the general pandemonium of horns and thumping trunk wheels and the distant shriek of train whistles. The interior was even more ornate than the exterior, with impos-ing marble columns that looked better suited to a Grecian temple than a train station. Rows of high-backed wooden benches filled the bustling space, the ticket counters lined up along one side of the waiting area.

Joana marched through it all with as much purpose as a knife cutting through soft butter. She leaned against the glass of the nearest ticket window with the studied boredom of a world traveler.

"We're looking for the train to New York, connecting to the RMS *Olympic* transatlantic steamer," she said, keeping her chin tilted up and away from the man behind the glass, as if she couldn't be bothered to make direct eye contact.

He gave her a weary look. "Which line?"

Joana frowned. "How should I know? That's why I'm talking to you."

The man's breath was heavy through the mouthpiece. "Miss, if you don't know the line and the time of departure, I can't help you. We get hundreds of trains through here a day."

"Haven't you got some kind of schedule? What is it you people do all day back there?"

As Joana argued with the ticket agent, Sam scanned the crowds, her gaze snagging on every head of dark hair. She knew it was mostly hopeless to think she could spot Bennett in a crowd like this, even if she did know every curve and swoop of his wavy locks. He could already be on the train or halfway to New York by now. Joana was a bit fuzzy on the details.

Sam's breath caught in her throat as she spotted not Bennett's dark hair, but the ruffled edge of a robe. It was only a flash, so quick and distant she wouldn't have noticed were it not seared in her brain with the heat of a burning bookshop. How did they get there so fast? Did they know about Bennett? Had they spotted her? She clutched at Joana's arm, interrupting her mid-tirade.

"Jo," she whispered, her voice wavering and thick. "It's him. The man . . . the one from the shop. Brother Padraig. He's here."

Joana cut her a sharp look. "What do you mean? Where?"

Sam pointed a trembling finger in the direction of the train platform. "There. He just . . . Jo, what do we do?"

"We follow him," Joana said, taking Sam by the arm and dragging her away.

"Jo, we can't follow him!" Sam whispered, throwing apologetic looks to the people she jostled. "What if he sees us?"

"Train platforms are always crawling with coppers," Joana said. "All you have to do is shout and wave and they'll bundle him up faster than a South Side pickpocket."

The train shed vibrated with noise, the metal ceiling arching a hundred feet overhead. Giant windows filtered in light at the top of the shed, great puffs of steam and coal burn filling the place with a dusty glow. Sam ducked around a woman waving to a departing train.

"Where is he?" Joana asked, squinting against the haze.

"I don't . . . There!" Sam pointed toward a train at the far end, the flash of a dark brown robe slipping in between the grays and blacks. "That train!"

Joana hustled through the crowd. Under any other circumstances Sam would have admired her fearlessness, but she almost tumbled off the edge of the platform two different times, and she wished Joana would let up just a little. The sound and heat and volume of people pressed in, and without the tether of Joana's hand on her wrist she was sure she would drift into the sea of humanity forever.

"Excuse me, ma'am," said a porter to Joana as they reached the end car in the last train, an elegant Pullman sleeper. The porter wore a deep-red suit and a pillbox hat, marking him as an employee of Pullman. "I'll need to see your ticket before you can board."

Joana stopped, giving him her best impression of Mr. Steeling in full business mode. "We need to get on that car."

"Surely, ma'am, but you'll need to buy a ticket to do so."

"We don't have time for tickets, my brother is on that train along with an arsonist and attempted murderer," Joana said loudly, collecting the nervous stares of approaching passengers.

"Ma'am, I'm sure that's not—" the porter began as a window slid open and Bennett's head popped out.

"Joana, what are you doing here?" he demanded. His gaze swiveled to Sam, his frown deepening. "Sam, what has my sister dragged you into?"

Joana pointed a triumphant finger at Bennett. "See? I told you my brother was on board."

"Where is the porter?" demanded an older woman with a strident voice and a bouncing peacock feather in her hat. "We need our luggage loaded!"

"Yes, ma'am, right away," the porter said, his gaze lingering on Joana doubtfully. But he moved toward the impatient woman and her oversize suitcases.

Joana wasted no time, hopping up the steep steps into the train car. Sam hesitated only a moment before following suit, sending a silent apology toward the beleaguered porter. The interior of the car was cramped and narrow, several of the compartment doors already closed and the shades pulled against prying eyes. But one of the doors at the far end slid open, and Bennett's imposing figure stepped out.

"Joana, what trouble are you in this time?" he asked, his voice drawing the attention of the two older women in the nearest compartment.

Joana skirted past them, pushing her brother back. "Just tell the whole world, why don't you, brother?"

"What are— Sam, what is going on?" Bennett turned his exasperation in her direction.

"I . . . We . . . There's . . . something's wrong," she stammered, words failing her at the most important time.

"What's wrong?" Bennett asked, more bewildered than afraid.

"Somebody burned down the bookshop," Joana said, all business. "And Sam thinks it's you and some book they're after."

"What do you mean someone burned down the shop? What book are you talking about?"

"The one from your professor," Sam said.

Bennett frowned. "The diary? What does anybody want with the diary? Wait, did the shop really burn down?"

"That's not the point of any of this," Joana said with a dramatic sigh. "The point is there's a murderer after you and this book, and you need to get off the train."

"Someone was murdered?" Bennett said, alarm ringing through his tone.

"Well, no," Sam said. "But they tried."

"What—" Bennett began, but a shrill whistle cut off his next question. The train lurched, jostling them against each other as another whistle blew through the open window.

"What is that?" Sam asked in a voice one decibel below a shriek.

Joana leaned over the small table in the compartment, glancing out the window as the lurch gathered momentum. "The train is pulling out. We're leaving the station."

CHAPTER SIX

"**W**hat?" Sam asked, her voice now reaching full shriek.

She pressed in beside Joana, her breath obscuring the glass. Faintly through the fog she made out the figure of the smaller man from the bookshop. His eyes opened wide in shock as they locked on hers, and he shoved his way through the crowded platform toward their train car. She could do little more than watch, her heart climbing up her throat, as he leaped from the platform and down on the tracks to chase after the departing train, the edge of the shed cutting off her view. She wrestled the window open and stuck her head out, wincing against the sting of the freezing January morning as several railroad employees restrained the man and dragged him away.

"That's one of them," she said with a gasp, her breath passing over her face like a cloud. The train picked up speed, rocking the car back and forth and knocking her head against the window.

Joana peeked out beside her. "See, I told you. Bundled up like a South Side pickpocket. Problem solved."

"But what are we going to do?" Sam asked, drawing back inside. "We can't be on this train!"

"We could jump," Joana said, though she didn't sound confident in their chances.

"No one is jumping," Bennett said, exasperated. "You're both going to sit down right now and tell me what is going on, or I'll call the train officer on you myself."

Sam slid meekly into the seat opposite Bennett, folding into herself to make room for Joana and trying to contain the panic squeezing her heart. If she closed her eyes, she could imagine she was back in the bookshop, and all her precious works were still there, and none of this was happening. The screeching sway of the car didn't really lend itself to the fantasy, though.

Bennett fixed his gaze on Sam in a way that made her aware of every nerve ending of exposed skin. "Start from the beginning."

"Well, it started with that strange package at the shop, the one your professor sent, though I guess you already know that part," Sam said, knotting her fingers together. Now that she was sitting on such a plush seat—without the jarring threat of Joana's driving to keep her awake—all the energy that had sustained her through the last several hours evaporated like the steam puffing past their window. She was dreadfully tired. She should have slept in the car when she had the chance.

"Yes, I already know that part," Bennett prodded when she didn't go on.

She snapped up from the half second of oblivion. "Yes, right. So, after I brought the package to you, I went back to the shop. Except . . . there were men. In the shop. They had torn the whole place apart, my books were . . ."

A lump rose in Sam's throat and she paused, the sheer terror of that first flame eating into the pile of books washing over her again. Joana grabbed her hand and squeezed it tight.

"Are you sure it wasn't the butcher's boys?" Bennett asked. "They're always tearing things up around town."

Sam shook her head. "No, I'd know them. They're terrible, but they wouldn't do *this*. These men were strangers. And they had Irish accents."

Bennett crossed his arms, sitting back. "What did Chief Higgins say about all this? Surely he's got men searching Clement for these . . . Irish intruders now."

"Oh, well, I tried to tell him," Sam said. "But he was distracted by the fire, and then we had to get here and warn you. We didn't have time to tell anyone else."

Bennett's expression darkened. "How exactly did you get here?"

Joana cleared her throat, leaning forward with a smirk. "I'll field this one, Sam. We borrowed Daddy's Phaeton."

"Joana Rose Steeling," Bennett thundered in his father's exact tone. "Of all the irresponsible, idiotic—"

"It was my idea," Sam said hastily, glancing at Joana. "Bennett, you don't understand. These men left me in the shop to burn. I couldn't think what they would do to you. We had to!"

Bennett closed his eyes, pinching the bridge of his nose. "What a mess you two have made. And you, Sam, I'm most surprised at you. Letting Jo drag you into her antics like this."

"Hey, this time it was the other way around," Joana protested. "She dragged me into these particular antics."

"That doesn't matter," Sam cried, slapping her hands down on the table and drawing their attention. "What if there were more of them? What if they're in Clement now? They know who I am. If they try to go to the farm, my mother . . ."

Sam imagined one of these faceless men looming over her mother in the laundry room where she spent her days, suds cascading on the floor as her mother tried to fight them off. Her mother had no one else to protect her, and here Sam was running off and abandoning her like she always did. Choosing the Steelings over her own blood. Her mother never said as much with words, but she didn't have to—Sam knew it in the quiet spaces whenever she was home, the times when her mother could have made conversation and turned away instead. And now she'd left her to the machinations of an arsonist and would-be murderer.

"I'll send Father a telegram as soon as we reach a stop," Bennett said. "He'll make sure your mother knows where you are and that you're safe. But I still don't understand why these men were after the diary Professor Wallstone sent me. It looks to be more than a hundred years old, and in terrible condition. What could they possibly want with it?"

Sam shook her head. "They didn't really take the time to explain. And I only did a cursory cleaning before I brought it to you. Do you have it now?"

"Of course," Bennett said, standing up and reaching for the trunk stored above the table, digging through its contents.

"Your professor didn't mention the diary or these men in any of his previous letters?" Sam asked as he pulled out the beaten package, setting it on the table between them.

Bennett hesitated. "No, but that's not . . . Professor Wallstone's correspondence has been inconsistent since he arrived in Dublin. He was never the best at keeping up, but now it's like he's . . . hiding something. I haven't had any communication from him in weeks. The last letter said only that he'd stumbled across something." Bennett spread his hands. "He must have meant the diary, but why not just say so? What was he afraid of?"

"Based on the condition of Daddy's shop, I have a tall guess and a short guess," Joana said.

"Maybe the diary has the answer," Sam said, though she made no move to touch the package.

"Or maybe it'll just make us a target like the shop," Joana reasoned.

"We're already targets," Bennett said. "Better to know what we're going into. Knowledge is always the higher path."

"You sound like my classics professor at the academy," Joana muttered.

"Shouldn't we give it to the authorities?" Sam asked, chewing at one corner of her lip. "Like the police? If we keep it, people could get hurt."

"Us people," Joana said.

But Bennett was already sliding the diary out of the package. "If the professor took the trouble to send it to the shop, it was for a purpose. The police would only lock it up and treat it like evidence of a crime. I need to know what's in the diary."

Joana rolled her eyes at Sam, slouching back in the seat. "There's no reasoning with him when he gets on a tear like this. He's never met a problem he wouldn't love to take responsibility for, especially if it's not really his. It's his fatal flaw. If Atlas ever got tired of holding up the world, Bennett would be the first to volunteer to take his place."

"Someone's got to keep the world turning, don't they, Jo?" Bennett said. "We can't all go jiving through life. There's always someone responsible."

That was all well and good back in Clement, and one of the things Sam most admired him for, his ability to take control of any situation. But here it felt foolish, even to Sam. These men were dangerous, and she had no intention of facing them again. But she could hardly let Bennett go careening into danger by himself. If she could help in any way, she would.

Even if it meant looking at that hideous diary again.

It looked more fragile now, if that was possible. Sam flinched away from it, her resolve to help shrinking under the weight of the memory of that frantically sketched picture. Joana gave her a questioning look, and Sam forced her fingers to unclench beneath the table.

"It's only a picture," she muttered to herself, taking the book gingerly from Bennett.

A picture that got no less disturbing on a second viewing.

"What in the devil is that thing?" Joana asked, a healthy quiver in her words.

Bennett leaned forward. "Ah, that's the Hellfire Cat."

"The what?" Sam and Joana asked simultaneously.

Bennett put one finger on the edge of the book, turning it toward him to get a better look. "The Hellfire Cat; it's a local legend among the Hellfire Club. It was supposedly spotted whenever the Hellfire Club was meeting at the lodge, only they claimed it didn't look like any ordinary cat. It was the size of a Dalmatian, they said, with ears shaped like horns and glowing red eyes. It was meant to be a sign that the club was conspiring with the devil."

"So, I wasn't far off," Joana said.

Bennett nodded. "This must be why the professor sent the book to me, to have it repaired. I've told him about the shop before. He couldn't have done this level of repair in the field, and he has a bit of a rivalry with the professor who's in charge of the department while he's gone. Whoever this Father Jacob was, he must have had something to do with the Hellfire Club. This could lead to proof that the lodge was built from a passage grave. It's exactly what Professor Wallstone needs to secure a license to dig there."

Sam thought it meant something entirely different, but she wasn't going to argue with Bennett. He tried to turn the pages, but they were lumped together, turned to a pulpy mess along the edges where moisture and dirt had fused them. He dug his nail under one side, trying to separate the pages, and the paper gave an ominous tearing sound.

"Oh, please don't!" Sam cried, reaching out without thinking and laying her hands over his. The contact sent electric sparks along her nerve endings as Bennett met her gaze in surprise. He was so close she could make out the small flecks of gold in his eyes.

"What is it?"

"You'll damage it, doing it like that," she said. "See, you've already torn the edge there. The book is in a significantly deteriorated condition. Any force or pressure you apply now could ruin it completely."

Bennett sat back, spreading his hands wide. "I don't know any other way to open it. If you still had the shop . . ."

Sam drew her hand back sharply, which made Bennett wince. "Sam, I'm sorry, I didn't mean to be —"

"It's okay," Sam said hastily, hugging her arms around herself. She chewed at one corner of her lip, weighing her desire to help Bennett against her desire to never have to look at another page of the diary again. "I might know a way. But I would need tools, and time."

"What kind of tools are we talking?" Joana asked.

Sam shrugged. "For this level of repair? I'd need my humidifier, a set of brushes, a scalpel, wheat-starch paste, glue. But those are all specialty items I order from Mr. Peltingham's shop in London. I suppose I could try to find a place in New York that could provide a substitute, but I wouldn't even know where to start. I'd have to ask your father. Though I suppose that's not the best idea either."

Joana stood up, setting her feet apart like a sailor bracing on a ship. "Give me ten minutes. I'll see what I can scrounge up."

Sam blinked in surprise. "But you don't know what any of those things are."

"I didn't know the combination to the dean's private safe either, but here I am, persona non grata at the academy. You two play nice while I'm gone."

Joana slid out of the compartment, which suddenly felt three sizes too small as the door slammed shut, and left Sam alone with Bennett. Her fingers were clunky and unsure on the pages, the hem of her borrowed skirt riding up her knee and leaving her bare skin dangerously close to brushing against him under the table. She tucked her legs together and pressed them sideways, out of potential contact range. Even though all her feet wanted to do was slip free of their sensible loafers and slide up his calf.

He could see the course of her thoughts, surely, in the drop of her eyes and the flush of her cheeks. But he said nothing, only continued to squint at the Hellfire Cat sketch. His fingers brushed hers and the air in the compartment heated and expanded from the friction of that touch. For a moment Sam couldn't remember what she was doing there.

"It must be a dream, to be immersed in knowledge like this every day," Sam said, turning her gaze out to the pristine landscape beyond the train tracks to break the tension rising in her. "And with a professor renowned in the field, no less. To have access to such minds every day, all the time . . . All my confidants are long dead, their opinions and decisions as set as the type on the page. But to be living it, now . . ."

"Sam . . ." Bennett hesitated, his fingers flexing and relaxing where they rested on the table. "You could go, if you wanted. The University of Chicago is co-ed, and prides itself on being so. With your mind and your skills, they would be fools not to admit you to the college. The knowledge you have from repairing the books alone . . . Do you understand the value? Father would happily sponsor you. He's said it often enough. It would certainly be a better return on investment for him than Joana's tuition at the academy."

Sam shook her head resolutely, drawing her attention back in from the open fields beyond. "No, I couldn't ask Mr. Steeling to do that. He's already given me so much. He's been like a second father to me, especially . . . after."

Bennett's fingers flexed again, closing some of the distance between them. "Sam—"

The door to the compartment slammed open, and Joana slid in, her arms filled with a bizarre collection of items that she let tumble onto the tabletop. The last item, a large silver pitcher, she set down more carefully.

"What is all this?" Bennett asked, drawing back to his side of the table.

Joana sat beside Sam, tossing one elbow over the seat back and cocking her head at a jaunty angle with a smirk. "Supplies. Just about everything Sam said she needed. I've got boiling water here in the pitcher, so don't let it tip unless you're looking to poach yourself. Some makeup brushes I swindled out of a girl three compartments down, and some kind of shoe-repair glue I bartered from the shoe-shine boy. Lips like sandpaper on that one. I don't know what wheat-starch paste is, though, so you'll have to do without on that one. Oh! Almost forgot."

She pulled a small knife from the bodice of her dress, flipping out the blade as she set it down. "And one scalpel. Well, closest I could find, but that tip's freshly sharpened. You won't find a finer blade on these tracks."

Sam spread the items out on the table, touching each makeshift tool with reverence. "Jo, this is . . . How in the world did you get all this, and so fast?"

"This is nothing, I once traded three cigarettes for the keys to the dean's office."

"Was that before or after you got the combination to his safe?" Bennett asked with a frown. "I think the reasons for your expulsion are becoming clear now."

Joana kicked at him. "Worked in your favor today, didn't it?"

"That remains to be seen," Bennett said. "Sam, can you use any of this?"

"I think so," Sam said, taking one of the smaller makeup brushes and using it to clean the outer edges of the paper. A tidy pile of brown dirt gathered on the tabletop. "I can't promise much, but I'll try."

Bennett and Joana watched as she carefully loosened the spine enough that she could prop the book open over a bowl Joana had brought, waiting for the train car to rumble past a boisterous piece of track before pouring the hot water. She held the book in place as the steam went to work, softening and rehydrating the damaged pages. She lifted it after a few minutes, smiling as she examined the results.

"The edges are loosening," she said, reaching for the knife. "I might be able to pry them apart."

Carefully, painfully, slowly she worked the knife around the edge of the paper, prying it loose from the leather grain of the cover. Her nerves quieted and her focus became as sharp as the knife tip, same as it did within the safety of the shop. She could not control anything else on this train, but she could do this.

"This is incredible, Sam," Bennett said, his voice a surprising vibration in the otherwise-quiet compartment. "An entire team of conservators at the university couldn't do what you're attempting now. This is brilliant."

"It's only brilliant if it works," Sam murmured, all of her attention on the delicate edges of the paper. She knew it took only one careless flick of the wrist to ruin everything.

Joana sighed. "I know that look; we'll be cramped in this compartment huddled over that lumpy thing all day until she gets it right. Meanwhile I've had nothing but cocktail shrimp and champagne in the last twelve hours, and I could use a plate of eggs Benedict and the strongest coffee they've got on board."

"I'll have the porter send for something," Bennett said, his attention drawn to the careful movement of Sam's hands. "I'll have to speak with the ticket taker about purchasing your fares when he comes by as well. Sam, do you think you could turn the book around so I can start copying and cataloging the pages you've already opened?"

"I could try," Sam said, frowning at a particularly sticky section of paper. "Give me a minute, this seems to have fused with the leather cover, and I think if I just get my knife—"

Sam stopped as the chunk of paper popped free with a tearing sound, a loose section of the book fluttering free and falling on the table. It was folded in half, and unlike the rest of the pages it seemed untouched by the dirt and water. It was warped a little at the corners and the bottom edge was jagged, but the lettering was at least legible.

"Oh no," Sam sighed, running her finger softly along the feathered edge. "I must have torn it when I pulled it open. I shouldn't have used so much force. If I had paid more attention . . ."

"You did a sight better than I could have done," Bennett said, taking the folded paper and gently opening it.

"Still, I should have been more careful," Sam said, reaching out instinctively. "Let me see if I can repair it. Maybe the other half is stuck to the diary here."

She glanced at the book, but it was hard to make out any distinct edges in the rumpled topography of the ruined pages.

"Sam, it's a wonder you even got it out," Bennett said, leaning over the paper and scrutinizing the text. "Don't be so hard on yourself. It looks like it might be a letter, but I can't . . . The ink is smeared. It's hard to make out anything."

Sam leaned forward, willing herself to ignore the tickle of Bennett's hair against her temple as she craned her neck around to consider the words. Bennett was right, the lettering was jumpy and smudged, like the words were written in a hurry and the paper folded before the ink could dry. She could just make out a date at the top of the letter, the strokes ornate despite being written in haste, and her heart gave a little thumping thrill.

"This letter is from 1741," she said softly. "It must be from Father Jacob."

She squinted at the rest of the letter, trying to see through the smears to read on.

"'My Brothers in Light,

"'What we feared is true. The club has taken their debauchery to the ultimate low. I have overheard them in the tavern making preparations to enact the curse I have feared. It can only occur during a momentous passage of the moon. I have stolen the ritual artifact they require to complete the curse, and I will never allow it to fall back into their hands. I will do what I must for the safety of the world.

"'May the hazel bring you wisdom, and the aspen guide and protect you' . . .

"The rest is missing," Sam said, fretting with the torn edge. How could she be so careless and let such damage occur? She was supposed to fix these kinds of problems, not cause them.

"What curse is he talking about?" Joana asked.

Bennett shook his head slowly. "I have no idea. The Hellfire Club has long been associated with the occult. Locals believe the building itself was cursed by the devil. But those are just superstitions."

Sam knew they were—of course they were, right? But that didn't stop the shiver that ran over her skin and penetrated deep to her bones. If they were just superstitions, then what happened to Father Jacob and his diary?

Bennett carefully lifted the letter and turned it over. "There's more on the back here."

Sam leaned in, squinting at the few cramped words. The ink on the back was in worse condition than the front side, most likely from its exposure to the rest of the ruined pages. "It looks like some kind of list. Are those . . . ? Does that say *oak*?"

"They're plants," Bennett said in surprise. "I think this says holly, and oak again. And this one says whitethorn."

"Why plants?" Sam asked.

Bennett shrugged. "No clue. Several of these are repeating, too. Oak, oak, holly, whitethorn, aspen."

Joana slouched against the seat, dropping her head back with a groan. "It sounds like those ridiculous codes Daddy would make Sam solve before we got to the good treasure bits when we did the hunts at the Manor. It used to take you *days* to figure out whatever it was he was trying to say. Remember all those papers you would tack up on my bedroom walls, scribbled with all your guesses? Mother used to scream when she found the little holes. Me, I was only interested in the rewards. And the petty thievery, of course."

Sam sucked in a breath as she reread the scant words on the back of the letter, Bennett's gaze finding hers across the table.

"Oh, Jo," she breathed. "You're a *genius.*"

"I know," Joana said with a shrug. She rolled her head to the side to look at Sam suspiciously. "Wait, about what?"

"It's a cipher," Bennett said, his voice coming alive with excitement. "He's coded a message here."

"Well, what does it say?" Joana asked. "And who are these Brothers in Light he's sending it to?"

"More importantly," Bennett said, "what was Father Jacob trying to hide?"

CHAPTER SEVEN

"It must be this artifact he mentions," Sam said, tapping a line in the letter. "The one he stole. Maybe it's the location; that's why he encrypted it."

"Can you decipher it?" Bennett asked.

Sam took a deep breath, letting it out with a worried sigh. "There's not much to go on here. It's not a transposition or substitution cipher, because the words are clearly readable. So they must represent something. Maybe they're code words? But they could reference anything—a letter, a number, a letter and a number that reference a book cipher. It could be encrypted in multiple layers. Without knowing the key . . . I'd need more than just these few words to go on."

"We could check the diary," Bennett said, picking up the clump of paper still welded together. "If he used the code here, he might have used it elsewhere in the diary."

"The level of repair it needs could take me hours," Sam said.

Joana snorted. "Good thing you're trapped on a train headed for New York for the next twenty-two of them."

"You're both on the train back to Chicago from the next stop we reach," Bennett said sternly. "You should never have gotten on in the first place."

Joana crossed her arms, staring him down. "And you're going to figure this thing out all on your lonesome, without Sam's help?"

Bennett hesitated. "Fine. Then you're going straight to Aunt Neem when we arrive. I'm not setting you loose in New York City."

Joana gave him a sweet smile. "Of course, brother."

"I can't promise anything," Sam said, even though her eyes were drawn back down to that stained and blotted list of plants. Something that felt like hunger, but burned hotter, stirred up her gut, the intensity of it dislodging a slew of other emotions she didn't yet want to examine. For now, Joana was right—they had nowhere to go for the rest of the day. She had a perfectly good mystery on her hands, and twenty-two hours to immerse herself in it.

"I'll give it my best," Sam said, the gears in her brain already clicking and turning. "Bennett, you wouldn't happen to have paper and a pencil, would you?"

"Of course I do," Bennett said, sounding offended. "I'm an academic."

"I'll need all you've got," Sam said, staring up at the meager wall space in the sleeper compartment. "There's not much room to work with in here, but we can improvise."

"I certainly know *that* look," Joana said, sliding out of the way so Bennett could reach his trunk once again. "I think I'll make my escape before you wallpaper me in. How about I go scrounge up some breakfast for the three of us while you two toil away at the boring, non-treasure-y bits. I'm the only one who ever remembers to eat during these things."

"You're not going anywhere," Bennett said, pulling out a small notebook and two freshly sharpened pencils. "It's not safe for us to split up. I can ask the porter to have someone bring us a few pastries to tide us over."

"It's not me he's after," Joana pointed out. "It's that book. So really, the farther from it I am, the safer I am. The dining car is on the opposite end of the train, and they have bacon."

"We stay together," Bennett said, sitting back down and pointing to the seat beside Sam.

Joana crossed her arms, ready to dig in, but the safety latch on the compartment door rattled, interrupting their impending battle of wills. Sam stiffened in alarm, the pencil in her hand scratching across the paper with a jolt. Bennett stood and pushed Joana behind him, where the rocking motion of the train knocked her into her seat. Sam gathered the diary and the letter quickly, tucking them both under the table in the gap between the cushioned seat and the window, out of sight.

The door rattled again, more insistently, and Bennett wielded his own pencil like a knife, holding it high and at the ready as he stood beside the door, grasping the handle. He gave one last look of warning to the girls before wrenching it open, hoping to catch the potential intruder off guard.

Sam tensed, but it wasn't a large Irishman in dark robes who fell through the door. Instead it was a young man with light-blond hair and a neatly trimmed mustache that twitched in surprise at the sight of Bennett ready to deal him a graphite blow.

"Ho there," he said in a congenial tone, his eyebrows arching upward. "A bit early to be so tense, huh, Steeling? Another research-paper reference section giving you trouble?"

Bennett lowered the pencil with a huff of annoyance. "Phillip. What are you doing here?"

Phillip tucked his hands in his pockets, rocking back on his heels with the movement of the train. "Thought I'd come check on you," he said in a crisp New York accent. "Make sure you caught the train all right."

"Of course I caught the train all right," Bennett said, irritation laced through his tone. Sam noticed his grip on the pencil didn't lessen in the other young man's presence. "I booked our tickets, didn't I?"

Phillip peered around the edge of the door where Bennett still held it, raising his eyebrows once again in surprise. "Who's this with you? Steeling, you sly dog, already making friends on the train?"

"That's my sister," Bennett said, his tone ominous.

"Joana Steeling's the name, though the handsome boys call me Jo," Joana said, taking in the fine cut of Phillip's cotton day suit. He was a few inches shy of Bennett's height, but he made up for it in meticulous style, his hair swept back in careful waves. Her spine curved in an alluring arc as she sat up, crossing her legs and tilting her chin with a flirtatious smile.

Bennett pointed the pencil at her. "Don't even think about it. You're off to Aunt Neem's the second we reach New York."

"Oh, don't be a stuffed shirt, Steeling," Joana said with a smirk.

Phillip gave her a bemused smile. "Phillip Montrose. I'm a student of Professor Wallstone's as well, along for the adventure. Pleased to meet you, Jo."

Sam sighed. Poor Phillip. There was no escape for him now. He was just Joana's type, good-looking enough to please without stealing her spotlight.

"Say, Phillip, you wouldn't let a poor girl starve, would you?" Joana asked. "I'm famished, and my brother's being a brute. Care to escort me and Sam to the dining car?"

"Sam?" Phillip asked with a frown.

"Hello," Sam said from where she kept her seat. "I'm Sam."

Phillip looked to Bennett. "Another sister?"

"No," Bennett said, sounding uncharacteristically flustered. "Sam is a family friend. Jo's best friend."

Joana went a little stiff at that, which made Sam go stiff, but she didn't deny the association. Which gave Sam hope that the gulf between them was still traversable.

"Now that all the proper introductions have been settled, how about breakfast?" Joana asked. "Phillip, are you game?"

"It would be better if we stayed here," Bennett said. "The three of us. All things considered."

Phillip didn't miss the pointed exclusion, though he seemed to take it in stride, as if it weren't the first time Bennett had made one. Joana put her hands on her hips, steeling will against steeling will. "I'm not a child and you're not Daddy, Bennett. I go where I like, and right now I'd like to eat before I wilt like some pasty-faced starlet. Sam, you'd better come along as well. And don't say you're not hungry, I can hear your stomach grumbling from here."

Sam *was* hungry; her mother always said her stomach was more reliable than a dinner bell, and it was proving no less punctual, despite the chaos of the previous evening. But the cipher wouldn't reveal itself while she gorged on bacon and biscuits. There was the book to clean and repair and search for clues, and any number of decryptions she could try. There was the double entry, for instance—oak followed by another oak—that could stand for the same letter twice. Which narrowed the field of options it could represent, if she assumed Father Jacob's cipher was in English. It was a guess, and a weak one at that, but decryption was built on guesses, intuition, and time. Time she couldn't waste on breakfast, even if she was famished.

"I'm all right, really," she said, her stomach betraying her with another loud grumble. "It's like Bennett said, I can just ask the porter to bring me something."

Joana turned accusing eyes on Bennett. "You're doing it again, look at her."

"Doing what?" Bennett asked defensively.

"She'll work herself into the ground for you."

Sam flushed bright red, opening her mouth to protest, but Joana held up a hand to silence her.

"Don't bother denying it, Sam; I'm on a roll here. She needs to eat, you need to eat, and most importantly, *I* need to eat. What good is a brain half-starved? Besides which, you're being unconscionably rude to Phillip here."

Phillip gave a congenial smile, spreading his hands wide. "I do hate to disappoint a lady, Steeling."

Joana glared at Bennett. "So, what is it, are you going to let poor Sam starve?"

"Really, I'll be all right," Sam said weakly.

But Bennett sighed, his shoulders sagging. "No, of course not. All right, we all go to breakfast. Together. Besides, I have to purchase tickets for the two of you from the train officer before you get us all kicked off."

"All right," Phillip said, stepping back and sweeping out an arm for Joana to pass by. "An unexpectedly delightful turn of events. Shall we?"

"Such a gentleman," Joana purred, giving him a pat on the chest as she passed.

Sam stood and cast one long, agonized glance down at the diary tucked between the seat and window, its secrets still unexcavated, but there was no denying the Steeling will. Besides which, bacon sounded heavenly at the moment. She still had time, even if it felt like every second that ticked past was another one wasted. She had solved more difficult encryptions before, though never ones with such high stakes as this one.

"Sam," Bennett said, his hand brushing the small of her back. She fought the urge to curve her spine toward that hand. "You'll figure it out. You always do. Jo is right, though don't tell her I said so. You need to eat."

"I know," Sam said, letting out a gusty sigh.

The narrow hallway of the sleeper car teemed with passengers making their way toward the dining car. Several of the compartments they passed had the shades opened, the passengers within reading newspapers or chatting with each other or already sleeping, hats pulled low over their faces. At the end of the car the porter stood beside the woman in the giant peacock-feather hat, her shrill tone more grating than the screech of the train wheels against the tracks. Her hands glittered with jewels as she flung them around.

"I can barely stand with everything in there," she said as the porter looked patiently on. "Is there really nowhere else for you to stow our luggage for this dreadfully long trip?"

"I apologize, ma'am, but there's not," said the porter, a portrait of patience.

"Well, I shall have to let Mr. Pullman know next time we see him at dinner. This is unreasonable," the lady proclaimed.

"What a dreadful woman," muttered a young man with a British accent behind Sam. "Are all Americans like that?"

Sam glanced over her shoulder at him. "Only the wealthy ones," she said.

The young man looked flustered, his eyes widening in surprise before crinkling into a smile. "Ah, well, I shall have to cross the Waldorf Astoria off my list of accommodations, then. I thank you, for you've saved me from a future earache."

Sam returned his smile. He was good-looking in an unassuming way, with soft brown hair swept back, but not overly styled. He wore a light pinstripe suit with a matching vest beneath his coat. That made for two well-dressed, handsome men she'd met on the train so far who weren't Bennett. Maybe Joana had a point about broadening her horizons.

"Sam, are you coming?" Bennett asked, snagging her attention and bringing her back to the present. He held open the heavy exterior door.

"Oh, yes, sorry!" she called, turning hastily to the young man. "Enjoy your trip!"

"I shall, if we meet again," he said with a smile.

Sam flushed, hurrying after Bennett. He frowned down at her as she slid by him out onto the small platform.

"Who was that?" he asked.

Sam shrugged. "I have no idea."

"Sam," he said in a heavy tone, laying one hand on her shoulder. "You have to be careful who you talk to out here. Not everyone is trustworthy."

"I know," Sam said, fidgeting with the sleeve of her coat. "I was only being nice."

"Being nice can get you in more trouble than you think," Bennett said. "You're not in Clement anymore."

Sam shivered against the whipping wind that tore at them out on the tiny connecting platform. The meager morning sunlight didn't do much to warm her, and neither did Bennett's words. Because he was right; she didn't know what she was doing. She'd never been farther than the watering hole outside of Clement, much less on a train bound for New York with no extra clothes and no money. She shrunk down into the collar of her coat, wishing she could disappear inside its warm folds entirely.

Bennett seemed to sense the shift in Sam's mood because he reached out, putting an arm around her and giving her a brotherly squeeze. Then he stepped back with a cough, looking like he already regretted the embrace.

"Come on, let's get something to eat."

CHAPTER EIGHT

"Tell me, Philly, where has my brother been hiding you all this time?" Joana asked, leaning into him on the plush velvet seat they shared at the dining table. "Most of the fellas he brings home from the university are too much substance and far too little style for my taste."

"Only you could make a compliment sound like an insult, Jo," Bennett said.

Joana arched an eyebrow. "Only you would assume that was a compliment, Bennett."

"I actually only started attending the University of Chicago this past year," Phillip said, spreading a thin layer of butter on his toast. "I was at Oxford the year before that."

"Oxford," Joana said in surprise. "And you left that to come here? Why in hell would you do that? Did you lose a bet?"

"The University of Chicago is the highest-rated university in America," Bennett said, stabbing at his pile of scrambled eggs a little too forcefully. "Oxford might have prestige, but the university has progress."

"What's that bit from Shakespeare?" Joana asked, biting into a soft pastry. "You're arguing too much."

"'The lady doth protest too much, methinks,'" Sam and Bennett said simultaneously. Sam dipped her head to take another bite of eggs while Bennett glared at Joana. But it was Phillip who spoke up in his defense.

"Your brother is right about Oxford," he said. "The lads there are more concerned with their titles and inheritances than they are with making progress in the field. The only way they can keep their aging power is to suppress real change, real improvements. They're so afraid the world is going to leave them behind that they can't see they're already stuck in the past, holding on to a way of life that isn't possible anymore."

"What took you to Oxford in the first place?" Sam asked.

Phillip hesitated, his knife slipping off the edge of his toast. "My mother died."

Sam drew in a soft breath at the complication of emotions that passed over his features. She knew those emotions. On instinct she reached out and laid a hand over his. "Oh, I'm so sorry."

The contact seemed to startle him out of whatever depths he'd plunged into, because he shook his head with an empty little laugh. "It's still such a strange thing to say out loud."

"It gets better," Sam said softly. "It never goes away, but it . . . it hurts less. Over time."

"You say it like you know," Phillip said.

Sam withdrew her hand, curling her fingers into her palm. "I do."

Joana cleared her throat, shifting her posture. "Well, it sounds like you turned your tragedy into something positive."

Phillip's lips curled in an approximation of a smile, but his gaze was still clouded. "I wouldn't define my time at Oxford as positive, but it was . . . productive. And edifying. I learned that fellows like that will never accept me because of my parentage. My father is a count, in England, not that it means more than an open seat at the club these days. But my mother and father were never married. His influence might have gotten me in, but it never got me accepted. Those boys at Oxford built their high walls out of the stones of their reputation; they would never let a bastard come and knock them down."

"Are they really still so obsessed with birthrights and all that over there?" Joana asked. She rolled her eyes. "As if being a bastard were some kind of defect."

Phillip stiffened slightly, a cough overtaking him. His body shuddered as he pulled a handkerchief from his pocket and pressed it to his face. "Apologies," he said, lowering the handkerchief again. Sam saw a monogram on the edge, the letters RR stitched in a looping script. "The cold always aggravates my lungs. My mother was the same way; it was what weakened her and invited the pneumonia. As I said, it wasn't the place for me. I'm far better off at the university with Professor Wallstone. The man is a genius, and what we find at the Hellfire Club will change the world."

"It must be quite an honor, for both of you, that your professor invited you along on the survey," Sam said.

"*Invited* is a strong word for some of us," Bennett muttered into another forkful of eggs. "You offered to finance the entire trip when the university rejected his request for funds. What else could he do but include you?"

Phillip shrugged one shoulder. "We all find our ways to achieve our goals. I wasn't able to inherit my opportunities. I earned that money by my own hard work."

Joana choked on a sip of coffee as Bennett ground his teeth together so loudly it made Sam cringe.

"What are you hoping to find at the Hellfire Club?" Sam asked hastily in an attempt to redirect the conversation.

"I'm less interested in the old club and far more interested in the Neolithic passage tomb and what secrets it might divulge," Phillip replied, his demeanor calm in spite of the tic in Bennett's jaw. "As I said, what we find there will change the world, and I aim to be at the forefront of it."

"And how fortunate you were, to bribe your way into such an opportunity," Bennett muttered.

"Bennett," Sam said in surprise.

"Oh, let him go on," Joana said with a dismissive wave. "He's just jealous."

Bennett gave her a glowering look. "I have never been jealous a day in my life. I am only wary of people who think they can buy their way into historical significance instead of doing the hard work."

"I think you've misunderstood the history of archaeology, then," Phillip said wryly. "It's full up on men who bought their way in."

"Bennett's just afraid of ending up like Daddy," Joana challenged. "Aren't you? Always so disdainful of the money that pays your tuition. You could do worse, you know."

"I don't think that's what he meant," Sam started, but Joana cut her off with a look.

"Of course you'd take *his* side."

"That's enough," Bennett said, putting on the special big-brother tone he saved for reprimanding Joana. "I've lost my appetite, and Sam and I have work to get back to."

Phillip lifted a brow. "What kind of work?"

"The kind you can't buy your way into." He stood up, tossing his napkin on the table. "Sam? Jo?"

Joana leaned back and draped one arm across the seat behind Phillip's shoulders, staring Bennett down. "It's not my skills you need, is it? I think I'll loiter a bit here with Phillip, spend some of Daddy's hard-earned money. What do you say, Phillip?"

Phillip, to his credit, hesitated only a moment as he glanced between siblings. "It would be my pleasure."

Joana cocked an eyebrow at Bennett. "It would be his *pleasure*. So run along, both of you."

"I'd rather we stay together," Bennett said tightly.

"And I'd rather we spent some time apart," Joana said, her tone like a knife's edge.

"Jo—" Sam started, but Bennett interrupted.

"Fine, throw your tantrum. A few days with Aunt Neem will cure you. Sam, are you coming?"

Sam hesitated a moment, not wanting to leave Joana alone. Bennett raised an eyebrow at her in expectation. It reminded her of both Joana and Mr. Steeling, and she could do nothing but follow the siren call of the Steeling willpower. She took his hand, letting him wrap his long fingers around hers and pull her up out of the seat. It was a visceral loss when he let go.

"Phillip, don't let her do anything wild," Bennett said, every word sounding like it had to be physically extracted from his gut.

"He couldn't stop me if he tried," Joana said, her words a hard promise. Phillip gave a halfhearted shrug and a conciliatory smile as Bennett turned and walked away, leaving Sam to hurry after him.

"And that is . . . nothing," Sam muttered, scratching out her latest attempt with enough force to tear a small hole in the paper. "Complete gibberish."

Bennett raised an eyebrow from across the table, where he held

Father Jacob's diary opened to the latest page Sam had been able to loosen. "Not *F*, then?"

"No," Sam grunted. "And probably not *G* either, unless he wrote a secret message about haggis. It might not even be a double letter, for all I know. My hunch might have been wrong. It could be a decoy, an extra character meant to fool someone trying to decrypt it. Or he could have used a Vigenère cipher, and the letter shifts each time. Without more text or knowing the key, I could play around with this for years without getting it right. It took Champollion three years to completely decipher Egyptian hieroglyphics, and he had the Rosetta Stone to aid him. This is thirteen random words on the back of a two-hundred-year-old letter. Maybe Father Jacob truly was a genius ahead of his time, inventing a cipher so complex no one could ever break it. A true chiffre indéchiffrable."

"Or maybe he was just a madman," Bennett said, pushing the book back and rubbing his eyes tiredly. "His diary certainly makes it seem like he was."

"No luck finding any more examples of the code?"

"No, but I've found plenty of other things to worry me. I've read the local legends of the Hellfire Club, but this is . . . something different. Blood rituals, human sacrifice, some kind of spell book they kept with all their exploits. I'd always assumed the reports of the locals were fantasies invented by scared and ignorant townspeople, but Father Jacob writes like he witnessed these actions firsthand."

Sam suppressed a shiver of apprehension. "Have you found anything else about the curse he mentions in the letter? Or the relic he says he stole?"

Bennett shook his head, running a hand through his hair and sending it curling in all directions. "Not yet. I don't understand why Professor Wallstone didn't send some sort of instructions to tell me what he wants me to do with this book. I feel as if I'm trying to fly a plane blindfolded with one hand tied behind my back."

Sam well understood that sentiment as she gazed down at the letter. By the time of their last failed treasure hunt at the Manor, Mr. Steeling had been using three to four encryption techniques to challenge her skills. Those had been feverish days spent in a haze of code books and maps spread across Joana's bedroom walls, marked with all Sam's attempts at discovering the latest piece of treasure. It had fired her from a place deep within, like the molten core of the earth, a place that turned cold as stone the day she learned her father had died.

And now she couldn't even crack the code of a mad local priest from two centuries ago. Maybe it had been for the best, walking away from the treasure hunts when she did. The field of archaeology required brilliant minds—minds like Bennett's and his professor's—and her own was proving as weak as the brown-tinted swill Mrs. Morton served at the Steeling Mill cantina, passing it off as coffee.

Bennett glared at the book in frustration. "Half the pages are so badly damaged I can't even turn them without tearing the whole thing apart."

"Let me see," Sam said, setting the letter aside to take the book. She reached for the supplies still left from Joana's raiding excursion, taking the knife and working the edge of the blade gently between the lumped pages.

"What I wouldn't give for half an hour in the humidifier and a surgeon's blade," Sam murmured, rocking the handle of the knife back and forth to coax them open. They gave with a little rending sound that she felt deep in her bones. But she managed to get the pages apart, for all the good it did her. The ink had run in rivulets down the page, sloppy and indecipherable. She gave a little grunt of disappointment.

"It's useless," Bennett said, glancing out at the dying rays of sunlight tinting the blankets of white snow a deep shade of orange. The light spilled into the compartment, highlighting every ripple, dip, and curve of the ruined diary. Sam frowned at the topography of the paper, the faintest impressions of lines showing in the slanted light.

"Maybe not," she said, plucking his pencil from his hand and laying the graphite against the page. "I have an idea."

She lightly colored, covering the area in wide swaths of gray that eclipsed the ruined ink. The more she colored, the more the lines stood out, deeper impressions in the paper made by Father Jacob's writing. It pained her to do such damage to an already battered book, but in this case, it was the information that mattered, not the book itself. She sat back once she was done, both of them sucking in a breath.

"'Curse of the Specter Queen,'" Bennett read. He grinned up at her. "Sam, you did it."

Sam flushed with pride. "It worked. But who is the Specter Queen?"

Bennett scratched at his chin. "I think it must be a reference to the Morrigan. She was the Celtic goddess of war and death, as well as the sovereignty of the land. It's said that no man could be king of Ireland unless she chose him. She was a shapeshifter, often taking the form of a beautiful young maiden or an old crone, or sometimes even a crow or a raven. She would influence the tides of battle by whispering in the ears of men on the field, confusing them or causing them to turn on each other. She also often prophesied the death of a warrior by sitting on his shoulder in her raven form."

Sam looked down at the diary, the chill of the window seeping into her skin. "What does the Hellfire Club have to do with a Celtic goddess? I thought they were supposed to be consorting with the devil."

"Religious types think all forms of pagan worship are devil worship," Bennett said dryly. He spun the book and read aloud. "'I have borne witness to the club's attempts at their most foul, depraved act yet. A ritual they call the Curse of the Specter Queen. The curse would call forth the Specter Queen's powers to whisper in the ears of men and turn the tides of war. The poisoned minds of men would bring about great strife across the land, turning brother against brother, father against son, and friends to foes; the soil would run with the blood of those who would not bow to the sovereign king. The last great war of man.'"

Something cold and heavy dropped down in the pit of Sam's stomach, sending its ripples out to the tips of her fingers and toes. "The last great war of man. Why would anyone want to do that?"

Bennett gave a shrug. "War was a way of life for the Irish Celts. A sign of their power and virulence. In one of the Irish stories, the *Cath Maig Tuired*, the Morrigan supposedly prophesied the end of the world, when the seas returned no bounties and the morals of man decayed. So maybe they thought this curse was meant to bring about that prophecy?"

"Do you think that's what those men from the shop wanted?" she asked, not able to bring her voice above a whisper. "To . . . to invoke this curse and start the last great war of man?"

"It could be," Bennett said, a deep crease of concentration forming between his brows. "There's more here, though it's far less legible. Seems like he wrote it in a hurry, or in the dark."

"Or both," Sam said. She leaned over the table, turning her head to get a better look at the words.

Ritual requires significant passage of the moon (Winter solstice? Solar eclipse? Further research required)

Unholy relic (bowl found in rubble of destroyed passage tomb)

Ritual words spoken over unholy relic (word magic)

Sacrifice

"What kind of sacrifice do you think he meant?" Sam asked, her heart rate picking up.

Bennett shook his head. "It doesn't say, but considering the club's reputation . . ."

Sam shuddered at the savagery of the idea.

"It's all superstitious nonsense, of course," Bennett continued. "None of this is real. They could never start a war that would wipe out all of humanity."

But Sam knew what a great war looked like; she had lived through one. She watched it make her home a ghost town, filled with shadows of the men who never returned. Men like her father. She knew Bennett was probably right—it couldn't possibly be real, the power of this curse. But she knew the power of men dedicated to their ideology, however real or imagined it might be, who were willing to go to any length to make such a ritual reality—these were men to be feared. Men who believed they could reshape the world by sacrificing all those who stood in their way and slaughtering those they viewed as unfaithful.

"We can't let this happen," Sam said, her voice so much smaller than she wished it to be. Still, she used it. "We can't let those men do this."

"Of course not," Bennett said, his concentration on the book. "This bowl he mentions here, the unholy relic, that must be what he said he stole from the Hellfire Club. If it was truly recovered from the deconstructed passage tomb, it could be the greatest archaeological find in Ireland since Newgrange. We can't let it fall into the hands of a few grave robbers."

The crease between his brows deepened. Sam knew that crease, had wanted to smooth it away with her thumb during plenty of treasure hunts when the answers to their quest had eluded them. It was a crease of frustration, appearing when Bennett wanted to control the uncontrollable.

Sam shook her head. "No, Bennett, I mean we can't let them . . ."

But how to explain it to someone like him? Bennett could never wrap his mind around something until he could wrap his hands around it. He was an adherent of facts and findings, not fantastical fictions. If she was thinking at all rationally—which she must not be, to consider any truth in a madman's rantings—she would know she sounded ludicrous. She probably *was* ludicrous; sleep-deprived, crispy around the edges, in shock from the loss of her books.

And surely whatever madness fell upon Father Jacob must be beckoning her from the great beyond, because she still wanted to decrypt the letter. She needed to; it was a compulsion, a series of electrical impulses under the skin that made her fingers twitch for a pencil and her eyes look for patterns in the plain carpeting of the sleeper compartment. The cipher was harder than ever, the stakes as high as could be, and her mind was on fire.

Because if she didn't solve the encryption, those men from the shop would. And they would use it to try and end the world.

"We need to keep working," she said, reaching for a fresh scrap of paper. "Keep trying new methods until we find one that cracks Father Jacob's code."

"Only until we reach New York," Bennett reminded her. "I don't want you and Joana getting any more mixed up in this than you have to."

Sam nodded, though she didn't say what she really thought— that they were already far too tangled up to ever come unknotted again.

CHAPTER NINE

Sam jolted awake with the disorienting notion that her bed-room walls were rattling like a tin roof in a rainstorm. She didn't remember there being a table in the middle of her bedroom, though, the edge cutting into her hip where she half slumped over it. Nor was there a window above her bed, showing the faintest traces of light in the distance. And she definitely did not remember Bennett ever being there, asleep across the table with his mouth slightly open, the softest of snores coming out.

She snapped up as the train took another jostling turn, her foot meeting with a spongy object on the floor below. The object grunted and rolled over, giving her calf a pinch.

"Watch it," Joana grumbled, rolling herself up in a makeshift blanket of all their coats and promptly falling back asleep.

Sam wasn't home; she was on a train that was less than an hour away from New York City, the greatest city in America. Two days ago she was hanging laundry before the long walk to the book-shop; now she was bundled into a sleeper compartment with her estranged best friend and childhood crush, trying to decipher a two-hundred-year-old letter and find a missing relic to stop a ritual to raise an ancient god that would end the world. A ritual she couldn't quite convince herself was superstitious nonsense, not that she would admit such a thing to Bennett.

He looked younger in his sleep, the furrow between his eyebrows softened and relaxed in his vulnerable state. He looked more like the Bennett from childhood, the one who could be lured into their treasure hunts if she let him take charge of the map. Those were gilded memories, highlighted in precious tones of golden summer sunlight and the deep, rich scent of freshly turned earth. She fit with the Steeling siblings—the calm to Joana's storm, the creativity to Bennett's practicality. The three of them together were unfettered, unflappable, unstoppable.

It hadn't occurred to Sam at first that what she felt for Bennett was anything more than an appreciation for those of his skills that she lacked. The breadth and depth of knowledge he could carry on any subject never ceased to astound her. Mr. Steeling had a penchant for working hints from the classics into his treasure hunts, but even he could never outrun Bennett's knowledge on the subject. Bennett soaked up dates and names and details like the parched earth after that first summer rain, filling every nook and cranny of his gray matter with Greek war heroes and French philosophers.

She had always considered him handsome—which of the schoolhouse girls did not?—but he'd held himself apart, even more than Joana. The girls thought him a snob, but Sam saw the dedication he had to his future. He would let nothing derail his plans, the least of all a country dalliance with a local girl. And she tried—oh, how desperately she tried—to keep her own growing feelings from taking up every waking breath.

But he was like the sun, her neck the stalk of a sunflower. Where he went, her gaze would follow; what he read, she would inevitably borrow from Mr. Steeling's library; when a clue would stump her, it was his input she sought first. Joana used to say that hers was the only set of braids he noticed in Clement, but it was never true. He appreciated the chance to apply his knowledge, that was all. And eventually, even that wasn't enough. He pulled away from the hunts, away from her. And then her father died and she stopped doing the treasure hunts completely, and there was nothing holding the three of them together anymore.

Papers were scattered over the little table where they had fallen asleep. Bennett had never even called for the porter to pull down the sleeper bunk, all of them too caught up in the contents of the letter and diary to admit defeat. For all those swaths of paper taped to the walls and covered in her handwriting, she still had nothing. Somewhere deep in the dregs of night, when her eyelids were more sandpaper than skin, she had pushed the letter away and succumbed to the vital need for rest. And now, with the breaking of dawn, she had to admit that time was up, and she still had no answers.

The train gave a shrill whistle, jostling Bennett out of his sleep as it announced their imminent arrival at New York's Grand Central Terminal. He frowned at her, still caught in the web of his dreams, but Joana's groan from the floor brought him fully awake.

"Tell them to shut that damn thing off or I'll crash this train myself," she groused.

"We're almost in New York, Jo," Bennett said, straightening up and tugging his clothes back into proper alignment. "Morning, Sam."

"Morning," she said softly. If she didn't know him any better, she would have thought there was a slight reddening around his ears as he tried to make himself presentable. But she did know him, and she knew Bennett never blushed. Certainly not on her account.

"Oh blast," Joana groaned, sitting up with half her hair plastered to the side of her face. "You're not really shipping us off to Auntie Neem's, are you? I think I'd rather face one of Mama's lectures than sit through another one of Neem's salons. Everyone smells like lavender and they only drink tea; it's like living in a dollhouse."

"It's only until you can catch another train back to Chicago," Bennett said. "I won't make the mistake of leaving you to your own devices in New York of all places."

"But what about the letter?" Sam asked, her throat scratchy from lack of sleep. "We still haven't decrypted it."

"I've got the rest of the steamer trip to figure it out," Bennett said.

Joana snorted as she tried to shake her hair into some manageable shape. "Good luck figuring anything out without Sam."

"I've studied Celtic lore," Bennett said defensively. "Besides which, I was sometimes the key to solving those treasure-hunt messages from Father."

"Sure you were," Joana muttered, crimping the edges of her hair around her fingers. "When Sam let you think you solved it."

Bennett frowned at Sam, who turned pink. It was far too early in the morning for her to come up with an adequate response. "Oh, that's not . . . I mean, there were times when you . . . when you figured it out. Before me."

Joana chuckled. "Good at puzzles, terrible at lying."

"Yes, well," Bennett said, clearing his throat and straightening his shirtsleeves unnecessarily. "I will have to do my mediocre best to figure it out, because you are both going to stay with Aunt Neem."

"Are you really sure you should be going alone?" Sam asked, scooting out of the way as Bennett rose to pull his steamer trunk down from the overhead rack. "Those men from the shop won't stop until they get the diary and decipher the location to the missing artifact. You're still in a great deal of danger, and we don't know what the cipher says."

"They have officers on the ship," Bennett said matter-of-factly. "If I spot anyone questionable, I'll be sure to alert the first mate. And I won't be alone; Phillip will be along with me. I'm sure between the two of us we can handle anything."

"Phillip, yes," Joana said on a sigh. "What a waste of a perfectly handsome friend."

"Neem will be along to collect you at the station before long," Bennett said, directing his frown at his sister this time. "Try not to get kidnapped before then. Or kicked out."

Joana shot him a sinister smile. "No promises, brother."

"But, Bennett, what if something happens to you?" Sam asked, that warning flare sparking hotter in her chest at the thought of the men from the bookshop finding him. "What if you and Phillip . . . ? What if you can't stop them? You don't understand what these men were like. If something happened to you . . . do you know what it would do to your father? Or your mother? Or Jo and me, for that matter. You don't know . . ." She swallowed hard against the feeling rising in her throat. "You don't know what it's like, for somebody to never come home."

Bennett paused, letting go of his steamer trunk to put both hands gently on her shoulders. "Sam, I'll be all right. All that nonsense in the diary is just that, superstitions of a local priest. The Hellfire Club was just a bunch of rich young drunks, nothing more devilish than that. There is no great ritual, no Specter Queen, or last great war of man. I promise."

"Bennett—" Sam started, but he held up his hand.

"I've got to get my things transferred to the *Olympic* before the baggage car leaves." He leaned in closer, dropping his voice. "Can you keep an eye on Joana while I'm gone? I'll be back in a few minutes."

Sam sighed, pressing her lips together tightly as he lugged the trunk toward the door. But she could never deny Bennett anything, and so she gave him a wordless nod. He smiled in relief, pulling the trunk out the door and leaving the two of them alone. Sam sat down, her stomach churning and the gears of her mind turning. "He can't get on that ship, Jo," Sam said. "It's too dangerous. He has to see that."

Joana snorted. "You'd have better luck keeping the ship from leaving port than keeping Bennett from being on it. He's stubborn as a mule in mind, you know that."

Sam did know that—in fact, his determination was one of the qualities she admired most in him. Only not when it was aimed in her direction, as it was now.

"Does he not understand how dangerous it is for him to try and go to Dublin, after everything that's happened?" Sam asked, pacing back and forth. It proved unsatisfactory in such confined quarters, though, and she soon had to stop or risk toppling over in dizziness.

"He's Bennett," Joana said with a wave of her hands, like that explained everything. "He's always going to do what he thinks is right, which is of course just whatever he wants to do anyway. If you want to put those spinning wheels to good use, why don't you figure out a way for me to avoid going back to Chicago?"

"You don't want to go home?" Sam asked in surprise. "Why not?"

Joana laid her head back against the seat, rolling her eyes. "So that I can do what? Trot along behind Mama like an obedient show dog? Sit with Daddy while he does his ledgers at the mill? Drink bathtub giggle juice with Georgie Heath and the boys? The only thing worse than being at the academy is being back in Clement."

"Why get yourself kicked out, then?" Sam asked, before she

could consider saying something better. Which would have been anything, really, judging by Joana's reaction.

"Listen, Miss Priss," she said, sitting upright. "Not all of us want to preserve ourselves between two pages like a wilted old flower all the time. You and Bennett might get your kicks reading about old dead men and their old dead men thoughts, but I want to live a little before all the good living is used up. You used to feel the same; I saw it on your face every time you figured out one of Daddy's little codes. And now here you are, stumped by a mad old priest."

"That's not fair," Sam protested, the casual observation cutting deep. "With your father, I knew his tells. Every code has a weakness, even the most unbreakable ones. The weakness is the human using it—people will reuse old keywords for convenience, or they'll choose keys that mean something to them. With your father, I knew how much he loved Greek antiquity, so I always knew the key would be something from the classics. But with Father Jacob, I don't know anything other than his diary. Which is, frankly, more disturbing than helpful."

Joana waved a hand over the papers on the compartment table. "Didn't you say he was a Catholic priest? Maybe the key is something simple, like 'Jesus' or 'eternal damnation.' You know, all the things the Catholics love to harp on."

Sam shook her head. "It's not just that he was Catholic, Jo. It's that he was Catholic in secret. Catholicism was outlawed at the time in Ireland, and they would execute anyone they found practicing. He was already outside of the law when he learned about the Hellfire Club and their . . . extracurricular activities. So, who would he go to? These Brothers in Light that he wrote the letter to, who were they? Other hidden priests, practicing in secret out in the woods, risking their lives every time they preached?"

Joana shrugged. "Maybe that's why all the words are trees, because that's all he ever saw. Now there's your terrifying existence. Imagine no indoor plumbing."

"Trees," Sam said, the gears clicking into place and turning fiercely. "A secret language of trees. Oh, Jo, that's it! Of course, that's it, it's so simple. It's right there! I've been making it too complicated."

"The Samantha Knox way," Joana muttered.

"They're not just plants; they're trees!" Sam exclaimed, scrabbling through the mess of paper Bennett had left behind until she found one where she had made a clearer copy of the back of Father Jacob's letter. "Look here, whitethorn, rowan, oak. They're not just trees; they're characters."

"Characters of what?" Joana asked, wrestling to fix her skirt under the table.

Sam grinned at Joana, her face glowing. "It's ogham. The Celtic Tree Alphabet. He used ogham. Oh, but I'm going to need more paper, and definitely more wall space. I don't remember all of the aicmí; Bennett will have to help with that. And I won't know it's ogham for sure until I've applied all the characters. But it makes sense. It finally makes sense."

Joana watched her dig through the papers looking for empty margins to start scribbling new notes, the corner of her mouth curling into a small smile.

"There she is," Joana said.

"Hmm?" Sam hummed, still sorting the scraps. "There who is?"

"The Samantha Knox I know," Joana said. "You've been gone a long time. Welcome back."

Sam paused, taking in the goose bumps along her arms, the flush in her cheeks. Joana was right; it had been a long time since she'd felt this rush of discovery. Seven dark years since her father died and she gave up the treasure hunts for good. She had forgotten how all-consuming it was, the fever. Now it burned in a deeper way, thawing the core of her and threatening to unleash a river of molten feelings that terrified her more than anything in Father Jacob's diary.

"This could take a while," she said quietly, taking a long breath to cool the heat rising in her. "You'd better go catch Bennett before he buys our train tickets."

"Oh, I'll do you one better," Joana said with a wicked smile. "I'll get you on that ship."

CHAPTER TEN

"Absolutely not," Bennett said, shaking his head as people streamed around them on the docks, headed toward the massive ocean liner obliterating the skyline behind them. "You're not coming to Dublin."

"But I know how to solve the encryption," Sam said, jostled into his shoulder by a man in a long coat. "At least I think I do. I need time, and paper. And your help remembering all the characters."

Bennett took her arm, steering her out of the path of an oncoming cart loaded high with trunks and bags. "If it really is ogham, as you say, then I can do the decryption myself, on the ship. There's no need for you and Joana to come along as well. I promise to telegram you from the ship as soon as I have it. I'll make sure Professor Wallstone knows how helpful you've been. I'm sure he'd put in a good word for you with the admissions board at the university if you ever change your mind."

"I told you, stubborn as a mule in mud," Joana muttered to Sam. She gave a small smile to Bennett. "Can't say we didn't try, though, big brother. We'll just be shuffling off back to the station, then. Wait for Auntie Neem's driver to pick us up."

"Good," Bennett said, though he frowned at her. "I'll walk you back."

"Oh, no need," Joana said, waving him off as she linked her arm through Sam's and backed up, nearly colliding with a woman chasing a giggling collection of children. "We wouldn't want you to miss your ship. We'll find our way back just fine."

"You're headed in the wrong direction," Bennett said, taking a step toward them. "You're not thinking of running off, are you?"

"With what clothes and what money?" Joana asked, though she didn't stop moving in the direction of the massive steamer.

"Jo," Bennett said, his voice dropping down into a threatening range. But he was interrupted by Phillip calling from the crowd, pushing his way toward their small cluster.

"All right, Steeling, you've had your fun," he said, dragging his trunk with one hand while waving at Bennett with the other. "Now give it back."

"Give what back?" Bennett asked.

"We should go," Joana said in a low voice to Sam, tugging her more forcefully toward the ship's gangway.

"What? Why?"

"My ticket, Steeling," Phillip said, his congenial tone fraying. "It was gone from my coat this morning. You've made your point—you don't want me on the trip. But I'm going to need that ticket."

"Jo," Sam said, suspicion prickling the back of her neck.

"Move," Joana hissed.

"Don't be ridiculous, Phillip," Bennett said, crossing his arms in disapproval. "I don't have your ticket. You must have lost it."

"I never took it from my coat pocket, which means someone stole it. If it wasn't you, it must have been some grifter on the train."

Bennett took a deep breath, turning in what felt to Sam like slow motion, his expression darkening.

"Sam, get the lead out," Joana growled, pulling her deeper into the thick of the crowd.

"Jo, what did you do?" Sam asked, stumbling after her.

"Listen, I told you he wouldn't let us on the ship," Joana said, her expression resolute as she forced her way through the crowds. "And I have no intention of staying at Auntie Neem's. Did you not hear the part where I said everything smelled like lavender? So, I had to make a different way for us."

"Joana!" Bennett shouted, lost somewhere back in the crowd.

"You stole their tickets?" Sam hissed, though she hurried to keep up with Joana. "How will we get on without passports?"

Joana flashed the inside pocket of her coat. "Picked them up from the safe at the Manor before we left. Never know when you might need to flee the country. It's a good thing Daddy made you get your passport for that trip to visit the bookseller in London that you've been putting off for the last year."

Sam swallowed guiltily. "What if the steamer is all booked up and Bennett and Phillip can't get on?"

Joana cocked her head to one side. "Now, that would be unfortunate. Bennett's too stubborn to let a little thing like that hold him up, though. Come on, I want to see what kind of room he booked. Probably a glorified broom closet, knowing him."

"Jo, I don't know if that's—"

"You want on the ship or not?" Joana demanded.

"Well, I guess . . . yes? I suppose?"

Joana rolled her eyes, pulling a pair of tickets out of her coat. "Then hand this to the man and look innocent."

Sam had spent a good chunk of her childhood in the grandiose trappings of Steeling Manor, but none of those visits could have prepared her for the majesty and opulence of the RMS *Olympic* steamship. The sheer size of the ocean liner took her breath away as they approached the docks crowded with people who had come to wave good-bye to those departing. Men and women were dressed in their finest despite the whistling January wind, waving long white handkerchiefs at those already on board. The steam stacks filled the air high overhead, the tops painted a brilliant red. Sam's breath caught as they started up the gangway, her neck refusing to go any farther back to take it all in.

"How do people . . . ? Where do they even . . . ? How can we . . . ?" She wasn't quite sure what she was trying to ask, or understand. It was only that the feeling inside her, looking up at such a magnificent structure, couldn't be bound by words or linguistic concepts.

"Wait until you see inside," Joana said, slipping an arm through hers and huddling in to steal her warmth. "The *Olympic* was the *Titanic's* sister ship, you know. Built at the same time, almost the same design. I've heard the grand staircase looks exactly like the one they had on the *Titanic*, before it . . . you know . . ." She made a cracking noise with her mouth, simulating a stick breaking in two.

Sam winced. "Are you sure it's . . . safe? After what happened to the *Titanic*?"

"That was over ten years ago," Joana said with a wave. "The *Olympic* is a tough old girl. She took a torpedo in the war, didn't even crack the hull. We'll be fine."

"Maybe from the ship, but not from Bennett," Sam said as they reached the promenade and looked back down at the gangway, where Bennett and Phillip were arguing with the ticket taker. He caught her look, glaring up at them with murderous intent.

"Eh, as soon as you figure out that little riddle, he'll be over it," Joana said with a wave. "Now come on, I want to find the bar on this thing. The second we're in international waters, I'll be popping the first bottle of champagne. We might actually have some fun on this dull little diggy thing."

The ship's horn gave a great blast, rattling the boards of the promenade beneath their feet. Sam startled, her nerves already on edge, but everyone gathered at the railing cheered and waved to the crowd below. The passengers jostled for the best view of New York's impressive skyline, craning their necks about for any celebrity sightings.

But Sam was far more interested in reaching Bennett's room and beginning their decryption than she was in the shuffleboard decks and badminton nets. Her mind teemed with fragmented memories of the articles she had read about the ogham stones in *Archaeological Digest*, images of weather-worn stones standing in fields with deep notches carved into the edges. She needed paper, and space, and time to put it all together. But she was sure that was what Father Jacob had used to encrypt his letter. So simple; it had been right there all along, but Sam had been looking for complicated answers.

Still, even she had to pause in admiration when they reached the forward Grand Staircase, with two sets of stairs leading from the promenade up to the boat deck and wrapping around in a balcony. It was exactly as she imagined a distinguished European manor—the look Mr. Steeling was always chasing with his carved balustrades and marble floors. A statue of a cupid crowned the bottom of the railing, holding aloft a crystal torch twinkling with electric light. A glass dome overhead flooded the stairs with early-morning light, a delicate and intricate pattern of ironwork holding it up.

"Come on, slowpoke," Joana said. "Before Bennett catches us out here and tries to chuck us overboard."

She followed Joana up the staircase and through the hallways of the ship until they reached the first-class deck. Compared to the cramped quarters of the sleeper train, Bennett's stateroom on the steamer was like a deep breath of air. There was a sitting room with couches and a fully stocked bar in one corner, the edges of a bed showing crisp white linen off to the right. There was even a glimmer of a private bathroom just beyond, the oval mirror reflecting her surprise. Bennett might disdain luxury, but he clearly didn't abstain from it.

"Now this is what I'm talking about," Joana said, her voice like a live wire as she snaked through the room, running her hands along the velvet back of the couch. "I could get used to these digs. No more bathtub gin for this gal."

Sam knotted her fingers together, frozen near the entrance to the stateroom. Everything was so nice she was afraid to even bump a piece of furniture. At least at Steeling Manor she had always been a welcome guest, but here she was a true interloper—the consequences of which she would have to face as soon as Bennett arrived. *If* he arrived.

"Jo, what if they were full up?" Sam asked, cracking the door to peek down the hallway. The ship gave another enthusiastic blast of its horn, and the cheers of the travelers on deck and the onlookers at the dock filtered down the hall and into their room. "What if Bennett and Phillip don't make it on? We can't go to Dublin by ourselves! Two young women with no money, no chaperones, no place to stay. Do you know what could happen to us, out there all alone? We don't even know where their professor is staying. Or what he looks like, for that matter. We don't know the man at all."

"Oh, stop worrying," Joana said, getting up and sauntering over to the bar to check its contents. She gave a little pout. "Of course they left the crystal empty, what a bunch of stuffed shirts. Look, Sam, my brother is a lot of things—a pain in my rear end, an utter bore at parties, and a surprising snob about dancing—but he's nobody's fool. He'll get on this boat. You should be far more concerned with this translation business of yours. The tree thing."

"Ogham," Sam said absently, pacing the small open space by the door.

"That's what I said, the tree thing." Joana shuffled through the back of the bar, her voice muffled through the thick wooden doors. "And why is it the answer to the letter?"

"Oh, good question," Sam said, her worry giving way to excitement as she pulled the few scraps of paper from her coat pocket. She crossed to the small table beside the couch, kneeling down and laying them all out in order. "See, in ogham each character represents a letter, but it also represents a tree. The Celts worshipped trees. In fact, there are several sources that claim the word *Druid* means *people of the oak*. And some of these trees, like furze, these aren't even common names anymore. They're symbolic. Look, here, the first tree in the list. *Alder*. I remember that character. I think it represented *V*."

"Or *F*," Bennett said from the stateroom door.

Sam gave a soft gasp as Joana bumped her head trying to scramble out of the bar. Bennett filled the doorway with both his height and his glowering presence, a muscle in his jaw clenching every time he inhaled. Sam bit her lip, shrinking back against the velvet couch and wondering if the space beneath it was small enough for her to fit. Joana straightened up with a brilliant smile, putting one hand on her hip.

"Brother, there you are!" she said brightly. She swept a hand to Sam, who was doing her best to blend in with the pattern of the carpet. "Sam was just getting started with all that letter business. You should dive right in."

"The only diving anyone will be doing around here is the two of you out the porthole window," Bennett ground out, dragging his trunk into the room and letting it drop with an ominous *thump*. "I had to pay double the price to talk a married couple out of their tickets. This was their honeymoon, Jo."

Joana waved a hand at him. "They're newlyweds; I'm sure they'll appreciate the extra money more than a boat ride."

Bennett pinned her with a glare that would have incinerated a lesser woman. Even Joana's bulletproof smile slipped a bit. But she cleared her throat and straightened up, grabbing for the handle and pulling the door open. Sam wondered if she was trying to escape or make sure they had witnesses. But if it was an escape she was planning, Phillip's presence at the door impeded it.

"Oh! Phillip, there you are." Joana's hasty smile only shone brighter. "You made it on as well, excellent."

"It seems I'll have to watch my back with both Steeling siblings," Phillip said, the barest edge of frustration peeking through his placid tone. He pulled his handkerchief from his pocket, an aggressive cough racking his shoulders. "And my pockets as well."

Joana put a hand on his arm. "Desperate times and all that, Philly, you understand. Let me make it up to you with a cocktail at the bar."

"You and I are not done here," Bennett said, taking Joana in a firm grip and steering her toward the bedroom. He closed the door, but it did little to muffle his raised voice as he launched into a lecture. Sam crept up to the couch, her legs tingling from being folded beneath her on the floor. Phillip watched the door in fascination.

"I never even felt it," he mused, shaking his head. "Where did a society girl learn to pick pockets like that?"

"Oh, that's just Jo," Sam said, scratching out more ogham characters with a pencil she found in her winter coat. Maybe if she had the aicmí figured out by the time Bennett was done dressing down Joana, she could avoid his censure.

Phillip lifted an eyebrow, moving closer to the table where she worked. "And you never thought to ask why a girl with that much money feels the need to steal?"

Sam paused halfway through a character. "I . . . No, I suppose I never thought to ask. She's just always done it, as long as I've known her."

Another thing to add to the list of ways that Sam had failed their friendship. It really never had occurred to her to ask why Joana had such a compulsion to take things when she had enough money to buy them. Phillip had only known them a day and he'd seen it straightaway. Sam hesitated over the ogham character. Phillip crouched down, studying her paper.

"What's that you're working on?" he asked.

"Oh, it's from the diary," Sam said, tapping the edge of her pencil against the half-done character.

Phillip rocked back on his heels. "What diary?"

"The one your professor sent from Dublin." Sam looked up. "Bennett didn't tell you?"

"I think it should be clear by now that Steeling doesn't tell me anything unless it's tortured out of him," Phillip said with a wry laugh. "If he had his way, I wouldn't be on this trip at all. He prefers to do everything himself."

Sam echoed his laugh, tilting her head in concession. "That's certainly Bennett. You shouldn't take it personally, though. He's always been like that. Even when we were children, he was so serious and responsible. The other girls would tease him about it, call him Bennett the Bore. But I thought it set him apart. He's always known what he wanted and gone after it."

"I can certainly admire a trait like that," Phillip mused. "I don't suppose you'd do me a favor and let me in on this diary business? I wouldn't want to come between you and Bennett, of course, but

I just thought . . ." He took a deep breath, letting his head drop a little as he continued. "I thought it would all be so easy. Going to Oxford, being part of my father's world after longing to know him my whole life. And instead it was . . . isolating. Lonely. I thought I could outrun it, losing my mother like that. But you can travel the world over and never leave yourself behind."

Sam nodded, her chest swelling with sympathetic emotion. "I know what you mean. I thought I could lose myself in the books at the shop. Like if I could fix them, even the most damaged among them . . ."

"Then maybe you could fix yourself, too?" Phillip finished gently.

Sam huffed an empty laugh, looking down at the papers spread before her. "It sounds silly, I know."

"On the contrary, it sounds far better than what I chose. But I'm hoping if I help Professor Wallstone, if I make my choices mean something . . . I could honor her."

"Oh, that's . . . What a lovely sentiment." Sam reached out again, an instinct to comfort as she placed her hand over Phillip's where he rested it on the table. "I'll talk to Bennett about the diary. He's stubborn, but he's not mean-spirited. He can be made to see reason."

Phillip started to reply when the door to the bedroom slammed open and Joana swept out, her lips set in a thin line.

"Say, Philly, be a gent and show me to the bar," she said, her tone like ice. "I could use that cocktail now more than ever."

Bennett glowered in the doorway behind her. "You will stay here, Jo."

Joana cut a look over her shoulder. "You've said your piece, brother. I've got nowhere to go on this ship. Come on, Philly."

Phillip hesitated, looking back at Sam. He tapped his fingers where they rested on the table, reminding Sam that she still had her hand over his. She pulled it back, blushing.

"Don't get yourself into trouble on my account, Sam," Phillip said in a low voice. "I'll deal with Steeling myself. Thanks for the talk. It feels good to meet someone who knows what I've been through."

"Of course," Sam said as he stood up.

He smiled at Joana, holding out an arm gallantly. "Come on, Jo. They don't start serving until we reach international waters, but I bet if anyone can convince them to pop a bottle early, it would be you."

Joana gave him a dazzling smile. "Your money would be well placed."

Sam watched Bennett silently drag his trunk into the bedroom and begin unpacking his things, stalking past the open door with menacing intention. She wasn't sure how much time passed, but Bennett had fully emptied his trunk and neatly packed everything away by the time he returned to the sitting room. "My sister has dragged you into some questionable outings in her time," Bennett said, bringing the full weight of his disapproval on Sam. "Not the least of which was hopping on a train with no ticket like a drifter yesterday. You both got lucky the train officer allowed me to purchase your tickets in transit. But this, Sam, this is beyond . . ."

"I know, and I'm sorry," Sam said anxiously, scrambling up on her knees and twisting her hands together like a mendicant at church. "And I wouldn't have done it—well, I guess technically I didn't do it, since I had no idea Jo had taken your tickets—but, Bennett. Look, here, the first tree. Alder. It represented V, or F as you said, right? And down here, the hawthorn. That was the letter H, wasn't it? I think these trees, they're characters in ogham."

Bennett didn't stop glaring, but he did take a step closer. "What else?"

Sam looked down to her scraps excitedly. "There are repeating patterns, too, look. Rowan and rowan, side by side. What letter is the rowan?"

"L," Bennett said suspiciously.

"And furze, that was . . . what? O?"

Bennett nodded. "I'd have to check the aicmí to be sure, but I believe so."

"Look," Sam said, glowing in triumph. "If we're right, this first grouping, it says F-O-L-L-O."

"Follo?" Bennett said, the lure of the trees pulling him closer. He knelt beside Sam. "What is follo? Is that anything?"

He pronounced the vowels in their long form, but Sam searched through her memories for the images of the article she had read. "There's no W in ogham," she mused.

"What do you mean?" Bennett asked.

"Well, the letters, they're representative of the Celtic language, right? So, it's not a true ratio of one to one to the English alphabet, because they weren't speaking English. Any English approximation would be just that, an approximation. What if it's not *follo*, but *follow*?"

"Follow," Bennett said thoughtfully, turning the word over in his mouth like a sip of fine wine. "But follow what?"

"I don't know, but now we know how to find out," Sam said. "We need the rest of the characters, though. And I need your help. I don't remember all of the aicmí."

Bennett took a long, slow breath, tapping one finger on her list of trees. "If you're wrong, you and Jo are both on the first lifeboat back to shore."

Sam grinned. "I can take that deal. Get your survey papers; we need more space."

CHAPTER ELEVEN

By the time Joana returned several hours later, Sam and Bennett had plastered the open spaces of the stateroom walls with survey sheets covered in their attempts at reconstructing the aicmí of ogham. They had even covered the porthole, the gray light mottling the paper. Joana frowned from the doorway, where a long-suffering cabin boy pushed a rack of clothes wrapped in bags.

"When the steward said make yourself at home, I'm not sure he meant for you to re-wallpaper the digs," she said, touching the edge of the nearest survey sheet.

"It's only tape; it should come right off," Sam said, scribbling something on the paper beside it. "Bennett, do you remember if *N* had four or five strokes?"

Bennett paused where he was in the process of taping up another sheet of paper. "I think it was *S* that had four, and *N* that had five. Or was it the other way around?"

"I'll leave it blank for now," Sam said, making a note with her pencil.

"Oh good, I was afraid you might have gotten into too much fun while I was gone," Joana deadpanned. "Meanwhile one of us was more useful. I smoothed things over with Philly *and* procured a new wardrobe for the two of us. It took six hours and several testy conversations about waist-to-bust ratios with the ship's tailor, but we have new threads!"

She indicated the clothes rack with a flourish, the cabin boy straightening hastily from where he had been leaning against the rack.

"Who exactly paid for those things, Jo?" Bennett asked.

"The queen of England. Who do you think? It's not like we thought to grab our purses on the way to saving your hide."

Bennett pinched the bridge of his nose. "Those funds are coming out of my personal account, Joana. This isn't some tourist outing with Father in the French Riviera."

"I bought the bare-bones basics," Joana said, tucking a new pair of patent leather heels under the garment bags. She waved the cabin boy toward the bedroom.

"You and I have very different definitions of *basic*," Bennett growled.

"Speaking of the basics, have you two figured out the clues yet?" Joana asked, following the cabin boy into the bedroom and unloading the clothes from the rack into the armoire.

"We've started it," Sam said, stepping back to survey the aicmí they had accumulated.

"Started it?" Joana called, poking her head out with an armload of shimmering fabric. "I've been gone a cocktail and two wardrobes' length of time. What have you been doing?"

"It's not that simple," Bennett said, a touch defensively. "We had to assemble all the aicmí with the characters and make sure we had the correct corresponding English letters. There were some we disagreed on."

"Because you were wrong," Sam murmured without thinking, crossing off a letter from one of the survey sheets. She paused, realizing she'd spoken out loud, and turned bright pink. "I mean . . ."

But Joana's uproarious laughter cut across Sam's attempt to backtrack. "Just like the old days, isn't it, brother? Tell me again, which of the Plinys died when Vesuvius erupted?"

Sam groaned. "Don't bring it up."

"That was an honest mistake," Bennett grumbled.

"An honest mistake that cost us three days and ended with you getting pneumonia because you insisted on diving in the swimming pond after a snow squall to prove you weren't wrong," Joana said. "Mama had to stay home to take care of you while Daddy went to Greece. I've never seen her more furious. She scalded your tea every time out of spite."

She came back out of the bedroom with the cabin boy wheeling a now empty clothes rack, nudging Bennett to hand over a tip before the boy made his hasty escape. She stood before their walls of work, hands on her hips.

"And just like old times, you two need me to execute while you bicker about semantics," she said. "What have we got so far?"

"F-O-L-L-O," Sam said, pointing to the first translation she had written several hours ago.

"Follo?" Joana said, pronouncing it as Bennett had. "Who is that?"

"We think it's supposed to be *follow*," Bennett said, glancing at Sam.

"Follow what?" Joana asked.

"Well, we don't know that part yet," Sam said. "We were constructing the aicmí."

Joana rolled her eyes. "I swear, if it weren't for me you two would *still* be debating whether or not the Roman cloak pin was in the back shed or the kitchen hearth."

"Your father changed encryption methods halfway through the message on that one!" Sam protested. "And how was I ever supposed to know your family called the kitchen the 'burrow'? It was an understandable mistake."

"I wasn't wrong that time, was I?" Bennett said smugly.

"Give me a pencil," Joana said, holding out a hand to Sam.

"Why?" Sam asked, clutching hers closer.

Joana snatched it from her fingers. "Because we'll lose three days to another Pliny debate if I don't intervene. What's next?"

"Holly," Sam said slowly. "But you don't even know how the characters work—"

"Sure, sure," Joana said, squinting at the list of aicmí. "But it says here holly is *T*. Right?"

"Well, yes, but that's not—"

"It's trees, Sam, not the Pythagorean theorem," Joana said. "Give me the next one."

"You know the Pythagorean theorem?" Bennett asked as Sam rushed back to the letter.

"I know plenty of things that would surprise you," Joana said with an arched brow.

Joana made short work of the remaining list of trees, cutting through each of their philosophical arguments with a bold pencil stroke. When she was done, they all stepped back, surveying the string of letters.

"F-O-L-L-O-T-H-E-O-R-D-E-R," Sam read out loud.

"Who is Theorder?" Joana asked. "Is that a person or a thing? Maybe he meant Theodore. Who is Theodore?"

"It could be someone's name, or a location," Bennett said. "The professor will know."

"I don't think it's Theorder," Sam said. "I think it's *the Order*. *Follow the Order*."

They all sank into a pensive silence, soaking in the realization that they had done it. They had translated the hidden message on the back of Father Jacob's letter.

And it meant nothing.

"Okay, so," Joana said slowly. "What is the Order? And how are we supposed to follow it?"

"Who could possibly say?" Bennett asked, his voice dropping down into the lower registers of disappointment.

"It must be another code," Sam said, touching the letters.

Bennett spread his hands wide. "If it is, we've got no idea what it means. Or how to solve it. We've been operating under the assumption that Father Jacob was some kind of ciphering genius. But maybe he wasn't. Maybe he was wrong about everything."

"Or a crackpot," Joana added. "A lot of those back in the day. Practically everybody had syphilis."

"I think he was scared," Sam said quietly. "Of what he saw. Of what he knew."

She looked down at the letter in her hands, the handwriting telling its own story. The strokes that had been trained to be neat and tidy instead jagged and uncertain. The care he took to address and date the letter despite his haste.

"Whoever—or whatever—he was afraid of, he wanted to be sure they could never get the missing relic back. Just think of it. If you could have stopped the Great War, wouldn't you have done everything in your power to do so?" She dropped her eyes. "I know I would have."

"Well, okay, but what do we do about it?" Joana asked, bringing Sam out of her own head and back to reality, as she always did. "We're not the ones he left the letter for, so how the hell do we figure out what he meant by *Follow the Order?*"

"Professor Wallstone will know," Bennett said resolutely. "He'll know what the Order is and what we have to do to follow it."

It was a great deal of faith to put in a man she had never met, but Sam hardly had any other choice. It wasn't as if this was her area of expertise—she solved the cipher by happenstance, a collection of half-remembered magazine articles and a stroke of dumb luck. If any of them could find the missing relic, it would be the professor.

But the itch was still there, just under her skin, too deep to ever scratch. She had solved one puzzle only to find another. It beckoned her, laying out cryptic clues and drawing her in like a trap. Every reasonable barrier she had erected within her heart and mind screamed at her to stop, to consider the consequences of succumbing to the fever.

"What if there are more of those men from the shop waiting for us in Ireland?" Sam said, frowning at the aicmí lining the walls of the stateroom. "Or what if they're on the ship now? We didn't even consider the danger. We don't know who they are, what they look like, how many of them there might be. We just . . . I just leaped into this, without thinking about . . . There's no one to help us, no one to protect us. What have we done?"

She looked to Joana and Bennett helplessly, reality crashing into her like the waves beating against the hull of the *Olympic*. With the triumph of the translation fading, the cold certainty of dread settled into her bones, squeezing them like a vise. They had no idea who they were dealing with, or what they were capable of. The closer Sam got to an answer, the greater the threat she and Bennett and Jo posed to these men and their agenda.

Joana clapped her hands, making Sam jump. "What you need is a tall glass of champagne and a good swinging brass section, make you forget all your troubles. And it's almost dinnertime anyway. We'd better start getting ready."

Bennett frowned, looking at his watch. "Dinner isn't for another two hours."

"Yes, and this look doesn't happen with a snap of two fingers," Joana countered. "So, if you could scurry off and leave us a modicum of privacy, that'd be splendid."

"This is my room, Jo."

"Technically, it's ours now," Joana said with an apologetic grimace. "According to your ticket, yours is now . . . ooh, steerage class. Bad luck, brother."

Bennett crossed his arms, his teeth set so tight it made his jaw tic. "Joana, if you think I'm going to let you take over this room after the stunt you pulled this morning—"

"Fine, brother, twist my arm and make me say uncle. I'll make you a deal. You give us two hours, we'll give you the bed for the first night."

"The first night?" Bennett said incredulously.

"Obviously we'll have to negotiate the rest of the trip; there's two of us and only one of you," Joana said, giving him a healthy push toward the stateroom door. "Now, Sam and I need some girl time and you need to skedaddle. Phillip said there's a library on this thing. I can't imagine how it's functioning without you to correct their shelving methods. You can stare out at the sea and contemplate what Order the batty old priest might have been talking about."

"Jo, you can't honestly expect me to let you take over the whole—"

"That's exactly what I expect you to do," Joana said, throwing a glance over her shoulder at Sam. "We've all been through a lot, Sam most of all, and the girl deserves a little pampering. Would you really be the one to deny her?"

Bennett glanced at Sam, his expression softening. "No, of course not."

"Perfect, then we'll see you for dinner."

"Jo, I still need to get dressed—" Bennett protested, right as she pushed him out the door and swung it shut. She twisted the lock with a flourish, turning bright eyes on Sam.

"Come on, come see what I bought." She moved into the bedroom, dragging Sam along with her. "I'm pretty sure I got your measurements right, although heaven help you if you need an alteration. I'm pretty much banned from the tailor's shop at this point."

"I'm sure they're perfect," Sam said, happy to finally get out of the skirt she'd borrowed from Joana back at the Manor. It had been too tight when she first put it on, and after a full day of travel, her skin was starting to rub raw in patches where the unforgiving fabric squeezed her more ample figure.

"Of course they're perfect, I picked them," Joana said, pulling out several dresses and draping them over the bed. "And, while we're trying things on, drumroll please . . ."

She reached into the bottom of the bag, fishing out a bottle of wine and holding it aloft. "Ta-da!"

"Oh, Jo, I don't think we should—"

"Relax, Do-Right Sam, it's legal now. We officially crossed into international waters a couple of hours ago. The man in the shop just handed it over to me, no fuss, no code words or revolving rooms. No slipping a fiver to a thug with a hollow leg." She paused, tilting her head to the side. "It was anticlimactic, really. But the least we can do is toast your first foray outside of Clement. It only took a fire, some threatening fellas, and a nasty old book to do it."

Sam hesitated as Joana moved to the bar, digging through the cabinet until she came up with the foil cutter and a corkscrew. "I don't know. We've tested Bennett's patience enough as it is."

"My whole existence is testing Bennett's patience, you know that," Joana said, popping out the cork and dashing off a few fingers of ruby-red liquid into two glasses. "Come on, a toast. To Samantha Margaret Knox, finally flying the coop for more exciting pastures."

"I don't think that's the saying," Sam murmured, but she took the glass and swirled the liquid in time to the gentle movements of the ship. She took a hesitant sip, the wine dry and slightly bitter. It sucked all the moisture out of her mouth. Why did people enjoy this so much?

"Don't make that face, Sam, this is a fifty-dollar bottle of Bordeaux," Joana said, taking a long drink of her wine.

Sam choked on her next sip. "How many dollars? Jo, tell me you didn't."

"I won't tell you a thing," Joana said. "Besides, I had to celebrate my first real drink with my long-lost friend."

Sam took a sip, letting the warmth of the wine loosen the knot of tension Joana's words coiled in her gut. "I wasn't lost. You knew where I was the whole time."

"Yep, right where I always left you, buried in a pile of books," Joana said, draining her glass. "You know what? I need another one."

"Jo," Sam said as Joana poured herself another full glass, but she didn't know what to follow it up with, so she took another long drink of her wine instead. The last dregs trailed into her mouth, though she didn't know how that was possible. Joana had just filled the glass for her, how could it already be drained?

"Come on, I've had just the right amount of wine to give me the courage to attempt taming those unruly locks of yours," Joana said, standing abruptly and nearly sloshing said wine on the carpet. "Besides, you'll scream when you see what I've bought you."

"Tell me you didn't go all out on my account," Sam said, frowning at the sumptuous garments laid out on the bed.

"Of course not," Joana said, digging through the pile. "I did it on *my* account. Five years of trying to convince you to let me doll you up for Mama's Christmas party, and now I've got you trapped with no clothes of your own. Here we go."

Sam sucked in a breath as Joana held a dress aloft, the golden fabric draping over her arm and slithering down to the floor. Delicate lace overlaid the gold sheath underneath it, the arms bare and the drop waist gathered with a bit of tulle. The hem draped in folds, the patterns of tiered lace overlapping and shifting with each movement. It was a dress made for a goddess, not a washerwoman's daughter. Sam didn't dare touch it.

"Jo, I can't," she said, shaking her head. "I could never pay you back, not in a hundred years. I can't take this dress."

"It's not from me; it's from Bennett," Joana said, thrusting it toward her. "And trust me, it will pay for itself once he sees you in it."

Sam turned a deep, furious red at the arch in Joana's voice. "I have no idea what you're talking about."

"Sam, I may not be able to solve Daddy's puzzles, but I can certainly do basic math," Joana said, pulling another gown from the pile and hanging it up beside the gold dress. "I put two and two together a long time ago about the massive crush you've harbored for Bennett. I won't pretend to understand your fascination with my terribly boring brother, but I won't talk you out of it either. Now you can put on that dress, or we can keep talking about this until all the blood in your body rushes to your head and you pop like a mosquito."

Sam took the dress meekly. "I'll wear the dress."

"I thought you would," Joana said, digging through the armoire and pulling out a pair of heels. "Don't forget the shoes. A dress is only as good as its corresponding footwear."

Sam collected everything Joana held out to her and retreated to the washroom. She was happy enough to get out of her borrowed shirt and skirt, finally taking a deep breath. She considered locking herself in the bathroom and refusing to come out until dinner was over, but she couldn't put it past Joana to break the door down if she did. So instead, she put the dress on.

If it looked like a dream, it felt like a sin. The fabric was whisper soft, the sparkling gold underlay keeping the scratchier edges of lace from touching her skin. Only the barest sigh of lacy fabric brushed against her shins, and the dress left her arms completely exposed. She caught a glimpse of herself in the washroom mirror and gasped, the color of the dress transforming her hair from a dull brown to a shining mahogany, shot through with accents of complementary gold. She didn't recognize herself, and she wasn't sure how she felt about that.

"I know you're done in there, quit lollygagging," Joana called, rapping sharply on the washroom door. "Come out, I want to see how it looks."

"I don't know, Jo," Sam called, though she couldn't stop looking at her reflection.

"Come on, if nothing else I know you're starving."

She *was* starving, actually, and her stomach reminded her that it was dinnertime back home. She reluctantly left the security of the washroom, ducking out quickly before she lost her nerve. Joana stood beside the bed in a brilliant scarlet dress, looking like a model as she always did. She gave Sam a triumphant smile.

"I knew that color would suit you; you look an absolute dream," she said snatching the shoes from Sam's hands, and waving her over to the bed. "Come on, I'll strap you in and then we'll do something about your hair."

"What's wrong with my hair?" Sam asked, touching a hand to her head self-consciously.

"Nothing," Joana said. "Once I get through with it."

CHAPTER TWELVE

All in all, it took the full two hours for Joana to finish her ornamentations, and by the end Sam felt plucked and prodded within an inch of her life. It was no wonder Mrs. Steeling had always been so particular about her children not being overly affectionate with her and mussing her hair or makeup. If this was what she went through every day, Sam could hardly blame her. Bennett had returned to the stateroom to get ready for dinner in the mean time, grumbling all the while about being relegated to the fringes of his own room. Joana ignored him, tossing out his evening suit and shoes when his grumbling got too loud.

"It took every pin I could scrounge up, but it's done," Joana said to Sam, directing her toward the washroom mirror. Joana had pinned Sam's hair up in an elegant twist, little tendrils framing her face.

"Oh," she breathed. She'd never felt more beautiful, even if her toes already ached and her temples were throbbing from the pull of the pins in her hair. "Thank you."

"I've been begging you to let me do this for years, so I should be thanking you," Joana said. "Now, are you ready for the big reveal?"

Sam flushed in the sudden cloying warmth of the room. "I don't think that's necessary."

"Nonsense, this much work deserves an entrance." She moved to the door and cracked it open a hair. "Bennett, we're coming out."

"They sounded the dinner bell twenty minutes ago," Bennett said from the other room by way of response.

"As ready as he'll ever be," Joana muttered, before throwing the door wide and sweeping an arm back to where Sam stood self-consciously. "What do you think?"

Sam forced herself to meet Bennett's eyes, even though every fiber of her being wanted to sink down into the ship's boiler room and dissipate with the steam. His gaze landed on her, the irritation that crinkled his brow smoothing out as his eyes skimmed her face, down her dress, and back up again. Something in his expression shifted, warming and expanding, and she thought her skin might burst from the combustion of feelings it was trying to contain.

She was used to seeing him in a tailcoat for the annual Steeling Christmas party his mother held for all their employees, all buttoned up and proper with perfectly crisp collars. But she had never met him as an equal in opulence, since she had always insisted on wearing her own dresses to the affairs. She didn't want to feel like a charity case to the Steelings, a self-sufficiency inherited from her mother. Those dresses were built for function, though, not form. They had never made her feel the way the lacy edges of this dress did as they tickled her collarbone. Nor had they ever made her feel as exposed as she did now, standing before Bennett in a dress that amounted to a slip.

"Doesn't she look fabulous?" Joana prompted, when no one had said anything for several long moments.

"Like a vision," Bennett said softly, the words slipping out before he could take careful stock of what they might reveal. Sam's breath caught somewhere between her mouth and her lungs in a painful lump that got beaten about her chest by her rapidly thrumming heart. Bennett pressed his eyes closed, his ears turning red around the edges, and shook his head. "I mean, yes, of course. You look . . . very nice. They'll be giving away our seats soon if we don't hurry. Maybe I'll just go down and hold them myself. I'll see you both down there, yes?"

It wasn't until he was gone that Sam could catch a proper breath again, and Joana grinned at her in delight. "Didn't I tell you it would pay for itself? Come on, I need a quick touch-up and then we'll go down. I'm famished."

Sam worried she would look silly and overdressed for dinner, but by the time she and Joana reached the dining room, she wondered if she might actually be underdressed for the occasion. The gathered diners of the RMS *Olympic* put every Steeling party to shame, decked out as they were in furs and jewels and sporting elaborate hand fans with feathers along the edges. It was like someone took all the wealth of New York and put it on display in a moving exhibit. Now she understood why everyone had crowded the docks to see the *Olympic* off; these people gave an impressive show.

The dining room was no less grand than everything else on the vessel, and they even had a live brass band and a singer to keep the dance floor packed. If it weren't for the windows with their curtains thrown wide, showing the sparkling blue lines of the horizon outside, Sam never would have believed she was on a ship.

"I heard a rumor there's an actor on board," Joana said as they made their way between the tables. "The tailor was all in a twist about it because apparently the fella needed his coat mended for dinner tonight and sent it down last minute. Who do you suppose it is? Mr. Fairbanks? Or that little fella, what's his name? The one who's always doing those ridiculous stunts with a stone face."

"Buster Keaton," Sam said.

"That's him," Joana said, snapping her fingers. "Keep an eye out if somebody suddenly falls into the punch bowl or takes a tumble down the staircase. Those are always his bits."

"Ah, ladies, don't you both look fantastic," Phillip said as they reached the table, standing up to pull out a chair for Joana. He took in the flare of her red dress appreciatively, giving her a wry grin. "Whose trunk did you steal that out of?"

"No one's," Joana said primly. "Though now I'm disappointed it never occurred to me to go hunting. Especially after dealing with that unpleasant little tailor all afternoon."

Joana bumped Bennett's shoulder hard as she sat down, looking pointedly at Sam's chair, which was still tucked under the table.

"Bennett," she whispered through clenched teeth.

"What?" he asked, annoyed, before noticing Sam was still standing there. "Oh, Sam, I . . . Let me get that for you."

He pushed his chair back and stood up quickly, which brought him too close, their chests brushing against each other and the lacy ends of her skirt clinging to his pants.

"Here you are, Sam," Bennett said, pulling out the chair and stepping clear to the other side of it to avoid any more collisions.

"Thank you," Sam said quietly, taking her seat and letting him push it back into the table. "I could have done it for myself, but I wasn't sure of the protocol."

"Nonsense," said a crisp voice from the other side of the table. "A gentleman should never let a lady such as yourself pull out her own chair. It would be uncouth."

Sam perked up in surprise at the young man, the same one she had spoken to about the rude woman with the peacock hat. "Oh, it's you! From the train."

"You saved me from a potentially perilous medical situation," the young man said with a wink.

"Oh, I don't know about that," Sam said, flushing with a smile. "But it seems you didn't need the advice after all, seeing as how you're on the *Olympic*."

He returned the smile. "I didn't know you would be here either."

"To be fair, I didn't know I would be here until this morning," Sam conceded.

"What are you, stowaways?" asked the young woman beside him before taking a drag from a cigarette in a long, thin holder. She wore a black sequined dress with a plunging neckline, showing off the perfect curve of her collarbones and the swan-like length of her porcelain neck. Her hair was short like Joana's, but instead of finger curls she kept it straight and black, framing her high cheekbones and red-stained lips. Sam had never seen anyone so glamorous outside of a movie screen, not even Joana.

"More like bootleggers," Joana said, giving her skirt a flare as she settled the layers of fabric in her lap. "We're far too dashing for plain old stowaways."

The young woman arched a perfect brow. "I was under the impression you had to be smuggling something people want in order to be considered bootleggers."

Joana's flippant smile froze. "Who are you? I didn't catch a name."

"Ah, Jo, this is Veronica Fitzgerald," Phillip said as the waiters brought around their soup course, something creamy and earthy-smelling that made Sam want to slurp it straight from the source. "And her brother, Alistair Fitzgerald. They'll be our tablemates this evening, since the dining room is full up."

"Half brother," Veronica said, the word like a sharp wind.

Alistair gave a small smile, his gaze drifting to the band as the musicians segued into a slower number, the clinking of spoons against bowls like a background accompaniment. "Yes, half brother. My father died when I was an infant, and our mother remarried Veronica's father and had Veronica a year later. As Veronica likes to point out whenever it comes up."

Veronica gave him a cool smile. "I like to keep the record straight, dear half brother." She turned that same cool attention to Joana. "And who are you? What was that name—Jo? What a perfectly American name."

Joana's spine snapped ramrod straight. "Joana Steeling. Of Steeling's Textiles."

Veronica made a little humming noise. "I'm sure I haven't heard of it."

"Ah, so, Alistair," Sam said, eyeing Joana's death grip on the bread knife. "What brings you and your . . . half sister to the *Olympic*?"

"Ah, that," Alistair said with a nod. "It was Veronica's idea, actually, to do a Grand Tour. Like all the fashionable youths today."

Veronica gave a smoky sigh, the edges of it dissipating against the jacket of a passing waiter. Joana flagged him down by raising her empty champagne glass in a desperate swirl. "You're twenty years old, Alistair. Stop talking about yourself as if you were a decrepit pastoral vicar. All the lads at Oxford are taking a gap year these days to explore the world and widen their horizons. The university gets absolutely stuffy with the same names year in and year out."

Phillip gave a soft grunt of agreement as he sampled the soup.

"Oh, you're at Oxford?" Sam asked Alistair in surprise. "Then you must know Phillip, from before."

Phillip stiffened slightly in his seat, pasting on a smile as he waved off the bottle of champagne the waiter offered. "I wouldn't think so, Sam. Alistair and I ran in different circles."

Alistair frowned at Phillip like he was trying to put the pieces of an incomplete puzzle together. "You're an Oxford lad?"

"Was," Phillip said succinctly. "I didn't care for it. I attend the University of Chicago now."

"You're smarter than most of the Oxford lads, then," Veronica said.

Alistair's frown deepened. "Now I'm sure you look familiar. Did you take ethics with Professor Fuston?"

Phillip's smile grew taut around the edges. "No. As I said, you and I ran in different circles. I wasn't part of the Bullingdon Club."

"Ah, well," Alistair said, sounding embarrassed as he accepted another glass from the waiter. Sam would have liked more, but her head was still swimming from the red wine Joana had shared with her back in the room. "That business is so old-fashioned. I don't care much for it myself, truth be told. But it's important to my stepfather that I keep up his tradition."

"Tradition is overrated," Joana said flippantly. "It's just another way to keep everyone in their place."

Veronica looked her over carefully. "What a very nouveau riche mind-set. Out with the old, in with the new, isn't that what you lot say? The baby with the bathwater?"

"We value innovation," Bennett said. "Even as we mine the past to understand our own history better. It's important to know where we came from, of course, but we should also recognize how we can be better. Sometimes to preserve the past, you have to change the future."

"George Santayana said, 'Those who cannot remember the past are condemned to repeat it,'" Sam said. "I think tradition is just as important as innovation. We focus so much on moving forward, we convince ourselves that where we are isn't good enough. But sometimes it's okay to stand still."

Alistair leaned forward, the lapels of his jacket dipping dangerously close to his consommé. "You read Santayana?"

"I work in an antique bookshop," Sam said, her words faltering at the end. "Well, I worked. There was a fire, and it was destroyed."

"Your own Library of Alexandria," Alistair said sympathetically. "What a terrible loss that must have been."

Sam's eyes filled with unexpected tears. "Yes it was."

"Father will rebuild," Bennett said confidently to Sam. "You'll have everything back the way it was, I promise. Better than before."

But how could she explain to him that it wasn't the building, or the job? It was every single book she had put her hands on and her heart into, each one she had nursed back to prime condition. Those books, that work, would never come back to her. Bennett had never known such loss. But it seemed to be the only constant in Sam's life, to lose those she loved.

"Some things can't be replaced," Sam said softly.

"Some things shouldn't be," Phillip said. "But Santayana also said to be happy you must have taken the measure of your powers and learned your place in the world and what things in it can really serve you. We make our own traditions, even from the ashes of nothing. My ancestor Richard Rosewood did just that, built himself a life around the time of the Revolutionary War with nothing more than a bastard heritage."

"Is that where your handkerchief is from?" Sam asked, pitching her voice above the band as it struck up a brassy, swinging number. "The embroidered one? I saw it had R.R. on it."

Phillip nodded. "It's all that remains after his children squandered his wealth, but I fancy myself a new Richard Rosewood, building my empire."

"I can toast to that," Joana said, lifting her champagne glass high.

Veronica gave a curling smile. "How perfectly American you all are."

Joana returned the smile. "What perfume is that, Veronica? Lavender? Reminds me of my Aunt Neem."

Sam choked on a sip of her water, spluttering through a cough as Bennett patted her on the back. Several nearby tables looked over in alarm, but Bennett waved off their concern with a hasty smile.

"Still, I'm sure I must have seen you somewhere, even in the dining hall," Alistair said to Phillip, shaking his head. "Oxford's not so large a place as to swallow a person up whole. Which college were you in?"

"Alistair, for the love of the queen let the matter drop," Veronica said. "Perhaps Phillip doesn't want you to remember him."

Phillip gave a forced chuckle that convinced no one at the table. "It was a . . . difficult year for me. Great deal of change. I'm afraid I spent most of the time in my dormitory at St. Hugh's College avoiding the social goings-on. That's probably why you don't remember me."

"St. Hugh's?" Alistair said in surprise. "Isn't that where they had that unfortunate business last year, some sort of childish hazing incident that ended with the missing—"

"Alistair," Veronica said sharply. "Drop it."

Phillip's smile looked brittle enough to crumble, and Alistair went pale. "Right, of course. Sorry, Phillip."

"As I said," Phillip continued, his voice tightly controlled. "Not the place for me."

The table fell into an awkward silence, everyone jumping in their seats as the trumpet hit a high note. Joana perked up, putting on her most dashing smile.

"Oh, I love this tune," she said, shimmying her shoulders hard enough that one strap of her dress slipped down her arm. "What do you say, Philly? Care to give the boards a good stomping with me?"

The tightness in Phillip's smile eased. "I'm not sure I can keep up."

"I'll go slow, just for you," Joana said with a wink.

"That sounds like fun," Alistair said, clearly relieved to have moved beyond the previous awkwardness. "Even with two left feet like mine. Say, Sam—"

"Sam, would you like to dance?" Bennett asked, a little too forcefully.

Sam drew back in surprise. "Oh, I . . . Well, I don't really know the steps."

"I'll lead you," Bennett said, holding his hand out to her expectantly. "I'm used to it after all of Joana's failed dance lessons. You can't be any worse than she was."

"Because I should have been lead," Joana said, giving her skirts a toss.

Sam looked hesitantly at Alistair, who gave her a game smile and a shrug. "I'll take the next song, if you're not too tired."

"Okay, yes, of course," Sam said, putting her hand in Bennett's and letting him lead her to the dance floor.

CHAPTER THIRTEEN

Bennett kept his grip on Sam's hand firm as he navigated her past the dining tables. Whether it was the aftereffects of the wine or the heat of his touch, her head spun as they took a place on the edge of the wooden floor, Joana and Phillip already deep among the other dancers. The band wound down from a swinging number to a slow, sweeping waltz as Bennett pulled her in close, sliding his hand over her hip to fit it into the curve of her lower back. Sam took quick, shallow breaths, trying not to think too much of the press of his hand or the span of his fingers or how there was nothing more than a thin weaving of silk between his skin and hers.

He moved like a dream, like *her* dreams, sweeping her around the dance floor as if her feet were only brushing the tiled surface. She tried to keep up, to move as gracefully and elegantly as he did, but her feet lagged a half beat behind, and her neck had a disturbing tendency to bend toward him every time they twirled.

"Sam, I don't think you should be associating with Alistair," Bennett said, his voice rumbling through her chest.

"Oh, that's . . . I'm sorry, what did you say?" The dreaminess faded as she spotted the crease between his brows. That wasn't the crease of someone who had been waiting to dance with her. That was the crease of someone preparing a lecture, and not knowing the proper opening salvo.

"Alistair Fitzgerald," Bennett said, his voice deepening along with the crease. "I don't think you should be encouraged by his attentions. I don't trust him."

"What are you talking about?" she asked as he moved her across the floor. The song had come to an end, much to her disappointment, and he guided her near one of the wide windows. The setting sun glared off the water's surface, throwing rays of light at her like knives.

"You're young and inexperienced, and you don't know fellows like him," Bennett said, his tone growing flat and scholarly. "He might act cordial now, but boys like him . . . they're used to getting whatever they want, whenever they want it. You wouldn't want him to get the wrong impression of you."

"What impression is that?" Sam asked, her face growing warm.

Bennett hesitated, chewing on his next set of words. "You're a good girl, Sam. And smart. Book smart. And you're kind, and you want to give people the benefit of the doubt. You want to believe everyone is as nice as you are."

How was he making so many compliments sound like insults? Sam fidgeted, her feet growing tired and swollen in her new shoes. She *had* thought Alistair was nice, and genteel, more so than any of the boys back in Clement. Bennett was wrong about one thing, though. She knew people weren't nice.

"I am . . . perfectly capable of taking care of myself," Sam said, though she didn't sound like it right at that moment. She straightened up. "And anyway, Alistair has been nothing but kind to me. I have no reason to suspect he's anything but. Why are you so suspicious?"

"Because I know his kind. I've met them plenty of times over at Mother's endless galas and Father's Archaeological Institute meetings. These fellows know how to play nice until they need to get mean. I don't think you should spend any more time with Alistair."

"Well, that's not really up to you, is it?" Sam said, growing frustrated. "You're not my big brother, are you?"

"I practically am," Bennett insisted, growing red around the ears. "And I'm in charge of this whole excursion. I'm trying to look out for you. And I say that you're not to be around Alistair anymore."

Sam huffed out a long, angry breath "Well, you might be in charge of this excursion, but you're not in charge of me, Bennett Steeling. The only person around here I think I should avoid is you, seeing as how you've ruined my evening and my appetite. I'm going back to the room."

"Now hang on, Sam," Bennett started, but she stepped back.

"Don't you . . . Don't 'Sam' me," she said, pointing a shaky finger at him. "You just leave me alone, Bennett."

She fled the dining room before he could say more, her toes throbbing and her ankles weeping, but she didn't stop until she had reached the A deck. The waves had turned rolling and high by the time she returned to the room, tilting the ship back and forth in nauseating movements. She held on to the door frame, steadying herself as she fumbled for the key Joana had given her, and managed to get the door unlocked. The room was dark, the sunlight long gone. It took her a few tries to locate the light switch, but eventually she managed it. She wrestled her way out of the shoes, tossing them in a corner and wishing she could do the same with Joana's beautiful golden dress. But she didn't know what other clothes Joana had bought or which were hers, and she refused to squeeze into that borrowed skirt again, so she was stuck with the dress for now.

"The . . . the absolute nerve of him," Sam muttered, stomping through the sitting room into the bedroom and plopping on the mattress only to pop back up a second later and pace into the sitting room. "Who does he think he is, telling me . . . I can talk to whoever I want! I'll talk to Alistair if I please, he can't . . . What does he even think is wrong with Alistair? He seems perfectly nice to me. Bennett is just . . . Well, he's acting . . ."

She couldn't quite finish that thought, though. Had it been one of Joana's flings, she would have said *jealous*. But that couldn't possibly be what Bennett was. Jealous of Alistair? Because of *her*? It wasn't . . . It just wasn't possible.

"He's simply being a . . . a brute," Sam said, frowning hard at the ogham characters still taped to the walls. It had been so exciting, working through another puzzle with Bennett and Joana. It really had felt like old times, all the treasure hunts at Steeling Manor filling their idle childhood days. She had let herself believe things were that good again, that pure.

But she should have known better. They'd all grown up, and apart. Maybe Joana was right; maybe Bennett was stodgy. He was trying to control her like he tried to control everything else. He didn't see her as Sam; he saw her as a problem to contain.

She dropped onto the sofa, burying her head in her hands and sending an array of pins scattering across the rug. She should have stayed in Clement, even with the bookshop burned. This was all too much. The strange men, the terrifying images in Father Jacob's diary, the last great war of man, even the social dynamics of their dinner table. She wasn't equipped for this. She should have stayed where it was safe.

Not that Clement was safe anymore either.

She shivered, sending a few more pins scattering, as the ship crested a high wave and rattled the door to the stateroom.

Except it rattled again, even after the ship leveled out.

Sam froze, peering up through her fingers as the doorknob gave a shake. She had locked it behind her—a habit from working at the bookshop—and for a moment she thought it might be Bennett, coming after her to apologize or put his foot down harder. Or maybe it was Joana, too many glasses in to remember Sam had taken her key. The knob stilled, and she held her breath as she waited for Joana's voice to call out for help.

But the knob rattled again, this time accompanied by a scratching noise. Someone was trying to pick the lock.

Sam shot up, swallowing back a scream. Her heart, so painfully stopped a moment ago, was now working overtime to catch up, doing its best to beat its way out of her chest. She glanced around in a panic, looking for any means of escape, but it was a ship. There was nowhere for her to go.

She backed up beside the bar as the scratching continued, the paper on the wall crinkling behind her head and stopping her heart once again. Did the person on the other side of the door hear that? Did they know she was in there now? Someone had to come along the corridor soon, she was sure of it. Dinner must be wrapping up, right? Someone would come and save her, wouldn't they?

What should she do? What *could* she do? Hide in the bathroom? Shimmy up the air vent? Corkscrew him in the neck as soon as he came through? She couldn't breathe. She was going to suffocate before the intruder ever got in. She needed air, not this stale, recycled air but fresh, real, mind-clearing air. She moved to the porthole behind the couch, tearing away the paper covering it and wrestling with the mechanism to get it open. It stuck, forcing her to push so hard she nearly fell out once she finally got it to swivel.

The frigid ocean air slapped her back to reality, shrinking her skin and expanding her lungs. The ship crested another wave, sending a spray of salt water into her face. The lights of the promenade deck twinkled overhead, so calm and peaceful and mockingly distant in her current panic. If only she could get up there. Maybe if she shouted for help, someone would come running. She looked down and spotted the porthole window beneath hers open.

"No," she whispered, shaking her head at the ludicrous idea that formed in her mind. She couldn't go out the window of a moving ship. It was freezing, she was in a dress, and she had no shoes on. It was impossible.

The doorknob rattled again. They weren't giving up, whoever it was. Which meant she was . . . She was going out the window.

Okay, she could do this. Well, she had to do this. But how to do it without plunging into the waters below? It might have been over a decade since the *Titanic*, but she didn't care to experience that terror on its sister ship. Joana would know a way—she always knew the way. She'd scaled every portcullis and drainpipe at Steeling Manor. Once she'd even escaped the third-floor nursery after being locked in for cutting up all the stockings the dressmaker had brought by making a rope out of old blankets and climbing down to the garden.

Sam sucked in a breath—that was it. She needed a rope.

The scratching stopped again, the handle of the door rattling. Sam's heart squeezed, her eyes falling on a nearby chair left askew from the small desk in the corner. On instinct she darted forward, grabbing the chair and shoving it under the door handle to keep it from opening. That would buy her a few seconds, which she hoped would be enough.

She ran to the bedroom, stripping the pristine sheets from the bed and running back to the open porthole still blowing frigid air into the stateroom. She spotted Bennett's travel coat laid out across the back of the sofa and snatched it up, stuffing the pockets with Father Jacob's letter and the ogham figures on the wall before wrapping it around herself. Underneath it was a beautiful umbrella, presumably part of Joana's new acquisitions, and Sam knotted the bedsheet around it a few times with shaky hands as the doorknob turned all the way around. She cringed as the door opened a half inch before meeting the stiff back of the wooden chair. It slid forward another inch before catching on the carpet, stopping the door. It held, but it wouldn't for long.

Sam swung one leg up and over the lip of the porthole, the metal exterior of the ship infinitely colder than she anticipated. She sucked in a sharp breath, her bones hurting as she tossed the bedsheet out and stuck the umbrella at the bottom of the rounded window, pulling hard on the sheet to make sure the umbrella would hold. It wasn't nearly as stable as, say, a ladder, but it was better than nothing. And the chair scraped forward another inch, so she didn't have time for more doubts.

"Just don't look down," she whispered as she forced herself to swing her other leg around and lower herself out the window, gripping the bedsheet for dear life.

For a terrifying moment, Sam hung suspended between two worlds, welded to the side of the ship like a barnacle. She had absolutely misjudged the distance between the portholes, and as she tightened her fists around the bedsheet and pressed her face to the side of the ship, her feet scrambled for a foothold but couldn't find purchase. The ship crested another wave and she yelped as it loosened her hold on the sheet, dropping her down a few inches and bringing her feet in blessed contact with the frame of the porthole below. The wind and salt spray cut through Bennett's coat like rice paper, soaking her beautiful new dress and numbing her extremities.

She forced herself to climb down the sheet until she had both feet on the bottom lip of the lower porthole. She leaned out a little, slipping her feet into the safety of the window and trying to lower herself all the way down. But the change in position made the sheet slip where it was tied to the umbrella, and another rising wave knocked the umbrella sideways so that it clattered to the ground and the sheet went sailing out the window. Sam gave a strangled cry as the backs of her knees caught the bottom edge of the window, the rest of her flying past until she was hanging upside down out the window by her knees, the lacy edges of her dress blowing in her face and Bennett's jacket tangling up her arms. Something tickled her nose and she swiped at it, only to hear the telltale crinkle of Father Jacob's letter and her hard-earned translation as they slid out of the coat pocket.

"Oh no, no, no, no!" she cried, snatching at them as they flew past. But the wind was faster, sending both papers on a downward swoop toward the black waters below. From her inverted position she could only watch, helpless, as they landed in the cresting foam of the waves made by the ship's passing.

She might have hung there the rest of the night, her thighs freezing and her head slowly filling with a rush of blood, but voices drifted out the porthole above. The chair had given up its valorous defense, and if she didn't move quickly, the intruders would spot her—much more of her than she wanted to share.

She squirmed and slithered her way up the side of the ship, her fingers so numb they barely held to the lip of the porthole as she hauled herself inside, dropping into a puddle of shimmering silk on the floor of the room. The lights were out, the only illumination a thin slit under the door from the exterior hallway. Not much had gone her way so far that evening, but at least there had been no one here to witness her humiliation. She sat on the floor a few minutes, regaining her breath and trying to slow her racing heart while stretching her fingers to work some sensation back into them. Oh, how she wished she could stay here, in the comfort of the dark. But someone was still in their stateroom. She couldn't stand to think of what might become of Bennett and Joana if they returned and surprised the intruders.

She gathered herself up, stumbling through the dark of the unknown room, letting the thin strip of light serve as her guide. She ran into a few soft edges and one hard one, hissing a curse as the pain shot through her shin. But finally, she reached the door, turning the lock and wrenching it open.

Only to run right into Alistair Fitzgerald, knocking him back and sending the key he held clattering to the floor. Sam put up both hands with a gasp.

"Oh, Alistair, I'm so . . . What are you doing here?"

"I suppose I should inquire the same thing," Alistair said, a bit out of breath. He pushed himself away from the wall, shaking his head slightly as he pulled his lapels back into place. "What are you doing in my room?"

CHAPTER FOURTEEN

"Your room?" Sam echoed, glancing over her shoulder.
"Yes, well. I—"

Sam whirled back around, grabbing Alistair by the lapels and giving him a shake. "Oh, thank you for leaving your window open! But wait, where are the others? They haven't gone back to their rooms, have they?"

Alistair gave her a look of wild confusion. "What others? Were there more of you in there? Did I miss an invitation to a party in my own room?"

Sam shook her head. "You deserve an explanation, and I promise to give one, but I need to find Bennett and Jo first. Please say they're still at dinner."

"When I left, everyone was headed to one of the smoking rooms," Alistair said. "I only came to retrieve my pipe."

"There's no time for that," Sam said, starting down the hall and inadvertently dragging Alistair along by the lapels, which she had forgotten she still had ahold of. "Which smoking room was it?"

"I'm not sure . . . Your tall friend made a joke about the poop deck," he said, stumbling after her. He looked down. "But wait, you haven't got any shoes!"

"No time!" she said, turning the corner and whipping Alistair along behind her. Alistair, to his credit, managed to keep up at a hopping pace. She paused as they reached the lobby of the deck. "Up or down?"

Alistair pointed to the stairs leading up. "That way to the promenade. But, Sam, what's going on? Why the rush?"

"Someone broke into our stateroom," she said breathlessly, letting go of Alistair to climb the stairs.

"What?" Alistair said, his voice shot through with alarm. "Shouldn't we alert the first mate? How did you get to my room?"

"I jumped," Sam huffed, reaching the top of the stairs.

Alistair gave her a wild look of surprise. "You did what?"

"Well, technically I climbed down a bedsheet," she replied, looking left and right. "Which way?"

"Did you say you climbed down a bedsheet?" Alistair asked, bewildered.

"Which way?" Sam prompted.

He shook his head a little but pointed to the left. "That way, I think."

Sam nodded, rushing around and following the faint strains of music and the heavy smell of tobacco until she found the entrance to the smoking room. The lights were low, the men in their evening clothes crowding leather booths with their shirts slightly untucked and their grins expansive. Sam proved an entertaining sight for them, barefoot and wrapped in Bennett's coat with her hair in complete disarray, but she ignored their laughter and pointing. After all, none of them had just climbed out of a porthole on a ship.

A boisterous, full-throated laugh shot up out of a thick crowd of passengers near the bar, and Sam headed straight for it with a sharp sense of relief. She found Joana sitting up on the bar, several young men draped around her like petals on a rose. She was in top form, head thrown back, shoulders shaking with another laugh. But when she opened her eyes and spotted Sam, it was like something switched on, or off. She reached out both arms, wiggling her fingers at Sam.

"Oh, Sam, there you are! I thought my scoundrel brother had put you back to work." Her mouth turned into a little pout. "Oh, but what have you done to your hair? It's all fallen down and messy, and your dress! Two hours of my hard work out the window."

Sam didn't have time to tell her how literal that statement was. Instead she pushed through the gathered admirers, reaching for Joana's hand. "Oh, Jo, I'm so glad you're okay."

"Of course I'm okay; I'm in the prime of my life," Joana said, throwing her arms wide and knocking one boy's hat off his head. "Come on, come play. Oh, let's dance! What do you think, boys? Clear the bar and crank up the Victrola; I'll teach you the Charleston."

"No!" Sam shouted above the raucous cheers from the collected admirers. "We've got to find the first ma— Wait, where's Bennett?"

"Bennett who?" Joana asked, stepping up on a barstool and testing her balance. Several pairs of hands reached up to assist.

"Bennett! Your brother! Where is he?"

"Oh, that old stuffed shirt," Joana said with a wave. "Who knows? He disappeared right after you did. And then Phillip, the complete cad, offered Veronica a tour of the ship's library. Like I don't know what that means. So here I am, once again, making my own fun."

Sam clutched at Joana as she made a perilous sway to the right. "Did Bennett go back to the room?"

"How should I know? You two never tell me anything. One minute you're dancing, the next you've disappeared like a pint of gin from a police lockup."

"We need to find him! There were . . ." She glanced around at the assembled crowd, not keen on making more of a scene than Joana already was. "Something happened. Is happening. We need to find Bennett before he goes back to the room!"

"Boo!" Joana called, and her gathered petals echoed the jeer. "Tonight is for dancing and danger, not boring lectures."

"Jo!" Sam said sharply, giving her a tug that brought her crashing down from the barstool into the waiting arms of her followers. But Sam pushed them all back, grabbing Joana by the shoulders and giving her a good, sharp shake. "Someone broke into our stateroom."

Joana's eyes popped open and she made a small O with her mouth. "Sounds exciting."

"Jo!" Sam said, her voice pitched up with exasperation. "I think it might be one of the men from the shop, looking for the diary. If Bennett went back to the room and that man is still there . . ."

Joana's eyes narrowed as her expression slowly wrinkled into a frown, her brain lagging a second behind. "Oh, that could be bad."

"Very bad," Sam said. "We need to find Bennett. Now."

Joana clapped her hands loudly. "Come on, boys, we need to form a posse. There's a murderous arson thief on board!"

Sam groaned in frustration, but the boys were only too happy to oblige. They formed a crush around Joana, propelling her forward through the crowds like a battering ram headed for the door. Sam could only trail along in their wake as Joana called out orders, Alistair still trailing behind her in bemusement.

"Oh, Alistair, can you find the first mate?" Sam called to him as she tried to keep up with Joana. "Tell him to come to our stateroom. With backup!"

"But what are you going to do?" Alistair called after her.

"I'm not sure!" Sam shouted down the hall, rounding the edge of the stairs and climbing to keep pace with the posse. "Tell the first mate to hurry, please!"

"All right," Alistair said, before he was lost to sight completely.

At least if the intruder was still in their stateroom, he would get plenty of warning to escape before the noisy gathering of Joana's followers reached them. Sam had to practically run to keep up, shouting directions when they started down the wrong hallways. Joana led the charge with boisterous glee, most especially when she steered them in the wrong direction. If they all made it out of this alive, Sam was personally going to throw every bottle of booze on the ship overboard.

"Here we are!" Joana announced, stopping before an entirely different stateroom.

"It's that one, down there," Sam said, a sick dread filling her stomach at the wide angle of the open door and the busted wood of the broken lock. When she pointed at the door, she realized her hand was shaking.

"Somebody's left the door hanging wide open," Joana said. "That's awfully rude. I have a brand-new wardrobe in there."

Sam advanced slowly, her heart pounding as she reached the edge of the door. She waved back Joana and the boys, not wanting to startle anyone if they were still inside. She should have waited for the first mate and his men to arrive. They would know how to handle this, far better than her and this drunken posse. What did she think she could do? What if the man from the shop was still there, or worse—what if Bennett had already returned and caught him?

It was that last thought that propelled her around the door, with nothing more to defend herself than a set of untrained fists. The room was a mess, furniture tossed around and all their things scattered along the floor. She stood there, shaking and fearful, but determined to take a stand, when someone came rushing out of the bedroom. She raised her fists, with no idea what to actually do with them.

"Sam!" Bennett said, his voice wild and uneven. He strode through the wreckage of the room to wrap her up in a tight embrace. She couldn't tell where her shaking ended and his began.

"Bennett! Are you all right?"

"Yes, of course. Oh god, Sam, I thought someone had . . ." His voice drifted off as he squeezed her tighter.

"I escaped," Sam said breathlessly. "Before they got in."

Bennett drew back. "How?"

Sam nodded at the porthole window, still standing open and pouring freezing-cold air into the stateroom. Bennett gave a huffing laugh, shaking his head.

"Of course. That explains it."

Sam frowned. "Explains what?"

Bennett held up a scrap of gold lace. "I found it, torn on the edge of a rivet. I thought . . . I thought they had . . ."

Sam shook her head. "No, Bennett. I'm okay. I'm safe."

Bennett nodded, closing his fist around the piece of fabric. He cleared his throat, stepping away from her a healthy few feet. "Good," he said gruffly. "I'm glad. . . . That's good to hear."

Joana peeked her head around the door. "Are we storming the castle, or . . ." She trailed off as she took in the sight of the ruined stateroom. "Oh, what a mess. Bennett, what have you done?"

"What is it, Jo? We're ready to fight!" came a voice from around the door.

Bennett frowned at Sam. "Who is that?"

Sam sighed. "Joana formed a posse."

Bennett echoed her sigh. "Of course she did."

"At least they took down all your tacky wallpaper," Joana said, leaning against the doorjamb. She gave a little pout. "Not that this maroon-and-green motif is much better."

Sam looked up in surprise. Her attention had been so focused on Bennett and the mess on the floor that she hadn't even noticed the walls. "Oh, Bennett, she's right. All of our work—the ogham, the aicmí—they're all gone."

"That means . . ." Bennett trailed off as he stormed into the bedroom, returning a few seconds later, his expression grimmer than before. "It's all gone. All my letters from the professor, my notes on the Hellfire Club, everything. Including the diary."

Alistair arrived shortly after with the first mate and a contingent of men, as well as an official representative of the White Star Line. Joana honed in on the tweedy little man immediately, demanding to know what the cruise line was going to do to resolve their inconveniences and make them feel safe and valued aboard the ship now that their stateroom had been vandalized. While the man made increasingly more desperate hand gestures as he tried to assure Joana that this was all an anomaly and they would be well compensated, Bennett walked through the compartment with the first mate to catalog everything that was stolen.

"And this porthole window was left open?" the first mate asked, the censure in his tone evident.

"Of course not," Bennett scoffed. "We read about the disaster on the *Titanic* like everybody else. We know to keep the portholes shut so the ship doesn't take on water in the event of an emergency. Nobody would be so foolish as to forget that."

Alistair winced, turning with a sheepish smile to Sam where she huddled on the couch.

"If I promise to never let it happen again, do you think we could leave the bit about your daring escape into my open porthole between ourselves?" he whispered. "I don't think it would improve my standing at the Bullingdon Club any if I got the reputation as the fellow who almost caused the second *Titanic* disaster."

Sam gave him a tired smile. "Of course. For what it's worth, I appreciate your lapse of judgment. It saved my life."

Alistair returned her smile. "Then I shall consider it an inadvertent act of heroism."

"Say, are you all holding a party without us?" Phillip demanded from the doorway, Veronica trailing behind him. His expression slackened when he took in the full extent of the damage. "Good lord, what happened here?"

"Is this another American tradition?" Veronica asked from beside him, waving a hand at the overturned furniture. "Tossing the place about?"

Joana sobered up with lightning speed at the sight of the other young woman, abandoning her attempts to finagle a larger stateroom out of the White Star representative to drape herself over Phillip's arm.

"Oh, Philly, it's just awful," she said, her eyes going big and dramatic. "Look at the place! Somebody broke into the stateroom, and with us still inside it!"

"What?" Phillip asked, his voice shot through with alarm. "When did that happen? Are you all right? What did you do?"

"She was down in the bar," Bennett said, crossing his arms. "It was Sam that was stuck in here alone."

"Sam?" Phillip said in surprise. "You were stuck in the room when this awful thing happened? Did you catch sight of the culprit?"

Sam shook her head. "No, I . . . I went out the porthole window before they got in."

"You did what?" Phillip asked, his eyebrows shooting up.

"The important thing is that everyone is all right," Alistair said hastily. "No harm done. Well, apart from the stolen items."

"Irreplaceable stolen items," Bennett said, with a look at Alistair and Sam. Sam had the urge to scoot away from Alistair, but instead she set her jaw and met Bennett's gaze with a stern look of her own. She'd just been chased out the window of a moving ship by intruders; she wasn't about to let him cow her.

Phillip looked around at all of them. "Sounds like your evening was far more exciting than ours touring the library. I do hope they're not making a run on other rooms in this corridor, though. Maybe I should check my room to be sure."

"I assure you, sir, that's not the case," said the White Star representative hastily, stepping forward. "This is an anomaly, and one we will rectify immediately. We will find the culprits and recover any stolen items. That's the benefit of being on a ship—the thieves have nowhere to escape."

"I'm not so sure about that," said the first mate, returning from the bedroom. He looked at them gravely, his uniform lending him an air of authority Chief Higgins back home in Clement could only dream of. "There is a lifeboat missing from the decks. We're using the spotlight to sweep the waters now, but if they had arrangements to meet up with another boat, they could be long gone by now. We've seen it before, with smugglers and pirates. They've got a fishing boat or some similar vessel that follows our wake, flashing lanterns in Morse code with drop locations. It happens more than we'd like, but the rumrunners have the Coast Guard all tied up, and nobody notices a stray fishing boat at night."

Sam looked at Bennett, all defiance gone out of her. Was he thinking the same as her? If they stole a boat and escaped, it could only have been the men from the bookshop. No other rooms had been burgled, and nothing else of value had been taken. As the others trailed off to Phillip's room to confirm it hadn't also been broken into, Bennett pulled Sam and Joana aside with a grim expression.

"Without those papers, we have nothing," he said with a shake of his head. "They have everything. The letter, the translation, all our work. They'll find the missing relic before Professor Wallstone can."

"No, they won't," Sam said. "I took the letter, and the translation, before I went out the window. They might have the aicmí, but they don't have the letter."

"You're an utter genius, Sam," Bennett said, taking her by the shoulders and kissing her forehead. They both paused, the moment blooming between them like a little flame, as Bennett seemed to realize what he'd done.

"I, uh . . . I shouldn't have—"

"That's all right," Sam said hastily, looking at the floor because she couldn't stand to keep looking at him.

Joana gave a snort. "You two are more transparent than a gin neat, you know."

"The letter," Bennett said gruffly. "Where is it?"

"Ah . . ." Sam tucked her hands in her coat pockets before remembering they were actually his, which only seemed to make her embarrassment worse. "I lost it. It fell out of my pocket when I went out the window—well, your pocket, I suppose. Do you want your jacket back? I only took it because it was cold; I wasn't planning to keep it. Here, I'll give it back now."

"Sam," Bennett said, giving her a soft shake. "Keep the jacket. I won't add you freezing to death to the list of hardships you've had to endure this evening. But without that letter, we have nothing. I've failed the professor."

"Not nothing," Sam said. "We finished the translation. We know the next piece of the puzzle."

"What good does it do us, though?" Bennett asked despondently. "We don't know anything about this Order, or what it means to follow it."

"But Professor Wallstone will." Sam took his hand impulsively. "Right?"

"Right," Bennett said, though the crease between his brows didn't lessen any. "Of course. Professor Wallstone will know what to do. We just have to make it to him before anything worse happens."

CHAPTER FIFTEEN

By the time they arrived in Dublin Port five days later, Sam wanted nothing more than solid land under her feet and a proper bed to lay her head on. The ferry that had brought them from England had been far less luxurious and far rockier than the RMS *Olympic*, and Sam was sick of anything that moved. It took all her manners not to shove the other passengers out of the way to be first on land. She could have planted herself in the sprawling emerald hillsides of Ireland like an ogham standing stone and never moved again.

She'd barely had time to register the splendor and movement of the docks in New York, but now she took her time cataloging her first impressions of Dublin as the passengers shuffled down the gangway like sheep. The sky hung low and gray, the late-afternoon mist obscuring the roofs and towers in the hilly distance. Chicago had been a city of modern giants, but Dublin felt older, like the roots of its buildings went deep down into the earth. Even the roads were different, built in uneven cobblestones worn down around the edges and slick with the heavy moisture in the air. In a way, it felt like stepping back into the past in the most inspiring sense.

Despite the looming threat of the bookshop invaders, Sam's

heartbeat picked up at the wild sense of the unknown greeting her there on the docks. She had never been farther than the eastern edge of Clement, and now within a week she had been to Chicago, New York, and Dublin. It took her breath away, even as her stomach churned with worry and her eyes scanned the crowds gathered on the docks looking for familiar or unfriendly faces. She was truly out in the wide world now, without the safety of her books or the climate-controlled interior of the shop. It was like finding herself on the upside-down portion of the Harvest Festival roller coaster, a death-defying turn that would either rocket her to an exhilarating conclusion or dump her out on her head.

"It's very . . . gray," Joana said beside her, her lips twisting into an uncharacteristic frown. Sam would never tell her she looked exactly like Bennett when she did that, but the thought made her smile.

"I think it's fascinating," Sam said, drinking in the sights. "Hundreds of years of history you can trace along every eave and doorway. I could spend my whole life just studying the architecture here."

"Of course you could," Joana muttered. "But at least they have pubs. They do have pubs, right?"

"Enough to drown in," Phillip said with a chuckle. "The Irish have come by their reputation honestly. Though don't tell an Irishman that to his face."

"Did you visit Dublin while you were at Oxford?" Sam asked.

Phillip shook his head. "Ah, no. Regretfully, I'd say. But I'm glad to be here now with a greater purpose than a pub crawl with the Bullingdon Club."

"So, a drinking contest here might be an actual challenge," Joana said, a wild light creeping into her eyes.

"Luckily for your liver, we're not staying in Dublin proper,"

Bennett said, his tone filled with censure. "The professor's accommodations are outside of the city."

"Who stays outside of the city?" Joana asked in bewilderment.

"Someone looking to get actual work done," Bennett said. "Professor Wallstone needs access to the location of the Neolithic passage grave he's surveying, which is up in the Dublin Mountains. Staying in the city would have required significant delays traveling out there, so he found closer accommodations."

"Tell me it's at least a country house," Joana said. "With servants?"

"It is a country house," Phillip said, but he gave her a chagrined smile. "Though you might find the 'servants' a bit lacking in their manners. They're monks."

Joana stopped so suddenly the woman behind her stumbled over the lip of the gangway, muttering curses under her breath. She shoved past Joana with a glare, which Joana gamely returned.

"What does he mean, they're monks?" she asked as Bennett took her by the arm and dragged her out of the way of the other departing passengers.

"We're staying in a place called Orlagh House," Bennett said. "Though it used to be called Footmount, if you can believe it. It was built by a man named Lundy Foot. He was a famous snuff producer here in Dublin."

Joana gave him a dead stare. "I swear, brother, if you start in on a history lesson with me right now—"

"All right, all right," Bennett said hastily. "The point I'm trying to make is, the house was eventually sold to Augustinian monks, and they turned it into a school for their novitiates. It's quiet, so Professor Wallstone can work, and it's close enough to the Hellfire Club that he can walk up there. And it will be more than suitable accommodations for us, as we're here to work."

"Speak for yourself," Joana muttered, the wild glint in her eyes turning hard and calculating. "These monk fellas probably won't take kindly to a couple of skirts staying on with them, will they? Sam and I should arrange our own place down here in Dublin, give you boys some breathing room."

"Not a chance," Bennett said flatly.

"Jo, we've got to stick together," Sam said, adopting a more soothing tone. She looked around at the remaining passengers departing the ferry, moving in closer and lowering her voice before continuing. "Those men from the bookshop could still be after us if they've figured out the letter is missing. We're safest together, all of us."

Joana gave a dramatic sigh. "Fine. But if the mattresses are lumpy, I'll raise hell."

Bennett and Phillip went to hire a car while Joana argued with the man unloading the ferry about whether or not he was required to haul their trunks all the way to the street. Sam waited on the docks, swaying unconsciously to the gentle movements of the ships coming in and out of port. A bird gave a shrill cry from the walls of the wharf above her, drawing her attention up to the rough stones. A raven perched there, cocking its head to one side to watch her with a beady eye. There was something unsettling about the bird—much larger than the cardinals and robins they had back home. It wouldn't stop watching her, craning its head to track her movements as she shifted nervously from one side of the dock to the other.

"Sam, there you are!"

Sam nearly jumped out of her skin at the greeting, turning to find Alistair giving her an enthusiastic wave from amid the last of the straggling passengers.

"Alistair," she said, breathing out in relief. When she glanced back, the raven had disappeared. "I wondered where you got off to on the ferry."

He gave an exasperated chuckle. "Veronica insisted I sit with her things on the lower deck. She said the men working down there had a disreputable look. Really I think she was just sick of having to talk to me."

"Well, that's her loss," Sam said with a smile. "I enjoyed our talks together at breakfast on the ship."

Alistair nodded. "As did I, though I think your friend Bennett was a bit less enthusiastic about me on the whole."

"That's just Bennett," Sam said. "So, Dublin is the last stop of your Grand Tour."

Alistair nodded, smoothing back his hair in the chilly wind. "Yes, a week here, and then we return to Oxford. To be honest, I was rather dreading the whole tour business when Veronica first suggested it, but it has been a surprising delight. Particularly this last leg."

"Really? I think that's wonderful. What has been your favorite thing to discover so far?"

Alistair grew slightly red along his cheekbones. "Ah, well. Meeting you—I mean to say, all of you—on the RMS *Olympic*. Veronica is not always the most generous conversationalist, so it was nice to have such enthusiastic dinner tablemates. Especially one that shares an interest in Santayana."

Sam laughed. "Well, I can't say that I agree with your opinions on Locke and his theory of mind, but I respect your research."

Alistair stuffed his hands in his pockets, hunching his shoulders up against the cold. "Say, Sam, this might be . . . terribly forward of me, all things considered. But . . . well, if you find yourself lacking in things to do—which I'm sure you won't, you all sound like you have a very busy schedule. But if you . . . if you'd like, we could meet up. For tea. Or is it coffee you Americans always drink?"

"Oh," Sam said, surprised. "I think . . . Well, I don't know how long I'll be here. And we will be busy. Sorry, that sounds like I'm pushing you off! I'm not, I just genuinely don't know. But coffee—or tea—sounds wonderful. Maybe I could bring you around on Locke."

Alistair's smile broke wide open. "That's fantastic. Just great. Here, this is where Veronica and I will be staying in town. If you're interested, just call or send a note round. I'm sure Veronica will appreciate the break."

He handed her a card with an address written out for a hotel, the card stock thick and woven and embossed with his name and title on the other side. Sam tucked the card in her coat pocket, rubbing a finger absently over the fine quality of the paper.

"Sam," Bennett called, looking stormy as he approached them. He gave Alistair a barely civil nod. "We've got to go."

"Oh, all right," Sam said, making up for Bennett's brusque manner by giving Alistair a warm smile. "It was really a pleasure to meet you, Alistair."

He nodded enthusiastically. "And you as well. I hope to see you soon?"

"I don't think that will be possible," Bennett said, taking her by the arm and moving her toward the road, where a car idled. "We're extremely busy. Good-bye, Alistair."

"Bye, Alistair!" Sam called with a wave, before dropping her voice to a hiss. "That was very rude, Bennett."

"I told you to stay away from him," Bennett said, the furrow deep between his eyebrows.

Sam felt a similar furrow forming between her own. "And I told you that you're not in charge of what I do. Alistair was only being nice."

"They're always nice," Bennett growled. "Until they're not."

"You're the only one around here I see being rude so far."

Bennett sighed, his expression softening. "I . . . apologize, Sam," he said, the words sounding stilted and unfamiliar in his mouth. "This trip has not gone the way I expected, and the harder I try to keep everything on track the farther it seems to go off the rails. I just want to make sure everyone is safe. We've got to find the professor and work out the location of the missing relic before those men do."

Sam could hardly argue with that, even though she felt a lingering urge to do so. She climbed into the back of the car, refusing Bennett's outstretched hand on principle, squeezing beside Phillip and Joana. The drive through the city passed quickly, the buildings falling away into rolling hills of patchwork green and jagged fences, tufts of white sheep dotting the green like dandelions. Even in the descending gloom of an early evening the hills were breathtaking, like someone took a quilt in every shade of the forest and laid it out over the whole island.

The road wound along a stand of trees on either side, obscuring their views of the sprawling greens beyond. A few loose animals grazed the fields, horses covered in blankets against the chill and great woolly sheep who provided their own cover. Sam was grateful to still have her father's winter coat, for even though Ireland was not buried under mounds of snow like Clement, it still carried a wicked chill in the air borne along by the mist settling on everything in sight. Joana complained about the terrible effects the damp was working on her finger curls, but Sam loved the way the drops of mist settled on her own hair and sparkled like diamonds.

She was also grateful that Joana's more practical side had selected the rest of her wardrobe on the ship, as everything was sensible button-up shirts and sturdy wool skirts and hose. Joana had even gotten her a pair of pants for their explorations into the mountains. She'd called them jodhpurs and claimed they were all the rage in New York. Sam loved them; she felt just like a real explorer when she put them on. She had no use for silk and lace, even though she did carefully fold and package the golden dinner dress in the bottom of the trunk Joana had gotten for her in Southampton. She'd felt like a fool saving it; the hem was torn and the lace still damp from her impromptu escape, and she had nowhere to ever wear it again. But it was too lovely to part with, so she didn't.

They turned a corner in the road and a stretch of white stood out against the green, lengthening and expanding the farther along they drove. At first it looked like only a house, but as Sam counted the windows and the floors, she realized it was much larger—three stories high and at least fifteen rooms across. It stood at the top of a little rise with a small forest arranged behind it like the ruff on a Victorian collar.

"I could certainly make this work," Joana said with a hum of approval, leaning forward to catch a better view of the house as the hired car pulled up to the front stairs.

"So glad it meets your standards, Jo," Bennett said dryly.

They climbed out of the car, Sam's legs gone wobbly from being cramped for so long. The driver killed the engine, the sudden stillness of the surrounding lands so absolute that Sam could hear every pop and creak of her joints. As she stared up at the house, the windows wide and dark, the sky heavy and gray overhead, something felt . . . off. There was nothing inherently wrong that she could point to; the trees were green and sparkling, the house a cheery yellow, and the collection of horses grazing the front lawn watched them with the placid detachment of work animals. But the longer the four of them stood there, the heavier the silence grew, until the skin prickled on the back of Sam's neck with an overawareness. Something brushed against her ear like a whisper, a desiccated echo of her name. When she turned to look, though, she saw nothing but the horses.

"You'd think they would crank up a Victrola or something," Joana said, sidling next to Sam. She stared up at the house. "It's too damn quiet. Makes my skin crawl."

Sam nodded in agreement, shaking off the feeling that someone was watching them. "I'm used to the quiet of the country, but this is something else."

Joana nodded at the trees looming over the back of the house, thick and dark in the fading light. "If they try to put me in a room that looks out that way, I'll have the whole place turned upside down by midnight."

"Bennett," Sam said, glancing up at the array of windows overhead. "Are you sure people . . . live here?"

"It *is* quiet," Bennett admitted as he paid the driver. The temporary crank of the engine shattered the stillness, though it did nothing to assuage Sam's unease. "But Professor Wallstone said that was why he sought lodging here, along with its proximity to the Hellfire Club. He tried staying in a hotel closer to the city, but he couldn't hear himself think with all the traffic noise and the chatter from the pub below. And I think the students mostly keep to themselves inside the house, where it's warm and dry."

Sam wouldn't have minded a nice crackling fire just then and a warm mug of cocoa like they served in the reading room on the *Olympic*. She shook her head, imagining her mother hearing her go on about fireplaces and cups of cocoa. She had always warned Sam not to let the extravagances of Steeling Manor go to her head because she'd still come home to the same one-bedroom farm-house in the evening. And now here she was; one week of sharing their finery, and already she was spoiled.

Phillip stood in the drive, staring up at the front of the house with an intensity that belied the week of traveling they'd endured. "We're finally here. Orlagh Country House. After all this time."

Sam couldn't quite share his enthusiasm, but she did have to admit a fascination with the history of the place. "You must have had your fill of country houses in England. Did your father have a family home?"

Phillip gave a snort. "More like a run-down apartment on the rougher edges of London. He preferred to spend his meager allowance on clothes and clubs. But Orlagh is . . . an altogether different thing."

"Well, I'm not getting any drier standing out here in the mud," Joana said, taking the lightest bag from the top of the stack. "You fellas have got the rest, haven't you?"

"Can I help ye young ones?" asked a voice from nearby. Sam didn't have fond memories of that accent, even though the man coming around the corner of the house was obviously not one of the bookshop intruders. He was average height, dressed in plain work clothes with a shovel propped over his shoulder. Sam wasn't sure what she thought Augustinian monks would look like, but this man wasn't it. He could have been a hired hand on any of the farms back in Clement, except for the soft waves of his Irish brogue. "This is a private residence, ye know. We're not open to the public."

"Oh, we know," Bennett said, taking on the professional Steeling tone. He stepped forward to meet the man, thrusting out a hand. "Bennett Steeling. We're students from the University of Chicago. We're here for Professor Wallstone."

"I see," the man said in a voice that concealed more than it conveyed. He shook Bennett's hand slowly, sizing each of them up in turn as he took off the cap he wore and scratched at the thinning brown hair along his temple. "Well, I'm Noah. I tend to the land around the house. What is it ye want here?"

"We've come to assist the professor with his survey," Bennett said, doubt creeping into his tone. "He should be expecting us. Where can we find him?"

"Ye can't," Noah said.

"What do you mean, we can't?" Phillip asked. "What's happened to the professor? Where is he?"

"In the basement," the man said gravely. "Locked up, as it were. For his own protection as much as ours."

"What?" Bennett said, his voice tight with alarm. "Why?"

"Because he's gone completely mad."

CHAPTER SIXTEEN

"**M**ad?" Sam cried. "What do you mean, he's gone mad?"

"Do people even still go mad?" Joana asked. "I thought that was a Victorian, Edgar Allan Poe–talking-to-ravens type of thing."

"What happened?" Bennett asked succinctly.

"He attacked one of our students," said Noah, swinging the shovel off his shoulder and letting the blade bite into the dirt so he could rest his arms against the handle. "The lad caught the professor trying to break into our private records here, and when he confronted him, the professor attacked. Like a beast, he was. Took the boy near a week in the infirmary to recover."

"No," Bennett said, shaking his head. "Professor Wallstone would never do anything like that. He's one of the most respected academics in his field. He has students of his own, for god's sake! He would never attack anyone."

"I don't even think he'd know how," Phillip added.

"'Tis that place," Noah said gravely. "The Hellfire Club. The wickedness of it, it's seeped into his blood. No one should be walking that cursed earth anymore, much less trying to dig it up. The professor had been complaining for weeks about hearing voices out in those woods, people following him. Birds watching him. Even went so far as to say he thought we were the ones doing it to drive him off. He'd started setting traps in his room, accusing our students of going into his personal things when he was out. He'd take elaborate paths through the woods to get to the club and back, claiming it kept the shadows from finding him. When he went missing for two days a few weeks ago, we had to form a search party to find him. He was lost in the hills muttering about making the find of a lifetime. Later that night he attacked our student and we had no choice but to restrain him."

Sam shivered, moving closer to Bennett and dropping her voice to a whisper so only he could hear her. "Do you think he meant the diary?" she asked. "The find of a lifetime?"

"If he did, then he wasn't so crazy as these men think for being afraid that someone was following him," Bennett murmured back. He raised his voice. "I need to see him. I'm positive this has all been a misunderstanding that can be sorted out immediately."

Noah shook his head. "I don't know as how that's a good idea, lad. Your professor's gone near feral in his madness. He won't let us come in the basement without trying to attack us. We can't even give him utensils with his meals anymore since he tried to break a window with a fork."

"Then let me speak to whoever's in charge here," Bennett said. "I'm not leaving without the professor."

Noah glanced over at their trunks stacked up on the front lawn. "Suit yourself, but Father O'Connell will tell you the same thing."

Noah led them up the stairs into the grand front entryway, the wooden slats of the floor gleaming softly in the electric sconce lighting. The walls and light fixtures were elaborate, but the furniture was spartan and functional. He deposited the four of them in a sitting room that was more *room* than *sitting*, considering it only had two chairs. But Sam had far too much energy to stay stationary anyway, so as Joana and Phillip took a seat in the chairs, she paced the room.

"You'll forgive the necessity," Noah said, wielding a ring of keys. "But I'll need to secure this door while I'm away. We're responsible for the care and safety of the lads here, and we've already made the mistake of trusting outsiders once."

"You're locking us in?" Bennett asked in alarm.

"Only until I return with word from Father O'Connell."

"Just let him go," Phillip muttered. "We can always knock the door down if we have to. These old country houses are half-rotted anyway."

"Fine," Bennett said, though he didn't look pleased about it.

The lock clicked like a declaration of intent in the small space, and Sam tried not to pay attention to how much closer the walls felt now. Instead she studied their décor, examining the leaf patterns of the wall sconces.

"You said this was a country house?" she asked Bennett, tracing a finger through the inside of one large whorl. "When was it built?"

"In 1790," Bennett said, his pacing concentrated on the same path along the hard floor. "You can see the Georgian influence in the sconces and the framed doorways. The Augustinian monks took it over in the late 1800s, though it seems they maintained much of the house's original décor."

"Except for these backside-numbing chairs," Joana muttered. "This must be how they keep their students awake during lectures on morality."

Noah returned shortly, unlocking the tension in the room along with the door. "Father O'Connell can see you, but ye must make it quick. It's near on dinner, and he's got to preside over blessings and the evening meal for the novitiates."

"It shouldn't take that long," Bennett said, moving toward the door. "I'm sure we can get this all sorted out immediately."

"I don't suppose you've got a facility to make use of," Phillip said, giving the man a sheepish grin. "It's been a long trip from the ferry, and the drive up here was bumpy enough to rupture something."

Noah gave a grunt before nodding. "Come along, then."

"Unless the father has a leather couch, I think I'll stay right here," Joana said, stretching out her legs and crossing them at the ankle. "Do you fellas do a tea service around here? I could nibble."

Noah gave her a thin smile. "I'll see what we can do."

"Sam, you'll be all right with Jo?" Bennett asked, looking at the two of them doubtfully.

Sam looked away from the wall sconce she was studying, the fixture obviously converted from gas to electricity sometime in the recent past. "Hmm? Oh, yes. Sure. We'll be here."

"Don't go anywhere," Bennett said, pointing a finger at Joana.

She spread her arms wide. "Where would I go in a locked room?"

"If anyone could find somewhere, it would be you," Bennett muttered, following Noah and Phillip out. The lock clicked again, the sound of it like a spring coiling in Sam's chest.

Sam continued her examination of the Georgian features of the room, making mental notes about certain repeating motifs she could read up on later. A gleaming spot of metal caught her eye from the far side of the room, a bronze plaque fixed to the wall. She gravitated toward it, squinting to make out the raised lettering. She assumed it must be some kind of historical marker, identifying the significance of the house or the previous owners, the kind of thing Farmer Mason was always trying to get the Clement city council to put on his barn, which he swore his great-great-grandfather built over 150 years ago. But as she got close enough to make out the writing on the plaque, it wasn't the words that made her heart pound and her mouth go dry.

It was the symbol at the top, a smooth bronze depiction of a heart with a flame above it. A heart on fire. The same symbol she had seen pinned to the robes of the men who had caused the fire in her bookshop.

And under it, the plaque read in tidy letters: THE ORDER OF SAINT AUGUSTINE.

Follow the Order.

"Jo," she whispered.

"Hmm?" Joana murmured, twisting and turning as she tried the other chair. "Honestly, this one is even worse. How is that possible? These things are barely above a torture device."

"Joana Rose!" Sam hissed, glaring at her.

"What's wrong with you?" Joana asked, rising out of the chair and arching her back with a grimace. "What's going on? You look like you swallowed glass."

"Look at this," Sam hissed, jabbing a finger at the plaque.

Joana stared at it. "It's a heart."

"On fire," Sam said. "This is the symbol the men were wearing at the bookshop."

Joana lifted both eyebrows in surprise. "You don't say. What are the odds it's a coincidence?"

"Your father would say coincidences are patterns you haven't learned to recognize yet," Sam said.

Joana took a deep breath, holding it for a second before letting it out in a whoosh. "Well, what in hell is going on here, then?"

"I think the men who broke into the shop must have been from here, from Orlagh," Sam whispered. "That must be why they're holding the professor, and why they don't want Bennett to see him. Because he found the diary, the one they stole back on the *Olympic*."

"So you're saying he might not be mad after all," Joana said, finally catching on. "That they're actually . . . What? Holding him prisoner?"

"And now Bennett and Phillip have gone off with Noah," Sam said.

"And we're stuck here alone," Joana continued, her voice going flat. "In a locked room."

Sam gripped her friend's hand. "What are we going to do, Jo?"

Joana's gaze narrowed on the heart, the wild gleam she always had honing into a blade. "We need an escape plan."

"But how? We don't know anything about this house, or where they took Bennett and Phillip, or even if the professor is here at all."

"But if they got that diary like you said on the *Olympic*, what do they care about us? Why lock us up?"

Sam looked to the door, the handle suddenly appearing large and heavy and ominous. "Because we're a liability for them now. We know about the diary, and there's still the letter. Without it, they won't know how to find the relic Father Jacob stole. The bowl they need to invoke the curse."

Joana frowned at her. "I thought you didn't know how to find it either."

Sam threw her hands out. "Well, I don't, but it's not like they know that!"

Joana set both hands on her hips, squaring off with the door handle. "They might have locked us in, but there are plenty of other ways to escape a room. Look at that right there, a perfectly good window with easily breakable glass."

She stalked across to the window, snatching up one of the torture chairs on the way and raising the legs with intention.

"Jo, wait!" Sam said, hurrying forward and throwing herself before the innocent glass. "If we break that window, we'll have half the place down on our heads. Let's see if we can open it first."

The sash was old, the paint thick and glossy in the corners where it had obviously been applied many times over the centuries. But there didn't seem to be any kind of lock, and when she tried to lift the window, the wood groaned and protested, but it wiggled up an inch.

"I think," she grunted, digging her fingers in between the sash and the sill to get better leverage. "I think if we both give it a good shove, we can get it open."

Joana sighed, elbowing in beside her to slip her fingers into the narrow opening. "You know, if I had my trunk this wouldn't be an issue. I've still got that knife I found for you on the train. This paint could use a good cutting and scraping."

"If you want your things, you've got to get through this window," Sam said, heaving upward and buying them another inch or so. Her knuckles cracked, the chill wind seeping in through the slit in the window and tightening the tendons in her fingers. She pulled them loose, shaking them out for relief.

The light outside had disappeared completely in the time they had spent locked in the waiting room, the glass of the window acting as a mirror to reflect the tight draw of her mouth and the pale gleam of her skin. Even if they managed to get the window open, where would they go? What would they do? They didn't know where Bennett or Phillip were, they didn't have a car, all their possessions were still piled on the front lawn, and they were more than half an hour outside of a town where they knew no one. Even if they escaped this room, they were still trapped.

A faint light bobbed across the darkness outside, marring her reflection as it drew closer to the house. At first it seemed like a wayward firefly, or maybe the mythical fairy lights she'd read of in the ancient Irish lore. But the closer it drew, the more definition it took on, until it solidified into the rectangular shape of a lantern. She leaned forward with a frown, cupping her hands around her eyes to block out the light of the waiting room.

Four men in dark robes approached their trunks in the driveway out front, crowding around them and hauling them up by their handles. Sam's frown deepened as she watched them lug the steamer trunks away, and for a moment she thought maybe Bennett had worked something out with Father O'Connell, and the brothers meant to let them stay at Orlagh. But they weren't bringing the trunks toward the front entryway; they were carrying them toward the back of the house.

"What do they think they're doing?" Joana said beside her, squinting. "Are they stealing our things?"

"I think—" Sam began, but her breath caught on a smothered gasp that sounded like a gunshot in the oppressive quiet of the waiting room. The last man had straightened with her trunk, his height and breadth eclipsing the other men around him. He was the one who had carried the lantern, a light that he had set on top of the trunk before lifting it, a light that now illuminated the stony crags of his face.

It was Brother Padraig, the man who had burned down her bookshop.

CHAPTER SEVENTEEN

Sam spun around and dropped below the window in a crouch, her breath heaving in and out and making her chest rattle. Joana looked down at her in bewilderment.

"What's gone off with you now?" Joana asked.

"Get down!" Sam whispered, glancing up at the sash. "Now!"

"What? Why?" Joana asked, even as she squatted beside Sam.

"That's him," Sam whispered, looking up again as if Brother Padraig might be looming outside the glass, hunting them. "The man who burned down the shop. Brother Padraig. That's him out there, taking my trunk."

Joana peered through the small crack in the window. "Do you think he saw you?"

"I don't think it matters," Sam said, checking outside again. The trunks were gone, and so were the men. "They know we're here now, and I don't think they plan on letting us go."

"They may not be planning on it, but I am," Joana said, straightening up with grim determination and lifting her chair. "Get back, Sam."

"Jo, I still don't think we should—"

"Get back!" Joana said, shoving the chair forward and shattering the glass. Sam scrambled away just in time to avoid the shards as they clattered to the ground. Joana knocked the chair legs into all four corners of the window until the jagged edges were gone, then set it back down.

"If they expected us to hang around here locked up all night, they should have given us more comfortable chairs," Joana said, dusting her hands together. She used the toe of her shoe to move the bigger pieces of glass aside. "You round up the boys, and I'll find transportation."

"How are you going to do that in the middle of nowhere?" Sam asked, looking out into the darkness. If anyone heard the window break, they weren't running to stop them.

"I'll figure it out as I go," Joana said.

"Jo, these men are dangerous," Sam said doubtfully. "Whatever you're thinking . . ."

"Too late, already thought." Joana threw one leg up and over the empty windowsill. "Come on, Sam, you ought to be used to going out the window by now."

Sam sighed, following her out. "At least there's solid ground to catch me this time."

"Like I used to say at the academy, good luck and don't get caught." Joana gave her a mock salute before disappearing around the side of the house.

Sam moved in the opposite direction, toward the main entryway. Noah might have taken the precaution of locking them in the sitting room, but luckily he hadn't been so careful with the front door. She slipped back inside, pausing in the foyer as the stillness of the place prickled at her nerves. She wasn't nearly so confident of their chances of escape as Joana, but she couldn't let that deter her now. They were in danger; she could worry about being afraid once they were all free.

All the rooms on the first floor seemed to be classrooms, dark and empty in the evening hours. The more halls she went down, the more her concern increased for Bennett's and Phillip's welfare. Maybe she should have started with the basement, not that she knew where to find it. Or how to get in if they kept it under lock and key. She came upon a set of double doors she assumed led to the dining hall, doing her best to crack the door silently to check inside.

Two long tables filled the room, the boys seated at the table ranging in age from seven to seventeen, their backs straight and their heads down over the plates. The hall was so quiet she wasn't even sure they were chewing. There was a small table in the front of the room, where a group of stone-faced men ate their dinners in equal silence.

Off to the side three men talked urgently in low tones, the rumble of their voices carrying through the stillness. The biggest of the men she recognized with a sickening lurch—Padraig's face was no less menacing in the soft light of the dining hall. Beside him stood the groundskeeper, Noah, his arms crossed and his expression stern. The third man she didn't recognize, but based on the differently colored rope belt tied around his robes, she guessed he might be Father O'Connell, the man in charge of the monks. Which only made her stomach feel worse, since she didn't see any sign of Bennett or Phillip.

Brother Padraig was talking now, holding up a piece of clothing. Whatever he was saying, the other two weren't responding well. Brother Padraig gave the clothing item a shake and Sam recognized the cut of the collar. It was Bennett's coat—the one she had borrowed when she made her hasty escape out the porthole window. The tail had gotten caught on the rivet along with her gold dress and ripped, so Bennett had packed it away until he could have it repaired.

What were these men doing, going into Bennett's trunk? Were they looking for the letter? What had they done with Bennett and Phillip? She should have never split from Joana. What did she think she could do, wandering the house alone with no idea where anything was?

Brother Padraig reached into one of the pockets of the coat, pulling out a scrap of paper and holding it up like a piece of evidence in a jury trial. Sam couldn't read what was on the paper, but she could hazard a guess. It must have been a scrap left over from their attempts to decipher the code, an ogham character or an alcmí. Everything else had been stolen or washed away, but somehow that little piece of paper had survived in Bennett's pocket. And now these men knew they had found the letter.

"Sam? What are you doing?"

Sam gasped as she snapped upright, drawing the attention of a few of the students closest to the door. She shoved the door closed, the latch catching with a loud click as she whirled to face Bennett standing behind her, his arms crossed.

"I told you both to wait in the sitting room," he said. "How did you even get out? And where is my sister?"

"Bennett, thank goodness you're okay," Sam said instead of answering his questions. She glanced back at the door. Had Brother Padraig spotted them? "We need to get out of here."

"Why? What's happened?"

Sam took him by the arm and hustled him away from the dining hall. "Those men in there, all these men—they're the same ones that burned down the shop. That stole the diary. And we walked right into their trap."

"Wait, these men are what?" Bennett stopped, taking her by the shoulders. "Sam, what's going on? What do you mean these are the men who burned down the shop? I thought you said they were on the train platform in Chicago."

"They were," Sam said, looking back toward the dining room. She was sure she heard heavy footsteps, creaking the floorboards like a warning signal. "But the big man, he's here now. Brother Padraig. He must have found a way back here after he stole the diary on the ship and took the lifeboat. We need to leave. Jo went to find transportation."

Bennett shook his head, gently pulling his arm from her grasp. "I'm not leaving without the professor. If these men are holding him hostage, he's in danger, too."

"Right now we're in greater danger if they catch us!" Sam said, but she knew that look on Bennett's face. There was no convincing him otherwise—he wasn't leaving Orlagh without the professor. She sighed in resignation. "We need to find the basement."

They hurried down halls and past more empty rooms until Sam was sure they had passed the same lamp four or five times. But Bennett soldiered on as if he knew every twist and turn. If Sam had less faith in Bennett, she would have guessed he was completely lost. He didn't deign to show it, though.

Somehow, they found their way to a set of stairs that led down to the basement level. Bennett's steps slowed, the light of the electric lamps not extending below. Sam felt along the wall as they descended, wishing she could take Bennett's hand for guidance. He halted a few steps short of the bottom, the stop so abrupt that Sam bumped into him. She couldn't see a thing, but she could feel the tension radiating off Bennett. And somewhere just beyond him, she could see a shape darker than the rest of the shadows, taking on the lines of a person. Her heart seized up, filling her ears with a roar.

"Phillip?" Bennett whispered harshly. "Is that you?"

The shape straightened up, a faint gleam of teeth lighting the darkness as Phillip grimaced. "Ah, Steeling. You nearly gave me a heart attack."

"What are you doing down here?" Bennett asked. "You said you were going to use the facilities."

"That was a ruse." Phillip looked around, tapping on the basement door. "I came to find the professor. It's clear these fellows are up to no good, claiming old Wally is mad."

"And when were you planning on telling me?" Bennett asked in his censorious tone.

"We don't really have time to argue," Sam whispered, glancing back up the steps. "If the professor is down here, we need to get him and go."

Bennett gave a thin sigh. "Fine, but we're not done discussing this, Phillip. Have you got your lighter?"

Phillip rustled around in his jacket and handed over the lighter. Bennett struck the flint and a tiny flame cast a halo of light around them, just enough to outline a plain wooden door with a keyed handle.

"Locked," Bennett said grimly, giving the handle a rattle.

"Sam, have you got a bobby pin on you?" Phillip asked, leaning in for a look. "I'm not a master picker, but I've finagled my way into a few off-limits rooms at the university."

Bennett gave a huff. "That's how you got the answers to Atchinson's last exam."

"You'd have to prove that," Phillip said with a grin as Sam fished a bobby pin out of her hair. He knelt beside Bennett, elbowing him out of the way. For a few minutes it seemed as if his only secret was wiggling it around in the lock in random directions, but then something deep in the mechanism clicked and the knob turned freely.

"There we are," Phillip said, sitting back on his heels triumphantly.

"I'll remember this next time scores get posted," Bennett said, pushing the door open.

The smell of the basement physically knocked Sam back a step. It was as if someone had taken their travel-stained clothes, dunked them in a puddle of stagnant rainwater, and left them to molder in a rusted metal tin. It was strong enough to make her eyes water, and Phillip raised the sleeve of his jacket over his mouth with an indelicate cough. Bennett held up the lighter, advancing a few steps into the dank interior.

The sight wasn't much improved from the smell. It looked like her mother's laundry room on Mondays when she brought in all the town's washing, old hulking forms of furniture heaped with piles of sheets, and clothes twisted in grotesque shapes and covered with a layer of feathery dust. In the far corner was an empty cot.

"Where is he?" Sam asked, just as someone let out a blood-curdling scream and rammed into her from behind.

CHAPTER EIGHTEEN

Sam could do little more than squeak as the weight knocked her into Phillip, who in turn fell against Bennett and sent all of them sprawling to the floor. The lighter sputtered out, plunging them into a darkness that threatened Sam's sanity. Whoever ran into her scrabbled to stand up, climbing over them.

"You won't find me this time, you devils," the voice growled.

"Professor Wallstone?" Bennett called out after the fleeing figure.

And though Sam could hardly believe this . . . this *wildling* was Bennett's professor, the shadow hesitated just long enough to show stark tufts of hair and a flash of glass lenses.

"Master Steeling?" the shadow asked, the tone shifting to a genteel British accent. "Is that you, my boy?"

Bennett struggled to a kneeling position, searching blindly until he grasped Sam's arm and helped her stand.

"It's me, Professor," Bennett said, advancing carefully toward the wild shadow. "Bennett Steeling. And Phillip Montrose. We're here to help you."

"Oh, but you can't be here!" the professor proclaimed, his voice taking on an edge of hysteria. "If they've captured you, then they must have . . . No, but you wouldn't be that foolish. No, no, no, I trusted you, I would never trust where it was not warranted. The diary, my boy. Where is the diary?"

Bennett hesitated, and Sam could feel the weight of his gaze on her. "It was stolen. On our way here."

Professor Wallstone dropped his head back with a primal wail. "Then all hope is lost! All my care, my secrecy and sacrifice, all for naught! These scurrilous knaves have won. They'll have us all trussed up and forgotten down here while they hoard the glory for themselves."

"Professor, what are you talking about?" Bennett asked, bewildered. "What happened?"

"What always happens when small men grow suspicious of the aspirations of their betters," the professor growled, shoving his hands into his hair as he paced about. Sam couldn't help comparing him to a jungle cat in a Rudyard Kipling novel. "I sought lodging here under the impression that these were men of the Christian god, humble and honest even if their judgment of creation lacked substance. But it became evident, straightaway, they lured me here under false pretenses. They sent their spies after me, all the time following me up the mountain and making note of my progress on the survey of the Hellfire Club. I thought they might protest on religious grounds, knowing the Irish for the staunch Catholics they are—but then I found the remains."

"Remains?" Phillip echoed.

"Human remains," said the professor in a tone that raised every hair on Sam's arms. "I took great care to obscure my routes up and down the mountain in an effort to shake these would-be provocateurs, traveling the denser parts of the trees until I felt much as John Muir must have exploring the wilds of Yosemite. It was on one such circuitous route as I swept leaves to obscure my passage that I uncovered the long-decayed remains of a human. There wasn't much left except a half-crushed skull and a patch of brown wool, and of course the diary."

"Oh, Father Jacob," Sam said softly.

"Who's there?" the professor demanded, crouching into a defensive stance.

"Professor Wallstone, this is Samantha Knox," Bennett said, a note of exasperation in his tone. "She works at my father's bookshop, where you sent the diary."

"Ah, the repair girl!" Professor Wallstone exclaimed.

"You . . . you know who I am?" Sam asked, surprised.

"Of course, Master Steeling spoke so highly of the young female who conserved the antique tomes at his father's shop," said the professor. "As soon as I recovered the diary and gleaned its contents, I knew I couldn't risk leaving such a momentous find in the lair of the beast. I had to get it away from here, but where? To Professor Atchinson at the university?" The professor snorted. "A greater thief there never was, I'd be reading of *his great discovery* in the *Daily News*. But the girl, she would know how to restore the diary without stealing the credit."

"Oh," Sam said softly, looking to Bennett. She couldn't have read his expression, even in the full light of day. "You spoke to your professor about me? Highly?"

"I might have mentioned you," Bennett said gruffly, before clearing his throat and infusing his tone with Steeling grit. "Professor Wallstone, we have to get you out of here. We can talk about the diary later, but these men are dangerous."

"I can't leave!" the professor protested. "What about the bowl?"

"What bowl?" Phillip asked.

"*The* bowl, my boy," the professor said, his voice filled with reverence. "The most important bowl in the history of Ireland. A bowl of petrified wood, allegedly carved from the Tree of Life. Or the Tree of Knowledge, if you believe the biblical version of things. A ritual vessel, used for sacred rites."

"Is it here?" Phillip asked intently. "Have you seen it?"

"Not yet, not with these ruffians keeping me chained down here like an animal. But it's here; it must be. The eclipse is only three days away. A total solar eclipse, the first one on Irish soil in two hundred years."

"A significant passage of the moon," Sam whispered, reaching for Bennett's hand. It couldn't be a coincidence.

"I was so close," the professor continued. "I found their secret archives. But that boy interrupted me, and they locked me up down here in punishment."

"We're here to get you out," Bennett said.

"Hang on, Steeling," Phillip said in a conciliatory tone, pulling Bennett aside and lowering his voice. "If that bowl is here like the professor says, we should try and find it. If they were willing to lock him up over it, it's got to be worth a pretty penny. This'll be the best chance we get."

"It's not worth our lives," Bennett said flatly. "We can discuss what to do next once we're safely back in Dublin."

"Once we're gone, they'll lock this place up tight," Phillip said, his polite tone edged in frustration. "The professor risked his life for that artifact, we owe it to him to find it."

"Phillip, I know the only language you speak is greenbacks—"

The ceiling above them rumbled with the threatening cadence of footfalls, interrupting Bennett's reprimand. Sam shrank back against Bennett and he wrapped an arm around her, his muscles tight with tension.

"Never mind, we need to go," Bennett said. "Now."

"But the bowl, Master Steeling, the bowl, the bowl!" the professor muttered, pulling at the ends of his hair.

"You can worry about the bowl from the safety of a hotel in Dublin," Bennett said, exasperated. "Right now we've got to get you away from these kidnappers."

"Professor," Phillip said, turning to the older man. "Where were these secret archives? Could we find them on our way out?"

"Phillip, give it up," Bennett said in a tone that brooked no refusal.

Phillip paused for a moment, his features taut, as if he wished to continue arguing. But then his expression relaxed into an easy smile. "You're right, Steeling. Lost my head there for a minute. We need to get the professor safe; everything else can wait."

They filed out of the room, Sam taking a deep breath for the first time since entering the rancid basement, and crept up the stairs. The previously silent house was filled with noise now, heavy footsteps and creaking doors as rooms were methodically checked. Bennett paused at the top of the stairs, making sure the way was clear. He waved the others forward, and they headed toward the front of the house.

Sam's stomach muscles tightened every time they turned a corner, sure they were going to hit a dead end in the shape of a massive man in robes. But by sheer luck or a miracle, they reached the front entrance and slipped outside, the darkness so complete she stumbled down the last few steps and nearly sprawled across the gravel drive.

"What was your plan from here?" Phillip asked. "To commandeer a few horses?"

But Bennett didn't have to answer, for a roar filled the air and a motorcar came swinging around the side of the house. Sam

shielded her eyes from the sudden intrusion of headlights as someone threw a door wide open.

"You look like you could use a lift," Joana said, her cocky grin
appearing behind the headlights.

"Where did you get a car?" Bennett asked. He couldn't help it,
the reproach was baked into his tone whenever he spoke to Joana.
But even he seemed to sense it, because he cleared his throat and
started toward the car with the professor in tow. "I can overlook
it this time."

"How generous of you," Joana said dryly. "Come on, before they
figure out I let their horses loose, too."

"Stop!" called a familiar voice from the front steps.

Sam glanced back, her heart spiking right up her throat at the
sight of the big man filling the door frame. She could almost smell
the ash of her books still drifting into her lungs, making it hard to
breathe. Bennett took her by the arm, dragging her into the car.

"Sam, now!" he said, the urgency in his tone breaking the spell.

"Get back here!" Brother Padraig thundered, hurtling down the
stairs. "That car is private property. Thieves!"

"Turnabout is fair play!" Joana called out as she threw the car
into gear, knocking Sam against the driver's seat as it lurched forward. The car roared down the lane, the Augustinians spilling out
the front door and giving chase. But they were no match for Joana's
lead foot, and they shrank in the distance as Joana took reckless
turns back down to Dublin.

"So, where are we headed?" Joana shouted over the roar of the
engine. "A pub?"

"We need to find somewhere to stay for the night," Bennett said.
"Which we can't do if we flip over in a ditch, Jo."

"You can't make a getaway at posted speeds," Joana called back.
Sam dug her hands in her coat pockets, seeking some small

protection from the whip of the wind against her skin. Her fingers brushed a corner of heavy card stock, the one Alistair had given her just a few hours ago that felt like a different lifetime by now.

"I know somewhere we can go," she called.

It took all of Joana's charm and a hefty chunk of Phillip's and Bennett's wallets to secure lodgings for the five of them, but they managed to book two rooms—one for the girls and one for Bennett, Phillip, and the professor. Sam briefly considered asking the desk manager which room Alistair might be staying in, but she didn't think Bennett would appreciate it. And it was far too late to make a social call, especially after the evening they'd had.

The desk manager looked askance at the professor, who spent the check-in process circling the lobby and muttering about eyes in the wallpaper and relics hidden under the floorboards. Joana paced the length of the front desk, her adrenaline still high. Sam seemed to be the only one ready to topple over with fatigue. But at least they would have beds to sleep in, even if the brothers had stolen their trunks.

Not that any of them were going to get any real rest.

"Bennett," Sam said in a low voice as they climbed the stairs to the third floor. "Professor Wallstone, he —"

"I know," Bennett said grimly. He shook his head. "I don't . . . This isn't like him. The professor I know, he . . . They've done something to him, Sam. Drugged him, or tortured him. He wasn't like this, I swear. He's become so obsessed with this passage tomb, and now the bowl . . ."

Sam chewed one corner of her lip as Phillip helped the man up the stairs, his grip on the professor's jacket the only thing keeping the man from stumbling. Several times Phillip had to lean down and murmur in his ear to draw his attention back to the present, his head snapping up and his eyes refocusing each time. There wasn't a mark on him she could see, but she wouldn't put it past those men at Orlagh to have employed more devious means besides physical torture.

But . . . none of that explained his obsession with the bowl. Whenever he had discussed the professor on their trip, Bennett had painted the portrait of a consummate academic—intelligent, thorough, a bit eccentric, but dedicated to science. And Sam had read enough of his articles to believe it; his arguments were always well reasoned, a bit chiding, but exuding a love of the field and the progression of its practices. This man was nothing like that. He seemed fully absorbed in finding the bowl, and his singular fixation didn't seem remotely academic.

"Bennett, Professor Wallstone said he was sure the Augustinians had the bowl." Sam paused on the third-floor landing, her legs like lead. She dropped her voice to a near whisper so only Bennett could hear her. "Father Jacob's letter said to follow the Order. What if he meant the Augustinians? This isn't over."

"It is for tonight," Bennett said resolutely. "There's nothing we can do in the dark without our things."

Sam could hardly argue with that, considering how she swayed on her feet like a sapling in a strong wind. But they were here in Dublin—finally here, after so many days on trains and ships and cars—as close as they had ever been to solving Father Jacob's riddle. She had hoped the professor would know what to do, but he hardly knew which way was up.

"I'll just get old Wally situated," Phillip said, plastering on a smile.

The professor seemed to go through some sort of fit, swatting at

Phillip's hands like they were tongues of flame. Phillip met Sam's gaze, giving a little shrug as if to say *What can you do?* Sam gave him an encouraging smile that withered a bit as the professor grabbed the door frame with both hands.

"You'll not lock me up again, you scoundrels!" the professor exclaimed.

"Bennett, a bit of help?" Phillip grunted. "He's got a grip like an alligator's bite. All those academic papers he writes, I suppose."

Bennett hesitated, looking between Sam and Joana. "No antics, you two. All right? No hopping trains, stealing ship tickets, or midnight joyrides. Do you both understand me?"

"We're not children, Bennett," Sam said, an odd defiance rising up.

"I'll stop treating you like children when you stop taking unnecessary risks behind my back," Bennett said, his voice in full big-brother mode. "No antics tonight."

"If there's anyone you should be worrying about, it's that stuffed sausage of a man trying to bite Phillip's fingers," Joana said archly, nodding at the professor as she shoved Bennett out of the way to open their door. "Sam's halfway to beat and I've still got a ringing in my ears from the car ride."

"No trouble tonight, Jo, I mean it." Bennett's expression took on an edge of desperation as he turned to Sam. "Please, Sam? I've got my hands full already."

Sam relented and followed Joana into their room, all her resolve undone by his ragged tone. "Of course."

He let out a deep sigh of relief. "Thank you."

"Night," Joana called out cheerfully, shutting the door in his face and throwing the dead bolt. "So! We're going back out there, right?"

CHAPTER NINETEEN

"What?" Sam asked, startled. "Of course not. We just . . . *I* just promised Bennett we wouldn't do anything."

"Oh please," Joana said with a wave. "I know that look on your face. You've figured something out."

"I don't know that I have," Sam said slowly.

Joana put her hands on her hips. The Steeling gaze was as inexorable as the machinery in their mill. "You can't bluff a card sharp, Sam, so don't try. What is it?"

Sam shook her head. "Maybe it's nothing. Bennett's right; we have to be careful."

Joana scoffed. "Bennett is never right, even when he is. Quit doing that."

Sam frowned. "Doing what?"

"Shutting me out," Joana said, turning away as she said it so Sam couldn't see her expression. "I want to help, so let me help."

"Jo, I wasn't—"

"What is it?" Joana interrupted. "What did you figure out?"

Sam took a deep breath. She knew she really should listen to Bennett—not just because she didn't want to let him down, but because she knew he was right. She had already experienced what these men would do to get what they wanted. Sam was nautical leagues out of her depth here, drowning with every attempt to catch her breath.

But they were so close to an answer. It prodded at her like needles under the skin, this drive to solve the puzzle. To prevent the curse.

"The letter," she said finally, letting her breath out. "From Father Jacob. The transcription said *Follow the Order*. I think he must have meant the Augustinians. I don't know how they're connected yet, but it's all we've got to go on right now. The answer to what we're looking for has to be at Orlagh."

"Not to mention our stuff," Joana said. "I don't care if they are murderers, I want those suede heels back."

Sam chewed at her lip, the skin raw and tender from how much she had worried it over the past week. "Bennett will kill us. I mean, absolutely kill us."

Joana's eyes gleamed. "I know, it's worth it for that alone."

What they were considering, it was . . . well, it was madness, wasn't it? The same madness that had infected the professor, and those men at the bookshop. If she had any sense left, she would call the police right now.

But what could the police do? What kind of story would she tell them? That the Augustinian monks were seeking a ritual bowl carved from the Tree of Life, a bowl meant to call forth an ancient Celtic goddess to lay waste to the current age of mankind? They would never believe her—she hardly believed it herself. They'd have her locked up and the key tossed in the trash before she got to the end of her complaint.

No, there was no one else to help them now. Certainly not the professor. They would have to help themselves. And so Sam found herself buttoning up her jacket as Joana cracked open the door to the hallway. She peeked out only to straighten up in disgust.

"Oh, for Pete's sake," Joana muttered, throwing the door wide as she caught Bennett sneaking out of his room next door. "Bennett, you complete sap."

"Jo, what are you doing?" he asked.

She set her hands on her hips. "I could ask you the same."

"I was . . ." He looked up and down the hall. "Getting something for the professor."

Sam peeked around Joana. "You need your coat for that?"

"Sam!" Bennett crossed his arms, looking down on both of them. "I'm disappointed. I would expect something like this from Joana, but you promised me."

Sam shrank back behind Joana as if the other girl could physically protect her from Bennett's disappointment. But Joana thrust a finger against his chest, pushing him back.

"Don't you lecture her when you're the one we caught sneaking out," she said.

"I am not . . ." He took a deep breath, lowering his voice. "I am not sneaking out. I was going for a walk."

"I thought you were getting something for the professor," Joana countered.

"You're going back to Orlagh to follow the Order as well, aren't you?" Sam asked.

"That is none of your— Wait, what do you mean, as well?" Bennett asked.

"Oh, stuff it, Bennett, the jig is up," Joana said. "We caught you, you caught us, we've all been properly chastised. Let's get on with it. We've got some shady characters to stalk and a real treasure to steal. Plus, I've got the car keys, so you can ride with us or find your own way."

"I can't allow either of you to put yourselves in harm's way again," Bennett said.

"Oh, but you're happy to do so yourself?" Joana asked, squaring off with him.

"I am responsible—"

"Oh, not this again," Joana said, rolling her eyes.

They were wasting time, treading the same old arguments that always cropped up when they disagreed. Sam stepped past Joana, squaring her shoulders and doing her best impression of a Steeling gaze. "You listen to me, Bennett Steeling. You're not in charge here anymore. Those men burned down my shop, threatened the people I love, and made me climb out the window of a moving ship. Professor Wallstone is no help, and the police wouldn't believe us if we tried to involve them. We're the only thing standing between those men and another world war, and I won't step aside and let them invoke this curse any more than I'd let Frank Mead kiss me at the Spring Dance."

"I told you this is all— Wait, Frank Mead kissed you?"

"Tried to," Sam said with grim determination. "Now, Jo and I are going to Orlagh to investigate the Augustinians, and you can either get on board or we can leave you here."

"Well . . ." Bennett blew out a stream of air through his nostrils, looking at her as if he were just meeting her for the first time. "Fine. We go together. But I'm driving."

"Like hell you are," Joana said, grinning at Sam.

"What about the professor?" Sam asked. "And Phillip?"

"The professor fell asleep in the bathtub, and Phillip's gone to the pub downstairs," Bennett said. "I've locked the door and taken the room key, just in case. But from the looks of him, the professor won't be awake until tomorrow afternoon at the earliest."

"Good." Sam nodded, her newfound sense of determination feeling nice, if awkward, much like the jodhpurs Joana had gotten her. "Let's go, then."

"Where did that come from?" Joana whispered as they headed down the stairs.

"I don't know," Sam whispered back. "I was a little terrified Bennett would lock us in our room like the professor."

"Good thing you know how to climb out the window," Joana said with a wink.

They found their way back to where Joana had haphazardly parked the car. Sam scrambled into the backseat, but at least this time she had more room to breathe without Phillip and the professor scrunched in with her. That didn't stop her from jumping as Bennett slid in beside her, his knee pressed against hers.

"Are you sure you want to do this?" he asked.

She nodded hastily, her face flushing in the dark. "Yes, of course."

"The pants look fabulous, by the way," Joana threw over her shoulder as she cranked up the engine. "I knew they would."

Sam gave a tentative smile that quickly turned into a frown as they left the populated streets of Dublin and started toward the mountains again. Sam had been so sure they were doing the right thing when she was arguing with Bennett in the hotel hallway, but now the old fears came crawling back up her throat. They were barreling headfirst into real danger, worse than anything she had ever imagined, with no plan and no reinforcements. They were three kids from rural Clement; what chance did they stand against these men?

What if, instead of leading them to the answers, she was leading them to disaster?

CHAPTER TWENTY

They hid the car in a stand of trees, a mile or so out from the main house for fear the Augustinians might hear the uproarious engine. The clouds obscured the moon, dropping them into darkness, but none of them had thought to bring along a lantern. At least the lights were blazing in the windows at Orlagh despite the late hour, and they stumbled toward it like pagans drawn to a distant bonfire.

"Do we have a plan here, or am I scuffing up my new heels for no reason?" Joana asked.

"There's something we're missing," Sam said as they continued toward the house, keeping her steps as silent as possible. "Something these men know, something they're hiding. I don't know how all the pieces fit together yet. But Father Jacob said *Follow the Order.*"

She had puzzled over his words during the bracing car ride out there, tacking up each scrap of a clue on her mental mystery board. She could feel the patterns emerging, just as they did when she deciphered encrypted messages. Those little pieces that lined up just right, chinks in the impenetrable armor that guarded the truth. Father Jacob, *Follow the Order*, the Order of St. Augustine, the ritual bowl—they were all tied together. But she didn't know how, not yet.

She just had to keep digging.

Sam had to practically run to keep up with the Steeling siblings—who both had a few inches of height and stride span on her—all of her breath concentrated on not hyperventilating in the creeping dark. She didn't even like making the long walk from Steeling's Rare Antiquities to her family farm once the sun set, and she'd walked the Clement back roads her whole life. Out here was just chaos. Even the ground felt different, spongier and slick from the steady mist, threatening to make her turn her ankle every time her heel found a stray rock.

They gave the house a wide berth as they reached the woods bordering the back, their steps slowing and growing more deliberate. If the trees had seemed oppressive during their previous flight, they were downright invasive now—snatching at Sam's coat sleeves, sprouting hidden roots to catch her toes, and hissing warnings through their leaves. Even when they found a thick stand of trees in which to hide and watch the house, the branches seemed to bend toward her, making her hunker down into her coat in a crouch. Silhouettes occasionally moved across the brightly lit windows of the house, stopping her heart every time.

"Probably doesn't bode well for us that all the lights are still on at this hour, does it?" Joana whispered.

"It will certainly make investigating the house more difficult," Bennett conceded, the illumination highlighting his profile as he watched the windows. "But it makes spying on them easier."

"Do you think it's odd, the entire house being lit up?" Sam asked, the still woods putting her on edge. Shouldn't there be night birds calling, or creatures rustling? It seemed as if even the wind had died away, despite the fact that it had gusted steadily on their drive.

"Could be they're planning to come after us," Bennett said with a frown. "We'll have to be on guard. We don't want to give them any reason to suspect we came back."

"Could be," Sam said, rubbing at her neck where wisps of her hair felt like spiders crawling over her. She needed to keep it together, but it was just so *quiet*.

"Or maybe they all sleep with the lights on because they realize how spooky it is out here otherwise," Joana said, just as the lights along the top floor went out one by one. A second later the lights along the lower floor went out, again one by one, leaving only the bottom floor illuminated. Shadows moved across the windows, form after form, trooping along in a single line. Sam counted at least a dozen of them as the lights along the ground floor flickered out.

"I think we should—" Sam started, her words cut off as a door on the backside of the house swung open, throwing a long rectangle of light across the grass. A dozen men in robes spilled out of the glowing mouth.

"Did they . . . ? Good heavens, are those *swords*?" Joana hissed as the men gathered in a circle, all of them holding axes and swords and cudgels. "What in hell do they need swords for? Do they think we're Viking invaders?"

A man moved through the group, sprinkling water over the weapons in a steady rhythm as he spoke words too low for Sam to make out.

"That's Noah, the man from earlier," Sam said. Noah made the sign of the cross on the foreheads of the assembled brothers. "I thought he was the groundskeeper."

"He probably said that to throw us off," Bennett said. "It looks like he's the one in charge here."

"But what is he doing? Why is he blessing them?"

"Maybe they're about to wage a holy war," Joana said darkly.

"This was a mistake," Bennett said, rising suddenly. "We should never have come out here. These men are too dangerous."

"But the bowl," Sam protested.

"Damn the bowl," Bennett said harshly. "We've got to go. Now!"

Bennett grabbed her hand and hauled her and Joana up, the three of them hurrying away from the house as the men broke for the tree line with grim determination, Sam's pulse spiking in her throat at the sight of their gleaming weapons. Bennett and Jo increased their speed, and Sam did her best to keep up as they angled toward where they had left the car, in the opposite direction of the men charging into the woods. Her breath came loud and close, the thickness of the air like an invisible hand pressed over her mouth. The men filtered into the trees, calling out to each other in urgent tones.

Sam's heart pounded, terrified as she was that she might step on a branch and give away their position. More than once she jumped at the sight of a hulking trunk of a tree, imagining Brother Padraig's harsh features etched across the bark. Except . . . the men were moving away from them, up the mountain. Why weren't they going down to Dublin? The men had watched Sam and the others drive away toward the city. So where were they going? And what were they after?

"Bennett, Jo, wait," Sam gasped. "Something is wrong."

"Is it the burly men with swords hunting us down?" Joana asked, exasperated.

Sam shook her head. "No, listen. The men—they're gone. They went up the mountain."

"Good, that means we can hightail it out of here without getting caught," Joana said.

"But why?" Sam pressed, resisting Bennett's pull on her hand. "They saw us drive toward Dublin. So why are they going up instead of down?"

Bennett paused now, too, straining to hear any sign of life in the woods. A soft breeze wended through the trees, stirring the hair along the back of Sam's neck even as the leaves behind her didn't so much as rustle. Sam took in a long, deep breath as her primal warning system sent a prickle of unease over her skin. It was the same prickle she'd felt just before she heard the men in the bookshop and the scratching at their stateroom door on the *Olympic*. Something was wrong.

"Sam, what is it?" Bennett asked.

"I don't think it's us they're after," she whispered.

A sound went up from the trees, a howling cry unlike anything Sam had ever heard before. It was like a human, but not; like an animal, but not. It was something wholly impossible, and yet viscerally real. It pressed the air out of her lungs like an iron weight, the urge to scream burning the back of her throat.

Only then did it occur to her that the woods might harbor something worse than the armed men.

"What in hell was that?" Joana asked sharply.

A scream ripped through the trees, cut off with a sickening gurgle. Sam smothered a gasp, her hand shaking. Bennett's grip on her other hand tightened until her bones creaked under the pressure.

"Come on," he said grimly, reaching for Joana.

They started through the trees again as chaos erupted around them, shouts in Gaelic and English shaking the leaves as the men of the Order thundered through the woods. Whatever had unleashed that howl was terrifying enough to send grown men fleeing for their lives, and Sam was certain she didn't want to find out what it was.

But she could barely see to put one foot in front of the other, much less make a hasty escape. She stumbled over more roots, turned her ankle stepping on loose stones, winced at softer patches of earth that sucked at her boot heels. Clement was flat and predictable, even in the pitch dark. These woods were a snarl of traps intent on bringing her low. A branch swiped at her hair and she frantically beat it back, missing Bennett's warning about a rock in the path. She hit it full-on with her toe and dropped to one knee.

"Sam!" Joana panted, reaching down to help her up. "Are you all right?"

"I think so." Her knee throbbed when she flexed it, but it didn't seem broken.

"We've got to keep moving," Bennett said tensely. "If those men—"

The trees fell into a hush again, robbing Bennett of his words as the prickle along Sam's neck turned to a buzz, and then a cold stillness that made her stomach turn. Her breath was too loud, grating against her ears; her eyes were too dry, burning when she pressed them closed. Something pungent and sulfuric singed her nostrils. She didn't want to turn around. She knew no good would come of it. But still her head swiveled, her shoulders following in a begrudging motion.

It came out of the trees in a half walk, half crawl, like a man cut short at the knees dragging himself on all fours. It was blacker than the night, absorbing the scant light around it, except for eyes that burned like coals at the center of a fire. Its ears curved up and glinted like horns, its mouth hung open and dripped a thick, dark liquid along the ground. The academic, remote part of Sam's brain noted that Father Jacob had done a good job drawing the Hellfire Cat's likeness. The rest of her brain, however, was screaming.

"Run!" Sam shouted, snatching Joana's and Bennett's hands and tearing off through the woods. The Hellfire Cat sent up that human/animal cry, so much worse at close range, and the earth shook with the thunder of its paws. It sent trees tilting and vines creeping, catching at them as they half ran, half tumbled through the woods. Sam had no idea in which direction she was headed, except away from the Cat.

Joana and Bennett kept pace with her, but soon they were all battling the landscape too much to keep hold of one another. Sam's grip on Joana's hand slipped, then Bennett's, and soon she could only tell where they were by the cracking branches and muttered curses. Sam tripped over a rock and scrambled to get clear of the brush where she fell. Her heart slammed against her ribs, her sides aching from stitches and her feet like wooden blocks in her new boots. Her knees began collapsing, protesting the sharp slant of the ground, and more than once she landed hard on a bare patch of earth that sent shocks of pain up through her legs. But the Hellfire Cat howled again, the sound cutting through the trees like a razor blade, and she found the strength to move.

"Bennett?" she cried in a loud whisper. "Jo? Are you there?"

Only the trembling of the leaves greeted her in reply, making her heart hammer harder. The ground leveled out, but all she could see in every direction was darkness. Somehow in their flight she'd lost sight of Orlagh. She slowed to a stop, backing up against a tree for protection while she looked for something—anything—to anchor her to the real world. She swore if she heard that terrifying howl one more time, she would lose her mind. But the longer she stood there, trembling and terrified and *waiting*, the more she became convinced she would never escape these woods. No one would ever find her.

Something rustled in the tree above her, making her jump away from the trunk with a smothered shriek. Black eyes glinted from the branch above where a raven perched, its head tilting in consideration before it let out a jarring *caw*. Sam stumbled back another step, the dark and the terror of the Hellfire Cat convincing her this raven must be the same one from the docks earlier that day. Had it followed her here? How?

A soft wind brushed against her, curling over her collarbone and creeping up through the inner curve of her ear, forming into a whisper as it dissipated against her skin. It was like a breath, a cold sigh, a luring promise. The raven watched her, its call rhythmic as a heartbeat, though not an echo of her own. Her heart was pumping far too fast, as if it knew better than she did that they needed to escape.

Because she was sure—as sure as the grave—that the wind had whispered her name.

She whipped around, praying to every deity that might listen that she would find Bennett or Joana waiting to lead her out of this nightmare. And then she prayed even harder that it wasn't them, because there was a body slumped against a tree across from her, eyes black and lifeless, its robes torn to shreds. The raven fluttered overhead, perching on the man's shoulder with another cry.

The wind whispered her name again.

Sam sucked in a breath to scream as rough hands grabbed her and dragged her back, clamping over her mouth. A strange scent enveloped her, spicy and deep and somehow ancient. It was how she imagined the old cathedrals of Europe might smell, like thousands of years of incense.

"Don't make a sound," said a rough Irish voice in her ear. "If you value your immortal soul, come with me now."

CHAPTER TWENTY-ONE

Sam had never given more than a passing thought to the value of her immortal soul, but just then she would have followed the devil himself to be out of his woods and away from his Cat. She gave a quick nod of agreement, and the man released her mouth and took her arm in a viselike grip, moving at a quick but quiet pace through the woods.

She nearly cried out in relief as a bob of light appeared in the distance, expanding into the solid outline of Orlagh Country House. They broke the cover of trees, the branches giving one last longing tug at Sam's coat sleeves before releasing her. Sam slowed her step as the light from the house illuminated her savior, his expression fierce and sour.

"What do you think ye're doing out there?" Brother Padraig demanded. "Ye haven't the faintest clue of the powers ye're dabbling in, and ye're going to get us all killed because of it."

Sam shook her head, too out of breath to truly answer, not that she had one to give. Brother Padraig kept tight hold of her sleeve and dragged her to the back entry, pounding on it with his fist. A young man opened the door, no more than fifteen or sixteen years old. His rusty-red curls flopped over his forehead as his eyes widened, taking in Sam's disheveled appearance.

"Is it true, then, Brother Padraig?" the young man asked, his voice part excitement and part trepidation. "The Hellfire Cat, walking these hills after two hundred years? Have you seen it for yourself?"

"Never mind the Cat, Amos," Brother Padraig growled, shoving Sam forward into Amos's arms. "Take this one to the sanctuary and hold her there until Brother Noah can see to her."

"Wait!" Sam protested. "My friends are still out there!"

"Then they're greater fools than you!" Brother Padraig barked. "Now do as ye're told and stay here while we try to drive the infernal beast from our land."

"But I have to go with you!" Sam protested again, wrenching free of Amos's grip. No part of her wanted to go back into those woods, but Bennett and Joana were still out there. "I have to save them!"

"There's nothing you can do for them now," growled Brother Padraig, shoving her back again. "Hold her, lad, or so help me I'll make sure ye never take the vows, next month or otherwise."

"No!" Sam cried. But this time Amos kept his grip, dragging her over the threshold into the warm interior of the country house. "Please! Find my friends. Please!"

"Miss, ye'll hurt yourself," Amos said. He grunted as one of Sam's elbows grazed his jaw. "Or me."

"Let me go!" she said. "You don't understand what's out there."

"Brother Padraig will find your friends, I've no doubt of it," said Amos, gently but firmly moving her down the hallway. "He can be a rough old codger, but he wouldn't let no harm come to them."

"I'm not trusting my friends to that arsonist," Sam said, pulling harder.

But the young man had the advantage of proper rest and the patience to wait out her struggles, and Sam soon exhausted her reserves. Her arms went slack as the adrenaline flushed out of her system, leaving her shaky and light-headed. She stopped pulling and dragged along behind him in a fog.

What was that . . . *thing*? It was certainly no cat. It was like someone's demented, perverted idea of a cat, as if a cat and a dog and a demon had been melted together in hellfire. Even here, in the warm bowels of the house, she shivered to think of its eyes glowing out of the dark.

But the raven . . . and the man . . . and that *voice*. Even now it lingered like a wisp of spiderweb on her ear, susurrating in the quiet of the wood-paneled halls of Orlagh. She scrubbed at her neck, her collarbone, scratching the inner whorls of her ear until she came away with skin and blood. She could have sworn the voice laughed, mocking her.

"Did you see it, then?" asked Amos, startling her and snapping the threads of the web.

"What?" Sam blinked, looking around. She thought they would take her to the basement, same as Professor Wallstone, but she seemed to be in some kind of chapel or . . . What had Brother Padraig called it? The sanctuary. It was empty, thankfully, and she sank down into the stiff embrace of the nearest pew.

The boy crouched beside her, his face shining up with unchecked curiosity. "The Hellfire Cat, miss, did you really see it? I never hoped to see it in my lifetime. Well, I suppose *hope* is the wrong word to use. Nobody hopes to cross paths with the devil's own offspring, do they now? Still, it's what they train us for. Cor, that would have put the heart crossway in me."

Sam looked down at him. "Who are you?"

"Me?" the boy said in surprise. He straightened up in pride, which was hard to do from his crouching position. "I'm Brother Amos, least I will be once I take my vows."

Sam shook her head. "Not you. Those men in the woods."

"Oh, you're after Solas Fíor, you mean."

"Solas Fíor?" Sam echoed. "What is that?"

"That's quite enough chatter for now, Amos," came a steady voice from the doorway. Brother Noah gave her a frosty look that she guessed put most of the novitiates here in a state of panic. It had a similar effect on her, and she curled deeper into the protective wool of her coat.

"You're the man from before, the one who met us outside," she said.

"I tried to warn you then, but circumspection is wasted on youth," said Brother Noah. He gave Amos a pointed look. "Why don't ye wet the tea for us, Amos?"

Amos popped up, giving an apologetic nod to Sam. "Yes, sir."

"What is Solas Fíor?" Sam asked, wishing her voice sounded stronger.

"I'll be asking the questions for now," said Brother Noah. "Where is it?"

"Where is what?" Sam asked.

"Father Jacob's diary," he said. "I know the professor sent it to you; he confessed as much when we caught him breaking into our archives. That diary is the rightful property of the Order of St. Augustine, and we'll have it back by any means required."

"Why, so you can call the Curse of the Specter Queen?" Sam demanded. "Start the last great war of man?"

"Start a war?" Brother Noah said in astonishment. "We're not trying to *call* the curse, ye daft lass. We're trying to *stop* it."

CHAPTER TWENTY-TWO

"What?" Sam said, feeling like somebody had knocked the pew out from under her. "That's not . . . No. Your men just chased us through the woods and kidnapped me!"

"We *saved* you in those woods, from your own fool selves," Brother Noah countered. "What were you thinking, tinkering with that kind of magic? Two hundred years we've watched this hillside, keeping it safe from the evils the Hellfire Club first stirred up with their Black Masses. And now tonight, that beast walks our woods again and we find you lot trying to make a hasty escape."

"A hasty escape?" Sam repeated. "We had nothing to do with that . . . that thing. I would never . . . None of us would ever . . . We're here to stop you!"

Brother Noah spread his arms. "And yet, the Cat left you untouched, when many of my men were not so lucky."

The empty eyes and shredded robes of the man in the woods came back to Sam in a wave of nausea that made the room spin. She took a deep breath, lowering her head and staring hard at the floor to keep control of her senses.

"You imprisoned the professor," she reasoned, grasping for the scraps of logic left to her. "Your men burned my books."

"That . . . was an accident," Brother Noah conceded with a tilt of his head. "An unfortunate one, to be sure. But truly an accident, lass."

"An accident," Sam said with a humorless laugh. "It didn't feel like one."

"What happened at your shop was a tragedy, but nothing close to the scale of disaster that will occur if we don't retrieve the diary."

"But you have it," Sam countered. "The diary. Your men stole it on the ship."

"The steamer?" Brother Noah said doubtfully. "My men were never on that ship. They chased you to New York and booked passage back on a freighter. Are you saying someone stole the diary on the *Olympic*?"

"Are you saying it wasn't you?" Sam said.

Brother Noah stared at her for a minute that felt like several small lifetimes stitched together as Sam's emotions swung from outrage to confusion to fear and back to outrage. What kind of game was this man playing, accusing them of raising the Hellfire Cat? Acting like *they* were the ones trying to invoke the curse? As if she would want another Great War to happen.

"Perhaps we've both made the wrong assumptions about the other," Brother Noah said finally, his tone shifting. "It's possible we're working toward the same thing, and maybe we should work together."

"Work together how?" Sam asked cautiously.

Brother Noah took a deep breath. "Come with me."

He led her out of the sanctuary to the sitting room in the front of the house. Sam cried out in relief at the two familiar figures occupying the room—Joana sprawled on a chair while Bennett paced the floor. Neither of them looked like they had given up the fight easily, and one of the brothers standing guard showed a darkening around the eye that would blossom into a full bruise by morning.

"Oh, damn," Joana said, straightening up. "They pinched you too, huh?"

"Jo!" Sam said, rushing across the room and wrapping her up in a fierce hug. "Oh, I'm so glad you're all right."

"Yeah, yeah, me too," Joana said, returning the hug. "Honestly, with all you two have dragged me into recently, we're going to have to skip these kinds of greetings or they'll take up our whole day."

"Are you all right, Sam?" Bennett asked, taking on his father's strident business tone. He brushed her cheek, the crease between his brows deep with worry. "These men didn't hurt you, did they?"

"Nobody's hurting anybody unless they need it," Brother Noah said, undercutting Bennett's authority with his superior tone. "Sit down, the lot of you. We need to talk."

"I'm not sitting anywhere until somebody tells me what in hell that *thing* was out there," Joana said, setting her hands on her hips. "And before you try putting any of that fear of god in me, you should know I've driven two bishops into early retirement."

"Jo, just listen," Sam said. "I think . . . we might have been wrong. About these men."

"They kidnapped the professor," Bennett protested. "Held him in the most deplorable conditions. I know exactly what I think of these men, and I'll be reporting it to the authorities."

"What do you know about Barnaby Wallstone?" Brother Noah asked.

"I know he's a respected and highly sought-after expert in the classics and archaeology," Bennett said, crossing his arms. "What you've done to him is a crime."

Brother Noah raised his brows. "What we've done to him? What's gone off with your professor is none of our doing. It's the Hellfire Club, got into his blood. Or didn't you see it yourself?"

"That's preposterous," Bennett said. "I have no idea what you're talking about."

"You didn't see his eyes, then?"

"Of course I've . . ." Bennett trailed off, looking uncomfortable.

"What?" Sam asked. "What is it? What about his eyes?"

Bennett shook his head. "It's nothing. It's ridiculous."

"Then why don't you answer her, lad?" Brother Noah asked.

"Bennett?" Sam said, touching his sleeve softly.

He looked down at her, his lips pressed into a thin line. "The professor has blue eyes."

Sam straightened in surprise. She thought back to her first good look at the professor, in the electric lights of the hotel. "But his eyes are . . ."

"Black," Joana said flatly.

"It doesn't mean anything," Bennett said. "We're all tired from a long week of traveling, and it's been dark everywhere we go. The professor has been under a terrible strain. That level of stress could easily lead to changes in the body."

Brother Noah shook his head. "It's no trick of the light, lad, neither is it stress. That's the magic, got into him. It eats away at you, rots you out. When you bite into the magic, it bites back."

"How is any of this possible?" Sam whispered.

"That's what we've dedicated our existence to finding out," Brother Noah said.

"Solas Fíor," Sam replied, repeating the name Amos had said in the sanctuary.

"What is Solas Fíor?" Bennett asked.

"We are a secret brotherhood within the Augustinian Order, not sanctioned by the Church but working in its holy name," Brother Noah said. "Founded by Father Jacob to combat the evils of the

Hellfire Club in our community. We keep watch over this land to make sure it never falls prey to the scourge of the heretical."

"What does that mean, keep watch?" Bennett asked. "What exactly is it you do?"

"There's something I ought to show you before I answer that," Brother Noah said.

He led them out of the front room and back through the maze of the house. Curious faces peeked around door corners and quickly disappeared after a disapproving grunt from Brother Noah, and before Sam knew it, they had returned to the stairs leading to the basement.

"Now hang on a minute," Bennett said, putting an arm out to stop Joana and Sam.

"Don't worry, I've no plan to lock you up," said Brother Noah, continuing down the steps. He produced a flashlight from somewhere in the folds of his robes, flicking it on and bathing the narrow staircase in light. "Yet."

When they reached the bottom, Brother Noah turned away from the basement to another, smaller door. It was painted black, same as the rest of the staircase, and if it weren't for the full light of Brother Noah's flashlight on the thin cracks and the small lock, none of them would have spotted it. He pulled a key from around his neck and fitted it in the lock. The door swung on silent hinges, nothing but a pitch-black room beyond.

"I don't want to go in there," Sam whispered.

"I can promise you do, Miss Knox," said Brother Noah, walking in ahead of them.

Joana strode in after him and Sam and Bennett followed reluctantly. Brother Noah flipped a switch and a series of pale lights came on overhead, the low ceiling lending a cramped feel to the space. But what really made it seem overstuffed were the rows of cabinets. Wooden cabinets, metal cabinets, even some ornate-looking trunks down at the far end of the room. The room itself wasn't that big—probably a storage closet at some point in its history—but it was overflowing with precious information. Sam reached for a stack of papers on top of the nearest cabinet that listed the moon cycles, including the upcoming solar eclipse.

"What is this place?" she asked.

"These are the Solas Fíor archives," said Brother Noah. "Anything anyone could ever want to know about the occult, the wicked dealings of the devil, the sources of power and magic across the island. We gather it all here."

"Why?" Bennett asked, lifting open a sketchbook with a drawing of an elaborate, bejeweled cross on the front page. The inside of the cross was filled with symbols Sam had never seen before. Beneath the image were scrawled the words *Hermetic Order of the Golden Dawn*.

"Because it's real, Mr. Steeling," Brother Noah said simply. "All of it. If it makes it into the archive, that is. Our members investigate every report of supernatural occurrence, and if we deem them to be valid, we make a record of them. This was where we caught your professor the night he attacked our student. He said he was looking for the ritual vessel and was convinced we'd secreted it away here. That's when we learned he'd found Father Jacob's diary and mailed it off to your shop. We never knew what happened to Father Jacob the night he disappeared. But now we think he must have taken that ritual bowl and burned down the Hellfire Club to make his escape. The club members pursued him into the hills and he died there, taking his diary and its answers with him. At least until your professor dug them up."

"But why are you showing us all this?" Sam asked.

"Because of this," Brother Noah said, holding up a thick leather-bound book he pulled from one of the shelves. "The reason for the formation of Solas Fíor. The Hellfire Club."

Sam took the book and opened the cover carefully, cradling it to protect the spine as her repair tendencies kicked in. Based on the type and quality of leather used on the cover, as well as the binding methods, she guessed the book must be at least two hundred years old. She recognized the writing on the first page straightaway. This was more formal, less rushed and harried, but those were the same swooping letters and compact writing style.

"Father Jacob wrote this," she said. She read the first line, the words instantly familiar from the benediction in the letter. "'May the hazel bring you wisdom.'"

"Father Jacob Donnell was just a local Catholic priest when the Hellfire Club first took charge of the hunting lodge on Montpelier Hill," said Brother Noah, his voice taking on a resonant quality that made Sam think he'd given this speech to plenty of novitiates. "The practice of Catholicism was outlawed in those times, and Father Jacob had to get creative in the ways he tended his flock. They often held their services in the woods, in secret, all over the Dublin Mountains. It gave him the unique opportunity to examine the Hellfire Club's activities up close. And he didn't care for what he saw."

"You all keep talking about the dark deeds of this Hellfire Club," Joana said in an exaggerated tone. "But they just sound like a bunch of rich drunks. Debauchery, sexual liaisons, a casual curse or two. You can find all that and worse in any speakeasy in Chicago."

"They were far more than just a bunch of rich drunks," Brother Noah said. "They might have begun that way, but their actions were cursed the moment they set foot on that profane ground. Soon enough they were carrying out unspeakable horrors under cover of night. Black Masses, blood rituals, burning people alive for their sacrifices. All in the name of the devil, they thought it. But those stones, they carry the power of a people much older than us. The Druids understood. It was why they held worship in the passage grave."

"But you said these fellas died two hundred years ago," said Joana. "And that Father Jacob burned their hidey-hole. So why all this cloak-and-sword business?"

"Because they're not so dead as we thought."

CHAPTER TWENTY-THREE

In the wake of her encounter with the Hellfire Cat, Sam's addled mind immediately went to ghosts, or the reanimated dead, or perhaps the immortal vampire. She would put nothing past some-one who could raise a creature like that Cat. But she was too afraid to say any such thing out loud, especially given the look on Bennett's face.

"It's not possible for any of those men to still be alive," he said.

"Not the founding members, no, but their offspring? Their descendants? Alive and well. And one of them is trying to call forth the curse. Two hundred years we've watched that hill," Brother Noah said. "And for two hundred years no more than a few fools have been willing to test their souls in that place. It stayed that way until five months ago."

"What happened?" Sam asked.

"At first it was lights at night," said Brother Noah. "We thought maybe it was young ones seeking their thrills braving the club by moonlight. But then we found the sheep."

"What sheep?" Joana said, in a tone that made it clear she didn't really want to know anything about the sheep.

"Two of them, buried in the woods," said Brother Noah grimly.

"Slaughtered by having their throats slit and their blood let out. Ritual sacrifice. And then we started getting reports from local farmers that their animals were behaving strangely. Sheep butting heads until one or the other died, cows breaking through fences and tumbling down the cliffs. Chickens pecking the eyes out of each other."

"That sounds horrifying," Sam said.

"It's only a portent of things to come if this curse is called down on the land," Brother Noah said.

"And you think Professor Wallstone is the one trying to invoke the curse?" Sam asked.

"It's not possible," Bennett protested. "I know how the professor has been these last few months, especially since he arrived in Ireland. But he wouldn't do something like this. He's an academic, not a . . . a pagan worshipper."

"We had suspected Barnaby Wallstone, yes, but that was before Brother Padraig brought word of other, more troubling new arrivals on our soil."

"What new arrivals?" Bennett asked.

Brother Noah opened a trunk filled with books of the same size and binding as the one Sam held, pulling out the topmost one and opening to the end, where a register of names was written in neat script that changed color and form, indicating that the list had been added to over the years by different people. He pointed to the last several rows of names, where the dates of birth were listed, but the dates of death were still blank.

"We've kept a watch on every known descendant of the Hellfire Club since its inception," he said. "For this very reason. There are roughly three hundred living descendants who share the bloodlines of the original members. Sixteen of them have been in

Dublin within the last five months since the first sightings up on Montpelier Hill."

Sam sucked in a breath at a line in light blue. "Alistair and Veronica Fitzgerald?"

Joana stabbed a finger at the line. "I knew she was full of dark magic the second I met her."

"But that doesn't . . ." Sam shook her head. "Alistair was so kind. He helped me! After the break-in. It couldn't have been him."

"I told you he couldn't be trusted," Bennett said grimly. He turned to Sam, an edge of triumph in his tone. "They're always nice until they're not."

Sam shook her head, everything she thought she knew slipping away from her. Alistair really had seemed kind. Could it have all been an act? What if he had been the one to break into the stateroom, and then pretended to help her? He disappeared to find the first mate, he could have cut that lifeboat loose and hidden the diary along the way. And he *was* in Dublin now, on this Grand Tour. The perfect cover for his actions. She had considered him a friend, but what if he wasn't?

"If Alistair Fitzgerald has the diary, things are even worse than we imagined," Brother Noah was saying. "He has all the means to find the bowl and invoke the curse."

Sam shook her head. "Not everything. He doesn't have the clues to where Father Jacob hid the ritual bowl. That page was lost."

"Lost? How?"

Joana sighed. "It's a long story that involves a bedsheet, an umbrella, and a perfectly good hairdo gone to waste."

"But the bowl is still hidden?" Brother Noah asked.

Sam nodded. "For now."

Brother Noah took a deep breath, the crags in his forehead

smoothing out just a little. "Then it's still anyone's game," he said, looking at each of them with resolve. "But we've only got three days more to play it. I've got men searching the city for the Fitzgeralds. Wherever they are, we'll find them."

Sam chewed guiltily at her lip. She knew where to find them— they were staying in the same hotel. She had planned to ask the front desk clerk which room Alistair was in so she could say hello. But now, now . . . she didn't know what to do. She could tell Brother Noah where Alistair was and end this whole debacle tonight. She probably should. But Sam had told Bennett she wasn't a fool, and she didn't intend to start playing one now. They had nothing more than Brother Noah's word that Solas Fíor was trying to stop the ritual. But between Alistair and Solas Fíor, only one of them had hunted her down, burned her books, and threatened her life. For all she knew, handing Alistair over to them could seal all their fates instead of saving them.

No, she wouldn't play the fool. She would find Alistair first thing tomorrow and get the truth out of him herself, one way or another.

CHAPTER TWENTY-FOUR

Sam was nearly cross-eyed with fatigue by the time Brother Noah sent Amos to drive them back to their hotel. The young man was even more apologetic about taking their only means of transportation away than he had been about holding Sam hostage, but they could hardly blame him. They had stolen the car, after all, and left Solas Fíor without any means of patrolling the mountains. A grave mistake Sam would never forget.

Tired as her body was, Sam's mind was alive with all the new information, the gears turning faster than even she could keep up with. Those she had thought enemies were now claiming to be allies, and those she had considered friends were under the greatest of suspicions. And those under suspicion were now the ones making accusations? How was anyone supposed to keep track of anything at this point?

She had her own suspicions, too. Suspicions that none of these men knew what they were doing. Not the brothers of Solas Fíor, who'd had two hundred years to find the diary and lost out to a madman stumbling through their own backyard; not Professor Wallstone, who was far too overcome with the magic to be trusted; and much as it pained her to contemplate such a betrayal, not even Bennett. Without her, he wouldn't have been able to open the diary, much less recover the letter or decipher the hidden message. He had put his trust in the professor, and what had that landed them in?

"A right mess," Joana said as they stepped out of the car, the horizon turning a barely perceptible shade of light gray.

"Yes, exactly," Sam said, still tangled up in her own thoughts. She paused on the sidewalk beside Joana as Bennett disappeared inside to find a bellboy to carry their recently recovered trunks up to their rooms. "Wait, what?"

"You," Joana said, reaching out to smooth down a flyaway wisp of hair. "I said you look a mess. That open top did a number on your hair."

"Oh," Sam said, patting self-consciously at the bun that had lasted her since the ferry ride that morning.

Joana chuckled, smoothing down her own curls. "Don't worry, I'm sure I look as if I stuck a finger in a light socket. I certainly feel like I did after tonight's outing."

Sam shivered. "That creature . . ."

"Let's not speak of it," Joana said with a wave that was far too cavalier to be real. "We're down in the civilized depths of society here, and I for one have no intention of setting a foot off of concrete again while we're in Dublin. Give me the seedy speakeasies on the South Side of Chicago any day of the week over a breath of mountain air."

"But there is still so much left unanswered," Sam said, frowning. "Where the bowl is, who raised the Hellfire Cat, what happens if we don't catch them before Saturday."

Joana tucked her hands in her coat pocket. "Not our problem, Sam. Those Solas fellas, they've got it all under control. You heard them, Alistair and Veronica Fitzgerald are the guilty ones. And can

I just say how vindicated I am right now? I never get a person's character wrong, and Veronica is the worst kind of bad news. If she'd gutted a cat and tried to call up a demon with its entrails right on the dinner table, I couldn't be less surprised."

"But Alistair was so kind," Sam protested, still not convinced. "And he helped me escape! How could he have helped me escape from his room if he was the one breaking in?"

Joana waved a hand. "Semantics I'm not interested in arguing. Somebody else is in charge now, which is just the way I prefer it." She leaned a heavy arm on Sam's shoulder. "If I promise you the entirety of my inheritance could you carry me up those stairs?"

Sam gave an exhausted sigh, the questions still churning her mind and her stomach. "At this point I'm not sure I'll make it up by myself, much less carrying anyone else. Even a lightweight like you."

Joana chuckled, knocking into Sam with her hip. "I'll have you know I have been referred to as 'statuesque' by the sons of two prominent Chicago families. Which is just a nice way of saying I'm too tall for them. Obviously their loss."

Bennett reappeared with a young man in a bellhop suit, directing him toward the trunks Amos had helped them unload. Their conversation shifted to the logistics of transporting their luggage, but that didn't stop Sam from continuing the arguments on her own as she hefted hers onto the cart. They managed to load all four trunks and the bellhop gifted them with a ride to their floor in the service elevator, which Sam's throbbing knee greatly appreciated. It had grown insistent in the car ride back into Dublin, a physical reminder of the unearthly horrors she had faced in those woods.

Joana gave a happy little noise when they reached their hotel room, tossing her coat on the floor and diving under the fluffy duvet covering the bed.

"I'm so sorry I ever accused you of being lumpy; you're a cloudy slice of heaven," she said, her voice smothered by the pillow.

Bennett stood just inside the door of their room, wearing his most foreboding Steeling frown. "I have half a mind to lay out a pallet right here and block your door to keep the two of you from trying to sneak out again."

"That's not necessary," Sam said, heat flushing her cheeks. It had been one thing to fall asleep in the same space from exhaustion on the train; but if she knew Bennett was in the same room as her, could hear his chest rising and falling in deep sleep, could watch his profile as he slept without the fear of being caught staring . . . she would never sleep again.

"I pinky swear never to leave the delicious comfort of this cocoon unless wild dogs drag me from its embrace," Joana said from under the duvet, her words heavy and slurred in half sleep. She paused a moment, her next words slightly sharper. "Although I suppose it would be a wild cat in this case, wouldn't it?"

"Jo," Bennett said in a warning tone.

"I already swore it, Bennett, you despot."

Bennett moved his gaze to Sam. "Sam? What about you?"

Sam took a breath. "Shouldn't we discuss it?"

Bennett's brows lifted. "Discuss you sneaking out?"

"What? No, I don't mean . . . Of course I won't sneak out. That's . . . No. Not after tonight."

"Good," Bennett said. "I wasn't relishing the idea of sleeping on the floor after tonight either."

"But," Sam said, lurching forward and putting a hand on his arm, "shouldn't we talk about what happened tonight? The Hellfire Cat, the brothers, whether or not we trust them, and what we're going to do now?"

Not to mention the raven, and the voice that still haunted her even now that it had gone quiet. But she couldn't bring herself to tell him any of that. It felt more like a hallucination at this point, a trick cooked up by her terrified mind. Even if she now watched all the shadows around them obsessively.

"What we're going to do now is get some much-needed rest," Bennett said, turning and putting his hand over hers. He'd done it unconsciously, but the contact caught them both by surprise and he quickly dropped his hand. "Everything else can wait."

"But the eclipse is only three days away," Sam said, chewing at one corner of her lip. "Two, really, considering it's after midnight. If Solas Fíor is wrong, if it's not Alistair—"

"Of course it's Alistair," Bennett said with a frown. "He fits the bill perfectly. A descendant of an original Hellfire Club member, the timing of his trip here. I never bought that Grand Tour business anyway."

"But that still doesn't—"

"Sam," Bennett interrupted, taking her by the shoulders. "There's nothing to do tonight, and you're practically swaying on your feet right now. We all need sleep. I need . . . I want to know you'll be safe. Otherwise I won't sleep. Promise me, please? And mean it this time."

"Of course I promise," Sam said. She had to admit he had a point, even if her lips twisted into a frown, working on more arguments. She did feel light-headed from fatigue.

Bennett's shoulders sagged in relief as he dropped his hands. "Good. Thank you. We'll discuss what to do next in the morning. Good night, Sam."

"Good night, Bennett," Sam said, closing and locking the door. She had half a mind to put a chair under the knob, just as she'd done on the *Olympic*, but she had a feeling it wouldn't stop someone with the power of the Hellfire Cat. If they wanted in, they would get in. A thought that did little to settle Sam's mind for sleep.

She took her time getting undressed, carefully hanging her coat in the armoire and setting her boots neatly beside the bed. She needed to think, even if she agreed with Joana that the bed looked like a puff of heaven right now. She could rest when the puzzle was complete.

Whenever a cipher eluded her, she had to go back to the basics. Back to the patterns, to those threads that tied the incomprehensible together. The sense in the chaos. Sometimes those patterns were purposely placed to throw her off—repeating letters or characters that seemed to indicate an answer when really they were red herrings, inserted into the text to imply an answer that wasn't there. Like the brothers and the diary—she had been so sure they were the ones who stole it because they wanted to invoke the curse. But after tonight, she had to admit the reason might have been quite the opposite, that they were as afraid of the curse as she was. She had also been so sure the professor would be able to solve all their problems, but he was just one more burden to add to the pile. And then there was her opinion of Alistair . . .

She considered herself a good judge of character, same as Joana. She didn't give her trust away easily. Alistair hardly seemed the kind to destroy the world to set himself up as king of a new one. But there were the facts, plain as day. His family history, the timing of the trip, the convenience of it all. Still, it felt like those red herrings in the cipher—patterns placed purposefully to throw her off the truth. But if everyone else was convinced, who was she to say they were wrong? And was she only helping him with his plans by not revealing his whereabouts to the brothers? It had seemed like the right thing to do a few hours ago, being held captive at

Orlagh by Brother Noah and his men, but now she wondered if she should have just told them where to find Alistair and washed her hands of the whole business.

A pang of homesickness sharpened into a blade, stabbing at her with a longing for the safety and security of her books. It wasn't her mother or the farm that she thought of—as much as she cared for her mother, that life had never fit her either. Her mother was far too practical, too focused on the physical needs of food and shelter after her father died to ever indulge Sam's intellectual needs. The shop had been a gift, an oasis Sam could escape to when the outside world and its hurts grew too overwhelming. And she had come to rely on that shop, more than her life with her mother at the farm, more than her friendship with Joana, more than anything.

But her books were gone. And so was her safety and security. Sam could keep mourning their loss, or she could make it mean something. Because as terrifying as the evening had been, it had delivered a rough and timely lesson- -Sam could survive it. Same as she survived the break-in on the *Olympic*; same as she survived the fire at the shop. She was not helpless, nor was she hopeless. She had knowledge and skills of her own. Skills she could use to help herself. To maybe even save the world.

After all, it wasn't as if anyone else was lining up to do it.

"Samantha Margaret Knox," Joana groaned from deep in her covers. "You're going to wear a hole in the floor pacing like that, and that creaky floorboard is about to drive me as mad as the Telltale Heart. Go to bed."

"Sorry," Sam murmured, crawling under the covers. She couldn't possibly sleep, but at least Joana would leave her alone if she stayed quiet. Although she might close her eyes, just for a moment. They did feel as if they were made of grit and fire by this point, anyway. They needed rest, even if her mind couldn't possibly manage it. She had so much to plan—a cryptic clue to unpack and a ritual bowl to find if she was going to save the world. She had no time for sleep.

CHAPTER TWENTY-FIVE

Something sharp and insistent prodded her side, snapping Sam awake what felt like only a few moments later. She shot upright, swinging blindly at whatever was attacking her. Joana jumped back, just out of range of Sam's arms, putting up her hands.

"Whoa there, Jack Dempsey," Joana said. "You're not in the ring, champ, quit your swinging."

"Jo," Sam gasped, trying to scrub the fuzz of sleep from her mind. "You scared me."

"And yet I'm the one getting the hard right," Joana said, putting her hands on her hips. "You sleep any longer and we'll miss lunch."

"Lunch? What happened to breakfast?"

Joana waved a hand. "Passed us by looking. Come on, get up, I'm starving, and Bennett and Phillip are waiting."

So much for finding Alistair first thing in the morning. She'd have to make an excuse to slip away from the others soon and find a way to talk to him, get everything sorted. Sam crawled out of bed, pulling on the same pair of pants that it seemed like she had taken off only minutes ago, Joana making impatient little humming noises all the while. Sam had always admired her friend's ability to shake off the night before, even when they were children and would stay up late into the evening telling ghost stories and daydreaming about when they would move to Chicago together. But right in that moment, she would have sold her friend to the first traveling circus for five more minutes of sleep.

The boys met them in the hall, Bennett looking as put together as always in his tweed pants and button-up shirt and coat. Phillip looked paler than usual, the circles dark and deep under his eyes. He clutched his handkerchief in his hand, finishing up a coughing fit just as Sam and Joana appeared.

"You two look like I feel," he said with a weak smile. "Tied one on a little too tight last night down in the pub. Bartender had to kick me out around midnight. I don't even remember what bed I ended up sleeping in."

"It was mine," Bennett said flatly.

Phillip gave him a sheepish grin. "Thanks for the loaner, Steeling. Hope it wasn't too much trouble sleeping it off in mine."

"Your mattress was lumpier," Bennett grumbled.

"What about the professor?" Sam asked.

Bennett pinched the bridge of his nose. "He's barricaded himself inside the bathroom. Claims someone tried to, and I quote, 'breathe in his essence' last night."

"It's made using the facilities damn difficult," Phillip added with a grimace. "We had to make do with the public lavatories in the pub across the street. Luckily I'm on a first-name basis with them by now."

"Well, he's safer barricaded in there than running loose in the streets," Bennett said. "And it's only for today."

"Why?" Sam asked in alarm as they headed down the stairs.

"Because we're going home as soon as I can book passage on a steamer," Bennett said.

"Come again?" Phillip asked in surprise, pausing on a stair as another coughing fit overcame him. He balled up the handkerchief when the fit passed, but not before Sam saw a dark stain on the linen.

"Phillip, are you okay?" she asked. She knew that kind of stain, had watched her *oma* die from blood that filled her lungs when she contracted pneumonia. "Shouldn't we take you to a physician? You said this runs in your family; isn't there anything we can do?"

"No, I'll be all right," Phillip said with a weak smile. "Steeling caught me by surprise with that joke."

"It's not a joke," Bennett said, charging down the stairs. "We're leaving Dublin."

They arrived at the dining room, their conversation falling into a temporary lull as they were ushered to their seats and ordered lunch. The waiters brought out an Irish stew, the restorative power of the dish acting like some kind of miracle. The meat was tender and soft, the gravy thick and rich, the vegetables like a tonic for Sam's soul. She had nearly licked her plate clean by the time Phillip leaned in to the table with a low, urgent voice.

"What's this about leaving Dublin?" he asked, trying to keep a cheerful tone even as lines of tension pulled his mouth tight. "What's got into you?"

Bennett raised both brows. "Are you posing that question seriously? Did you tie one on so tight you forgot the events of yesterday evening?"

"Well, the run-in with the Augustinian fellows was unfortunate, but you said they brought our things back last night and apologized for the whole debacle." Phillip spread his hands wide. "So I fail to see the problem."

"The problem is that the professor is unwell," Bennett said tersely. "You've seen the man, the last thing he needs is to stay here and try to conduct the survey. Once we get him settled safely back in Chicago, we can discuss the opportunity to resume the survey at a later date."

Phillip tapped a finger restlessly on the tabletop. "Now listen here, Steeling. I've put a great deal of money into this venture, and I was promised a return. We can't just pack up and ship out because the professor got a little twisted before we got here."

"A little twisted?" Bennett echoed incredulously. "Phillip, you've seen him. The man is ill. He needs help. This trip has been a mistake from the start, and I can't continue to put everyone in danger. Especially not my sister and Sam."

"You don't speak for me, brother," Joana said, draping an arm over the back of her chair. "But, speaking for myself, you're not getting me up on that hill. What about a nice, long tour of London instead?"

"We're returning to Chicago," Bennett said. "And that's all there is to say. I'll book the tickets this morning. Sam and Jo, pack your things."

"I think we should stay," Sam said quietly.

Bennett's brows lowered dangerously. "You what?"

She straightened, unwilling to be cowed by the Steeling stare. She had given it plenty of thought last night, the debate weaving its way into her dreams until she had a vivid memory of arguing with a younger version of herself about code words and Vigenère ciphers signaling the end of the world. But she had awoken with her mind made up.

"I'm staying," she said. "Until we see this thing through."

"Have you lost your damn mind too?" Joana blurted out.

Sam took a deep breath. "We started this, even if we didn't mean to. The diary, the letter . . . There's more we can do. And we have a responsibility to fix this. I . . . I have a responsibility. I have to fix this."

"Diary?" Phillip said, looking between them in confusion. "You mean the book that you said got stolen on the ship? What's that got to do with anything? What's this about a letter?"

Sam kept her concentration on Bennett, willing him to understand her reasoning. "If we don't do it, who will? Who could? I can't just leave, not like this. Not knowing what's at stake."

"It isn't our concern," Bennett said. "This is a . . . local matter."

Sam shook her head. "You know that's not true."

"Sam," Joana said, her voice strained. "You don't know what pain it brings me that you're forcing me to play the responsible one, but we shouldn't be here. We don't know what we're doing, and we'd be a bunch of damn fools to try."

"Then I'll be a damn fool," Sam said. "But I can't walk away. Not now."

"This is ridiculous," Bennett said, cutting through the air with one hand. "No one is staying. The professor needs to return to Chicago, and I certainly won't leave you behind."

"Hang on, I haven't agreed to anything yet," Phillip protested. "And Sam has made some good points here. This bowl that the professor was on about last night, it could be a huge find if it's real. These kinds of disputes happen all the time. Hell, Howard Carter wrote about carrying a pistol on him down in the Valley of the Kings so grave robbers couldn't attack him! There are always opportunists looking to cash in on treasures. We can't let that deter us. I won't walk away from a potential discovery like this, and the professor wouldn't want us to either. Certainly not in his name."

"He's not well enough to argue his case, is he?" Bennett countered. He stood up, all business. "I'm not discussing it any further. I'm going to the docks right now to purchase tickets, and when I return, I expect everyone to be ready to go."

"Bennett," Sam protested, her chair scraping back as she stood hastily.

"No, Sam," Bennett said, his voice hard. "We're leaving. That's it."

He strode away, not giving her a chance to argue. Phillip chased after him, calling in vain for him to reconsider. Frustration and rebellion simmered under Sam's skin, even as her brain tried to convince her that perhaps she was being the unreasonable one. Bennett was right: To stay could be disastrous—it probably would be, if she was honest with herself.

But she couldn't leave. Not now. Not when she was so close to an answer. Not when the fate of the world might be at stake.

"Come on," Joana said, standing up and smoothing her skirt. "We'd better pack our things and have the bellboy bring them downstairs. I wouldn't put it past Bennett to leave our trunks behind if they're not ready and I'll be damned if I lose those suede T-strap heels."

Sam set her jaw. "This is a mistake, Jo."

Joana sighed, rolling her eyes toward the ceiling. "This isn't a treasure hunt in the back garden, Sam. I know these things get in your brain, but a few weeks touring the sights in London or Paris will shake it right back out. They've got that Rosetta Stone display in the British Museum; that's right up your alley. Bennett is right, and those are three words you'll never hear from me again. We need to leave. This isn't our problem to solve. Now, come on, I need to stash a few pairs of shoes in your trunk so Bennett doesn't yell at me about expenses."

"I'll be up in a minute," Sam said, glancing toward the front desk and contemplating her options. She needed to find Alistair now more than ever and get the truth out of him somehow.

Joana nudged her shoulder. "Don't mope, it sours your color. This is for the best."

"Is it?" Sam asked, swiveling her gaze around.

"Of course it is. We're in so far over our heads we'd have to sprout gills to keep from drowning."

They squared off, Joana's gaze so calm and sure it made Sam feel mad for even suggesting they stay. Which she probably was, considering that the voice from the woods still whispered through her dreams last night. She sighed, dropping her eyes.

"I'll be up in a minute. Really. I just . . . I need some space."

Joana shrugged one shoulder, turning to leave. "Suit yourself. But your trunk is communal property until you show up, and you know I'm terrible at packing neatly."

Maybe they were right. Staying in Dublin, trying to play hero in a game she couldn't begin to understand, it was ludicrous. And she certainly couldn't do it on her own, without Joana and Bennett. Brother Noah and the men of Solas Fíor could sort this out. They had to. Because if they didn't . . .

Sam shook her head. She couldn't contemplate it, another war. The last one had nearly destroyed her; this one would finish what was left.

CHAPTER TWENTY-SIX

Sam leaned against the front desk, waiting for the clerk to return so she could inquire after Alistair's room number, when a voice from behind caught her attention.

"Are you following me?" someone asked very sternly.

She spun around in surprise. "Oh! Alistair!"

He gave her a goofy grin. "Sorry, that was a bit sinister, wasn't it? I was trying to be clever, like they always are in the novels. But Veronica says clever isn't my strong suit."

Sam gave him a tentative smile while looking furtively around for other hotel guests. The lobby was empty, the front desk clerk still absent. But at least she had a clear path to the street and could make a break for it if Alistair tried anything—although he looked far more nervous than suspicious at the moment, toying with the brim of a bowler hat he carried.

"But look at you, here you are! In my hotel. I didn't know . . . You didn't say anything, about staying here. When I gave you the . . . the card."

"Oh!" Sam said, pulling out the card. "That's because I didn't know we would be staying here. Our original accommodations . . . fell through. Luckily, I had your card, so we had another place to stay. I was actually coming to ask after your room number so I could speak with you."

Alistair's grin widened. "So, you wanted to see me again as well? What a boon for me."

"I guess you could say that," Sam hedged.

"Excellent," Alistair said, almost to himself. "Because I thought you might like . . . Well, I suppose I don't know what you'd like. That's awfully presumptuous of me, isn't it? But I could ask, instead, couldn't I? And you could tell me if you'd like it."

"Like what?" Sam asked, her guard coming back up.

Alistair gave a hasty laugh. "I'm mucking this all up, aren't I? Veronica said I would, and I suppose she's right. I always do."

"Muck what all up?" Sam asked. She was having a hard time following the meandering path of his conversation, which distracted her from her own reasons for wanting to speak with him.

Alistair turned a light shade of pink. "Well, I was wondering if maybe you'd like to go to dinner with me? Sometime. If you have time. Which, I suppose maybe you don't, if you're here on that dig of yours. But seeing as how we're both in Dublin already, it might be . . . Well, I suppose I should just stop talking and let you answer instead."

"Alistair, are you . . . asking me on a date?"

"Oh, well, I don't . . . We don't have to call it that, if you're not . . . I mean, if you wanted to call it that, of course we could—"

"Alistair," Sam interrupted, feeling breathless once again. If this was some kind of trick to throw her off, it was working. "I wanted to find you because I need to know: What are you doing here in Dublin?"

"Oh, well, the Grand Tour business. You know, travel the world, see the sights, climb the heights." Alistair frowned. "Though really the suggestion struck me as strange when Veronica made it, considering she doesn't care to share a table at breakfast with me, much less an entire trip. Always been a slippery one, Veronica has. Hot and cold. Though our mother says she's less hot and cold and more cold and frigid. Always holding herself apart from the rest of us. I thought perhaps this trip was her way of, I don't know, trying to forge an actual connection? But it's been an odd one. First Veronica drags me to Chicago, then on this steamer to Dublin, and then we're meant to return home. Not much grandness in that tour."

Sam's stomach twisted. "Veronica arranged all of this?"

Alistair's expression cleared. "Oh, yes, down to the accommodations. Was really insistent on it, in fact. She said I'd only get it wrong, which maybe I would have. I've never been to Dublin before, but she has."

"When?" Sam asked in alarm.

Alistair scratched at a place just above his ear. "Not long ago, in fact. Maybe five or six months?"

"Oh, Alistair," Sam breathed, just as a hulking shadow fell over her.

"You should leave now, lass," came Brother Padraig's deep voice.

Sam whirled about, tilting her head back to meet the brother's eye. They were alone in the lobby, except for the five men in robes standing behind Brother Padraig.

"What are you doing here?" Sam asked, bewildered.

"Best get back to your room now," he said. "Our business is with the Fitzgerald lad."

"I'm sorry, who are you?" Alistair asked, looking between Sam and the men. "Do you know these men, Sam?"

"Sort of," Sam said, frowning. "But, Brother Padraig, please listen. It's not Alistair you're after. It's—"

"Don't tell me my own business, lass," Brother Padraig rumbled. "Now, go on, before ye make a poor choice."

"I'm sorry, but what exactly is going on?" Alistair asked, his polite veneer slipping into confusion. "I'm sure I don't know you, or what business we could possibly have with each other. I'm not . . . I'm not going anywhere with you."

"Ye will," Brother Padraig said, every word a threat. "By choice or by force."

"Please, Brother Padraig, if you would just listen," Sam said, trying to step between him and Alistair. But the other men surrounded them, putting their hands on Alistair's arms.

"Hey!" Alistair said, pulling at their grip. "Say, what is the meaning of all this. Sam? What's going on?"

"Alistair!" Sam said, trying and failing to get around Brother Padraig. "I'm sorry! I'll get you out of this somehow. I promise!"

"Don't you worry about me, Sam," Alistair replied. "Call Veronica! She'll get our mother involved, and these men will regret setting foot in here."

"Let's go," Brother Padraig said, pushing Alistair toward the hotel door.

"You've got the wrong person," Sam said resolutely.

Her only reply from Brother Padraig was a doubtful grunt. She had half a mind to punch him, or scratch his face for the damage he had done to her life. That wouldn't help Alistair, though.

But she knew something that might.

"I want to see your archives," Sam said suddenly, taking a risk and grabbing at Brother Padraig's robes. He glared down at her. "Please, ask Brother Noah if I can have access. You've got the wrong person, and I'll prove it."

"Ye'd do best to stay out of it, lass," Brother Padraig said. "Ye don't know what you're dealing with. You and your friends have done enough damage already."

"I know, but Alistair is not who you think he is. Please, ask Brother Noah if I can see the archives."

"That's Solas Fíor business," Brother Padraig said. "It's not meant for outside eyes."

"But I have something Brother Noah will want," Sam said, dropping her voice so only Brother Padraig could hear her.

He crossed his arms, standing before her like a brick wall. "What is it?"

Sam matched his expression. "I have the transcription of Father Jacob's letter. I know how to find the bowl."

He gave her a hard look. "The letter ye said ye lost?"

"We did lose it. But not before transcribing the clue he left behind."

His expression turned dark. "So, you've had the bowl this whole time? What kind of game have ye been playing at?"

"No, no," Sam said hastily. "We don't have it. But I know how to find it."

That was more than a stretch, but she needed to see those archives. Somewhere in all that history was the truth—the truth that would exonerate Alistair, and hopefully reveal the actual culprit. And maybe help her figure out what Order the letter had been talking about.

"Whatever ye know, tell it to me now," Brother Padraig said. "I don't have time for games."

Sam shook her head. "Not until Brother Noah grants me access to the archives."

He stepped forward, a menacing chill in the shadow he cast over her. "Ye know I could make ye tell me."

She tilted her chin up. "I don't have any more books to burn, Brother Padraig. If you want the transcription, you get me access."

He grunted, but he stepped back, giving her enough room to breathe. "I guess we'll be seeing each other again soon, then. My men will be watching in the meantime."

CHAPTER TWENTY-SEVEN

Sam hurried up the hotel stairs, planning her research attack as she went. Solas Fíor was convinced Alistair was their culprit, and she was just as convinced he wasn't. If anything, Veronica seemed far more suspicious. Maybe she was working with the other Hellfire Club descendants who had come to town, and Alistair had no idea of their plans. But how to prove it? Sam wasn't sure how, but she prayed the answer would be in the archives.

Somehow Joana seemed even more unpacked by the time Sam returned to the room, every conceivable surface covered in swaths of fabric and collections of shoes. Sam dodged a pile of nightgowns in the middle of the room, digging under an evening dress for her winter coat.

"What are you doing, scurrying about so secretively?" Joana asked, coming out of the bathroom holding up a day dress.

"I've got to go out," Sam said, pulling on her coat.

Joana snorted. "What, are you planning to fit a whirlwind tour of Dublin into the next thirty minutes?"

"I've got to go back to Orlagh and look through the Solas Fíor archives," Sam said. "Would you stall with Bennett for me, just for a few hours? I promise I'll be back before nightfall. Probably."

Joana tossed the dress on her bed, setting her hands on her hips. "You can't be serious, Sam. You're not going back to that cursed house."

Sam tugged on the lapels of her coat, trying to put all her half-formed thoughts into coherent words. "Look, I know what you all think, but Alistair . . . He's innocent. I just saw him in the lobby and he told me Veronica planned their whole trip. What if she's using him as a cover so she can get access to the Hellfire Club while throwing all the suspicion on him?"

"That sounds like a Veronica thing to do," Joana muttered. "I never trusted that dew dropper. But even if that's the case, let those Solas fellas handle it, Sam."

"But Alistair is in trouble now," Sam said, picking her way over mounds of clothes toward the door. "Brother Padraig just showed up and hauled him off. I'm worried they'll do something, and they're missing the real culprit right under their noses. If I can have a few hours to dig through their archives, maybe I can discover the answers. Where to find the bowl, how to stop the curse, everything."

"I guess the professor isn't the only one who's gone mad around here," Joana said, her tone hot. "I can't believe you're going to make me side with Bennett, of all people. What an unforgivable sin. Sam, you cannot go back to Orlagh. I don't care what your malarkey reasons are."

"I can't just let it go!" Sam exclaimed, pacing what little open floor space there was left. "You don't understand, Jo. If this curse is even half-real, if they really can raise the Morrigan and start a war . . . I have to do this."

Joana crossed her arms. "Then I'm coming with you."

Sam shook her head. "No, you have to stay here and stall Bennett. There's no way Brother Noah will let me look at the archives if Bennett comes storming in. I have to go alone."

"You have to, or you want to?"

"I don't . . ." Sam shook her head again. "Of course I don't want to, but I don't see any other way, Jo. And anyway, there's nothing for you to do. I'll just be digging through old documents. You'd be bored out of your mind, like you always say."

Joana tapped her foot against the carpet, her step muffled by a heap of silk underthings. She worked her jaw back and forth, her lips pressed tight together like she was afraid of what might slip out.

"This is the bookshop opening all over again," she growled finally.

"What? What do you mean?"

Joana threw her arms out, tromping over the clothes to the door and stalking back again. "I wanted to work in Daddy's shop with you, but you said it was a one-person job. I would just be bored shelving books and filling out inventory all day. It never even occurred to you that we could do it together, that I wouldn't be bored if I was with you. I really thought you had changed, Sam, but here you are, pulling this claptrap all over again. Sam the Solitary, an island unto herself. You're shutting me out all over again."

Sam floundered. "Jo, I didn't know you felt . . . You never said anything. I would never . . . I'm sorry."

"Yeah, you're always sorry," Joana said bitterly, her heel dragging through a cotton shirt. "You're sorry, but you can't come to the academy. You're sorry, but you don't want to do the treasure hunts anymore. You're sorry, but you're not ready to come back to Madame Iris's schoolhouse just yet."

Sam drew her arms around herself protectively. "Wait a minute, you're bringing up things that happened during . . . That's not fair."

"I don't care if it's fair!" Joana said, throwing her arms out. "It's how I feel. You're always sorry, but you never change! You just keep pushing me away, no matter what I do. No matter how hard I try. Ever since . . ."

She stopped, clamping her lips shut as if she were afraid the words might escape if she didn't physically stop them. But now Sam was shaking, and she wanted to hear those words. She wanted to make Joana say them. She'd forgotten all about Alistair and Solas Fíor and the bowl for the moment.

"Ever since what?" Sam said quietly.

Joana shook her head, dropping her eyes to the floor for the first time. "Never mind."

"No, say it. Ever since what? Go on. I've never known you to quit when you were on a roll; don't start on my account."

Joana raised her eyes defiantly. "Fine. Ever since your father died."

Sam had wanted to make her say it, but it didn't feel any better hearing it spoken out loud. Her face grew hot, her vision wavering.

"Was it really so hard for you?" Sam asked, her voice as watery as her eyes. "To let me be sad? To let me miss him? Was it really so hard to let it be about anybody else but you?"

"Anybody else but me?" Joana repeated in a disbelieving whisper. "You think that's what . . ." She gave a humorless huffing laugh. "You're unbelievable."

"No, *you're* unbelievable," Sam countered, standing up. She wasn't sure where these words were coming from, but that core was thawing, turning to hot magma again, spewing up seven years of frozen emotion. "You never understood. You couldn't possibly understand."

"Understand what?" Joana challenged.

Sam thrust a finger out at her. "Your father came home, and mine didn't."

Joana drew back sharply. "And are you going to keep on punishing me for that forever?"

"I'm not punishing you," Sam said, shaking her head. "I never was. I was grieving, and you couldn't just let me grieve."

"You've been grieving for seven years, Sam! I tried, honest I did. I left you alone for months after your father died! And when you didn't want to do the treasure hunts anymore, I let it be. When you took a whole year to come back to Madame Iris's classroom, I let it be. When you took the job at Daddy's bookshop the year after that and stopped coming around at all, I let it be. I came to you. But you didn't want me anymore. You didn't need me. You were all I had, Sam! You were the only good thing in all of Clement, and you shut me out. You shut yourself up in that shop and you shut me out."

Joana trembled so hard she had to sit down, tears streaking through her mascara and ruining it. Sam had never seen Joana cry, not once in their entire friendship. Not when she caught a rose thorn right through the pad of her thumb and had to have it stitched up; not when her dance instructor humiliated her in front of the whole debutante ball by stopping her mid-dance to correct her footwork; not even when she stood over the empty, symbolic grave for Sam's father. But here she was, crying now, because of Sam. Sam had made her best friend—her truest, oldest friend—cry, and for that she felt the worst kind of guilt.

"Jo," she said, not sure what to say to make her stop. A simple apology felt insulting at that point, but she didn't have anything else to offer.

"And now you've got this stupid bowl you're just hell-bent on finding, and Bennett to fawn over and the Solas Fíor archives to dig through. I'm sure I'll never see you again." Joana shook her head bitterly, standing up and waving Sam off. "Forget it, Sam. Just forget it. You've been trying to tell me for years, and I've been too stubborn and selfish to accept it. Plenty of girls shed their childhood best friends when they grow up, I don't know why I ever thought I'd be different."

"That's not . . . Don't say that."

"Why, because it's not true?" Joana gave a bitter little laugh, straightening up and flicking the tears off her face. Her mouth settled in a hard line. "No, that's all right, Sam. You go on grieving, long as you want. Keep grieving until you're dead, too."

"Jo," Sam breathed, the name coming out like a whoosh of air. It felt like that, too, like someone had put their fist right through Sam's chest.

Joana hesitated, a shade of guilt passing over her face. The moment hung between them, a chance for either of them to amend the things they said. To reset the score, erase the past, start fresh. But Sam didn't know how to shake the past; she had never known. Joana just didn't understand; she could never possibly understand.

Joana seemed to sense the direction of Sam's thoughts, because the guilt hardened into resolve and she set her jaw, wrenching the door open and storming into the hallway. Sam hurried after her. She should do something, shouldn't she? Call out to Joana, apologize, or demand an apology—*something*. Something to close the gap that only widened between them as Joana disappeared down the stairs.

"Jo, what—" came a voice from just below. Phillip appeared a second later, looking after Joana. "Where is she going?"

Sam shook her head, eyes flooding at the prospect of having to recount their fight. Phillip gave one more glance down the stairs before tucking his hands in his pockets, coming to stand beside Sam.

"Is this about earlier?" he asked, his tone soothing and sympathetic. "Because you said you wanted to stay?"

"Yes," Sam said softly. "And no. It's . . . complicated."

Phillip nodded knowingly. "Friendships often are. Listen, for what it's worth, I'm with you. We should stay, see this thing through. Bennett won't listen to reason. But people like us, we're fighters. We can't afford to give up and try again another day. It's hard for the inherited elite like Bennett and Jo, who get handed endless opportunities along with their trust funds."

Sam shook her head. "Jo and Bennett aren't like that."

At least she didn't think they were. Bennett was certainly a hard worker, even if it was his father's money that financed his education at the best institutions. And there was the business with Joana and the academy, of course. Another squandered opportunity Joana couldn't be bothered to appreciate. And the things Joana had just said to her, about her father, and their friendship . . .

Why couldn't Joana see? How frivolous and stupid and *painful* everything was after her father died? The treasure hunts, Madame Iris's arithmetic exercises, the garish parties at Steeling Manor. Why couldn't Joana see that it hurt Sam to set foot in that foyer—the last place she had stood thinking her father would come home. She'd been playing archaeologist and digging up rosebushes while her mother cried and her father lay in pieces on another continent.

Joana could never understand that kind of loss, and what it took for Sam to try to come back from it.

Phillip laid a comforting hand on her shoulder. "Why don't I go see if I can bring Jo around? If she has some time to consider it, she'll see you were right all along. We belong here. If anyone could convince the Steelings, it's you."

"I'm not sure Jo will listen to me right now." *Or ever again.*

Phillip gave her a crooked smile. "I've seen that mind of yours at work, Sam. You're capable of far more than you realize. Bennett might discount that, but I never would."

He disappeared down the stairs, leaving her feeling adrift. She couldn't have said what the right answer was just then, her churning gut telling a different story from the feverish defenses her mind made. Was she right about Joana? Or staying in Dublin?

She returned to the room and shut the door, collapsing on top of a pile of Joana's dresses that had found their way to her bed. Maybe if she lay there long enough, all of this would resolve itself and she could go on as she always had. Although now she wasn't sure that was what she wanted anymore. A heavy knock fell on the door, startling Sam out of her misery. Brother Padraig stood in the hall, striking an imposing figure. He grunted when Sam opened the door, but he made no mention of her red eyes or anguished expression. Instead his own expression turned even more pinched, like he'd just eaten an entire can of sauerkraut.

"The luck of the Irish is with you this day, lass," he said.

"It doesn't feel like it," Sam said hollowly.

He grunted again. "Brother Noah's given you permission to access our archives. I'm to take ye back to Orlagh on this fool's errand of yours. Get your things, I won't be waiting about all day."

Sam wasn't yet sure what to do about Joana, but she was the only one who could help Alistair and figure out who was really trying to invoke the curse. Her gut told her he was innocent, but the brothers would never listen to her without solid evidence from their own archives. She paused only long enough to dash off a quick note to Joana and Bennett telling them where she was going. "I've got everything I need already. Let's go."

CHAPTER TWENTY-EIGHT

Sam knew from her experience among the precious tomes of Steeling's Rare Antiquities that answers often revealed themselves only if you were patient and diligent, willing to do the work and dig to find them. And Sam was a digger. She never could resist a good puzzle, as Bennett had said. It was what had made her so good at cracking Mr. Steeling's cryptograms—her inability to give up, even in the face of insurmountable odds. Losing her father might have doused the flames of adventure, but it never changed the way her mind worked, looking for patterns in the chaos. She had simply turned the cogs of her brain away from the buried secrets of the earth to the buried secrets of antique books.

All those countless hours in the shop were serving her well now as she methodically made her way through the mess of the Solas Fíor archives. And what a mess it was. These men might be fastidious in their dedication to their Order, but they were not careful in their record keeping. There was no filing system, no reference key or intake form for tracking the entries, no update log for when new files were added or old ones taken out, and, most distressingly, no clear path through the collection of filing cabinets and boxes. They had pieces of stonework leaning on thin glass bottles filled with black liquid, piles of cloth that made an ominous squeaking noise whenever she disturbed the edges, and stacks of loose papers on top of cabinets, between boxes, and scattered on the floor, and one sheet had somehow found itself wedged in the beams supporting the ceiling.

If she had the time and cleaning supplies, Sam could have happily spent the rest of the month cleaning and organizing and restoring order to the chaos. No wonder these barbarians had destroyed her books; they didn't know any better.

But she didn't have time, and cleaning up this mess wouldn't bring back her old life. So she contented herself with straightening up a few loose stacks of paper before heading for the trunk that contained all their knowledge on the Hellfire Club. Brother Noah also provided the registry of living Hellfire Club descendants, which she had gone a little cross-eyed squinting over, but it had turned up nothing useful except for one poet laureate who was apparently descended from the wildest of the club's founders. Sam had given Brother Noah the letter's coded message—*Follow the Order*—in exchange for her access, though Brother Noah seemed like he felt he'd gotten the short end of the bargain when she could provide no further context.

"What's that you're doing there, miss?" asked Amos, the young almost brother who had aided in her kidnapping, from the door of the archive closet.

"Organizing," Sam muttered, pulling the scattered documents and diaries out of the trunk and placing them in piles on the floor. "At least, I'm trying to."

"You're making a bit of a mess," Amos said doubtfully. "Brother Noah won't like that."

Sam looked up, her gaze sweeping around the disorganization of the room. "I don't know how you could possibly tell."

"Oh, I suppose you've got a point there," Amos said, scratching at the tight weave of curls adorning his head. "We always mean to tidy the place up, but we never seem to find the time."

"I don't know how any of you have kept tabs on anything with this mess," Sam said, her voice taking on a chiding tone. "Look at the state of these logs. These must be at least a hundred years old, and wearing their ages poorly. This one's spine is badly damaged, and the binding is coming loose as well. You'll need it repaired if you don't want it disintegrating in your hands."

Amos picked his way through the mess to sit on the floor beside her. He studiously avoided looking at her folded legs in the jodhpurs Joana had picked out for Sam. She would have been annoyed if he wasn't so earnest about his attempts to be respectful. For her part, she thought the pants were fantastic. Comfortable and fashionable, functional and warm. And they had pockets. She wasn't sure she would ever go back to long skirts again.

"Brother Padraig told me you were some kind of book fixer," Amos said. He lowered his head. "We truly are sorry for what happened with your books. Brother Padraig is like the rough edges of an old stone, but he's not a bad man. He never meant for those books to burn. It were an accident."

"I know," Sam said, setting aside one book and reaching for the next. "But sorry doesn't bring them back. Sometimes apologies aren't enough."

She hesitated, her fingers stalling on a list of names as a wave of emotion rose in her throat and filled her eyes. She couldn't think about Joana right now. She had a job to do; she could worry about the state of their friendship later.

"What is it you're looking for, if you don't mind my asking, miss?" Amos asked, leaning forward to watch her fingers as they skated down the page.

"I don't know," Sam murmured. "And call me Sam, please. You did kidnap me, after all. I think we're on more intimate terms than 'miss.'"

"All right, Sam," Amos said, testing out the name. "If you don't know what you're looking for, then how can you know when you've found it?"

Sam reached the last page of the log, closing it with a sigh and noting the date on the cover. 1848. At this rate she'd be an old woman before she made it through all of them. She paused, considering the stacks of logbooks gathering dust.

"You might have a point," she said, frowning at the trunk. "I really do believe things will reveal themselves if you only go looking."

"But you've got to have somewhere to start, don't you?"

"Somewhere to start," Sam murmured, tapping one finger on her knee. "I've been going at this backward, literally and figuratively. Solas Fíor knows all about the descendants of the Hellfire Club today. I need to go back to the beginning, to the start of the club, and find whatever it is they've missed."

"How can ye be so sure we've missed anything, mis—er, Sam?" Amos gave a vague wave to the floors of the country house above them. "Brother Noah and the others know what business they're about. They wouldn't go accusing your friend without good cause."

Sam shook her head. "No, they're wrong about Alistair; I don't care what they say. He was kind to me. He helped me, even when he didn't have to. And I don't think it's Professor Wallstone either. The magic seems to have . . . infected him. Like it was done to him, instead of him choosing it. I know it sounds odd; I can't really explain it. There's something we're all missing. And I won't leave these archives until I find it. Or until somebody invokes the curse and starts a war. Whichever comes first."

"Solas Fíor won't let that happen," Amos said resolutely.

"Neither will I, if I can help it," Sam said, pulling the original Hellfire Club logbook Brother Noah had shared with her the previous evening. Father Jacob's neat script greeted her like an old friend, and for a moment she considered the history she held in her hands, the weight of skin and oil and breath these pages held. She read through the introduction on the opening page, citing the reasons for the formation of Solas Fíor and their purpose.

"So, the Dublin Hellfire Club was founded by Richard Parsons, the first earl of Rosse and grandmaster of the Freemasons of Dublin?" Sam said as she read.

"Aye, and what a cock-up he was," said Amos. He tilted his head to the side. "He was fed up with what he'd seen of organized religion, so he started the Hellfire Club as a way of thumbing his nose at the strictures of religion and society. Started as a bunch of drinking and whor—ah, well."

He cleared his throat, his face blooming into a bright pink that made his hair stand out. "It's not fit for mixed company. But it's enough to say their relations with women of a certain class weren't sanctioned by any kind of church. They were copying the English Hellfire Club, the original one founded by Sir Francis Dashwood. Wicked lads they were, the English. Bought an abbey and held all their meetings there, getting fluthered on wine in caves they dug beneath it. My guess is, old Parsons wanted to one-up the English by establishing his club at a place everybody considered cursed by the devil himself. Give it that extra flair of debauchery."

Sam thought it sounded far too much like Georgie Heath and the other boys getting plastered out at his father's barn every night and waking up cuddled next to the pigs in the morning. You could give men money and titles, but they'd all end up drunk in a field yelling their grievances at the sky.

"I suppose they weren't prepared for the lodge actually being cursed?" Sam asked.

Amos shrugged. "Whether or not they started out believing it, I couldn't say. But they certainly ended that way. So the story goes, the man who built it—William Conolly, a wealthy old crust of a man and speaker of the Irish House of Commons—had the lodge constructed by tearing out the stones of a tomb on the hill. The devil objected to the desecration by blowing the roof off the place. So, Speaker Conolly tore out more stones to put a new roof on. But he died only a couple of years later, and it was abandoned until the Hellfire Club took the lease on it. What started out as drinking and carousing soon enough turned into devil worship, Black Masses, and human sacrifice."

"It says here Richard Parsons had one son, the second earl of Rosse," Sam said, "But there's nothing after that."

"Aye, he was the last of them," said Amos. "Didn't have any children. The line died out with the son."

"But who is this?" Sam asked, pointing to an entry scribbled on the side, hasty and smudged. "What does that say? Elgor? Ehnor?"

Amos tilted his head to the side. "Looks like Eleanor. Seems I maybe recall something about an Eleanor. An Englishwoman, somebody important. Maybe a marquess's daughter? There were always rumors about proper women being associated with the club on the sly. Could be she was somebody's mistress."

Sam tapped the addendum. "I know this handwriting. Father Jacob wrote this. Why would he put her name here? Who is she? What happened to her?"

Amos shrugged. "Search me. There's nothing else in the register about her?"

Sam flipped through the next few pages, the dates moving into the late 1740s and beyond with no mention of Eleanor. "There's nothing. It's like she disappeared."

Amos's face cleared. "Disappeared, that's right. Now I remember, she was mistress to the earl of Rosse. I think it was her that ran off to America after he gave her the heave-ho. Probably too ashamed to go back to England. Or she got in the family way like me poor cousin Siobhán. Me aunt shipped her out to Galway for five months and she came back empty-bellied and mean as an alley cat."

"But if she had a child, wouldn't it have been included here, in the register?" Sam asked, flipping back to the first page. "There's nothing."

"Could be if it were a bastard, the brothers wouldn't have bothered with keeping tabs on it back then. If the earl didn't claim the child, then it didn't have any rightful claims to the lodge or the hill."

Those boys at Oxford built their high walls out of the stones of their reputation; they wouldn't let some . . . bastard come and knock it down. A sinking feeling started in Sam's chest, turning the register into a leaden weight that pressed on her legs. She couldn't be right; she hoped she wasn't. The evidence was speculative—flimsy and circumstantial. Just because Phillip had been born out of wedlock didn't make him a suspect. Just because he had come to Dublin to explore the Hellfire Club didn't make him a suspect either. Even if he had access to the professor all this time, to whisper influences and infect him with the magic. And that cough . . . What if those dark stains hadn't been blood? But these were just . . . ideas. She could be worse than the brothers, levying accusations without proper proof. She needed the whole truth. She was too close to an answer to let it go now.

"Amos, I need you to think very hard," she said, her voice soft and urgent. He was her best chance at finding the truth. "I need to know anything else you can remember about Eleanor. Where she was from, her family name, anything the brothers might have discovered about her when she went to America. Any of it. What else do you know?"

Amos scratched at his scalp, sending curls flopping about. "I don't know as how I know much more. Brother Noah is a better one to ask than me. He knows the Solas Fíor business inside and out. Shall I fetch him? Oh, but he might be up the hill with Brother Padraig."

"There's no time for that, Amos. Please, there has to be . . . You must know something. You've been training all this time to be a brother, right? You must know at least as much as Brother Noah by now."

Amos puffed up where he sat. "Aye, I have been putting in my time with the archives, sure enough. And I'll be ready for the orders come spring."

Sam leaned forward, taking both his wrists in a viselike grip. "Then prove it here, now. What do you remember about Eleanor?"

Amos scrunched his face up. "I might remember a name, something to do with plants. Thornwood, or Thornberg. No, that's not quite it, is it? Maybe Thornrose or Rosethorn? Do those sound like names?"

Sam's skin rippled into goose bumps, an electric current of warning. "Was it Rosewood?"

Amos snapped his fingers. "Rosewood, that's it! Eleanor Rosewood, she was."

Phillip's monogrammed handkerchief. He'd said it belonged to his ancestor. Richard Rosewood.

Sam dumped the book on the floor in her haste to stand up, the precious history no concern to her now. "Amos, I need you to drive me back to the hotel as fast as you can."

Amos scrambled up beside her, knocking over a box of papers and spilling them across the floor. "Why, what's gone off?"

"I think I know who's trying to invoke the curse," Sam said breathlessly.

CHAPTER TWENTY-NINE

Sam sprinted out of the car before Amos had time to turn off the engine, waving away his calls of concern as she sped through the hotel doors. Maybe she was wrong, but the sick churn of her stomach and the buzzing in her back teeth told the truth. The facts were all there, too conveniently lined up to be wrong. She knew how to see the patterns in the chaos, and this one was screaming at her.

"Jo," she said as she burst into their room. It was empty, which was no surprise, but it only made Sam's stomach rumble more ominously. Something was very, very wrong.

"Hi, Sam," said a voice from the far side of the room.

Sam gasped and whirled around as Phillip emerged from a darkened corner, the shadows slithering away from him like a cloak sliding off his shoulders. She stumbled back a step, her leg bumping the edge of Joana's bed, the linens still rumpled. A faint waft of Joana's shampoo rose from the twisted sheets.

"Phillip," Sam breathed, turning toward the door. But then Phillip was there, blocking her way out. It wasn't possible for someone to move that fast.

"Not yet," he said, his eyes intensely black as he stared down at her. His voice was darker, too, and rougher around the edges. Even his blond hair was tinged in wings of unnatural black. "You and I need to have a little chat."

"Where is Jo?" she asked.

"Oh, Joana is secured," Phillip said, trailing one hand across the mess of clothes Joana had left strewn on her bed, still unpacked after she stormed out. The fight seemed ages ago, Sam's reasons so flimsy and selfish. "I told you I would bring her around."

"Phillip, if you hurt her—"

"Oh please, don't insult either of us by making threats," Phillip said. "I know you've been to Orlagh and done your digging, which means you know I hold all the power right now. And I also know you have the answers I need. There was more to that diary, wasn't there? Something that slipped away with you when you went out the porthole."

"*You* broke into our stateroom," Sam said, the realization like an avalanche of snow down the back of her coat collar.

"And I saw the drawings on the wall." Phillip tilted his head. "Curious, that a Catholic priest would use ogham to hide his messages. Clever, really. Who would expect a holy man to use the secret language of the heathen Celts? Where is the letter?"

Sam shook her head. "It's gone. I lost it when I went out the window."

Phillip moved around her, surrounding her with a chill that lingered like a coat of frost. "But you know what it said. I've watched you, Sam. You're the only one of them with any brains in your head, like me. Joana and Bennett, they've grown soft, relying on their father's wealth to carry them through the world. But you and I, we've had to carve our own ways. It's made us stronger than they could ever hope to be, and smarter. Whatever secrets Father Jacob tried to hide in that letter, I know you uncovered them."

"Phillip, please, think about what you're doing," Sam begged, rubbing her arms to try and bring some feeling back in them. She edged toward the door when his back was turned. "This magic, it's not . . . Look what it's done to you, to the professor! It will destroy you if you don't fight it."

Phillip cut his gaze to her. "Why would I fight it? I was *born* with it."

Sam froze. "How is that possible?"

His lips curled into a grin, his teeth digging into the soft flesh of his lower lip. "It would be a boring story, if it didn't have such a satisfying conclusion. A young woman of good standing, infatuated with an earl, follows him to Ireland to become his whore."

"Eleanor Rosewood," Sam said. And although she had already put those particular pieces together, it brought her no satisfaction to have solved the puzzle this time. Instead it filled her ears with a low buzzing, a warning of what was to come.

Phillip's smile twisted. "Eleanor offered the earl the only thing of value she had—her virtue. And in turn, he introduced her to the depravities of his Hellfire Club. Any other daughter of a marquess might have fainted at their revelries, but Eleanor sank into the indulgence like a queen on silk sheets. These men shunned everything she loathed about proper society, and they had the time of their lives doing it. She drank and laughed and whored them under the table, playing the part of the fallen woman in their Black Masses with glee. And she wanted more. While most of those idiots were content to toast the devil, Eleanor knew the true value of the cairn. It was Eleanor that gathered its secrets—lore of the Druids who worshipped there, magic spells half-remembered by the locals. She kept them in a book and shared her secrets with her lover. She made him the most powerful man in Ireland, and in return he made her a pariah."

"He cast her off," Sam said, recalling what Amos had said.

"Grew cold on her, as men in power will do," Phillip said, hyp-notizing Sam with the fluidity of his movements. "Cast out by her family, spurned by her lover, she fled to the colonies and the hope of a new life there. But she didn't leave alone."

Sam couldn't help herself, as drawn into the story as she was. "She had a baby."

"Not just any baby. A bastard child, conceived on the grounds of the Hellfire Club during a Black Mass. A baby that carried the magic in its tiny, beating heart. She also took the spell book, which contained the unfinished details of a ritual that could restore her child to his rightful place at the earl's side. A curse that would call the Morrigan, Celtic goddess of war, to punish their enemies and grant the sovereignty of the high kingship to whoever called her. Eleanor thought she could make a new Hellfire Club in the wilds of America. But the magic wasn't what it was in Ireland. Here the stones are forged in it, the ground saturated with it. Ireland is the domain of the Morrigan as the goddess of the land. All Eleanor had left of the magic was the splinter in her baby's heart."

"A splinter that passed down to you," Sam said, realization set-ting in. "That's what you meant, that you were born with it. The magic has always been there, hasn't it? Inside you."

"See?" Phillip said. "I told you, you're worth more than the entire Steeling line put together. Six months I've known Bennett, and he never even suspected. He couldn't believe it, even with his own eyes telling him. I thought he would interfere with my work with Professor Wallstone, but he was so convinced of his version of the truth he was blind to the reality."

"You've been poisoning him all along," Sam said. "But why Professor Wallstone?"

"Because he was the perfect Trojan horse for my needs. He

already had a reputation for his tangential archaeological obsessions. I only had to give him a little nudge to send him in the right direction."

"You drove him mad," Sam said, her voice soft but accusing.

Phillip tilted his head in concession. "An unfortunate side effect, as it derailed my plans. I needed him to gain access to the archives, not get himself locked up. So I had to improvise. I needed a way to draw the brothers out."

Sam sucked in a soft breath. "It was you. You raised the Hellfire Cat."

"And what a glorious beast he is," Phillip said, a tendril of smoke drifting out of his mouth on a sigh as he lifted his gaze to the ceiling. "I didn't have the power to call him, at first. Eleanor's spells were often incomplete, or incoherent. A product of the revelry. But with Father Jacob's diary, I had a secondary source, Eyewitness accounts to the rituals they performed. Thanks to you."

"I would have thrown it out the window of the ship if I had known."

Phillip gave a laugh that dropped the air in the room ten degrees cooler. "I admire your attempts at fortitude, Sam. But there's no need to fight me. When I am made Divine King of a new world, I will remember your service, however unwitting or unwilling it was. I will be a gracious king to those who deserve it. Better than my predecessors."

"Phillip, this can't be what you really want," Sam said, begging him to see reason. "The last great war of man? It would destroy people's lives. Good people—people like my father—would die. You know what it is to lose someone you love, like your mother. You can't wish the same fate on others."

"Someone I love?" Phillip said incredulously. "I *hated* my mother."

Sam stumbled back a step from the viciousness of his words. "What?"

Phillip stalked closer to her, his entire presence a menace as he leaned in. "Do you have any idea what a monster she was? What the splinter in her heart had done to her? It poisoned us, all of us, punishing us for trying to deny it. Richard Rosewood thought he could redeem himself from his mother's shame by pulling himself up by his bootstraps, the American way. And for that he got a bayonet to the gut by a redcoat in the War for Independence. It withered our crops when we tried to farm; blighted our bets when we traded on the stock market; poisoned our sheep when we tried textiles. It made my grandfather shoot his best friend on a hunting trip; it made my mother poison the wife of her lover, my father; and it led me to that unfortunate business with the lad who disappeared in Oxford."

He snarled, a feral sound reminiscent of the Hellfire Cat. "I tried to be what they wanted. My father, a peer of the realm; my mother, hanging all her selfish hopes on me. But I wasn't good enough for them. I wasn't *pure* enough for them. I was a bastard, like Eleanor's son, and those blue bloods at Oxford tossed me into the cold like the earl did to Eleanor. Two hundred years of progress, and nothing has changed. I decided I would make the change myself."

"By invoking the curse," Sam said, glancing at the door. If she screamed, would Bennett hear her? Was he even there? What would Phillip do if she tried?

"Yes. But we can't have a ritual without a ritual vessel, can we? For that, I need you."

She broke for the door, but once again Phillip was there faster, pinning her against the wall with one hand beside her head and the other on the doorknob. She cringed, drawing up her shoulders as if that would protect her from the malevolence emanating off him.

"I need that bowl, Sam," he said, his breath like the dirt of a tomb. "And you're going to find it for me, or you'll never see Joana again."

"Phillip," Sam gasped, turning her head from him. "Please don't do this."

"It's already done, Sam. Almost. Two hundred years of scrabbling in the mud, every door closed in our face. But I am on the precipice of forging a new fate, and I won't let anything stand in my way."

He straightened up so suddenly Sam could only gasp in relief. "You have until sundown tomorrow to bring me the bowl at the Hellfire Club."

"No, Phillip, please!" Sam cried, reaching out to grab his jacket but coming away with only a puff of smoke.

"Don't fail, Sam," Phillip said, pulling the door open. In the dim light he was nothing more than a shadow, his eyes gleaming red. "Because if you do, Joana will be the one to suffer. You have one day."

CHAPTER THIRTY

Sam rushed into the hallway, but it was already empty. Where had he gone? *How* had he gone? It wasn't possible for him to move so quickly. None of this was possible, and yet she couldn't seem to wake up. It was worse than a nightmare come to life, because even in her worst dreams she never imagined losing Joana like this.

A figure appeared on the stairs, and for a moment Sam feared it was Phillip returning to deliver some worse ultimatum. But it was Bennett, back from the docks. His expression shifted in surprise the moment he set eyes on Sam, taking the last few stairs two at a time. He tucked the steamer tickets he carried into his coat pocket.

"What is it?" he asked, taking her by the shoulders. "What's wrong?"

She looked up at him, trying to anchor herself to the earth by the weight of his hands on her arms and the concern on his face.

"It's Phillip," she said, her voice rusty and shivering. "He has Jo."

He pulled back in alarm. "What do you mean he has Jo? What happened?"

"Phillip is the one trying to invoke the curse," Sam said. "It's been him all along. He raised the Hellfire Cat, poisoned the professor, stole the diary from our stateroom. Brother Padraig took Alistair, but they have it all wrong. Phillip's got it in his head about some Divine Kingship, that it's his birthright. I tried to talk him out of it, Bennett, I did, but he was . . . The magic, it's too much a part of him. And he's taken Jo, and if I don't find the bowl and bring it to the Hellfire Club before the eclipse tomorrow, he's going to . . ."

She tried to breathe, but there didn't seem to be enough air left in the chilly hallway to fill her lungs. She couldn't finish that sentence, couldn't even finish the thought. Never seeing Joana again . . . It wasn't possible. None of this was possible.

"Bennett, what are we going to do?" she gasped.

"All right, Sam, it's all right," Bennett said, drawing her in close and wrapping his arms tight around her. She buried her face in his chest, just for the moment letting someone else shoulder her burdens. How many times had she imagined—*dreamed*—of Bennett holding her like this? And now all she could do was use his strength to stop her own from fleeing entirely.

"We have to find the bowl," Sam said, her voice edging close to a sob. "If we don't, we'll never see Jo again."

"We can't just bring him the bowl," Bennett said, his words rumbling under her cheek. "If you're right about this magic, bringing him the bowl will give him everything he needs."

Sam pulled back. "It's Jo, Bennett. We can't abandon her."

"I know that," Bennett said, shoving a hand through his hair. "She's my sister, after all. But we have no guarantee he'll even free Jo if we bring the bowl. He could kill us all on the spot. I'll go to the Hellfire Club. I'll get Jo back somehow, without giving up the bowl."

Sam shook her head. "You're not going there alone."

Bennett frowned. "I won't put you in harm's way as well."

The terror of her encounter with Phillip was hardening into a stubborn resolve. "Well, I won't let you just . . . waltz into harm's way without me."

"I'm not waltzing into anything. I'll call the police, or Brother Noah, whatever backup I need. But he's already kidnapped Jo. I can't have anything happen to you, Sam."

"Phillip has Jo because of me. I should have been with her. I should never have . . . We're better together, Bennett. All of us— you, me, Jo—we're better together. I forgot that, for a long time. But I won't forget it now. We do this together."

"Sam—"

Sam held up a hand. "Even if you try to stop me, I'll just sneak after you. So you might as well agree to have me along now and save me the trouble of subterfuge."

Bennett took a breath, studying her face. "Then we need a plan. A real one. Following the Order of St. Augustine wasn't the answer."

Sam blew out a long breath. "I know. But we've got one day to figure it all out."

$$+ \ \vdash \ \overset{||||}{} \ {}^{||}\!\! \ \ \overline{||||} \ \ {}_{|||} \ /\!/ \ \vdash$$

Sam stood before the papers pinned to her hotel room wall, frowning at the ogham characters they had transcribed once more on scraps of hotel stationery. "We're missing something!" she cried, slapping a hand against the ogham character for the letter *E*, a vertical line down the middle with four lines drawn horizontally through it. "It's right in front of us, it has to be. But we can't see it. We need more information."

"What we need is the right information," Bennett said, standing behind her. He waved his hand to encompass the stretch of papers they had filled through the evening, snatching only a few hours of sleep between them and rising with the sun to keep working. Each minute that ticked down, bringing them closer to the eclipse, was like another needle dragging across Sam's skin, until her whole body prickled with awareness.

Sam shook her head. "But how do we get it? We followed the Order—that nearly got us eaten up by the Hellfire Cat. I went through the archives—that nearly got *me* eaten up by Phillip. Where would the answer be, if not in the archives?"

Bennett scratched at his chin, considering the aicmí. "Well, the Order of St. Augustine didn't purchase Orlagh until the 1800s. Which means that wherever Father Jacob kept those registers, it wasn't at Orlagh."

"Where did the Order of St. Augustine worship before they bought Orlagh?" Sam asked.

"I don't know, Professor Wallstone didn't say."

Sam hesitated, looking at the connecting wall like she could see through the wood to the other room. "Do you think we could . . . ask the professor?"

Bennett frowned at the wall, like it had somehow disappointed him. "I'm not sure that's the best idea. When I checked in on him earlier, he was trying to break the window open with the soap dish. He said the bathtub tried to possess him."

Sam turned to him, an edge of desperation to her voice. "He's all we've got right now, Bennett. We have to try."

Bennett heaved a sigh. "This isn't even remotely a good idea, but let's do it."

They quietly opened the door, Bennett holding a hand to keep her back while he checked to make sure no one else was in the hallway. Sam thought about how Phillip had somehow cloaked himself in shadows, hiding in plain sight in the corner of her room.

But the hall was bright from the early-afternoon sunlight, with no pockets of shadow deep enough to hide a full-grown man, even a magical one.

"Let me do the talking," Bennett said in a low voice, unlocking the door as quietly as possible. "He's still . . . fragile."

"That's fine by me," Sam said in the same tone. She had no interest in getting tackled again by the small British man.

Bennett hesitated, his hand on the doorknob. "And I hope you know, the state the room is in right now, it's not . . . my ideal."

Sam tilted her head to the side. "What do you mean?"

Bennett fidgeted, seeming uncomfortable. "I mean, if it were just me, the room would be . . . tidier."

"Oh, of course I know that," Sam said, shaking her head. "I've seen your room in Steeling Manor. Why does that matter now?"

"It doesn't," Bennett said after a moment. He shook himself. "Right, of course it doesn't matter. Okay, here goes."

The smell wasn't quite as strong as the basement in Orlagh, but it still charged out of the room like a wild creature set free as soon as Bennett pulled the door open. Sam stepped behind him, willing to let him take the brunt of whatever attack the professor had planned. Luckily there was no assault forthcoming, and Bennett advanced cautiously into the room.

"Professor Wallstone?" he called, loud and authoritative. "Professor, it's me, Bennett Steeling. Are you awake?"

The room was dim, and what little of it Sam could make out was in more disarray than Joana in mid-packing frenzy. There were clothes everywhere, furniture dragged into odd formations like protective walls, with blankets slung over the top of them like some kind of childhood fort.

"Did the professor . . . sleep under there?" Sam whispered, pointing at the odd arrangement.

Bennett's nostrils flared. "He's been calling it his office. He held hours yesterday."

That didn't do much to bolster Sam's confidence in the professor, but he was their only hope at the moment. Bennett lifted an edge of the blanket, peering into the dimness under the chairs before straightening up.

"He must be in the bathroom," he said.

Sure enough, a faint muttering trickled out from under the bathroom door, the professor's unmistakable cadence sounding even more anxious. Bennett met Sam's gaze, both of them frowning.

"Should we . . . open it?" Sam asked finally.

"I guess we'd better," Bennett said heavily. He raised his voice, knocking loudly. "Professor Wallstone, it's Bennett. I'm opening up, all right?"

Sam braced herself as Bennett pulled the door open, but the assault that greeted her was of a visual kind. The professor stood in the tiny bathroom in a button-down shirt, and a bow tie neatly tied with a matching pair of red suspenders. But instead of pants, his suspenders were clipped to his underwear, his legs and feet bare and showing the cracked and yellowed nails on his toes.

"Oh," Sam said softly, turning away.

"Professor, where are your pants?" Bennett asked in a pained voice.

"Too tight, couldn't think," the professor said. "Say, Master Steeling, is that you?"

Bennett took a deep breath. "Professor, do you think you could put on . . . something? Sam and I have some questions for you."

"What is a Sam?" the professor asked, bewildered.

"I'm a Sam," Sam said, holding up her hand.

"Master Steeling, you brought a female student to your quarters? How wholly inappropriate."

Bennett turned an appealing shade of pink. "It's Samantha Knox, Professor. The book-repair girl I told you about?"

"The one in your hometown? What are we doing back in Illinois?"

"Let's get you some pants, Professor." Bennett sighed.

"At least he sounds lucid," Sam murmured. "Well, intelligible."

Bennett managed to find the missing pair of pants and coaxed the professor to put them on, even though the British man complained loudly that his hair hurt from the static in the wool fabric. Bennett dismantled a few of the chairs of his "office" and managed to corral the professor into a seat.

"Professor, we need to ask you some questions about the Order of St. Augustine," Bennett said, speaking loudly and slowly.

"Why are you talking like that, Master Steeling? Is there a child present?" Professor Wallstone demanded.

"Professor Wallstone," Sam intervened, "what do you know of the Order of St. Augustine's existence in Dublin in the eighteenth century?"

The professor turned wild eyes on her, the smudges on his glasses obscuring the deep black of his irises. "What a fascinating question. Who are you again?"

"Professor," Bennett said, his voice strained. "What can you tell us about where the Order would have worshipped in 1741?"

"Ah, you mean where would *Father Jacob* have worshipped," the professor said, pushing up his glasses. "Astute, very astute. For of course you know that the Order of St. Augustine did not always hold their novitiate at Orlagh Country House. They only purchased the house in the late 1800s, long after Lundy Foot built it."

"Yes, we know all that, Professor," Bennett said. "But where would Father Jacob have worshipped before then?"

The professor scratched at the stubble on his chin, tilting his head thoughtfully. "I suppose that would have been John's Lane

Church. Though of course it wouldn't have been called such in Father Jacob's time."

"What is John's Lane Church?" Sam asked.

"Ah, a very grand affair, much too ornate for my taste, but of course that was the way of the Gothic architects. Edward Welby Pugin designed it in the 1860s. The spire was really the crowning glory, though, and that was done by William Hague."

"But if it was built in the 1860s, Father Jacob wouldn't have worshipped there," Sam said, disappointed. Another dead end.

"Well, no, not in the revival style, but he would have worshipped at the medieval Norman monastery on the original site. It was built by Aelred the Palmer for the Crossed Friars who served under the Rule of St. Augustine. There was also a hospital on the site, much more famous than the crumbling little church ruins."

The more the professor spoke, the more Sam could see the glimmer of his former self emerging. It even seemed like his eyes had lightened up, streaks of blue peeking through the deep black. She could understand Bennett worshipping this man.

"Where is John's Lane Church?" she asked.

"Ah, well, they call it John's Lane because it sits at the corner of John's Lane and Thomas Street in the heart of medieval Dublin. But it is dedicated to both St. Augustine and St. John."

"Thomas Street," Bennett said, turning to Sam. "I know that name, I passed it on my way back from the ticket office. It's only a few blocks from here."

Sam didn't dare to get her hopes up, but her heart raced faster. "Maybe we'll find what we're looking for there. It's worth having a look, isn't it?"

"Professor Wallstone, Sam and I have to step out for a bit," Bennett said, raising his voice again. "Will you be all right while I'm gone? Should I have someone come look after you?"

"How preposterous, Master Steeling," the professor chirped in an offended voice. "I am not a child to be looked after. Besides which, my office hours are about to begin. I'll be taking appointments from now until the evening, most likely."

The glimmer of blue faded from his eyes as the professor hunched over, sliding down to the floor and crawling under the remaining chairs. The crease between Bennett's eyebrows deepened.

"And do shut the door on your way out, Master Steeling," the professor said.

"I think he means the chairs," Sam whispered. "He wants us to put the chairs back."

Bennett sighed, pinching the bridge of his nose. "Let's check out John's Lane Church."

CHAPTER THIRTY-ONE

John's Lane Church was indeed a Gothic Revival masterpiece, the redbrick facade decorated with stone reliefs of various saints, and the church spire towering over every other squat building on Thomas Street. Statues of St. John and St. Augustine flanked the arched wooden doors leading into the church, both of them holding out their hands like a benediction. Sam stopped before the wrought-iron gates, hoping they were praying for her success.

"What are we looking for?" Bennett asked, studying the exterior of the building as if Father Jacob might have left a great big arrow somewhere.

"I don't know," Sam said, doing the same thing. "This structure didn't exist in Father Jacob's time, but this is the site of the old church. Maybe he . . . I don't know, buried the bowl? We could walk the grounds, look for clues."

"And if we don't find any?" Bennett asked.

Sam shook her head, staring up at the stone face of St. Augustine. "Then we try something else. We try everything else until we find the bowl and rescue Joana."

She felt Bennett's eyes on her, the corner of his lip curling up in a rare smile. She blushed. "What? Why are you looking at me like that?"

"Because if anyone else said it, I wouldn't believe them. But I know you will. You never stopped, no matter how difficult the encryptions or obscure the clues, you never quit a hunt until you found the treasure. Sometimes you wouldn't even sleep. It would drive Joana nutty. I always admired that about you, your determination."

"Oh," Sam said, caught by surprise at the compliment. She'd had so few of them in her lifetime, it was a greater gift than even the rarest books she'd ever received at the shop. "Thank you, Bennett."

He cleared his throat, suddenly finding an intense interest in the stone carvings over the church door. "We should probably start our search."

"Oh, okay, yes." Sam dropped her head, moving through the gate at the same moment that the main church doors creaked open and a boy in distinctive robes with curly red hair appeared.

"Amos?" Sam said in surprise. "What are you doing here?"

"Miss Knox?" he replied with equal surprise. "Oh, er, sorry. Sam. What're you doing here?"

Sam glanced at Bennett, neither of them wanting to reveal their true intentions. "Sightseeing," Sam said vaguely.

"Oh, aye, John's Lane Church is a fine destination, then," Amos said happily. He frowned. "Though it seems an inopportune time, with the eclipse this evening and all."

Sam smiled faintly. "Yes. We're actually . . . looking for somewhere to watch the eclipse. You know, experience it as they did two hundred years ago."

As far as excuses went, it wasn't her finest, but Amos seemed to accept it in his preoccupied state. He gazed up at St. Augustine's patient stare, a desperate tinge to his own expression.

"But what are you doing here?" she asked, hoping to redirect him from questioning their motives.

"Oh, that's not important, is it?" Amos said, suspiciously avoiding her eyes.

Bennett stepped forward, putting on his best Steeling business voice. "Amos, is it? What are you doing here, Amos, that you don't want to tell us about?"

Amos slouched a little, tugging at the sleeve of his robe like a young child would. It reminded Sam that he was still of a tender, in between age. "If ye must know, I was here on a personal matter."

"What kind of personal matter?" Sam asked.

"A personal one," Amos said.

Bennett crossed his arms. "How do we know you're not the one looking to invoke the curse?"

Amos popped upright in horror. "I would never, sir!"

Bennett lifted a brow at him "And yet here you are, all on your own and looking suspicious on the very day of the eclipse, which you yourself just pointed out."

"I'm not looking suspicious!" Amos protested, swiveling his gaze to Sam. "Honest, Miss Knox, I'm not! I was seeking the counsel of St. Augustine. Brother Noah said I showed poor judgment, blabbing to you as I did that night of the Hellfire Cat. He said he thinks maybe I'm not ready to take my vows so soon this spring if I would give away the secrets of the brothers to a stranger so easily. So, I was seeking the wisdom of St. Augustine, as a true brother would."

"Wisdom," Sam murmured, tilting her head back to take in the great height of the church. Something nagged at the corners of her mind, a thread left un-pulled. "What is the motto of Solas Fíor, Amos?"

"I don't know as how I should be telling ye, miss," Amos said. "Brother Noah already gave out to me once on your account."

He hung his head, and if Sam hadn't been in such a rush to save her best friend, she might have taken a moment to feel sorry for him. As it was, she needed his help, not his self-pity.

"Amos," she said, her voice as sharp and commanding as she'd ever made it. He jerked his head up in surprise at her tone, and frankly she was a little surprised herself. "I don't want to be a pill about this, but you owe me."

"I owe you?" he said. "Why?"

"For holding me prisoner," she said. "And for . . . for bringing the tea in cold."

"Well, it wasn't cold when I brought it," he protested, though he hung his head again. "I did feel bad about the prisoner bit, though."

"Well, now you can make it up to me," Sam said. "What is the motto?"

"'May the hazel bring you wisdom,'" Amos said glumly. "St. Augustine was praised for his wisdom."

"The hazel tree is also associated with wisdom in Celtic lore," Bennett said.

Sam closed her eyes, trying to envision the last lines of the letter from Father Jacob. *May the hazel bring you wisdom, and the aspen guide and protect you.*

She opened her eyes again, her heartbeat picking up to a rapid pace as she pulled Bennett aside. "What if he didn't just mean the Order of St. Augustine? What if he meant the literal *order*?"

"The benediction," Bennett said, his expression opening up in comprehension.

"What if it's not just a benediction?"

Bennett's eyes glowed. "It's a map."

Sam grinned. "Not just any map. A treasure map."

"But there were only the two lines," Bennett said. "The rest was missing. How do we know what comes next?"

Sam turned toward the street, looking up and down. "It's a clue. It must be. We need to follow his lead, one step at a time." She moved beside Amos, who was still fidgeting with his robe and staring imploringly up at his chosen saint. "Amos, what would have been here two hundred years ago? What would someone have seen, if they were walking down this street during the last eclipse?"

"Oh, figuring that out is no easy feat," he said. "Dublin's changed quite a lot in two hundred years. There was the Georgian period she went through, and all the damage done by the War for Independence and the Civil War. Plenty of architecture was lost from the bombings."

Sam shook her head, the gears in her mind cranking fast. "No, they would have to be places of great significance. Places that would be protected, places with history and weight. Where would you have gone when you left this church two hundred years ago?"

"Well, I suppose I'd start down toward the quay," Amos said thoughtfully, pointing to the east. "Toward the River Liffey."

Sam returned to the street, looking in the direction he pointed. Bennett ushered Amos after her, shutting the gate behind them.

"What would you have seen?" Sam asked as she began walking down the street. The buildings they passed were small and compact, made up of red brick and white stone and a dozen other varieties of materials, like they had all been constructed at different times. They probably *had* all been constructed at different times, which did Sam no good right now.

"Oh, I don't know," Amos said, sounding as doubtful as she felt. "Most of this would have been rebuilt since then. Maybe a few buildings? That chemist shop over there has been here for ages, but that's just what my mam says. Really it's probably only been forty years or so."

"What was the second line of the benediction?" Bennett asked her quietly.

"'The aspen guide and protect you,'" Sam whispered, closing her eyes to visualize the letter and immediately bumping into someone walking in the opposite direction. Bennett took her by the arm, steering her away from the road and onto the right path.

"You think, I'll lead," he said.

She smiled up at him gratefully. "Something that would guide or protect. What would that be? A street sign? Some kind of police station?" She pointed up at a three-story building made of grayish-white stone. "What about that building, Amos?"

Amos shook his head. "Georgian, would have been built during the late 1700s, maybe 1770 or so. Does that work for your timeframe?"

"No," Sam growled, pulling him along.

They continued down the street, Sam growing more frustrated with every structure they passed. How could she hope to possibly find whatever trail of clues Father Jacob left, even with Amos's help? They reached a small split in the road, the median widening out enough to allow trees. She spotted a random section of wall through the trees, a dark and musty gray against the redbrick building behind it, and stopped.

"What is that?" she asked, pointing to the structure on the opposite side of the street.

"Oh, that's the old Dublin City Wall," Amos said happily. "Or what's left of it, I suppose. It was built in the Middle Ages, went all around the city for protection."

"Protection," Sam echoed, taking off at a run across the street.

Several cars slammed on their brakes and their horns, but she dodged them.

"Sam!" Bennett called out after her.

"Protection!" she shouted back in answer, reaching the edge of the remains of the medieval wall. It was a gorgeous piece of work, still standing after hundreds of years, the modern city built up around it like it was an old tree stump. The top was stair-stepped in four layers, too far up for her to reach. Amos and Bennett jogged across the street once the traffic cleared, Bennett giving her a glare when he reached the other side.

"You could have been hit," he said, exasperated.

"Give me a boost," she said, by way of apology.

"You can't go up there!" Amos said, looking at the top of the wall.

"Why not?" Sam asked.

Amos scratched at his head. "Well . . . it just doesn't seem right, does it?"

"I'll be okay," Sam said, putting both hands on the stone as if she could feel the history of the people who toiled to build the wall emanating from it. "And anyway, I've got pants on, so if I fall, I won't embarrass myself. But I need to get up there. Bennett?"

"I'm already regretting this," Bennett said, but he laced his fingers together and held his hands out like a sling. She put her hand on his shoulder, squeezing once for courage, before setting her foot in the sling and pushing up. She could just reach the ledge of the lowest stair step and she grabbed hold, scrabbling against the rough rock until she climbed up. Several passersby gawked at her, commenting among themselves about the odd woman—in pants, no less—getting up on the old city wall.

"It's all right," Amos said hastily, holding out his hands to the gathering crowd. "She's a . . . What are you lot again?"

"Archaeologists," Bennett said authoritatively.

Sam climbed the remaining stair steps until she reached the top of the wall, breathless from her short ascent. But she had no time to waste, and she got down on all fours and climbed across the uneven stone surface. *The aspen guide and protect you*, that was what Father Jacob had said.

"Bennett," she called down, examining the face of each stone. "What was the ogham figure for aspen? Was that *E* or *R*?"

"Uh, that was *E*," Bennett called back, covering his eyes against the looming gray overhead to look up at her. "Four lines across the center line, I think. Why?"

Sam sucked in a breath as she reached the far end of the wall, where a small symbol had been scratched into a little stone, nearly invisible unless you were looking for it. A long center line with four lines through it, representing the aspen tree.

"May the hazel bring you wisdom, and the aspen guide and protect you," she whispered. She leaned over the edge of the wall, grinning down at Bennett. "I found it! The aspen, it's here!"

CHAPTER THIRTY-TWO

"What do you mean, you found it?" Bennett asked. "There's not a tree in sight."

Sam shook her head, pointing at the rock. "No, there's a symbol carved here, the ogham figure for the aspen."

"But then where . . . ?" Bennett looked around the sedate street. "This is just a piece of a medieval wall. What does it have to do with anything? And where is . . . *it?*" He glanced at Amos. "The best place to watch the eclipse, I mean."

Sam ran her finger over the ogham etching, following the direction of the center line to the east. "The center line is pointing in that direction. Maybe that's our next clue?"

But no, Father Jacob had taken great pains to etch the ogham character here. He'd gone to great pains to steal the bowl and write that letter, enciphering even the cryptic clue he left. He wouldn't be so casual with these final hints. There must be something more.

"I should have been more careful," she muttered, thinking of the tattered edge of the letter. If only she had the rest of it, and hadn't so roughly torn away the remaining clues.

Unless it had been torn on purpose.

"What if I didn't tear it by taking it out?" she said, leaning over the wall to look down at Bennett. "What if it had been ripped all along?"

Bennett frowned. "What do you mean?"

Sam looked around the weather-worn surface of the wall. What did she mean? Even if Father Jacob had torn the letter on purpose—severing the rest of the clues—how was she meant to find them now, two hundred years later? A little scrap of paper wouldn't have survived out here all that time, exposed to the elements.

"The rest of the clues," Sam muttered to herself, knowing she wasn't making any sense yet. The gears in her mind weren't clicking together, just spinning freely without anything to bite into. "They must be around here somewhere, but where? And how?"

"Do ye think ye might get down from off the wall now?" Amos asked, glancing around at the growing crowd of observers on the opposite side of the street. He lowered his voice. "They think you're drunk, miss. It's not the attention ye'll be wanting, I'd wager."

"There must be something else," Sam said, moving to the edge of the wall. She turned around to climb back down, feeling her way along the uneven stones in search of footholds and handholds. It really was a wonder the wall had stood the test of time for so long, the mortar between the bricks black and green in several places. She worried about sticking her fingers in those same crevices, some of them so deep she didn't know what they might hide.

Bennett reached up and caught her around the waist just as she came level with one of those deep crevices, something inside winking in the wan sunlight. She gasped, her grip slipping as she fell back into Bennett's arms. He lowered her to the ground, his grip tight.

"Careful, Sam," he murmured against her ear.

She paused, her skin growing warmer the longer he held her.

But she didn't have time to lose herself in daydreams yet, so she stepped away, brushing her shirt hastily.

"I saw something," she said, pointing to the stone. "There, directly below the ogham character on top of the wall. I need to get a better look. Can you lift me up again?"

The request made Bennett fidget with his coat lapel, an odd restlessness for him. He was usually so composed. "I suppose. We should make it quick, though. We still have an audience."

He took her in a firm grip and lifted her again. But this time, instead of scrabbling for the top of the wall, she clawed her way to just below it, squinting into its shadowy depths in search of that faint wink. She couldn't be sure, but it seemed like something was wedged in there, too far to reach with her fingers alone.

"I need something long and thin," Sam said. "Tweezers if you have them, or maybe a stick. I think there's something in here."

"Tweezers?" Bennett echoed. "Where in the world would we get—"

"I'm after it, miss!" Amos declared, jogging across the street, heedless of the honking cars. He ran back the way they had come, disappearing into a building and reemerging a few minutes later holding something high over his head. He trotted back across the street, handing up a brand-new pair of tweezers to Sam.

"Chemist shop," he said proudly. "Back that way. Remember I spotted it?"

"You're a treasure, Amos," Sam said with a grin. There was just enough room for the tweezers to fit around the object wedged into the wall, and she wiggled it back and forth a bit to loosen it until it came out.

It was a little leather tube with silver ends. Like the scroll holders monks used in medieval times, except it fit easily within the palm of her hand. The silver was dull and blackened with age, the leather wrinkled and brittle, but it looked in remarkable condition for having been exposed to the elements for so long. The wall must have protected it, as it protected the city for so many centuries. Sam's pulse thrummed with excitement.

"Sam," Bennett grunted, reminding her he was still holding her up.

"Oh, sorry!" Sam exclaimed, the thrill of finding a two-hundred-year-old clue making her forget the sensation of Bennett's hands on her hips. "You can let me down. I've got it."

Bennett lowered her as she unscrewed one of the silver caps, turning the tube over and giving it a gentle shake to dislodge the slip of paper within. It was torn on both edges, no more than a scrap, but she recognized the handwriting. Bennett blew out a breath.

"How in the world did you find that?" he asked.

Sam used one fingernail to carefully unravel the curl of paper. "You said it yourself, I never can resist a puzzle left undone. Look here, it's another clue."

Bennett tilted his head to read the line. "'May the holly grant you luck.'"

"Oh, my mam keeps holly around the house during the holy days," Amos chipped in. "Says it helps her get a bonus every Christmas from the factory where she works."

Sam looked around the little intersection. "But what would have been considered lucky in the eighteenth century?"

"The Lucky Stone," Bennett said suddenly.

"What is that?" Sam asked.

"It's an old gravestone," Bennett said. "People have believed it has magic powers for centuries and they touch it for good luck. It was stolen in 1826, but apparently the stone got so heavy it broke the cart of the thieves. They left the rock where it was, and it was found by workers twenty years later who tried to break it up with their hammers to use in a building. The legend says the stone moaned and rolled away."

"Where is it now?" Sam asked.

"At St. Audoen's Church," Bennett said. "It's the only surviving medieval church in Dublin."

"That's St. Audoen's right there!" Amos exclaimed, pointing to a small structure down the street.

"Let's find this Lucky Stone and hope it really is lucky," Sam said, setting off into traffic once more and ignoring the horn blasts and shouted curses that followed

St. Audoen's was a magnificent medieval structure, the kind Sam could have spent days—weeks, really—exploring. Silently she promised herself if they made it out of this whole debacle alive, she would come back and do a proper tour of these sites. For now, she had to content herself with a longing glance up at the exquisite turrets of the bell tower overhead.

"The bells date from the early fifteenth century," Bennett said, as if he could hear her thoughts.

"If I had more time," she said sadly, shaking her head.

The interior was cool and quiet, their clattering footsteps automatically slowing in reverence to the historical weight of the place. "Where is the stone?" Sam asked.

"This way," Amos said, leading them through the church.

The Lucky Stone was a slab of granite roughly the size and shape of a pillow, not that anyone would consider resting their head on it, with the weathered etchings of a cross inside a circle on its face. Sam brushed her fingers along the edge, just as she had with the city wall, trying desperately to absorb the history and significance of such a relic. Whose grave had this marked? What made it so lucky? And what had changed so radically in her life in the last few weeks that she now stood before it, considering its history?

"Sam," Bennett said softly, bringing her back to the present.

"Right," she said, refocusing on Joana and the bowl. She gave a frustrated sigh. "I forgot a flashlight."

"Here," Bennett said, fishing out the lighter he had taken from Phillip that first night at Orlagh.

Sam crouched beside the stone and flicked on the light. She moved it over the face of the stone, inch by painful inch, looking for any marks left behind by Father Jacob. The stone was so rough, it was hard to tell sometimes what was natural and what was man-made. Even the Greek cross engraved on it had been worn nearly smooth over the passing centuries.

Sam rose with a frown. "What's on the backside?"

"The same engraving," said Amos. "A Greek cross."

"There's nothing here," Sam said, frustrated.

"It has to be the Lucky Stone," Bennett reasoned. "'May the holly grant you luck.' What else could it mean?"

Sam shook her head. "There was a mark on the wall. There should be one here, too. If we're wrong, if this sends us down the wrong path . . . We don't have time for mistakes, Bennett."

Bennett nodded, looking down at the stone. He frowned, leaning in closer. "Did you check the top? Ogham was originally developed using standing stones. They didn't carve the center line; they used the natural edge of the stone as the center line. Look, right here."

Sam leaned over, her cheek brushing against his ear as she followed his finger across the top of the gravestone. Three shallow cuts in a line, right along the edge of the top. Invisible to anyone who wasn't looking for them.

"The holly," Sam breathed. "You were right. This was it!"

"What about the clue?" Bennett asked. "The stone wasn't installed here until the 1860s."

Sam turned to Amos. "Where was the Lucky Stone before they put it here?"

Amos tilted his head. "In a field, I think."

Sam took a slow breath. "Before the robbers stole it, Amos."

"Oh, that makes a wee bit more sense. Well, it stood outside the tower of St. Audoen's for centuries."

"Right," Sam said, nodding at Bennett. "That's where we go, then. Outside."

CHAPTER THIRTY-THREE

"Sam, this could take all day," Bennett said doubtfully, staring up at the exterior of the church tower. "We don't really have time to check all these stones."

"We don't have to check all of them," Sam said, crouching down at the base of the wall. The ground was soggy and the stones cold, making her fingers ache as she touched them to balance herself. "Most likely it would have been hidden near the Lucky Stone, right? It's only a foot or two tall, so we just have to check the lower reaches of the wall."

"Every single rock?" Amos asked doubtfully. He looked at Bennett. "Is she always like this?"

Bennett gave a faint smile. "You should have seen her when we finally figured out the location of the Roman coin my father brought back from a dig in Athens. She crawled under the porch of our old schoolhouse and terrified a family of raccoons."

"Ah," Amos said, before frowning. "What is a raccoon?"

"I found it!" Sam exclaimed, holding up her tweezers with a triumphant smile. Her face was flushed, her hair falling in wisps around her ears. Bennett's smile widened.

"Of course you did," he said. "What does it say?"

She unscrewed the silver endcap, extracting the slip of paper within and unrolling it. "'The elder drive out all evil.' What drives out evil?"

Amos rocked back. "According to my da, a proper hiding with a good switch."

Bennett helped Sam stand up before moving toward the gate that led to High Street. "Look, we started at John's Lane Church, down that way. And then there was the Old City Wall, and now St. Audoen's. Amos was right, we're heading down to the River Liffey. Amos, if we kept walking that way two hundred years ago, what would we have seen next?"

"Not sure," Amos said with a shrug. "Today it's mostly businesses and residential buildings."

Sam moved closer to the edge of the street, nearly stepping out into oncoming traffic again until Bennett grabbed her by her coat and hauled her back. But she had caught a glimpse of something, and she pointed down the street toward the triangular peak of a tower a few blocks away.

"What is that?" she asked.

Amos went up on tiptoes to see. "Oh, right. That's St. Michael's Tower. It was originally its own church, but it went to ruin and they rebuilt it in 1815. They left the original tower, though. Ninety-six steps all the way up to the top. Cor, ye'd need a nap after all that climbing."

Sam turned to Bennett. "Michael is an archangel, right?"

Bennett nodded. "One of the leaders of the angels. There's not much about him in the Christian Scriptures. He's mentioned in Revelations, of course, where he battles a dragon. There's also a reference in the Epistle of Jude that says he guards the tombs of Moses and Eve. Apparently, he fought the devil over Moses, had to drive him out . . ."

Bennett trailed off as his eyes locked with Sam's, realization dawning on both of them. "'And the elder drive out all evil,'" they intoned together.

Amos gave them a frown. "Ye're going to make me climb those steps, aren't you?"

The adrenaline surging through Sam's veins carried her forty-eight steps up the tower before reality set in, making her lungs burn and her calves tighten up from the strain. She leaned heavily on the handrail that had been installed, pausing beside a narrow window fashioned into the old stone.

"Bennett," she wheezed. "Can we stop for a moment?"

"Are you all right?" Bennett asked, laying a hand on her cheek and tilting her head up.

"Yes," Sam panted, nodding. His fingers were warm and strong, and even though her skin was flushed from the effort of climbing, she didn't want him to drop his hand. "Just tired."

"I could use a break, too," Amos called from below, around the corner. He waved one hand to let them know he was still there.

Sam slumped against a narrow window ledge cut into the ancient stone, the wan light of late afternoon softening Dublin into a vision fit for a postcard. What a sight it must have been in Father Jacob's time, the medieval architecture of the surrounding buildings carrying all that history. Had he stopped and gazed through this window with the same fascination, or had he just kept going until he collapsed at the top?

"I'll go to the top of the tower," Bennett said. "I'll find the ogham figure. You rest."

Sam shook her head, straightening up. "I can make it," she said, though her legs protested otherwise. She set her hand against the edge of the window, bracing to force herself up the rest of the steps, when her fingertips brushed over a set of divots in the stone.

She drew her hand back, then counted each cut. Five slanting lines, shallower than the previous ones and clearly done in great haste, but nonetheless there they were.

"Bennett, look," she breathed.

He touched the lines lightly, letting out his breath in a huff. "Ruis. R. The elder."

Sam nodded. "Father Jacob was here."

A little light winked in the corner of the narrow window, just below the glass installed sometime in the past few years to keep the tower from getting too drafty, unnoticeable unless you were looking for it. But Sam was, and she wielded her tweezers like a sword, extracting a small leather tube from the stones.

"Got it," she said triumphantly.

"You already look the part," Bennett said softly.

Sam glanced up at him. "The part of what?"

"Not even Howard Carter in the Valley of the Kings could be so precise with a pair of tweezers. You look like a proper archaeologist. But then, you always did."

"Oh," Sam said softly, a surge of emotion cutting off any other words. Not that she had any words to give. A proper archaeologist. It had been so long since she even let herself dream such a dream, yet here she was. On an actual treasure hunt, with real consequences.

Amos came chugging up the steps then, the curls of his rusty hair looking limp and bedraggled.

"Cor, but that's a climb, innit?" he huffed, leaning heavily on the railing beside Sam. He looked up the curve of steps with a despairing gaze. "And still more to go, is there? All right, Amos, let St. Augustine himself be our guide."

"It's okay, Amos," Sam said, holding up the small leather tube. "We found what we were looking for."

"Blessed be the saint," Amos breathed, collapsing again.

Sam pulled the paper from the tube, noting the clean line along the bottom. "This must be the last one, see? It's from the bottom of the paper."

Bennett leaned over, reading the last clue. "'May the oak remain strong, and the rowan guide you to the otherworld.' Not an upbeat fellow, was he?"

"What is that?" Sam asked, pointing to the medieval building where the lines of Father Jacob's *R* slanted down.

Amos peered out the window. "That's Christ Church Cathedral, that is. Oh, but that won't work for you. It was completely rebuilt in the 1800s, same as John's Lane Church."

Sam sagged against the railing. "None of the original cathedral remains?"

Amos scratched at his head, his curls springing back to some sort of life. "Oh, there were some artifacts that were preserved, I suppose. The tabernacle dates from the seventeenth century, I think, and the tomb of Strongbow. Oh, and the crypt, of course."

"Strongbow and the crypt," Sam said, the final pieces clicking into place. She straightened up, the revelation giving her new life. "That's it. The last two clues are 'May the oak remain strong, and the rowan guide you to the otherworld.' The oak must represent Strongbow's tomb."

"And the rowan represents the crypt," Bennett finished. "The Druids considered the rowan tree to be a symbol of death and rebirth. They often used the branches of the rowan to build funeral pyres."

"It must be there," Sam said softly, her words vibrating. "We've nearly found it, Bennett."

His hand brushed hers, their fingers wending together just as they had all those years ago when the two of them went in search of the pottery sherd from Athens. And just as it had then, Sam's heart gave a delightfully painful squeeze.

Amos leaned in, his whole face turning down in a frown. "You're not going to make me go down in the crypt, are you? It's full of dead people. Long-dead people, which I think are actually the worst kind of dead people."

Sam gave him an apologetic smile. "Maybe you could consider it part of your test of maturity, to find the strength to brave its depths?"

Amos sighed, turning to go back down the stairwell. "At least I don't have to climb anymore."

CHAPTER THIRTY-FOUR

The interior of Christ Church Cathedral was a Victorian marvel, with checkerboard marble floors and massive stained-glass windows depicting holy figures. There were several visitors milling about inside, paying their respects at the chapel of Saint Laurence O'Toole, the patron saint of Dublin, whose heart was supposedly enshrined in a wooden reliquary in the crypt. Other visitors wandered through the side aisles of the church, where two massive stone tombs had been placed. Amos pointed to the one to the right, a large tomb with a smaller, half-size tomb beside it.

"That's the tomb of Strongbow," he whispered in a reverent tone.

"Richard de Clare was his true name, second earl of Pembroke," Bennett filled in. "He led the Anglo-Norman invasion of Ireland in the twelfth century. He worked with Saint Laurence O'Toole to replace the original timber church with a stone building. That's not the original tomb, of course, that was destroyed when the roof collapsed in 1562. But they say his bones are still in there."

Sam nodded, running her fingers along the edge of the monument. The face was rather blunt and obscure, which surprised her for such an elaborately decorated cathedral, until a collection of visitors filed past the tomb and touched the statue's face, murmuring prayers for strength and courage. She imagined that wouldn't be the only time that day such a thing happened, which explained why the statue looked like it had almost no nose at all.

She found the notches in the stone almost right away, two small lines to the left signifying the oak. The most sacred tree in the Druid faith. And those two lines were pointed to the opposite side of the church, where the archway to the crypt was set just to the left of the entrance doors. A metal gate blocked the way down.

"That's where we need to go," she said. "The crypt. It's the last piece."

"It's not open to the public at the moment," said a man as he passed them. He wore a shiny gold name tag that identified him as a docent of the cathedral. "We're cataloging the artifacts below in preparation for a display of the tabernacle and candlesticks used under James the Second when they restored the Latin mass for a time. It'll be quite a treat to view once we've got it cleaned up and set up. Do come back."

"Oh, but we need to get down there today," Sam said, leaning in to read the name on his tag. "Uh, Seemouse?"

"Seamus," Amos said hastily, pronouncing it more like *shay-muss*. He gave the docent a nervous laugh. "Americans."

"Mm," said Seamus, giving Sam a distrustful once-over. "Well, wherever you're from, the crypt is closed. You'll have to come back another day."

A visitor called to him in German, pointing to the tomb of Strongbow with a questioning smile. Seamus frowned at Sam and the others but moved away from the gate, throwing several suspicious glances over his shoulder as he moved between the massive pillars holding up the arched cathedral ceiling. Sam smiled, giving a little wave, waiting until he had moved out of sight to grab the bars of the gate and give it a little shake.

"It's locked," she said in a low voice.

Bennett had the nerve to give her a small smile. "Did you think it would be otherwise?"

"Well, what do we do now?" she demanded. "We need to get down there, and the only two people I know who can pick a lock are *indisposed* at the moment."

Bennett fidgeted, for once looking almost guilty. "Perhaps not the only two you know."

Sam's jaw hung slack. "Bennett! You don't really!"

"In my defense, there are a number of unusual skills required in the study of archaeology to obtain the necessary access and data," Bennett said defensively. "I am a student of knowledge, not a treasure hunter. But sometimes, a treasure hunter's methods are necessary to gain that knowledge."

Sam shook her head. "Jo is going to have a field day with you when she finds out."

"I was hoping she wouldn't have to," Bennett said, digging through his coat pocket until he produced a small leather case. He unrolled it to reveal a collection of metal implements tucked into their own small pockets inside.

"Bennett," Sam hissed. "You have a lock-picking *kit*? Oh, Jo will definitely find out."

"Blame Professor Wallstone," Bennett said, pulling out two of the implements and rolling the case back up to tuck it away again. "He's the one who gifted it to me. Keep a watch, will you?"

Sam moved to stand in front of him, trying her best to look nonchalant as she blocked him from the prying eyes of other visitors coming in and out of the cathedral. Sam saw no trace of their docent inquisitor, but she suspected he would be making an extra round to check on them soon. Amos moved to stand beside her.

"Do you really think it's down there?" he asked in a low voice.

Sam whipped her head to the side. "What is down there?"

Amos frowned at her. "The missing ritual bowl. That's what we're after, isn't it?"

"What makes you think that?" Sam asked.

Amos's frown deepened. "Well, I don't think it's watching the eclipse you're after down in the crypt. You didn't really expect me to believe that excuse anyhow, did you? You've been following some kind of . . . secret trail. Pulling out clues, asking what landmarks were hereabouts two hundred years ago. I figured it was Father Jacob's clues you were following."

"Oh," Sam said, hesitating, "I . . . didn't realize you had put all that together."

Amos's brows shot up. "What did you think I thought?"

"Truthfully? I hoped you were distracted enough with your personal business that you bought the eclipse excuse."

Amos turned his gaze out to the cathedral, looking distraught. "Maybe Brother Noah is right. If you thought me a fool enough to dismiss me, maybe I'm not ready to join Solas Fíor."

"Not a fool," Sam said hastily, feeling terribly guilty. "Not at all. You've been the greatest help, Amos. We couldn't have gotten this far without you, honestly."

Amos still looked doubtful. "Really?"

Sam nodded firmly. "Really."

"Got it," Bennett said from behind them, the gate giving a soft click as it swung open on silent hinges.

"You did it!" Sam exclaimed, a little too loudly. A few other visitors glanced over at them, and she gave a hasty smile. "We'd better move quickly, before Seamus returns."

They passed through the gate, pulling it just so that the lock didn't catch but it still looked closed. Sam figured they would have a hard enough time smuggling out a petrified wooden bowl without having to pick the lock again on the way out.

The stairs descended into darkness, the air below the cathedral cool and still with the peculiar musty essence of the ancient deceased. The crypt ran the full length of the nave overhead, making it the largest medieval crypt still in existence in Ireland. Arching stone supports held the entire weight of the cathedral above them. Sam touched one of the columns, giving it a little push as if testing its strength. The last thing she needed was to bring a whole cathedral crashing down on them.

"Where do we go?" Bennett asked, his voice muted in the thick air. He squinted in the dim, the electric lightbulbs strung up for the workers few and far between, with deep pools of darkness between them. "What was the last line?"

"'The rowan guide you to the otherworld,'" Sam intoned.

"That's not much help," Bennett muttered as they began to work their way through the crypt. "Maybe we should split up to cover more ground."

"This feels more like a stick-together situation, though, doesn't it?" Amos countered, pressing in close to Sam and dropping his voice to a whisper. "Don't make me poke around down here all alone, miss. There was once a soldier got lost in the crypt and eaten up by the rats."

That did very little to settle Sam's nerves, but she had to admit that Bennett might have a point. The crypt was huge and dark, and filled with the treasures of the Christ Church Cathedral, which were stored behind more gates and locks. Not to mention everything down here was made from ancient stone. If Father Jacob had left them a clue, they could spend the rest of their lives searching and still not find it.

"We have to think like Father Jacob," Sam reasoned, passing the first set of arches. A figure emerged out of the gloom and she gave a strangled cry, stumbling back into Bennett. His arms tightened in a protective circle around her, drawing her into his chest.

"What is it?" he asked, his voice urgent.

Amos stopped beside them, peering into the shadows. "Oh, that's King Charles the First. And that's Charles the Second there."

Sam let out a gusty sigh. "They're statues."

Amos nodded. "Used to stand outside the Dublin town hall, but people kept defacing them and trying to set them afire. The kings aren't the most popular figures here."

"Not when they look like that, I imagine," Sam said, peering at the jagged hole in Charles's face.

"They weren't here in Father Jacob's time," Amos said helpfully. "They only moved them down here in the 1800s."

"Then we'd better keep moving," Bennett said, dropping one arm around Sam's waist and urging her forward. "I'll check these alcoves over here to the left. Amos, take those to the right. Sam, keep working on the puzzle. You got us this far; if anyone can find Father Jacob's last clue, it's you."

Sam wasn't feeling nearly as sure of that down here as she had been out in the sunlight. She hadn't expected the crypt to be so . . . cryptic. And now no one knew they were down there, which had been a necessity, but felt like a smothering kind of thing to think about now. She moved cautiously into the gloomy space, passing an elaborate monument set into the stone. The air grew even chillier as she lost Bennett's protective presence at her side, both he and Amos moving off in opposite directions to explore, the latter far more reluctantly.

Sam did her best to shake off the chill, focusing instead on what she knew of Father Jacob and his last hours down here. The priest knew he would need to put the bowl somewhere the Hellfire Club would never find it, never even think to look. Somewhere he considered safe, both from the club and from random passersby. Somewhere that wouldn't have been changed or gotten rid of over the passage of time. Maybe even something sacred, to counteract the magic of the relic itself.

She paused under a low arch, huffing a sigh. She was in the bowels of a church; they were full up on sacred places down here. She needed to think more specifically.

It was only as she turned around, scanning the pillars and stones surrounding her, that she realized how quiet it had become. Bennett and Amos were nowhere in sight. The light was dim to the point of obscurity—only a few rays of sunshine peered in from small windows at the far east end. They hadn't thought to bring a lantern down with them, and Sam shivered in the oppressive stillness. She couldn't give in to creeping thoughts, though. She needed to save Joana.

Something tickled at the back of her neck like the brush of a feather, and she nearly screeched in surprise. She slapped at her skin, whirling about, but there was nothing. Of course there was nothing; what did she think, a bird had found its way into the crypt? It was a ludicrous idea, though that didn't stop her from staring hard into the darkest corners as if a pair of beady black eyes might stare back out. Or worse—a pair of glowing red ones.

"Get it together, Sammy girl," she muttered, her voice harsh and loud in the utter quiet.

Samantha.

"No," Sam breathed, gripping the lapels of her coat tight as if it might bring her some level of protection against the voice that whispered into her ear. It had been an echo, surely. A product of the shape and dimension of the crypt. Or a product of her exhaustion and fear. It wasn't real. It couldn't be real.

But then it whispered her name again.

"Bennett?" she said weakly, looking around once more. But of course it wasn't him. She knew who it was, and it made her blood go colder than the bodies in the stones around her.

The featherlight touch ran down her arm, tugging at her fingers and drawing her forward a half step. The voice was leading her, guiding her deeper into the crypt. And though every instinct of self-preservation screamed at her to turn the other way and run, instead she took another step forward. She followed the voice into the darkness, her breath fast and shallow. Joana, she had to think about saving Joana. She couldn't go mad with fear, not quite yet.

The tugging on her hand stopped as she reached a small alcove set behind a gate, the space filled with various items stored there over the years. In the front of the alcove was a compact wooden structure, plain and unassuming, but something about it drew her attention. What was it the docent had said about their upcoming displays? There was a plate, and candlesticks. And a tabernacle.

A sacred Catholic relic with ample storage space that would have stood the test of time.

Sam pulled at the gate, surprised to find it unlocked, considering it housed such precious items. But then the whisper was back, drawing her toward the tabernacle, the pull now like a rope around her chest. The holy relic looked for all the world like a puppet stage, the kind that Madame Iris would use to tell stories with her marionette dolls to the younger children in Clement's schoolhouse. But this one had no bright red-and-white-striped curtain out front, and the energy emanating from it was a far cry from the cheerful display of Madame Iris's stage.

Sam ran her finger along the edge of the little drawer in the back of the tabernacle, finding two small cuts made along one edge, just like the oak symbol on Strongbow's tomb. Except these two lines were cut to the right, the symbol of the rowan.

"I found you," she whispered, her chest so tight it hurt to breathe.

One corner jutted out just enough that she could dig her fingers in and pull toward her. The drawer came open with a protesting groan, as if the wood of the tabernacle itself didn't want to give up the secrets it held. But it came open enough that Sam could dip in her hands, briefly entertaining terrifying visions of a drawer full of sewer rats or roaches or some other crawling monstrosity. She gave a little gasp as her hands bumped something within, something curved and solid and engraved.

She took hold of the object, trying her best to pull it loose. It seemed to stick along every edge of the small drawer, as if it had sprouted arms and legs and gripped at the wood to stop itself from being removed. She grunted, setting one foot to the top of the tabernacle to give herself leverage to pull it loose. The tabernacle groaned another warning, and for a moment she feared she would have to splinter the holy thing apart to get the bowl out.

But then it came loose all at once, sending the tabernacle tipping in one direction and Sam flying backward in the opposite direction. She gave a cry as the bowl landed on her midsection, knocking the breath clean out of her. It was so heavy—too heavy, even for a petrified wooden bowl. It pressed into her stomach like it wanted to go right through her, to scoop out her insides and devour them as a sacrifice. And it felt . . . *wrong*. Her hands stuck to it, like her skin had fused with the bowl. Her stomach turned, and she thought she might throw up or scream.

"Sam!" Bennett called from afar. He came rushing into the alcove with Amos close behind, his face swimming into focus as she struggled under the weight of the bowl. Bennett grabbed her by the arm and pulled her up, the bowl clattering onto the floor.

"Are you all right?" he asked, wrapping one arm around her waist. "What happened?"

Sam shook her head, too shaken to form any words.

"Sam!" Bennett tipped her head up, his golden eyes searching hers. "Sam, what is it?"

"The bowl," she gasped. "I found the bowl."

CHAPTER THIRTY-FIVE

"You found it?" Bennett said, his attention turning to the bowl, which had fallen facedown in a pile of silver candlesticks. He stooped to examine it.

"Don't touch it!" Sam cried, taking him by the arm and pulling him back.

"Why? What's the matter?" Bennett asked, his gaze still fixed on the bowl.

"There's something . . . wrong about it," Sam said, tightening her grip on his arm. "It's the magic, I think. Don't put your hands on it. We don't want anyone else infected like Professor Wallstone."

"I won't," Bennett said softly, crouching down and tilting his head to the side to examine the bowl. "It's exquisite."

"Is that . . . it?" Amos asked, crowding in beside them. "The actual ritual bowl? Cor, it's a sight, innit?"

Now that the thing wasn't trying to bore a hole through her midsection, Sam could admit the bowl was unlike anything she had ever seen. The details were intricate—carvings of oak leaves and juniper berries, interlocking Celtic knots along the border, clusters of spiral work that branched in three directions, and a triangular shape made up of interlocking arcs with a circle behind them.

But the true masterpiece was the figure dominating the center of these embellishments, a large raven with outspread wings. The eyes were polished to a shine, so lifelike she expected the figure to start cawing any moment. In its beak it held a spear, and its talons dug into the flesh of a beast below—a wounded hound, from the look of it. The violence it depicted only made the churning of Sam's stomach worse.

"What is that?" Amos asked in fascination.

"The Morrigan," Bennett said, his quiet voice a mix of wonder and wariness. "Goddess of war, of magic, of sovereignty."

Sam lifted a shaking finger to the creature grasped in the bird's claws. "What is that?"

Bennett squinted. "It looks like a dog of some kind. Could be a representation of Cú Chulainn. He was a mythological Irish hero. *The hound of Culann* is what his name meant. The Morrigan foretold his death when he insulted her before a battle."

And for that he paid the price with his eternal soul, Sam thought. But the longer she stared at the tortured expression of the hound, the more disturbing the image became. It reminded her of something.

"The Hellfire Cat," she breathed. Not really a cat at all.

"I recognize these marks here," Amos said, pointing to the symbols Sam had first noted along the border of the bowl. "These spiral bits, those are the triskelion, aren't they?"

Bennett nodded. "The spirals represent the three realms of existence: earth, sky, and water. They've found carvings of it outside the tomb at Newgrange. And this one here, with the arcs, is a triquetra. It's the symbol of the threefold goddess."

"Father Jacob gave his life for this," Amos said. "I never thought to lay eyes on it myself. Brother Noah will have to let me take my vows now, won't he?"

Sam gave Bennett an uneasy glance. This was the part she had been putting off, but they were running out of time. "We need something to carry it in."

They scrounged around the small alcove until they came up with a few burlap sacks that had been used for packing. Carefully Sam wrapped the bowl in as many layers as she could gather, grunting under the sheer weight of the thing. She worried the edges of the burlap might tear, but they held firm as she lifted the bowl. Bennett reached forward, wrapping his hands around hers to lend support.

"It's heavier than I expected," Bennett grunted. "Even considering the petrification process."

"The weight of the devil be upon it," Amos said solemnly.

"No one touches it," Sam gasped, pulling the edges of the burlap out of Bennett's grasp and hauling the bowl over her shoulder. It settled against her back like a leech, her head swimming as if it were sucking away her actual blood.

Bennett reached for her. "Sam, if any of us should be carrying that—"

"It's me," she snapped, stepping back from him. The irritation caught them both by surprise, but she shook it off. "We've got a long way to carry it and a short time to do it. We need to get moving."

"I'll send word to Brother Noah," Amos said, trailing behind them. "He can secure transportation back to Orlagh."

"About that, Amos," Sam said, following Bennett out. As soon as she cleared the gate of the alcove, she swung it shut, the metal clanging as the lock caught and trapped the young man within.

"Miss Knox?" he asked, staring at her in disbelief.

Sam pressed close to the bars. "Amos, I'm so terribly sorry about this. Please know, I feel awful. And I'll make sure you get out. But we need that bowl to free Jo from Phillip at the Hellfire Club."

"The Hellfire Club!" Amos exclaimed. "Oh, miss, ye can't. Not on the day of the eclipse!"

"I know, Amos, I know," Sam said. "If there were any other way, I wouldn't do it. But Phillip has kidnapped Jo and threatened to kill her if we don't bring the bowl to the Hellfire Club. I won't leave you down here, at least not for long. We just need to get a head start. When you get out, get to Orlagh and tell Brother Noah and the rest of Solas Fíor to meet us at the Hellfire Club before the eclipse. We'll need all the help we can get. And again, I'm really so sorry about this."

Sam backed away as Amos lurched forward, his hand shooting through the bars to try and grab her and stop her from leaving. She could hardly blame him, considering she was locking him in a crypt and leaving him to an undecided fate, but it really couldn't be helped. They needed the bowl to save Joana.

"Wait, please, Miss Knox! Sam! Please, don't leave me down here! The rats will get me!" Amos's cries echoed through the arches, fading as Sam and Bennett climbed the stairs and exited the gate.

"I told you the crypt was closed to the public!" shouted Seamus as they turned around, startling the other visitors in the middle of prayers. "How did you get in there?"

"You were right!" Sam called back, a fine line of sweat standing out along her hairline despite the chill of the cathedral. "We shouldn't have gone down there, and now our friend has gotten locked in. Could you help him get out?"

"Gotten locked— What in the saint's name—"

"Thank you!" Bennett called out, giving a wave as he put his arm around Sam and hurried her out the cathedral doors before Seamus could spot the sack tossed over her shoulder.

"You did the right thing," Bennett said as they retraced their steps to their hotel.

"Did I? It doesn't feel like I did. I'm using people to get what I want, just like Phillip."

"You're trying to save Jo. That's nothing like Phillip."

"But at what cost?" Sam asked, huffing out a breath as they walked, the weight and drag of the bowl making it feel like she was carrying it up a mountain. "What good have we really done Jo if we just hand over the bowl and let Phillip invoke the curse?"

"Maybe it won't work," Bennett reasoned. "Phillip said the details were unfinished in Eleanor's book."

"That's why he needed the diary," Sam said. She stopped to lean against a stone wall, panting. "What do you remember about the curse in Father Jacob's diary? What pieces were required?"

"A significant passage of the moon, which we now know is the eclipse."

"Not much of a chance of stopping that," Sam said. "What else?"

"The ritual bowl," Bennett said, nodding to the sack digging into her shoulder. "Ritual words, which I suppose would come from his spell book. And a sacrifice."

Sam straightened a little. "You don't think he means for Jo—"

"I won't let that happen," Bennett said, his voice like iron. "*We* won't let that happen. We'll get to her before then."

"How?" Sam demanded, the snap back in her voice. "What can we really do, Bennett? What can *you* do? You've done nothing but mess this up from the very beginning."

Bennett drew back in shock. "Sam, we're both under a great deal of pressure, I know—"

"What do you know about pressure?" Sam asked, leaning into him and narrowing her gaze. A hot bubble of contempt rose up the back of her throat, singeing her vocal cords. "Everything handed to you, every door opened for you. The only pressure you've ever faced is deciding what to wear to one of your mother's ridiculous parties."

"Sam," Bennett said, his voice cracking like a whip. "What's got into you?"

Sam felt a ridiculous and overwhelming urge to slap Bennett in the face, so much so that she raised her hand and in doing so lost her grip on the burlap sack. The bowl clunked to the sidewalk and all the fight drained out of her, leaving her sweaty and panting and horrified.

"Oh, Bennett," she gasped, clamping one hand over her mouth. She shook her head. "I'm so sorry. I don't know what came over me. I can't believe   I would never . . ."

What *had* come over her? She had never in her life felt such . . . anger. Such vitriol. And toward Bennett, of all people. It was like something had taken every stray observation in her brain and twisted it into a hard, cruel little lump. It made her sound like Phillip, a realization that chilled the sweat on her brow to a frost.

"Sam, you're pale as a ghost," Bennett said with a frown of concern. He reached out a hand, steadying her at the elbow. "Or you look like you've seen a ghost."

Sam's skin prickled as the now familiar whisper slithered over her shoulder and into her ear, drawing her attention down to the bowl. It wanted her back, and now she knew where that hatred had come from.

"Bennett, I think   . I think it's the bowl. Please, you have to know, what I said is not remotely how I feel about you, or your mother, or any of it. The bowl made me . . . It made me want to hate you. The complete opposite of . . ."

Well, she didn't need to go confessing her lifelong feelings in a moment of weakness, so she clamped her lips together instead.

But the hot, angry feelings lingered like an ache in her ribs, and for the first time she realized the full extent of what the curse could do. If it could make her hate someone she loved, imagine what it would do to the rest of the world.

"I should carry it," Bennett said, reaching for the sack.

"No," Sam whispered harshly, snatching it off the sidewalk. "I can deal with the bowl for now. One of us needs to save our strength to face Phillip. You're the stronger of the two of us."

Bennett looked at her with a strange expression. "I don't think I am the stronger of the two of us, Sam."

Sam flushed with pride, which helped push back some of the churning nausea in her gut. "Of course you are."

He took her face in his hands, his thumb caressing her cheek as his fingertips brushed through her hair. "Sam, you're the most incredible girl I know. And you're right, I can't imagine the pressure you've faced in your life. You survived more during the war than any of us. And you made a place for yourself at the shop, an oasis of books in a farming town. Even at a full run, my mind stumbles to keep up with yours. My father never invented a cipher you couldn't crack, and he was skilled enough to work at the Intelligence Bureau during the war. The care you have with the books, your passion for everything you touch, you don't understand how rare those things are."

Sam's heart threatened to come out of her chest in the best possible way. "Bennett, you don't have to—"

"I do," he said firmly. "Someone should have told you all of this ages ago. *I* should have told you all of this ages ago. I was so fixated on my own education, on what I thought I needed to achieve, I pushed you away when I should have . . ."

"Should have what?" Sam whispered, caught breathless in the moment.

One corner of his mouth crooked up. "When I should have told you how much I like when you wear your hair up like this. Don't ever let Jo convince you to cut it."

"Oh, Jo," Sam said, her smile fading. A cold wave of dread rose from her toes and burned the back of her throat, making her eyes water as the bowl fed off her misery. But instead of giving in, she let the heat of Bennett's words burn it back. "I have an idea, but it's very dangerous and will probably get us in worse trouble than locking Amos in the crypt. Do you still have your lock-picking kit?"

Bennett tapped his coat pocket. "Of course—what are you thinking?"

"I'm thinking we've already broken into one holy place today, why not make it two?"

CHAPTER THIRTY-SIX

"**Y**ou're right," Bennett muttered, staring through the trees at Orlagh. "This is not a good idea."

"We just need a couple of their weapons, for protection," Sam said, the collar of her coat damp and stuck against her neck with sweat. The pressure inside her skull lessened somewhat when she set the bowl on the ground, but her stomach still threatened to turn itself inside out if she moved too quickly.

"Their weapons are exactly why I don't think this is a good idea," Bennett said.

"Phillip's magic can easily overpower us right now. But if we've got some of Solas Fíor's blessed weapons, you can distract him while I get Jo away from the Hellfire Club."

He looked down at her, concern flattening his lips. "And what about you? Sam, you can't keep on like this. Let me take a turn."

"No!" Sam growled. The whisper pushed at her, curling her insides to anger, but she took a deep breath and did her best to block it out of her mind. She could feel its influence growing stronger, the closer to the passage tomb they got. It took all her strength to shove it away, and she was panting with the effort as she continued. "We're so close, Bennett. You need to get those weapons so I can find somewhere to hide the bowl out here in the woods until the eclipse passes. We need all the delays and distractions we can get right now."

Bennett looked up as if searching for the sun and any sign of the approaching eclipse, but the trees blocked their view. He sighed, the furrow in his brow deeper than ever. "I don't want to leave you."

Sam gave him a thin smile, hoping it looked brave enough. "I'll be all right, you'll see. Think of it as field training to be an archaeologist."

His mouth turned up at the corner. "We don't usually put the artifacts back."

"I guess I'm inventing a new branch of study, then." She pushed at his shoulder. "Go, we're running out of time."

He hesitated, as if he would say something more, but instead he nodded and rose out of his crouch, moving swiftly across the open space between the tree line and the back of the house. Sam held her breath as he went, terrified a face would appear in one of the windows or the back door would suddenly be thrown open and spout a stream of robed men. But Bennett reached the door without incident, setting to work on opening the dead bolt. Sam might have stayed longer, waiting for him to return, but she had a job to do as well.

It was a risk, of course, showing up at the club without the bowl. But it was their only real bargaining chip, and if she handed it over right away, they had no guarantee that Phillip wouldn't murder them on the spot. She'd read a few pulp novels, hard-boiled detectives and femme fatales chasing shadowy murderers through foggy city streets. She knew you always needed leverage going into the final showdown.

Her hands were slow and clumsy as she reached for the edges

of the burlap sack, her heart pounding and her neck breaking out in a cold sweat at the prospect of letting it near her again. But this was for Joana, and she would carry that bowl up every mountain in Ireland if it meant getting her best friend back. So she gritted her teeth and took hold of the sack, hauling it up and starting into the trees to look for a secluded place to bury it.

Samantha.

"No," she spat, directing the anger that bit into her mind at the bowl itself. "I know it's you, and I won't listen."

But saying that was easier than doing it, and every step that brought her farther up the hill also let the magic burrow a little deeper into her mind. Their plan was foolish, bound to fail. Bennett would get caught, surely. He could never do anything right. And why were they bothering to save Joana at all? The girl had never done anything but waste her opportunities in life. She didn't deserve Sam's friendship; Sam had been right to cast off her dead weight. Besides, Phillip was far too powerful now, with the magic in his heart and the stones of Ireland under his feet. They couldn't possibly stop him.

"No," Sam gasped, dropping to her knees on the rough path. The pain was an electric jolt of light in the dark, and for a moment the clouds parted and she could see the way through the bowl's influence clearly. "I won't let you. . . . You can't. You can't."

A raven swooped down to the path before her, landing so close she would have startled if she'd had the energy. It considered her with its beady black eyes for a moment before throwing back its head and letting loose a cry that seemed to shake the trees around her. Sam knew she needed to move—to run, to hide, to throw the bowl in the deepest hole she could find and pray it never resurfaced—but the bowl was like a titan on her back, pressing down so hard her ribs creaked. Still she tried, clawing forward on hands and knees, ready to barrel through the large bird if she needed to.

But the whisper turned to a laugh as a stick cracked nearby, the earth trembling with the passage of something large and unholy. Sam gasped as the bowl seemed to triple in weight, pressing her low enough that she could smell the fetid damp of the earth.

"Who's there?" she whispered, not at all wanting the answer.

The creature emerged from the trees, the rot of unnatural death wafting out of its fur. Sam thought her mind might have played tricks on her the night they'd arrived in Dublin. But this creature was far worse in the watery light of day. The Hellfire Cat was an abomination, like a botched science experiment, a tortured thing caught between two states of being. Were the bowl not greedily sucking all the energy out of her just then, Sam might have screamed. As it was, a trail of silent tears leaked out as she struggled to catch her breath. The Cat let out a thin, hollow howl at the sight of her, the kind of sound made to cleave a man from his own mind.

"Good boy, Cú," came Phillip's voice. At first there was nothing, and then there was Phillip, materializing like some sort of magician. He laid a hand on the Cat's head, his skin stark and pale against the black of his eyes and the deepening dark of his hair. But those black eyes glowed as they alighted on the sack still hanging off Sam's shoulder.

"After all this time," he breathed. "I knew you wouldn't fail me, Samantha."

Sam used what little strength she had to push back up to her feet, setting her jaw. "Where is Jo?"

Phillip's smile curled into sharp edges. "You waste your affections on those who do not warrant them."

The whisper echoed in her ear, digging Phillip's thoughts into her brain. Sam closed her eyes, filling her heart with all the love she had for her best friend. For all their shared adventures in the back garden of the Manor; for all the times Joana had rescued her from the cruel taunts of the boys in the schoolhouse; for all the love and vibrancy and fullness Joana had brought to her life.

"You're wrong about Jo," she said, swaying on her feet from the effort of staying upright. "And Bennett."

Phillip chuckled, the sound like rusty nails dragged across a glass windowpane. "And yet where is your white knight now?"

He didn't know about Bennett, then. Sam clamped her lips shut, hoping her face betrayed none of her lingering hope. Phillip took another step forward, the Cat moving in sync behind him. She resisted the urge to run screaming into the trees; Father Jacob's demise had already taught her what fate awaited her if she attempted such an escape.

"Now," Phillip said, smoke curling off his tongue. "Bring me the bowl, Cú."

Her fingers locked around the burlap as the Hellfire Cat approached. It stalked around her, the brush of its fur tearing at her coat like a thousand needles. She wanted to fight, but the power of the bowl was like a second heartbeat, strong enough to rattle her bones. When the Hellfire Cat sank its jaws into the burlap and stripped the bowl away, she breathed a soft sigh of relief even as a different dread spiraled through her.

Phillip pulled the burlap back slowly, like a gift, his gaze growing more intent as he shed each layer. When the bowl was finally laid bare, he set his hands to the carved surface with a deep sigh. A throbbing bass tone rumbled through the earth, the black death leaching up from his fingernails into his hands and his wrists, pulsing along the snaking pathways of his arteries. The whites of his eyes were obliterated by the inky black of his irises, threading out through the tiny veins.

"Yes," he said, his voice no longer his own. The raven fluttered up from the path, landing on Phillip's shoulder with a triumphant caw. Sam nearly dropped to her knees again, the image of the bird on his shoulder reminiscent of the body she'd found that first night in the woods outside Orlagh.

"Phillip," Sam croaked in terror. "Where is Jo? Please."

Phillip glared down at her like she was a cockroach scuttling across the floor and he had half a mind to grind her out with the heel of his boot. But then the black receded a bit, and he smiled instead.

"Yes, come bear witness, Samantha. Let me show you what I have accomplished."

Sam wasn't sure she could keep standing, much less follow him up the mountainside, but when she took a step, her bones felt lighter than air. What was more, it seemed as if the bowl was pulling her, drawing her toward Phillip. A whisper circled the whorls of her ear in a dark ecstasy, terrifying her more than anything she had encountered so far as they began the steep trek up to the Hellfire Club.

Sam had no idea how long they had been walking when they reached a wide path leading up the mountain. Phillip turned his face to the setting sun as the clouds scuttled away, revealing the dark disk of the moon beginning its eclipse of the sun. He inhaled deeply, his breath slipping out like smoke when he exhaled. The bowl gave a resonate vibration, making Sam's teeth chatter. The whisper was constant now, louder and more insistent, tangling her thoughts within it so that she didn't know where her own mind ended and the whisper began. Her scalp tingled and her shirt scraped against her arms, making her whole body feel as if it were engulfed by cold flames. She was beginning to understand why the professor had eschewed pants.

"Almost home," Phillip said.

They continued up the path until it leveled out into a wide grassy area, the burned-out shell of the Hellfire Club rising up from the surrounding hills like a pustule. She had been expecting something like the sprawling splendor of Orlagh, but the charred husk of the hunting lodge lurked on the hilltop like a menace. The stones were old and gray, the ones allegedly stolen from the Neolithic passage tomb. Patches of green moss clung to the craggy roof of the building two stories up, the enormous windows gaping black spaces that might have once let in the sun but now seemed like a safety hazard.

"A marvel, isn't it?" Phillip said expansively, opening his arms to encompass the building. "If only Speaker Conolly had understood what he would awaken, digging up those stones to build his hunting lodge. But I suppose I should be thanking him; without his selfish actions, I wouldn't be on the precipice of reclaiming my birthright."

"Phillip, this isn't—" Sam began, but her breath caught as a line of figures emerged from an opening on the roof, all of them dressed in long ceremonial robes. For a moment she thought it might be the brothers of Solas Fíor come to rescue her, but the robes were all wrong. These people were something else; something far more sinister. She couldn't see their faces as they took up their positions along the edge of the roof, glowering down like sentient gargoyles.

"Who are they?" she asked.

"They are the followers of the Divine King," Phillip said, the black of his eyes pulsating. The raven lifted off his shoulder with a cry, swooping over the Hellfire Club before taking a spot of honor over the main entrance. More birds swooped in, dozens of them, decorating the roof beside the robed figures. "Those that were worthy in the blood and answered the call. The new Hellfire Club."

Sam took in a sharp breath. "Descendants of the original members. That's why so many of them visited Dublin in the last six months. They weren't coming to the club; they were coming to meet you."

Phillip grinned. "A king needs his court, even a bastard king. I had Eleanor's spell book, with the register of the original Hellfire Club members conveniently written on the first page. I tracked down each living descendant and learned their wants and fears, the secrets they buried from themselves and society. I offered each of them what they wanted and needed most—a chance to reclaim their truest selves. They welcomed the magic with open arms and gave me the money to fund this excursion. And so they shall be rewarded in the new kingdom!"

The last sentence he shouted up to the roof, holding aloft the bowl in triumph. The club members threw their heads back and howled as one, the light shifting as the clouds scuttled past, the moon eating up more of the sun and casting a pall on the earth. Sam's skin crawled.

Phillip lowered the bowl. "And now, to call the Morrigan and curse the world."

CHAPTER THIRTY-SEVEN

Sam had no choice but to stumble after Phillip as he headed toward the Hellfire Club, her head spinning. There were several openings leading into the club, but Phillip steered her around a rock wall and into a hidden entrance behind it. The dark blinded her, and for a moment she thought the constellations of light behind her eyes had gotten worse until she realized there were candles. Hundreds of them, everywhere, clustered in corners and lining the stairs leading up to the second floor. The rooms were like caves, the light doing little to pierce the gathering shadows. Sam took a deep breath and nearly retched at the dank, musty tang of the air inside. There was something familiar and terrible about that smell.

"Sulfur," she whispered, looking closer at the nearest bank of candles. The flames didn't move despite the mountain wind cutting through the open windows.

"Come, come," Phillip said excitedly, urging her up the stairs as if they were touring his family's townhome and not a two-hundred-year-old cursed hunting lodge.

Sam paused at a window opening, the whole of Dublin spread out at the bottom of the hill, the gray ocean just beyond. It was breathtaking and surreal; the mundanity of city life within sight as they faced the end of the world on top of the mountain.

But that was nothing compared to the sight waiting for her at the top of the stairs. A wide, flat rock filled the center of the room, more candles clustered at the four corners of the giant slab, emitting clouds of black smoke tinged in purple, obscuring the ceiling. Several more robed members of the new Hellfire Club ringed the altar—for that was what the giant stone must have been —and among them Joana stood bound and gagged, her eyes wide and round in a terror Sam imagined must be reflected on her own face.

"Jo," Sam choked out, lurching forward. Phillip caught her in his iron grip, steering her around the altar to stand beside Joana. Another of the robed club members took her arm, holding her fast. The young man's hood fell back, revealing eyes as black as Phillip's, his forehead marked with one of the symbols from the bowl. What had Bennett called it? The triquetra. The mark of the threefold goddess. Sam reached for Joana, gripping her fingers.

"You both have the privilege of witnessing the restoration of the Divine Kingship to the motherland," Phillip said, holding the bowl out over the altar ceremoniously. "And a cleansing of her soil by the blood of the unfaithful. Let this first great sacrifice begin the wave."

"Sacrifice?" Sam said, her voice hoarse from the smoke.

More robed figures filed into the room, all of them marked with the same symbol on their foreheads, guiding a familiar figure that made Sam's heart plunge into a deep well.

"Alistair," she whispered.

"Sam?" Alistair said, blinking through the shadows. He coughed, waving away the smoke. "What are you doing here? What's going on? Phillip, is that you?"

"Thank you for coming, Alistair Fitzgerald," Phillip said in a deep, resonant tone. "Your sacrifice today will set right the imbalanced scales of time. Please bring him forward."

"Sacrifice?" Alistair echoed as one of the robed figures prodded him forward. He took in the odd arrangements of the room, his eyes going wide as he stopped before the altar. He gave a nervous chuckle. "Veronica, this is a bit beyond the pale, isn't it? When you said you were taking me somewhere safe after getting me out of that old country house, I assumed you meant the hotel or the Garda. This is . . . What is this?"

"I told you, Alistair," came a crisp voice from the deep folds of the robed figure behind him. Veronica pushed back her hood, her lips stained a deep red. The mark of the goddess stood out like ashes on her pale skin. "You would find your life's purpose on this trip. You've always been a shiftless, spineless young man. Given all the opportunities denied to my gender. And yet you would squander them on what? Studying the humanities? Taking lunch at the club with your idiotic compatriots? Attending the House of Lords as if it were a burden and not an honor? You never deserved the title or the inheritance. They should have been mine by blood right, but instead my father bequeathed them to you. All because of a world that views women as nothing more than brainless chattel. But that changes today. With Phillip, I will reclaim what is rightfully mine."

Phillip seized Alistair as Veronica stepped forward, wielding a golden dagger that flashed in the unnatural candlelight as it arced across his throat. Sam screamed as the hot spray of his blood streaked down his chest, spilling into the hungry depths of the ritual bowl, absorbing into the grain until it pulsed with his lifeblood. The stones of the Hellfire Club trembled, the moon fully eclipsing the sun.

"Good," Phillip breathed, the deathly black staining his teeth. "Now we can begin."

Vibrations rattled through Sam's feet, making her teeth hurt as the ringing of the bowl made the earth itself quake. Smoke poured from the candles, burning her eyes and clouding Phillip in darkness while he read from the book placed on the altar, the spell book Eleanor Rosewood stole from the Hellfire Club. His words were guttural and ancient, weaving into the sonorous dissonance surrounding them. The smoke filled Sam's nose and mouth, tasting of metal and rot and making her gag.

"Specter Queen, ancient goddess of the fates of man," Phillip called, lifting the bowl high. "We beseech thee, rise from your slumber and bring forth your army to cleanse this land with the blood of the unfaithful. Arise, Morrígu, and anoint this land anew!"

A roar rose from the earth outside, the new members of the Hellfire Club abandoning their grip on Sam and Joana as they rushed to the window. Sam tore at the knots on the cloth wedged in Joana's mouth, tossing it aside and going to work on the ropes that bound her wrists.

"Jo, I'm so sorry, I didn't know what else to do," she said, her fingers shaking. "I couldn't just let him take you."

Joana grabbed for Sam's hands as the bindings came undone. "You did what I'd never have the guts to do, Sam. Even after those awful things I said, you came for me."

"Of course I came for you," Sam said, squeezing her hand as tight as she could. "I'll always be there for you, Jo. I . . . I forgot myself, for a long time. I lost myself, and I lost you. It took the end of the world for me to figure it out, but at least we're together now."

"I'm not dying here," Joana said grimly. "Not with Phillip and

Veronica and their tacky robes that look like a community-theater production of *Macbeth*. Where is Bennett?"

"He went to Orlagh to steal weapons from Solas Fíor," Sam whispered. "I was going to hide the bowl, but Phillip found me, and I lost Bennett."

"Well, then, we'll just have to get ourselves out of this," Joana said. "Come on."

They skirted around the altar, the smoke obscuring their movements as they made for the now-abandoned door. The Hellfire Club members still crowded the window, raising their arms and cheering the chaos happening below. Sam and Joana stole out of the room and down the stairs to the first floor, the air so thick they could barely breathe. But they managed to stumble their way out of the club and onto the grassy field beyond.

Except that the field was no longer grassy. A great trench had opened along the site of the former passage tomb; a dark light spilled up out of the earth and settled over the hill like an unnatural mist, obscuring the sky. The mountainside filled with the cries and howls of animals trapped in the trees and confused by the sudden fall of night. The ravens perched on the roof cried out, their calls overlapping and echoing across the open field. Above them all came the howl of the Hellfire Cat.

"Holy hell," Joana breathed, pointing toward the crack in the earth over the passage tomb. "What is that?"

Something crawled out of the earth, a broken form scurrying along the ground with a snarl. It slithered and skittered over the grass before stretching and lengthening into a familiar form with open wings and a curved beak, its shadow sailing into the dark sky like a missing patch of night. It gave a cry like those of the ravens on the roof, and yet the sound was deeper and more ominous, the cries clashing and resonating until Sam had to put her hands over her ears to keep them from bleeding.

"It's the Morrigan," Sam shouted, watching the shadowy figure settle in the open window of the Hellfire Club before Phillip. "The Specter Queen. Phillip has called the curse."

Several figures burst from the tree line at the edge of the grassy field, clad in robes and carrying a variety of weapons. Sam spotted Brother Noah in the forefront, holding aloft a sword still glistening with holy water. Brother Padraig crashed through the trees behind him, wielding a wicked medieval mace. Amos's flop of curls appeared at the back of the group, and Sam sent a silent thank-you to Seamus at Christ Church Cathedral. She searched desperately among their ranks for any sign of Bennett, but didn't spot him.

"End this blasphemy now!" Brother Noah thundered, raising his sword. "In the name of Solas Fíor, the One True Light, we are sworn to protect the earth from this evil."

Phillip stood large in the glassless window, the power of the curse lengthening his bones and sharpening his tongue as it flicked out from behind a smile.

"There have always been those that cast their useless corpses in the path of true progress," he called out, his voice unnaturally magnified. He held out an arm and spoke a few words, the Morrigan's raven form dissipating and re-forming with her claws biting deep into the folds of Phillip's robe as she perched on his arm. "Let your bodies be the first to fall before the might of the Morrigan. Speak our victory into their unwilling ears, great goddess."

The shadowy raven threw her head back and sent up a cry that swept over the land as a wave of dark mist poured out of the crack like a pestilence, surging toward the gathered men of Solas Fíor. Brother Noah gave a shout, swinging his sword through the oncoming tide and splitting the mist in half. But more of the dark mist poured forward, slithering through the ranks of the men like a murderous whisper and growing tendrils that wrapped around their ankles and curled over their collarbones, insinuating itself into the ears and noses and eyes of the brothers.

Even from the other side of the clearing, Sam could hear the whispering. The Morrigan, working her influence on the enemy. Sam's throat was too swollen with fear to shout a warning. The brothers' weapons, raised to attack, hovered in the air as the whispering grew louder, the men's bodies shuddering and jerking as if they were fighting a battle in their own minds. Which, Sam knew, they were.

It was Brother Noah who turned first, his eyes black and his veins pulsing with magic, raising his sword against Brother Padraig with a snarl. It cut through the smoke in a gleaming arc, the reverberations as it met the sharp steel of Padraig's mace worse than the trailing rumbles of the earth. One by one, the members of Solas Fíor turned on one another, their weapons filling the air with the ring of violent metal. It was just as Father Jacob had described it, and yet so much worse. Brother against brother, friend against friend. Sam knew what the bowl had done to her own mind; she couldn't imagine what nightmares the brothers were facing as they fought with bloody savagery among their own kind.

"The last great war of man," Joana said, her voice hollow.

The dark mist kept coming from the crack in the ground as the men fought like rabid animals. It spread its poison farther, filtering down through the trees and infecting the wildlife as it went. It billowed toward Sam and Joana like the inexorable crest of an oncoming wave, forcing them back against the stones of the Hellfire Club. The smoke surrounded them, blocking out the trees below as the moon obscured the sunlight from above. The eclipse had reached its apex, and the Morrigan was turning the tide of the war.

CHAPTER THIRTY-EIGHT

"What do we do?" Sam asked, shaking. She pushed back against the stones of the old lodge until they dug into her scalp, the dark mist swirling around them.

Joana shook her head, her eyes wide and her face pale. "Beats the hell out of me. That . . . evil fog is everywhere. If it tries to stick one of its tendrils in my ear, I'll saw it off faster than van Gogh. I'm not getting possessed by any kind of ancient deity."

The new members of the Hellfire Club cheered their goddess from the open window above, for a moment drawing Sam's attention from the oncoming wave. The Morrigan beat her wings, her shrill cry cutting through the mist, driving it down the mountain toward Dublin. But the mist didn't reach the window overhead, the faces of the club members clear and stark in their triumph. Veronica leaned out, her teeth bared as she laughed at the brothers, and Sam caught a glimpse of the smudge of ash on her forehead.

"The mark of the threefold goddess," Sam whispered.

"Sam," Joana said, her voice tight with alarm. Sam looked down where the mist had completely surrounded them, cutting off any hope of escape. A long tendril twisted out of the mass, slithering over the ground toward their feet.

"Do you have a lipstick tube?" Sam asked suddenly.

Joana gave her a crazed look. "Why? So you can murder me in style when that thing possesses us?"

Sam shook her head, holding out a hand. "Please, Jo, quickly."

"Well, it's not like I had time to pack," Joana muttered, but she dug through her coat pockets and pulled out a small gold tube of lipstick. "Here, but that's my best color. Don't ruin it."

Sam ignored her chiding, tossing the cap and rolling up the creamy stick of lip color with shaky hands. She'd only caught a glimpse of the mark on the bowl and on the other Hellfire Club members, but it was the best and only idea she had. Quickly she scrawled a mark on Joana's forehead, praying it was clear enough. The mist lapped over their feet, climbing up their ankles.

"Please work," Sam whispered, though she didn't know who she was whispering to.

A shudder went through the mist, like someone had dropped a stone into its depths, reversing the course of the ripples as it drew away from Joana's feet. But the mist climbed higher up Sam's legs, her calf muscles seizing like she'd plunged them into an ice bath. The Morrigan's whisper scraped at her ear, making her shudder.

"Quick, Jo, draw the mark on me!"

"I don't know how!" Joana protested, taking the tube of lipstick. "I've never seen it!"

"It's three arcs laced together," Sam said, her irritation growing. "With a circle in the background."

"Well, sure, when you say it like that," Joana said sarcastically.

"We don't have time for your quips," Sam snarled.

"Sam," Joana said, drawing back in surprise.

In agony, Sam quickly swiped her fingers over the stones of the Hellfire Club in an approximation of the symbol. "Like that, Jo. Quick."

"You're a worse instructor than my art-history teacher," Joana grumbled, but she wielded the tube of lipstick and made the mark on Sam's forehead. "How's that?"

Sam opened her mouth to snap at Joana once again, but the irritation sharply abated. She sucked in a breath, her calves unclenching as the mist receded from around her legs. She grabbed Joana's shoulder, as much to hold up her own shaking limbs as to draw Joana into a hug.

"You did it," she gasped. "Jo, you did it."

"Sure, but what do we do now? There's not enough lipstick to go around."

Something glinted through the mist, and for a moment Sam feared it was the brothers of Solas Fíor hacking their way toward them. But then a figure emerged, wild-eyed and waving a pair of stolen knives.

"You two," Bennett growled, pointing the weapons in Sam and Joana's direction.

"Oh hell," Joana muttered. "I'll distract him; you mark him."

She slapped the lipstick in Sam's hand and stepped forward, holding her hands up and waving them to draw his attention.

"Nice of you to make it, big brother," Joana said with a smile.

"Bennett, you don't want to hurt us," Sam said, moving around Joana to get closer to him. He watched her like a cornered animal, his blackened eyes fixating on the mark on her forehead. "That's right, see? We're marked by the goddess. We're not an enemy."

"Both of you have done nothing but make trouble for me this trip," Bennett said, though he didn't snarl as he said it. Sam considered that progress.

"Brother, I wouldn't be doing my job as a younger sibling if I didn't make trouble," Joana said.

Bennett's eyes narrowed on Joana, his grip on the knives tightening.

"That's not helping," Sam hissed.

Joana blew out a breath, throwing up her hands. "All right, fine. Bennett, I'm sorry. You were right, we were wrong, we should have left everything to you, now we need your help to fix this mess. Is that better?"

"You could be more sincere," Sam said, testing Bennett by taking another step forward. His eyes bore down on her, the glassy blackness terrifying this close. "Bennett. Please. I know what you're feeling right now. The anger, the hatred, it's scooping out your insides to make space for itself. It's awful. But it's not *you*. You're patient, and methodical, and fair. You always try to do what's right. And you're the only boy who's ever noticed my hair. Please, fight it. Put down the knives."

Bennett's jaw tightened even as some of the shine went out of his eyes. Sam took another step, close enough that she could raise a hand and smooth away the frown lines between his eyebrows, something she had dreamed of doing ever since they were children. The gesture was like a soothing balm, and Bennett's nostrils flared as he let out a breath and closed his eyes, lowering his hands. Quickly she raised the tube of lipstick and drew the triquetra, marking him safe from the goddess's wrath. When he opened his eyes again, they swirled like warm honey.

"Bennett," she sighed, throwing her arms around him. He didn't hesitate as he wrapped her in a fierce hug, breathing in the scent of her along her neck.

"Thank you," he said. "It was . . ."

"I know," Sam said, holding him tighter. "I know."

"This isn't making me at all uncomfortable," Joana said dryly. "But we've got to get out of here."

"That mist is moving down the mountain fast," Bennett said, drawing back reluctantly. "We need to get to Dublin and find help."

Sam looked behind her. "What about the brothers? And Phillip and the Hellfire Club members? How do we stop them?"

Bennett shook his head. "We can't. I have to save both of you. It's my fault you were ever here in the first place. I can't stop them, but I can still try to save you."

Sam looked at the heavy mist still surrounding them, the cloud rising and coalescing like a storm overhead. She was stuck in place as she always was. Was this how her papa felt in his last moments? Did he feel this tightness in his chest, the terror snatching his reason as the world burned around him? Did he try to stop it, or did he curl up and give in to the terror, as she wanted to do just then? The telegram had told her mother nothing; he had died in the trenches, scattered to the earth by a bomb. Nothing left to bury. There had been one item recovered, a half-melted little metal horse he'd found in the rubble in France. He must have been waiting to bring it home to her.

Her papa, so quiet and steady. Always willing to listen to her lectures on the latest excavation techniques she used in her treasure hunts. He never rolled his eyes as the other children did, or shoved a load of laundry in her hands as her mother did. He was a gentle soul, a man of the land. Not a fighter.

But he had fought. He had been one of the first to volunteer. He didn't fight for the killing; he fought to protect Sam and others whose voices would forever be silenced without his help. He made a choice; to fight for those he loved. To die for them, if he had to. Joana had been right all along; Sam had thought to protect herself from the pain of that loss by turning away from life, but this half life was like its own death. In order to live—to truly, fully live—she had to embrace all aspects of life, even the danger looming over them now.

And she still had a choice. To fight for the ones she loved, like Joana. Like Bennett, and her mother, and Mr. Steeling. And maybe, most of all, for herself. Yes, the world could be a frightening place, but only she had the choice of what to do with that fear.

And today, she chose to be brave.

"I have to go back!" she called above the rising wind.

"Are you crazy?" Joana shouted.

Bennett shook his head furiously. "I won't allow it."

"Go to Orlagh and search the archives," Sam said. The wind was screaming now, cawing like the Morrigan's cry above. "They must have something to help."

"Then come with us!" Bennett protested.

"I found that bowl, Bennett. I put it in Phillip's hands. I have to get it back, if I can."

"Like hell we're leaving you behind," Joana said, snatching one of Bennett's knives and holding it up.

"You have to," Sam said, hugging her friend fiercely. "I love you, Jo. I'm sorry I ever made you doubt it."

Joana's jaw set in a stubborn line. "I never did, you fool. Not really."

"Sam—" Bennett said, but she went up on her tiptoes and pressed her lips against his to silence him. It was a kiss they didn't have time for, but she took it anyway. She let the warmth of his lips infuse her with the strength she would need for what lay ahead. When she pulled back, he sighed.

"I can't let you do this," he said.

"You can and you will, because you know I'm right. Get to Orlagh and find something to stop Phillip. I've spent seven years running away from my feelings, from life, from everything, Bennett. I won't run anymore."

"Sam, don't do this," Joana gasped.

Sam gave her a smile. "For once I get to be the reckless one, Jo."

She dashed through the open mouth of the Hellfire Club entrance before they could respond, ready to face Phillip and the fate that awaited her above.

CHAPTER THIRTY-NINE

Sam sprinted up the stairs to the second level, chunks of rock pelting her head and shoulders as the earth outside vomited the Morrigan's whispering mist into the sky. It obscured everything, pouring through the open windows and condensing into shapes that terrified Sam if she looked too closely. She hoped Bennett and Joana could make it to Orlagh before the scourge reached the city. Even if they could find nothing in the archives, at least they might be safe in the country house.

Her newfound sense of bravery was all well and good, but once she reached the top of the stairs, the logic of it faltered. She had nothing to defend herself with, no clue how to stop the Morrigan, and she could barely hear or see anything through the dense smoke. Everything tasted like rotted eggs. She felt forward blindly, the stone walls slick from the damp interior and pulsing like newly formed skin.

She had no idea which direction to turn, or if it even mattered, but she kept moving forward, one hand along the stone, looking for the ritual room. The wall cut sharply to the right and she stumbled forward into the abyss, her boot tangling in something soft on the floor and dragging her down hard on one knee. She braced for the impact, but it wasn't stone that she hit. It was something far softer, and still warm. The smoke swirled away just long enough for her to make out Alistair's face on the ground, the golden knife lying on the floor beside him. She scrambled back, gagging on the sulfuric fumes burning her nose, and a gleam on the altar caught her attention.

The bowl.

The damned bowl that had upended the carefully laid path of her life. The bowl that had caused Alistair's death, had driven the professor mad, had burned up her books, and had planted its splinter of darkness in Eleanor Rosewood's womb two hundred years ago. She dreaded ever touching it again, but it was her only chance to end the curse.

She snatched up the golden knife, tucking it into her boot top as she shrugged out of her father's winter coat. She turned it around and put her arms through so she could grab the bowl without letting the petrified wood touch her skin. But it still burned her arms as they wrapped around it. Using every last ounce of her strength, she tried to lift it from its place on the altar. It seemed to have gained a hundred times its weight since she set it down, and she couldn't help wondering if that had something to do with Alistair.

But there was no time to think about the British boy, because the bowl was angry. It bit into Sam, stabbing at her mind and making her skin feel like it would shred and her eyes like they would burst. Its power was like a punch right through her midsection, and she had never wanted to drop anything so much in her whole life.

But Sam was no weakling; despite her years in the bookshop, she was still a laundress's daughter. She was built like her mother, and her grandmother and great-grandmother before her, with sturdy shoulders and a wide rib cage perfect for lugging hundreds of pounds of steaming-hot, wet laundry out to hang on the lines. So she gritted her teeth, squeezing the bowl as hard as she could, and wrenched it free of the altar.

The smoke halted mid-swirl, thinning and paling enough that she could see the Hellfire Club members gathered at the window. They paused in their celebrations, turning as one to where she now stood at the foot of the altar, the bowl doing its best to destroy her.

"What are you doing?" Phillip snarled, his cheekbones showing through his skin.

Sam didn't answer, just broke for the door as they all screamed—an eerie echo of the Hellfire Cat, as if the magic of the bowl had bound them all together. She could at least see her way down the stairs now, with the smoke seizing up and shrinking back into the corners of the lodge. The farther she got from the altar, the harder the bowl fought her and the heavier it got, until it was slipping out of her grasp and crashing down on the stone floor, breaking through the rocks to topple to the first floor below.

"Get the bowl!" Phillip cried from the top of the stairs, opening his mouth and emitting that same terrifying scream.

Sam slipped down the stairs and swept up the bowl, stumbling out the door as the Hellfire Club members descended after her, some of them jumping from the windows to block her path. The dark mist formed a cyclone around them, turning Sam's hair to razor wire as it whipped across her cheeks. She barely knew where the ground was under her feet. While she was still trying to figure out which direction was *away*, the robed figures emerged from the mist, surrounding her.

"Give us the bowl," they said in one voice, deep and thrumming.

"No," Sam cried, hugging it closer though it felt like holding a glowing ember from the center of a bonfire.

Phillip stepped through their ranks, a good foot taller than he had been an hour ago. "Give us the bowl," he said, his voice a collection of all the terrors of the underworld.

"No!" came a cry from deep in the mist. Brother Noah stumbled forward through the smoke, his eyes clear of the pestilence now that Sam had taken the bowl and weakened the curse. Several others broke through the dark mists behind him; Brother Padraig's expression was murderous.

"In the name of the true light, we will not allow heretical demons to poison this land!" Brother Noah called, trembling as he lifted his sword.

"Your pathetic pieces of tin will never stop us," Phillip growled, his teeth crumbling as a black fire burned through him. He sneered at Brother Noah. "You're too late. You can't stop us. You can't stop her."

The club members fell to their knees and raised their arms to the chaos as a shadow swooped out of the mist, the raven form growing and stretching until bare feet touched the ground and a woman's face emerged from the dark feathers. Except it wasn't a woman's face, not quite. Her aspect shifted with every gust of the magical wind, first a beautiful young woman, then a fierce warrior, then a wrinkled crone. And over all of those aspects hung the specter of the raven, her favorite form. She was the Morrigan, the threefold goddess, the shapeshifter, queen of Ireland and goddess of death. And she was looking right at Sam with the intensity of a single ray of sunlight through a magnifying glass, making her whole body burn worse than the heat of the bookshop fire.

"Who among you dares to interrupt my awakening?" the goddess asked in a voice that tore open the clouds and shook the leaves from the trees. That remote, academic part of Sam's brain noted what a terror she must have been for the earliest Celts on the battlefield.

"She took the sacrifice," Phillip accused, leveling one bony finger in Sam's direction. She shrank back, still clutching the bowl.

The Morrigan's gaze swept over her like a rake over coals. "She bears my mark."

"She is not one of us!" Phillip cried, and for the briefest moment his true voice broke through in his human frustration. "She stole her way in and is trying to trick her way back out."

In all her life, Sam never imagined facing an ancient goddess of death on a cursed hillside. But if she had, she certainly never would have imagined the goddess *smiling*. But the Morrigan did, the expression folding the wrinkles of the crone's face like a rumpled bedsheet.

"I enjoy a trickster," the goddess said.

Phillip shook with rage, bringing a bloodstain of color to his cheeks. "She is unworthy. I am the one who has called you. I am the one who deserves your favor. Cleanse this land of the unfaithful and restore me to the Divine Kingship!"

The smile dissolved as the Morrigan turned black eyes on Phillip, the blood draining away from his face as he shrank several inches under her consideration.

"You do not command me, child of the oak. I am the protector of the land. No man shall be king unless I anoint him so."

"But I called you," Phillip said, straightening up. "I was the only one who could. You are my birthright. I will be king. If it is another sacrifice you require, I will happily make it. And no one will stand in my way, least of all a bookshop girl."

Phillip pounced on Sam, drawing another golden knife from the folds of his robe and pressing it against her neck. Something rammed into them, knocking them apart and sending the bowl spinning off into the grass. Bennett wrestled Phillip to the ground, his own stolen knife flashing as they rolled over in a heap of robes and weapons. Bennett had the element of surprise, catching Phillip across the face with the stolen knife. Sticky black tar bubbled up from the cut, hissing and popping as the other Hellfire Club members cried out and clutched their faces.

But Bennett was no match for the strength Phillip now possessed with the magic burning through him. Phillip threw him off, sending him flying into the other club members, who grabbed at his clothes and held him down.

"Bennett!" Sam cried, scrambling up.

"I should have killed you that first day on the train as I planned," Phillip snarled, standing over Bennett with his knife flashing. "You've been nothing but a hindrance. Always trying to insinuate yourself between the professor and me like a lost puppy looking for affection. So pathetic."

"You poisoned him!" Bennett shouted, fighting against the club members holding him. "You had to use magic to get him to listen to you. If anyone is pathetic, it's you."

Out of the corner of her eye Sam caught the flash of movement. There was Joana, running across the open field toward them. Sam almost cried out, but Joana put a finger over her mouth. She edged closer to the fallen bowl.

"You couldn't stand not being the favored one," Phillip said. "Like all the rest. Never been denied a thing in your pampered lives. You've never had a door closed in your face, or an opportunity taken away because you didn't have the right pedigree."

He raised his knife over Bennett, and Sam lurched forward, drawing his attention. "Phillip, I know this world has hurt you. It's . . . It has hurt me, too. I know how you're feeling, that this world doesn't deserve to go on when it's cost us so much. But this ritual, it won't fix what's actually wrong. It won't heal your heart. This is the magic working its madness on you. It's devouring you from the inside out, can't you see that? The magic doesn't care about you, it only wants to use you. It's no better than those boys at Oxford."

Phillip turned on her. "It is not madness to want what has always been denied to you. You have lost, Samantha. Would you not do anything to get back that which was unfairly taken from you?"

Sam's heart squeezed, and for a moment—just a fleeting, intangible moment—she imagined what it would be like to have her papa back. Never gone to war, never torn apart, never memorialized with an empty grave. What would it have meant to her life the past seven years if he had come home?

"We can't go back, Phillip," Sam said, her voice thick with tears. "And even if we could, it would never be the same. We have to learn to move forward, otherwise we'll always be stuck in the past."

"I'm not stuck in the past, Samantha," Phillip said. "I'm forging a new future. We will be better than those that came before us."

Sam shook her head. "The world doesn't belong to you."

"It belongs to those bold enough to take it," Phillip said. "I sacrificed everything to be here. I deserve it."

"Then get what you deserve," Sam said, pulling the golden knife hidden in her boot just as Joana took the ritual bowl, screaming in pain but keeping her hold long enough to stumble to where Sam stood. Sam lifted the weapon over her head with both hands and brought it down in the middle of the bowl.

The knife, still imbued with Alistair's sacrifice, cut deep into the ancient wood, cracking it in half.

CHAPTER FORTY

The crack in the bowl reverberated through the earth, new fissures opening up around them and sucking in the dark mist back to the underworld. The ground ruptured between Sam and Joana, forcing them apart as the split halves of the bowl tumbled into the darkness below. The Hellfire Club members screamed, clawing at their faces and tearing apart their robes as the magic that imbued their blood and bound them together called them down into the realm of the Specter Queen. The Morrigan shifted into a raven and swooped into the sky with a great, screaming caw, diving down and latching on to Phillip's shoulder.

"Phillip," Sam breathed, the image a visceral reminder of the body she stumbled over in the woods. What had Bennett said about the Morrigan? She foretold a man's death by sitting on his shoulder in her raven form. "Phillip!"

But the Morrigan had already sealed his fate, plummeting into the dark depths of the earth and dragging him along with her, the black mist swallowing his cries. The other Hellfire Club members were not far behind, stumbling into the fissures after the Morrigan, some of them scrabbling at the dirt and screaming as the magic drew them down into the earth. The Hellfire Cat stalked the edges

329

of the deepest trench, throwing up one last plaintive howl before plunging into the maw after its master. As the smoke disappeared, the cracks began to shrink, the earth swallowing up its prize.

"Sam! Jo!" Bennett shouted as two club members pulled him closer to one of the openings. Sam dodged the cracks as she made her way toward him, Joana sprinting past her with a large rock in her hands. She raised it over her head and chucked it at one of the club members. His arms dropped to his side as the rock bashed against his head.

"That's for tying me up, you bastard," Joana shouted as Bennett fought off the grip of the other club member. The dark mist crested over the edge in a wave, swallowing the two men before it disappeared back into the earth.

"Did you consider that you might have hit me with that rock, Jo?" Bennett asked, bewildered.

She set her hands on her hips. "Are you honestly about to lecture me on technique when I saved you from getting dragged into the Celtic underworld? Is 'thank you' really that foreign a concept to you?"

"Right," Bennett said, for once looking suitably chastised. "Thank you, Jo."

Joana puffed out a breath. "You're damn welcome."

"Help!" someone cried, and the three of them lurched forward as a figure clung to the edge of one of the recently opened fissures. Veronica scrabbled at the earth as the mist licked hungrily at the dangling edges of her robe. Her eyes were now a crystal blue and wide in horror. "Please, help me! Don't let it take me!"

"Oh hell," Joana muttered, but she was first to the edge and grabbed Veronica's hand.

"Please don't let me fall," Veronica panted. "I had no idea . . .

Every dark thought I'd ever had about my family, about Alistair . . . Oh, Alistair. What will I tell our mother?"

"Whatever you want," Joana grunted as Sam and Bennett took hold of Veronica's arms, trying and failing to pull her up. "Let's just get you out first."

"Tell her I'm sorry," Veronica said, her eyes shimmering. "Don't tell her what we did. What *I* did. Don't let her think of me that way."

The mist surged up, driving Sam and the others back with the fury of its presence. Veronica's arms slipped from their grasp, and when the mist receded, the girl was gone.

"That absolute wretch," Joana said, her voice hoarse. "Making me feel sorry for her by the end. Of course she would."

The earth gave an ominous rumble as the cracks shrank even more, further destabilizing the earth.

"We've got to get off the mountain," Bennett said.

"This way!" called Brother Noah, waving them toward a break in the trees. They ran in a single line, losing their footing as the earth worked to close itself up again, rattling the ground beneath their feet. Bennett reached for Sam's hand and took a firm hold, and Sam did the same with Joana, all of them forming a chain as they made for Brother Noah.

"Watch the trees!" Brother Padraig shouted as they passed.

"What's wrong with the trees?" Joana called.

An enormous pine towering over them shivered and tilted, its roots shoved up from below, before it gave a resounding crack and toppled toward the earth. Bennett pulled hard on Sam's arm, all of them just clearing the tree before it crashed onto the path behind them, blocking the way back to the Hellfire Club.

"I think that's what's wrong," Sam panted, stumbling past the tentacle-like roots of more trees as she followed in Brother Noah's wake.

They continued their descent, reminiscent of their journey the night of the Hellfire Cat, each rock and root and soft patch of earth conspiring to bring them down. But when Sam stumbled, Bennett held her fast; and when Joana stumbled, Sam kept her from falling. As long as they held on together, Sam knew none of them would fall. The smoke had cleared, the clouds scuttling away as the moon continued its journey and sunlight returned to the hills. By the time they reached the bottom, the sun was setting in brilliant tones of gold. Faint rumbles echoed through the ground under their feet, but finally the mountain gave one last sigh and settled back into place with nothing more than a few uprooted trees to note what had transpired at the Hellfire Club.

Sam heaved in a breath, the sound of it ragged and loud in the sudden stillness. They stopped in a thinner patch of trees, all of them panting and leaning against the spruces and firs that remained upright. Sam trembled and ached, and her head pounded like it never had in her life. But it also felt clear for the first time since she touched the bowl back in the crypt of Christ Church Cathedral. The magic was gone, retreated back to the underworld. Along with the new members of the Hellfire Club, and Phillip and Veronica. For the rest of her life, Sam didn't think she would forget the look of terror on that girl's face before the darkness took her.

"Is it really over?" Joana asked, sagging against the bark of a nearby oak.

Bennett nodded from where he rested on a large stone. "I think it's over."

"Good, because I could use a pint or two. Or ten."

"Brother Padraig, take two brothers and go back up the mountain to check the site of the Hellfire Club," said Brother Noah, waving them back up the hill. "None of us will rest tonight until we're sure the place has been cleansed of the dark magic. And bring down the bodies of the brothers we lost in the fight. They deserve a proper burial."

"And Alistair, too," Sam said, the words thick. "He deserves one as well."

Brother Noah gave a short nod. "The Fitzgerald boy as well."

"Aye," grunted Brother Padraig, giving Sam a glare. Had she not just faced down the Celtic goddess of war and death, it might have cowed her. But as it was, she met his gaze straight on, steady and cool. He gave another grunt and turned away, up toward the club.

"I should be cross with you, lass," Brother Noah said to Sam, wincing from a deep cut over one eye. "In fact, I *am* cross with you. I told you to stay out of our affairs and let us handle the Hellfire Club, and instead ye took the bowl and handed it over to the enemy and nearly cost us everything."

"I'm sorry," Sam said, though she wasn't quite sure she could bring herself to actually feel it. "They had Jo. I couldn't just let Phillip . . . I knew you wouldn't approve, and I was afraid if I didn't do something, he would hurt her. I had planned to give it to you, I swear it, after we rescued Joana. But it all went a bit . . . pear-shaped."

"Pear-shaped." Joana snorted. "More like ass-end-up." Sam shot her a look and she held her hands up. "Not that I'm not grateful for the intervention."

"We would have given ye aid, had ye but asked for it," said Brother Noah, his tone heavy. He heaved a sigh. "But ye did good in the end, and the bowl is returned back where it belongs, in the bowels of the earth, out of the hands of those that would use it for harm. So, cross as I am with you, we can consider this one a wash."

Sam looked through the ranks of the remaining brothers, her stomach twisting. "But where is Amos?"

"Oh, I'm still kicking about, miss—er, Sam," said a young voice. Amos came limping through the trees where Brother Padraig had disappeared. "Banged up a good bit, and I can't quite see out me left eye, but the bastards didn't get me."

"Oh, Amos!" Sam cried, pushing past the other brothers to throw her arms around the boy. "Oh, I'm so glad you're safe."

"Oh, well, I . . ." Amos gave her an awkward little pat on her back. "I thank you for that. Though I guess I should be crossways with you as well."

"Oh, please don't," Sam said, pulling away. "You really were indispensable. Without your help, we couldn't have rescued Jo and stopped Phillip. You saved the day."

"I don't know about that," Amos said, his cheeks turning a bright pink.

"All right, that's enough," Brother Noah grumbled. "You keep on like that, he'll think he's too good for Solas Fíor and go try and start his own sacred brotherhood."

Amos's eyes lit up as they landed on Brother Noah. "Does that mean you'll let me take my vows after all?"

"It means you're a sight closer than you were before this day, lad," said Brother Noah. "Though we'll have to discuss how the lass led you on a hunt and locked you up down in the crypt."

Amos's smile turned a shade darker and Sam patted him on the shoulder. "Don't let him scare you," she said. "If they don't let you in, you can always come back to America with us."

"I wouldn't go that far," Brother Noah said. "We thank ye for your help this day, all of you. And for your discretion when you leave, of course."

"If there's anything I'm known for, it's not discretion," Joana muttered. She held her hands up as Brother Noah glared at her. "But for you, I'll consider making an exception."

"What will you do now that the Hellfire Club is gone?" Sam asked.

Brother Noah grunted. "The bowl might be gone, but the Hellfire Club stands as strong and cursed as ever. As long as those stones are on that mountain, we'll be down here to watch over them."

"The professor," Bennett said, rising off the rock. "What about Professor Wallstone?"

"We'll have his things collected and returned to him," Brother Noah said. "As for the magic, I can't say. The madness your friend put into him could take a great deal of time to undo. He'll need care and looking after. And if the magic is still within him—"

"I will take care of him," Bennett said firmly. "I'll see to it that no more harm comes to him. There's no need for any of you to concern yourselves with him anymore."

"We shall see," Brother Noah muttered noncommittally. He looked around to the other brothers of Solas Fíor, his expression grim. "We've got more than enough to do this night, brothers, so we may as well get to work. And I hope you three don't take it as an insult when I say I hope to never cross paths with any of you again."

Joana leaned in with a thin smile. "The feeling is more than mutual."

The brothers of Solas Fíor dispersed into the woods to begin the long process of putting their world back to rights. In the ensuing silence, Sam took a deep breath, taking in the tranquility of bird cries and frigid January winds. The woods, at last, felt like woods.

"I should be cross with the both of ye," Sam said in a poor approximation of Brother Noah's accent, rounding on Joana and Bennett. "I told you to let me handle Phillip and the Hellfire Club."

Joana rolled her eyes and groaned. "Just say thank you, you lump."

"Of course I'm grateful, I was only teasing," Sam said, tackling her friend in a hug. She turned to Bennett, her expression softening. "We did it. We saved the world."

"And said some very revealing things along the way," Joana murmured.

Sam's cheeks turned a dusty rose, but she didn't look away. Neither did Bennett, though his ears took on a distinctly pink tone along the top edges. Instead he stepped forward, brushing one hand against her cheek.

"*You* saved the world, Sam. I told you, you're the most incredible girl I know."

"Save it for the hotel, you two," Joana said, tromping her way toward the path to Orlagh. "I'm going to need that pint or ten to process this new development. I'll let you know after whether or not you've got my blessing."

Sam chuckled, the feeling of it intoxicating. "Which of us do you think she's talking to?"

"Definitely me," Bennett said, at the same time that Joana called out, "Definitely Bennett."

EPILOGUE

Sam squeezed beside two young women bedecked in hiero-
glyphic jewelry and wearing dresses draped to look like the
linen folds of a mummy to take a seat in the second row of the
already crowded auditorium. She clutched the pamphlet that was
handed her when she arrived in the room, an unsmiling picture of
the featured lecturer taking up half the first page of the flyer. Howard Carter looked stern yet wise, knowledgeable yet approachable.
The title of the lecture read HOWARD CARTER REVEALS THE SECRETS
OF THE BOY PHARAOH'S TOMB in large block letters drawn to look
like hieroglyphics themselves. The two girls next to her huddled
together, the gauzy strips that made up their dresses no match for
the deep chill of the early February day. One of them cast a pitying
glance in Sam's direction.

"Do you belong to an Egyptology salon?" she asked.

"Oh, no," Sam said with a smile. "I'm a new student here at the
university. And a fan of Mr. Carter's work."

"I'll tell you who I'm a fan of," one of the girls said. "That fella that
sold us the tickets to this thing. Mr. Tall, Dark, and Handsome."

"I think you mean Bennett," Sam said, her cheeks growing warm.
"Bennett Steeling."

The other girl leaned over her friend. "Steeling as in Steeling Textiles? *That* Steeling?"

"My cousin went to school with his sister," the first girl said in a low whisper exclusively reserved for gossip. "Said she got kicked out of the Marquart Academy for getting caught en flagrante with the dean's nephew in her dormitory."

"Actually, it was the dean's office," came a voice from over their shoulder. Joana stood in the row behind them, dressed to the nines and wearing a peacock-feather headdress that brought out the flecks of blue in her eyes. "And it wasn't his nephew; it was his son."

The two girls grabbed at each other's hands, the prospect of being in the presence of a true gossip legend far more tantalizing than an afternoon's discussion on ancient Egyptian tombs. Joana plopped down in the chair directly behind Sam, pulling her lips into a frown.

"Would it kill Bennett to turn on the heat in here?" she groused.

"You'd better get used to it, Jo," Sam said. "They don't have heaters when you're out doing surveyor work in the field."

Joana pointed a rolled-up program at her. "I already told you and Bennett, I'm only taking jobs in places with beaches and lax Prohibition laws."

"And we told you they don't do surveys on beaches," came a deep, warm voice from above Sam. "The sand and shifting tides erode any possibility of a valuable survey."

Joana stuck out her tongue at Bennett as Sam whirled around, flushing pink with surprise. "Bennett! I was afraid you might get so busy selling last-minute tickets that you would miss the lecture."

Bennett matched her smile with a soft one of his own. "I wouldn't miss it for the world." He caught sight of the two girls in the mummy dresses, their mouths gone slack and their attention rapt. "Good afternoon, ladies. Thank you for coming."

"Good afternoon," the girl closest to Sam said faintly, making a tiny O with her mouth to her friend when Bennett glanced away.

He waved a hand over the empty seat on the other side of Sam. "Is this seat taken yet?"

"I was saving it for someone special," Sam said, her cheeks warming.

Bennett's mouth curled up at the corner. "Should I be jealous?"

Joana leaned forward between the seats. "You two aren't nearly as clever as you think you are. Sit down, Bennett. You're blocking the stage, and I want to see the death mask."

Bennett took his seat beside Sam, lifting her hand and lacing his fingers through hers. "You only want to see it because it's made of solid gold," he said over his shoulder.

"Maybe she also wants to see it because it's in near-perfect condition and will tell us so much about how Tutankhamen lived and ruled in one of the last great Egyptian dynasties," Sam countered.

"No, it's definitely the gold bit," Joana said.

"How is the professor?" Sam asked, lowering her voice so the mummy girls wouldn't hear.

Bennett tilted his head to the side, a slight crease forming between his brows. "Some days are better than others. The physician thinks he will make a full recovery, but it could take several months. The . . . *attention* Phillip paid him took its toll. He recognized me today, though, and lectured me for bringing him the wrong volume on Socrates, so there is still hope."

"I'm sure the professor is grateful for all you're doing. You're practically running his classes while he's recovering."

"It's the least I can do."

Sam squeezed his hand. "It's not your fault."

His jaw tightened. "I should have seen it. Phillip was right. I was so convinced of what I wanted to see, I didn't notice what was actually happening right in front of me. I won't let it happen ever again."

Sam leaned into him, bumping his shoulder with her own. "I know you won't. And you did a wonderful job setting up this lecture. I, for one, am excited to see the inscriptions from the Egyptian *Book of the Dead* on the back of the mask. Ancient legend says they include instructions for bringing the dead back to life."

"I think I've had enough of the dead walking the earth," Bennett said dryly. "I'm far more interested to hear his restoration process for the beaded shoes he found. Thousands of beads that they carefully glued to a pasteboard in their original positions so they didn't lose the shape of the sandals, since the thread had long since disintegrated. Fascinating work."

"You and I have very different ideas of what's fascinating," Joana said.

"I think it's fascinating," Sam said, smiling up at him.

"Well, of course *you* do," Joana said. "Everything is fascinating after you've spent the last five years gluing old books back together. I'm in it to explore the lawless wilds."

"Inside or out?" Sam asked playfully.

Joana shrugged. "I'm open to the possibilities."

"Well, I'm in it to make sure you don't make those wilds too lawless," Bennett said dryly.

"Spoilsport," Joana muttered.

Bennett looked down at Sam. "What about you? What are you in it for?"

Sam smiled up at the stage as a pristinely dressed Englishman stepped up to the podium, ready to begin his lecture. "I'm in it for me. And this is only the beginning."

ACKNOWLEDGMENTS

Well, well, well. The sophomore effort. I wasn't sure we would ever meet. But I want to thank you, Book Two, first and foremost for existing. And for being a pain in the ass about it the whole time, like a proper second child.

A huge thank-you to Anna Sargeant, Dryn Shulke, Christina Frost, and Lindsay Funkhouser for tearing this book apart and helping me put it back together. And for all your weird conspiracy theories and love triangles while you were doing it. You don't know it, but those ridiculous tangents made me think it was a story worth telling.

Thank you to my agent, Elizabeth Bewley, for not letting me give up on this story like I wanted to. You championed it like you do best, and made it something beyond my wildest dreams.

To my editor, Kieran Viola, thank you for taking another chance on me. You are truly a spectacular editor, and I don't even shudder when I get your editorial letters, because I know I'm in good hands. I love these characters and this story because of you.

To the team at Hyperion, a huge thank-you for taking my Word doc and making it a real book. Thank you to Cassidy Leyendecker for reinterpreting all my misinterpreted emails. Thank you to Guy

Cunningham, Dan Kaufman, Martin Karlow, and David Jaffe for catching my ignorance and making it look like knowledge. Thank you to Phil Buchanan for a spectacular design. It's a special thrill every time I see it. My thanks also to Sara Liebling, Marybeth Tregarthen, Dina Sherman, Elke Villa, Seale Ballenger, Holly Nagel, Monique Diman, and Vicki Korlishin for being excited about the project and for making up the village it takes to raise a book.

My thanks to the real archaeologist here, Neil Jackman, and to everyone at the Hellfire Club Archaeological Project and Abarta Heritage. Thank you for making your research and findings available to the public. For anyone interested in learning more about the true excavations carried out at Montpelier, check out *Sacred Skies and Earthly Sinners: The Hellfire Club Archaeological Project*.

To Max, who earned the dedication in this book. Thank you for teaching me what Sam found exciting about digging into the earth and the past. And for the working title *Sam and the Big Cliff*. I was a little sad to change it, but you have to admit *Curse of the Specter Queen* is pretty cool.

To Lily, who is my own little reckless Joana. You pick locks, steal my things, and give me cute smiles when I confront you about it. Truly a legend.

Joe, I won't even begrudge you this thank-you. 2020 was a horrible, tumultuous, bizarre non-year of a year. But you made space for my writing, listened to my crackpot Wallstonian story theories, and kept the kids quiet when I had Zoom calls. It's always you and me, kid.

To the rest of my family—Mom, Dad, and Matt, for reading and supporting and loving me. I love you right back.

And finally, to my readers—you exist! You're here! I literally wouldn't get to do this without you, and I'm so grateful to you for it. Thank you for wanting to come on this adventure with me, and I hope you enjoyed the ride. And maybe have wild hair to show for it. And if you lost a night of sleep over this, what can I say except YOU'RE WELCOME.

READ ON FOR A SNEAK PEEK
AT SAMANTHA KNOX'S NEXT
ROLLICKING ADVENTURE!

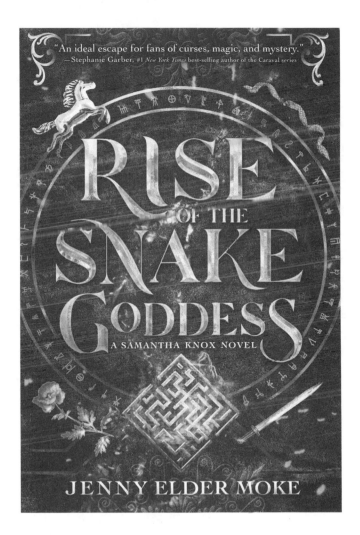

CHAPTER ONE

Samantha Knox was not lurking.

At least, she tried to tell herself she was not lurking. She was simply waiting. But the longer she paced the short stretch of hallway outside of Professor Atchinson's office, the less it felt like waiting and the more it felt like lying in wait. The paper she carried had long since crinkled into a withered white flag more suitable for blowing her nose than for triumphantly presenting to the professor as Sam intended. But it was the content of the paper, not its physical state, that mattered most to Sam.

"Professor Atchinson, good afternoon, so good to see you," Sam rehearsed softly to herself mid-pace. "I know we had a rocky start, sir, what with you kicking me out of your class on the first day of the semester and humiliating me in front of all my peers. You might be thinking I'm here now for revenge, but I assure you, sir, that hasn't occurred to me in months. Hmm, maybe not the most auspicious start."

Better not to bring up that awful day, already cemented in Sam's memory among other such denigrating experiences as falling in the mud pit outside of her schoolroom back in her hometown of Clement, Illinois, or that time she ate with the wrong fork at her best friend's house and had to be quietly corrected by the serving girl. No, if she wanted to win over the man who held her academic future in his hands, she would have to put aside the past and forge a new future.

Sam paused, her sensible loafers squeaking as she changed direction physically and mentally. "Professor Atchinson, sir, good afternoon! I am sure you are as excited as all your students are to begin your summer field school at Knossos. I know I am, because I will be one of them! Your students, I mean. For the summer. Because I did it! I made top of the class for first-years. Does that sound like bragging? That might sound like bragging. Professor Atchinson, if you would kindly read this paper for me, you will see . . . well, now it just sounds like I don't know how to read for myself."

She let out a sigh, slumping against the wall of the empty hallway. It was the end of the spring semester—her first semester at the University of Chicago—and the students had scattered faster than the pollen on the trees outside as soon as final exams were complete. She should have been off celebrating along with the rest of her peers—well, the ones that hadn't bought into the rumors about her—but instead here she was, certainly not lurking, but perhaps doing an approximation of it.

Sam fumbled with a little figurine in her pocket, drawing it out to hold it up in the electric lights of the hall. A misshapen lump of metal, nothing more than a bit of mangled tin. The front half of it was crushed and distorted, the back half giving the impression of hind legs. Once upon a time, it had been a toy horse, carried along in her father's pocket as he fought on the front lines in France, a gift he intended to send home to her. But it had been destroyed along with the rest of her father when a shell hit the hotel where his garrison had been sequestered.

"Oh, Papa," she said, petting the lump of tin where the horse's head would have been, the metal there tarnished and slightly indented from all the times she had invoked its comfort. "I wish you could see me now. At a real university, just like we always dreamed! And top of my class, besides. I know *you* wouldn't think I was bragging."

There had been a letter sent back along with the horse, half-written and half-burned. Her father had found the trinket buried under rubble, and he'd detailed to her how he had used the tip of his bayonet to excavate it using the techniques she had taught him. It had made him feel closer to her, the letter had said, on his own little treasure hunt just like the ones she was always so obsessed with back home.

He'd had dreams for her, Sam's father. Dreams she had put away for seven long years after he died. Dreams that hurt too much to have after he was gone. But that all changed six months ago, when a mysterious diary appeared at her shop and sent her on a journey that upended her life. Now all she wanted was to recapture that lost time and do right by her father's memory. She wanted to make him proud.

There was only one thing standing in her way, and he should have been done with office hours fifteen minutes ago.

"I should just knock, shouldn't I? I am a student with a question after all. Is that not what office hours are for?" Sam marched up to the door, lifting her fist and willing it to knock. Except all it did was hover there, uncertainly.

"Maybe I'll give him five more minutes," Sam said, pacing back toward the opposite wall. She dropped her forehead against the cool stones, shaking her head. "Or maybe you're just being a coward, Samantha Margaret Knox."

Or perhaps she was just hungry. She *had* elected to skip lunch in the hopes of catching Professor Atchinson after office hours. Her mother had often told her growing up that her stomach was more reliable than the dinner bell. And it was certainly ringing all the alarms now, gurgling loudly enough that a passing student gave her a worried glance.

"Happy end of semester!" she called to the boy as she hastily pulled her forehead off the wall to frown down at her stomach. "Hush, would you? I promise to give you an extra helping of mashed potatoes at dinner if you would just let me talk to the professor without embarrassing me."

"Too late for that" came an obnoxious male voice. Theodore Chapin, one of Professor Atchinson's graduate students, smirked at her from the doorway of the professor's office. He played full-back for the University of Chicago football team, and it showed in the massive span of his shoulders and the blunt thickness of his nose that had seen its fair share of breaks.

"Hello, Theo," Sam said to the boy, aiming for polite and landing closer to apprehensive. She had grown up around plenty of rude boys in Clement, but Theodore Chapin strained even her patience. Professor Atchinson had a reputation among the under-graduates for dispensing his favor to the students based on their worth to him, and Theo played the perfect heavy. He fell into the role now, crossing his arms and puffing out his chest so that she could hardly see past him into the professor's office.

She went up on tiptoe to peer over his shoulder, her hopes that she might have been spared some measure of embarrassment falling as she spotted Professor Atchinson standing just behind him. Still, she forced enthusiasm into her voice. "Professor Atchinson, hello!"

"Not you again, Miss Knox," said Professor Atchinson, his British accent lending a knife's edge to his annoyance. "I thought I made my feelings on your presence perfectly clear the day you attempted to infiltrate my anthropology lecture and sow your chaos among my students."

Well, so much for not bringing up the past. Sam cleared her throat of the lump that suddenly formed there, determined not to let it ruin her moment. "I know we started off on the wrong foot, Professor—"

"The wrong foot," Professor Atchinson snorted. "As if you did not conspire with Barnaby Wallstone on his harebrained scheme to undo all my tireless work here, traipsing halfway across the world to Dublin with no credentials and no experience and embarrassing the good name of our program at the University of Chicago."

That was not at all what had happened, or even how it happened, but she could hardly make that point to the professor. They had given their official version of what happened in Dublin enough times over to the authorities in Ireland and those here at home, to the official inquest opened by the school, not to mention in dozens of informal settings to gossip-hungry peers—and she couldn't claim anything to the contrary without opening herself to more questions that she did not want to answer. So she gritted her teeth, willed the corners of her mouth to lift in a smile, and focused all her energy on the future.

"I hope we can start fresh—well, start at all, really—this summer during the field school at Knossos."

"What could possibly make you think you would be part of my field school?" Atchinson asked with a sniff. "It is for graduate students only, Miss Knox, those handpicked by me for their skills and dedication. Students like Mr. Chapin here, who has earned his position among my elite disciples with hard work and dedication to the study."

And kissing up to you every chance he gets, Sam added silently.

But the thought must have made itself plain on her features, because Professor Atchinson's tight expression soured.

"This is what the prestigious University of Chicago has come to, letting in any riffraff from the cornfields on bloody scholarship," he muttered, as if to himself but loud enough that they could all hear.

Sam stiffened, her face going red as Theo let out a loud laugh. "Not going to start in with the tears now, are you?" Theo taunted her. "You're just like my girl, Evelyn, getting misty-eyed at the thought of a wounded bird."

Sam rather thought his girlfriend, Evelyn Hamilton, must get teary-eyed at the prospect of having agreed to date someone like Theodore Chapin. But Evelyn was not her concern today, and her attempts to start anew with Professor Atchinson were about as fresh as curdled milk.

"I made top of the class," she blurted out, thrusting the wilted piece of paper at the professor. He eyed it with distaste, and she gave it a little shake. Or maybe that was just her hand shaking with the attempt to keep her frustration at bay. "First among the undergraduates."

She waited for her meaning to sink in with him, waited to see it change his opinion of her. When he made no move to respond, her confidence faltered.

"The . . . the open position, in the field school," she continued, glancing between the professor and Theo. "For the undergraduate student who shows the most promise in the field. It's a tradition. Top of the undergraduate class gets to join the graduate summer field school excavations. Don't they?"

Theo's smirk only got smirkier, which didn't bode well for Sam. Professor Atchinson sniffed and straightened, the small motion as dismissive as if he turned his back on her. "That position has been eliminated."

Sam lurched a half step forward. "Eliminated? But . . . how? Why?"

"The costs would simply be too prohibitive," the professor said, looking past her at some distant point down the hall. "Were we making our normal excavations at the Kincaid Mounds, perhaps it would have been possible. But we are traveling to Knossos, on Crete, as part of the twenty-fifth anniversary of Sir Arthur Evans's discovery of the Minoan civilization that built the palace. There are a great many details to consider—passage to Crete, accommodations near the palace, invitations to the gala celebrating the anniversary. The undertaking is great, and we can hardly extend our scholarship considering the added costs of such an endeavor. Perhaps next year, if you can manage such a feat again."

"But I earned that spot," Sam said, her whole body trembling. She couldn't stand to look at Theo, whose haughty expression practically glowed. Instead, she focused on the professor. "I worked hard for it all semester. I followed all the rules. You can't just take it away from me now. It's not fair."

Professor Atchinson stepped past Theo to come toe-to-toe with her. He wasn't an impressive man by appearance—he was small and round, his hair grayed and drawn back sharply along a receding line from his temple, his nose slightly too large for his face. But what he lacked in physical prowess he made up for in presence. He knew how to hold a room's attention, whether it was a lecture hall filled with students or a board room of university trustees. He used that power now on Sam, giving her such a hard stare that she felt she must have shrunk three sizes in one look.

"What is not fair is that I have to contend with untried, over-eager amateurs like you, trampling through my carefully laid plans and disgracing all the hard work I have done. Your kind does not belong here, Miss Knox, no more than a cow would belong in the

White House or a chicken on the throne of England. The sooner you learn that your place is not here but out in those cornfields from which you grew, the faster this sinking ship of a department will be righted and set back on course."

Desperation sucked at Sam's shoes, holding her fast when all her wounded pride wanted to do was run and hide. "That's not true," she whispered. "I deserve to be here, same as everyone else."

"The only place you deserve to be is in that lunatic asylum alongside Barnaby Wallstone," snapped Professor Atchinson. "You've wasted quite enough of my time, girl, and I have no more of it to spare. Better luck next year. Come along, Theodore."

"Better luck," Theo echoed cruelly, trotting after the professor down the hall and disappearing around the corner, taking all of Sam's hopes along with them.

CHAPTER TWO

"**A**rsenic in his tea," said Joana Steeling, slamming her empty glass down on the bar top for emphasis. Her bright violet dress glowed in the dim light of the Green Mill speakeasy, drawing the attention of several of the young men in their pin-striped suits and spats along with the girls hanging off their arms. Joana had that effect on a room, that effortless Steeling charm like a magnet. She looked as fantastic as she always did, her dress fresh from next season's catalogs and her hair styled in short finger curls framing her gorgeous face.

"Jo, arsenic is a poison," Sam said glumly, swirling the full contents of her own glass. She wore a gold dress that was the height of fashion six months ago, before she tore the hem climbing out a ship's porthole window. The hem had been repaired, but the dress was showing signs of wear after being Sam's only evening attire for the past semester. "It would kill him."

"We don't give him enough to kill him, just enough to make all his weasely hair fall out," her best friend said, giving a little wave to the man behind the bar and shaking her empty glass at him.

Sam frowned. "Does arsenic do that?"

Joana gave her a determined look. "Let's find out."

"I don't want to poison him, Jo," Sam said with a sigh. "I just want him to give me a chance."

"The only chance that man will ever give you is a fat one," Joana said, giving the barman a winning Steeling smile. "Another one if you would, Leland. Sam, you know Atchinson's reputation. Self-thinkers need not apply. If you can't worship the ground he walks on, you might as well be made of wallpaper for all he'll see you."

"But it's not fair!" Sam protested, finding a new font of energy in her outrage. "I earned my place in that field school, same as every top undergrad who came before me. But it's only me that's being denied. And I don't believe it could be about the budget, do you? What difference would one student make among thirty others?"

Joana took her glass from the barman with a little wink, only wincing slightly as she threw it back in one gulp. "If you want to call his bluff, you could offer to pay your own way."

Sam gave her a flat look. "With what money?"

"You could always ask Daddy for the funds. He'd be pleased as punch to send one of us off on a dig."

Sam slumped back over her drink. "I couldn't ask that of him. He's already done too much for me. He's practically paying my room and board here, along with sponsoring my scholarship. Never mind that I can only afford the rest of it because of the money I saved working at the bookshop all those years. Taking any more from him would be egregious."

"It's practically your right," Joana said. "You know Daddy considers you a second daughter, and if you asked him after a few tumblers of the good stuff, he'd tell you that you're his favorite."

"But I'm *not* his daughter," Sam said. "I love your father, you know that, but he's my employer. It's not the same."

"Well, don't let Daddy catch you saying that—you'll break his heart."

"I want to do this for myself," Sam insisted, wishing she could make her point to Joana.

Their friendship had always managed to bridge several divides, but sometimes those gaps in their upbringing came to light with frustrating clarity. Sam was the daughter of a washerwoman and a farmer killed during the Great War, while Joana was the daughter of a textile magnate and a former actress turned socialite. Sam only owned the dress she now wore and drank the swill she now pretended to drink because Joana had bought them both. If it were not for the Steeling family's generosity, Sam would be burning her arms hauling out steaming piles of laundry to dry on the line alongside her mother. They had given her every opportunity she'd ever had except this one. This one she had earned herself, only to have it snatched right from under her.

"Well, good luck convincing that old windbag of anything. You know he hates us because of Old Man Wally and the Dublin incident," Joana said, surveying the club around them. The Green Mill was on the famous side of illegal, thanks to a payoff to the local police by the mobster who leased the place, Al Capone. His booth sat in the corner with a clear view of both doors, and legend had it the band would stop whatever they were playing when he entered the joint to play "Rhapsody in Blue," his favorite song. Luckily there was no "Rhapsody" in earshot tonight, just the easy croons of singer Joe E. Lewis. Sam didn't mind accompanying Joana on her law-breaking excursions, but she wasn't interested in getting mixed up with any real mobsters. She'd done her time with dangerous men.

"He thinks we conspired with Wallstone to try and make some great find in Dublin and take over the department from him," Sam said, shaking her head. "No matter how many times I tell him that's not what happened, he's convinced of it. And it's not like I can say what *actually* happened either. He had everyone's opinions of me set before I ever stepped on campus, and no matter how hard I work to change their minds, they choose rumors and lies."

"You and Bennett are going about this all wrong," Joana said, leaning back on her elbows against the bar as her tone turned expansive. "You keep looking at your reputations like a liability instead of an opportunity. You're not embracing all the possibilities. Just this past week I started a rumor that we were hired by the new Irish government to track down a cult of blood drinkers within their own ranks. I heard the Russo twins repeating it during library hours on Friday, and now I've got seven invites to end-of-the-year soirees this weekend, so you know it made its rounds."

"I'm glad you can find the fun in it," Sam said, turning her back on the room to glare at the clear liquor in her glass. Joana swore it would help ease her troubles, but Sam could never get past the dried-flower taste of it. "With Wallstone on indefinite leave and Atchinson firmly set in his intentions to blacklist me, I'll be lucky to have a career as a trench digger on an excavation site."

"Cheer up, here's Bennett," Joana said, taking pity on Sam's neglected glass and sipping from it herself. "If anyone can un-dol your drums, it's him."

Sam perked up and spun to face the room once again, her whole being coming alive at the sight of Bennett Steeling entering the Green Mill. He wore a suit that would have looked casual on anyone else but managed to look crisp and perfectly fitted on his wide shoulders and trim physique, his raven hair glimmering with deep rivers of warmer brown in the low light of the speakeasy. The lights flared a little brighter, the music swelled, the temperature of the early June night raised the heat in the bar. Or perhaps that was just Sam's reaction whenever Bennett entered a room, despite having spent plenty of time in plenty of rooms with him over the past six months. She wasn't the only female in the vicinity to notice him either, but his gaze skittered over the collected painted lips and sparkling dresses until they found her. His expression softened and warmed, his eyes swirling to a light golden brown as he sent her a small, private smile. Joana gave an audible sigh beside her.

"Hot looks," she said as Bennett moved through the tight crowd of the bar toward them.

"Hmmm?" Sam asked, the single sip of gin she'd taken that evening suddenly hitting her.

"If I stuck a marshmallow between the two of you, it would roast," Joana said, rolling her eyes. But her tone was good-natured.

Sam smiled shyly. "I'm mad for your brother and you know it."

Joana made a playfully retching sound. "I've told you not to bring that up with me. It's bad enough I have to experience it with my own peepers. I don't need you waxing poetic about his brain or other less appropriate parts."

Sam gave a dramatic sigh, looking dreamily through the swirl of lace and sequins and slick suits on the dance floor. "He really does have the best brain."

"Sam," Bennett said as he reached them, taking her hands to help her up off the stool. "You look incredible as always."

"Bennett," Sam said, shivering at the sound of her name spoken so intimately from his lips. Would there ever be a time that he called her name and she did not respond in such a manner? She doubted it.

He kissed her softly, his hands lingering at the base of her spine, his fingers warm and strong through the thin lace and silk of the underdress. Joana cleared her throat loudly, slapping her hand on the bar top.

"And I'm here, too, brother," she said, dry as sand.

Sam stepped back, a fierce blush crawling up her neck as Bennett gave a discreet cough. "Yes, Jo, hello to you as well."

Joana held up a hand. "I don't require the same greeting, thanks."

His expression flattened. "I hope that's a club soda, Jo."

Joana gave him a brilliant smile, swirling her glass. "Of course, brother. Alcohol is illegal after all."

Bennett's nostrils flared on a sigh before he turned back to Sam, his expression growing serious. "I heard about Professor Atchinson."

Sam deflated back on the stool with a groan. "It's all over the school already? I thought I'd at least have the summer to recoup my dignity."

"I bet it was Theo Chapin, that worm," Joana said. "He got that big by feeding on other people's misery. I'd lay money on it."

"Sam, I'm so sorry," Bennett said, running his hands along her bare arms and making her shiver once again. "I know how hard you worked to earn that position. It's unfortunate they didn't have the budget to include you this year."

Sam snorted. "You actually believe it's about budgets?"

"You think otherwise?" Bennett asked in surprise.

"I think it's flimsy at best and an outright lie at worst," Sam said. "Atchinson hates me."

"He doesn't hate you, Sam," Bennett said. "Atchinson is the old guard, and with the university president dying unexpectedly last month and throwing the administration into confusion, he's just trying to protect his position. I'm sure it's not personal."

"It felt very personal when he told me I don't belong here," Sam muttered, but her words were lost in the smother of Bennett's jacket as she burrowed into his chest.

He linked his arms around her back. "I know it's a low blow after all your hard work, but it's only your first year. Your first semester, really. And after the Dublin business, you were lucky to get into the university. But you overcame all of that, stuck to the rules, and came out top of the class. I'm sure you'll be top of the class next year as well, and the year after that, and you'll be so sick of the Kincaid Mounds by the time you graduate that you'll be begging them to send you anywhere else in graduate school."

"What good is following all the rules if Professor Atchinson is just going to rip the pages of the rulebook right out from under me?" Sam shivered at the idea of the worst torture she could imagine—purposely mutilating a treasured book.

"I'm sure that's not what he's doing," Bennett said, smoothing one hand down the little ripples of her spine. "Atchinson is a stickler for the rules, especially the ones he created himself. This is simply a budgetary constraint, you'll see."

"And anyway, why are we letting the old codger steal our joy?" Joana piped in. "Tonight is not a night for moping—it's a night for celebrating. Sam came out top of the class and I survived an entire semester without even the whiff of a scandal. Gold stars all around."

"You mean besides the rumors everyone keeps passing around about why we were in Dublin and what happened when we were there?" Bennett asked dryly.

"Those don't count," Joana said, pointing a finger at him around her fresh glass of gin. "That technically happened before the semester started."

"I can't believe I'm saying this," Bennett said, shaking his head. "But for once I agree with Joana. You did a brilliant thing, Sam, and you deserve to celebrate. Atchinson can go hang."

"That's the spirit, brother!" Joana declared, hopping off her stool and taking Sam by the arm to drag her upright. "Come on, kid, let's twist."

Sam sighed, doing her best to breathe out the disappointment weighing her down. It helped, maybe a little—or maybe that was simply the effect of being bolstered between the Steeling siblings. Either way, they made a decent point. Professor Atchinson could absolutely go hang. If he meant to deny her the opportunity she deserved, she would find a way to make her own.